FRISKY
BUSINESS

Clodagh Murphy was born in Dublin.
She moved to London in the 1980s and lived there for
several years. She currently lives in Dublin with her beloved
laptop. She is an aunt to five nephews and one niece.

Also by Clodagh Murphy
The Disengagement Ring
Girl in a Spin

FRISKY BUSINESS

Clodagh Murphy

HACHETTE
BOOKS
IRELAND

First published in Ireland in 2012 by
HACHETTE BOOKS IRELAND

1

Cataloguing in Publication Data is available from the British Library.

ISBN 978 1 4447 2623 7

Typeset in Sabon MT and Sakkal Majalla
by Bookends Publishing Services

Printed and bound in Great Britain by
Clays Ltd, St Ives plc

Hachette Books Ireland policy is to use papers that are natural, renewable
and recyclable products and made from wood grown in sustainable forests.
The logging and manufacturing processes are expected to conform to the
environmental regulations of the country of origin.

Hachette Books Ireland
8 Castlecourt Centre
Castleknock
Dublin 15, Ireland

A division of Hachette UK Ltd
338 Euston Road, London NW1 3BH
www.hachette.ie

To Trish and Emer, the best friends a sister could have

Acknowledgements

Huge thanks to:

My wonderful agent, Ger Nichol, for all the support and encouragement, and endless patience when I'm being neurotic.

Ciara Doorley and Claire Rourke for bringing out the best in the book.

Deirdre Mangaoang at Médecins Sans Frontières in Dublin for answering my questions about working with MSF.

Mark Stephens, RIBA MRIAI (www.MarkStephensArchitects.com) for all the property development advice. Any mistakes are mine.

Louise Clark for the use of the house in Leitrim Quay, where I wrote a large chunk of the manuscript, and without which this book would have had no middle.

Lesley Burke, who made the winning bid in the Authors for Japan auction to have a character named after her. Your generosity is greatly appreciated, and I hope you approve of your namesake. Thanks also to my lovely friend Keris who set up the auction, which raised over £13,000 for tsunami relief.

Everyone at We Should Be Writing for being supportive, chatty, clever, funny, and generally brilliant company online and in real life.

All the readers who loved my previous books and got in touch to tell me. It means a lot.

Finally, everyone who has bought this book. I hope you have fun reading it.

Chapter One

A strong wind blew down Curve Road, shaking leaves from the trees and rustling the bush at number 27 where Romy Fitzgerald was stringing pumpkin lanterns. She looked up at the sky, pleased to see it was still cloudless, promising a dry night for the trick-or-treating children. Despite the wind, it was surprisingly mild, and she had abandoned her jacket on the grass and was working on the garden decorations in just a sweatshirt. When she had finished stringing the lanterns in the bushes, she tied Hallowe'en balloons to the gate, winding the strings around its wrought green metal. Then she folded her arms and stood back, examining her handiwork. As well as the lanterns and balloons, fat pumpkins lined the gravel path to the steps of her big pink house, orange and black candles glowed in the windows, a large skeleton stood sentry at the door and a ghost hanging from the cherry blossom tree swayed eerily in the breeze. She knew it was a bit over the top, but at least children would be left in no confusion as to whether or not they were welcome to call.

Satisfied that the house looked suitably festive, she gathered her jacket, tools and baby monitor up from the grass and bounded up the steps to the front door. She was just letting herself into her flat when the hall door opened and her oldest tenant May came in, laden down with shopping bags.

'Romy, the house looks amazing!' she said slightly breathlessly as she unwound a colourful scarf from around her neck. 'Fair play to you for going to all this trouble. It's magical.'

'Thanks, May. Would you like a cup of coffee?'

'I'd better not, thanks,' she said, glancing at her watch. 'Frank's waiting for me and I'm already late. I got a bit carried away in La Senza.'

'Okay. I'll see you later then, for the party?'

'Yes, we're looking forward to it. What time would you like us to come?'

'Well, it's officially kicking off at seven thirty, but come over whenever you're ready.'

'Okay, we'll make it for seven thirty,' she said. 'That will give us plenty of time to do a bit of work on our project. We're almost halfway through the book now, but there are some pretty challenging positions coming up.'

'Oh?' Romy nodded interestedly, hoping May wouldn't elaborate.

'Yes, the next one is a sort of wheelbarrow. I have to get down on the floor on all fours, and then Frank lifts my legs up from behind—'

'Gosh, that sounds … strenuous. Well, be careful,' Romy said, turning her key in the door.

'Oh, we will. Safe sex has a whole new meaning at our age,' May said, chuckling. 'Luckily we're both quite fit and we do work at staying supple. I do lots of yoga, and Frank has his karate. But we're neither of us getting any younger.'

'You wouldn't think it to look at you,' Romy said, turning back to May. She didn't know how old May was exactly, but she guessed she must be in her late sixties. Still attractive, Romy thought she must have been stunning in her youth. With a figure that many twenty-year-olds would envy, and her silver hair cut in an elegant, shiny bob, she was a walking advert for growing old gracefully – at least until you got into conversation with her.

'Thank you.' She smiled. 'I do my best. Still, it's probably only a matter of time before arthritis kicks in. If we don't do these things now, we might never get another opportunity. Seize the day, isn't that right?'

'Yes, well – good for you!' Romy smiled brightly.

'Sorry, dear, is this TMI, as they say nowadays?' May seemed to have finally noticed Romy's discomfort with the conversation.

'No, not at all,' she said, smiling at May. 'I just need to start getting things ready.'

'Oh, of course. Well, see you later, Romy, love. I'll let you know how we get on.'

'Great! Bye,' Romy called, letting herself into her flat as May turned and headed for the stairs.

It was a spacious high-ceilinged flat on the first floor of the large detached house. Decorated in neutral shades of cream and taupe, it was saved from characterless blandness by splashes of red on accent walls and the large red sofa that dominated the room. She had originally decorated the flat for a quick sale, along with all the other flats in the house, but then the recession had struck and the bottom had fallen out of the property market. Romy had found herself with six beautiful upmarket flats that she couldn't sell without making a huge loss – and probably not even then. So she had decided to let them and live on the income. She had moved into this one herself, adding enough of her personal touches to it to make it feel more like her home than just a temporary stop on the property ladder.

The large living room had already been transformed for the party. Strings of orange and black bats flew across the ceiling, and the imposing mantelpiece was covered in an array of Hallowe'en knick-knacks interspersed with fat orange and black candles. A home-made pumpkin lantern stood in the grate.

When she had stowed her tools and jacket in the cupboard, Romy went straight through to the kitchen, which was filled with the warm, comforting aromas of cooking. A big pot of chilli was bubbling away in the oven and a toffee apple cake was cooling on a wire rack on the worktop. She put the baby monitor on the counter and turned the hob on under a pot of toffee she had made earlier. As she waited for it to heat up, she washed apples and stuck wooden skewers into them, lining them up on the counter ready for dipping. She knew Lesley thought she was daft going to this much trouble.

'Just get bags of those fun-sized bars,' she'd said earlier in the week when Romy had outlined her plans. 'Kids nowadays won't even know what a toffee apple is.'

But Romy thought that that was sad. She wanted kids to know what a toffee apple was. She liked things done properly. She was a firm believer in stockings at Christmas, and Hallowe'en absolutely had to include toffee apples. She had always loved this time of year – and she loved it more than ever now. As she stood calmly dipping apples in the warm toffee and placing them on a tray to cool, she thought about how much her life had changed since this time last year, her eyes flicking to the baby monitor, its red and green lights dancing in time with the snuffling and gurgling sounds that emanated from it.

When she had dipped the last apple, tidied the kitchen and loaded the dishwasher, she went to her bedroom and bent over the crib in the corner where her son Luke was sleeping, getting caught up as she always did in adoring his tiny curled fingers, his perfect eyelashes, his pillow-soft cheeks.

'Happy birthday, Luke,' she whispered, smiling down at him. Though he was only three months old, she couldn't help thinking of today as his birthday. It was the day she had got him, the day his life had begun – conceived in a cupboard at a Hallowe'en party. It wasn't a very auspicious start in life.

One year earlier

'Darth Vader's checking you out.'

Romy turned to Lesley, who nodded across the room. Following her friend's gaze through the throng of animals, robots and movie characters, she found herself eyeballing a very tall, imposing Dark Lord – at least she assumed she was eyeballing him. It was hard to tell beneath the shiny black helmet. He might just as well have been staring into space or had his eyes closed.

'Why don't you go over to the dark side and introduce yourself,' Lesley said, nudging Romy with her elbow.

'No thanks,' Romy said, grabbing another glass of champagne as a uniformed waitress passed with a tray. 'Who knows what might be lurking underneath that cloak?' She carefully took a

sip of champagne, cursing the dress code that had insisted on full fancy dress complete with masks.

'There might be something very nice lurking under there. You'll never know if you don't try. I bet he's really rich.'

'What makes you think that? It doesn't cost all that much to hire a costume.'

'He's here, isn't he? If he's a friend of David's, he's bound to be rich.'

'We're here, aren't we?'

'True,' Lesley conceded. 'Still, you have to admit that costume is pretty ritzy.'

'Maybe he owns it,' Romy said. 'He's probably some Star Wars nerd. Anyway, I don't care if he's Bill Gates, I'm not interested.'

'He's not Bill Gates,' Lesley said. 'He's too tall.'

'Well, I don't care if he's not Bill Gates either – I'm still not interested.'

Lesley turned to her with an exasperated sigh. 'When was the last time you got laid?' she asked, her hand on her hip. She might have looked mildly threatening if she hadn't been dressed as an Oompa-Loompa.

'It was … a while ago.'

'It was Gary, right? That was nine months ago, Romy. Nine months!'

'Well, I've waited nine months. I can wait a bit longer.'

'How much longer? Nothing's ever going to happen if you don't put yourself out there, take a few chances.'

'I am putting myself out there. I'm here, amn't I?' Romy said, waving a hand around to indicate the party.

She was here, but she really wished she wasn't. She had only come because Lesley was so excited about getting invited to a party at David Kinsella's house and hadn't wanted to come alone. She had begged and pleaded with Romy to come, until *eventually Romy had capitulated. It wasn't the sort of party they would usually be invited to. They had been at school with David Kinsella, but since then he had become an entrepreneur, and made billions from a business empire that had started out with a single bar, but had grown and diversified to encompass strings of nightclubs and restaurants all over the country as well as a vast property portfolio. He had consolidated his position by marrying an heiress and well-known socialite – a former model who now spent most of her time eating out for charity. Lesley and Romy no longer mixed in the same circles as David, but he occasionally threw the old crowd a bone and invited them all to one of his flash parties. Lesley had been gagging at the prospect of a night of free champagne, a nose around David's mansion and the chance to get a look at how the other half live. Romy was trying to get into the spirit of it for Lesley's sake, but it wasn't working. She really didn't want to be here.*

'I shouldn't have come,' she said to Lesley.

'Sure what else would you be doing?'

'That new tenant I was telling you about moved in yesterday. I could have had her to dinner, helped her get settled.'

'Romy, you're her landlady, not her mother.'

'I should hope not! She's old enough to be my grandmother.'

'That's a bit sad, isn't it – renting at that age? I hope I don't end up like that.'

'You could do worse. I don't think there's anything sad about May. I get the impression she's had a very interesting life – and still has. When she came to see the place, she asked me if it would be okay for her to have men stay over.'

'Fair play to her!'

'She probably has a more active sex life than I have.'

'That wouldn't be hard.'

'Well at least someone in my house will be getting some action.'

'A pensioner! Does that not make you feel even a little bit ashamed of yourself?'

'Nope.'

Romy took a sip of her champagne and glanced across the room. Darth Vader was still staring, and she looked away again quickly. 'Someone should have told that guy it's rude to stare,' she mumbled to Lesley. 'What's he looking at anyway? There's nothing to see here.'

'Maybe he just likes the cut of your jib,' Lesley said cheerfully.

'He hasn't seen my jib. He can't see my face and it's not as if I'm showing any flesh.' She had rejected all the slutty costumes in the shops and made herself a proper old-fashioned Red Riding Hood outfit.

'No, you could be a nun,' Lesley said.

'Why doesn't he stare at that Snow White right beside him? She looks like she'd be glad of the attention.'

'God, is that who she's supposed to be? I'd never have guessed.'

'Yeah – Snow White, the lap-dancing years.'

Lesley laughed.

'Damn!' Romy said as she tried to sip champagne through her mask. 'Why did David insist on these bloody masks? It's ridiculous.'

'He gave me some guff about how it would make us all equal and help break the ice – get everyone mingling. Otherwise, you know, us plebs might be too in awe of his cronies to talk to them – and they wouldn't bother to talk to the likes of us.'

'Huh! I think he was just trying to skimp on the champagne.'

'I bet he just did it so he can get off with anyone he likes and claim afterwards that he thought it was his wife.'

'Well, well, well, who have we got here?' A very fat Shrek suddenly loomed up on them. 'Your host at your service,' he said, with a little bow.

Crap, Romy thought. *Maybe David wanted the masks so he could sneak up on his guests and catch them bitching about him.*

'Hi, David, great party,' Lesley said. 'I'm Lesley, and Red Riding Hood here is Romy.'

'Ah, great to see you, girls. I hope you're enjoying yourselves.'

David may have done better for himself than his old classmates, but at least he wasn't ageing well. His hair was thinning, and years of good living had left him paunchy and bloated.

'So, what are you girls up to these days? Still dabbling in property, Romy?'

Romy seethed at his condescending use of the word 'dabbling'. He knew damn well that she was a full-time property developer. She may only be a one-man band, but she was very good at what she did, and was well respected in the business. She had a solid reputation as a first-class developer and her properties were always in demand and sold easily – or as easily as the market would allow. 'Yes, I'm still in the property business,' she replied, *determined not to let him get to her.*

David sucked his breath in through his teeth. 'Not a good time for anyone in that business. I was lucky – saw it coming and got out before the shit really hit the fan.'

And got bailed out by NAMA probably, Romy thought.

'You must be finding it tough?' he asked.

'Of course – isn't everyone? But I'm doing okay. I never over-extended myself in the first place, so I wasn't hit too hard. I'm just riding it out, living on rental income.'

'Good, good – glad to hear it,' David said, *but she could tell from his tone that he was disappointed not to have the opportunity to lord it over her.* 'I was sorry to hear about your dad, by the way.'

'Oh, thanks,' Romy mumbled. *Shit! She could feel tears*

stinging the backs of her eyes, and she was grateful now that she had the mask to hide behind.

'Was it sudden, or had he been sick for—'

'I was made redundant,' Lesley cut in.

'Oh, sorry to hear that,' David said, sounding delighted. 'If there's anything I can do to help …' he trailed off, glancing around the room.

'I'm grand, thanks. I'm doing freelance web design now, and it's going pretty well.'

'Great!' he said distractedly. 'I'm not going to be here much longer anyway. Katie and I are shipping out, moving to Canada. This country has had it.' His eyes roved around the room restlessly as he spoke. 'Well, nice to see you both. I'd better go and mingle. Enjoy yourselves, girls.'

'Yeah, thanks David,' Lesley called after him. 'Gobshite!' she said as soon as he was out of earshot.

'Thanks,' Romy said, 'for, you know, jumping in there …'

'No bother,' Lesley said.

Even through her mask, Romy could feel Lesley's uncomprehending look. She knew Lesley didn't understand why any mention of her father's death still filled her with horror and threatened to turn her into a trembling wreck. It was almost two months since he'd died, and it wasn't as if it was a shock – he had been sick for a very long time. She knew everyone thought she should be starting to get over it by now. But they didn't know her secret. No one knew what had happened the night her father died – which made her all the more grateful to Lesley for her unquestioning support.

'He's such a prick!' Romy said, her eyes following David as he worked his way around the room.

'Well, all the more reason to drink him out of house and home,' Lesley said cheerfully before draining her champagne glass and reaching for another as a waiter circulated with a tray.

'It'd take a long time to drink David out of house and home,' Romy said, glancing around the huge reception room. Light from the massive chandeliers overhead danced off the crystal champagne glasses, and banks of fresh flowers stood on marble tables with ornate gilded legs, releasing their heady perfume into the room. Lesley had gasped earlier when, after they had driven through the electronic gates and up a long, sweeping drive lit by flaming torches, their taxi had been waved to a stop on the crunchy gravel in front of the entrance by a uniformed attendant. In the vast entrance hall, a string quartet was positioned on the balconied landing at the top of a curved double staircase, the gentle strains of Mozart floating down to greet the guests as they arrived. David's home was a monument to the Celtic Tiger, a remnant of an era that already seemed light years away. It was like visiting the Palace of Versailles – so opulent and ostentatious, and so far removed from real life.

'Well, we've got all night,' Lesley said now. 'Drink up!'

Romy grabbed another glass of champagne. Maybe she should get drunk. It might help get her in the party mood. She felt antsy and agitated, and she regretted letting Lesley talk her into coming. She just wanted to go outside and scream her lungs out; or race home, curl up under her duvet and cry herself to sleep. Maybe drinking herself into oblivion would be a suitable alternative.

'Right, we should get mingling,' Lesley said.

Romy looked around at the sea of blank anonymous masks and her heart sank. There were probably people she knew here – other people from the old neighbourhood – but she had no way of knowing who they were, and she was in no mood for making small talk with strangers. She wondered which of her old friends were here, and suddenly she realised she was wondering about one person in particular – Kit. It wasn't likely he would be at David's party. She knew he was home from

New York – her mother had told her – but as far as she knew, he never got in touch with any of the old crowd when he was back. He'd certainly never contacted her.

She shook her head, annoyed with herself. She was being ridiculous. What difference would it make if Kit was here? They didn't even know each other anymore. He lived in New York, and they hadn't seen each other in years. It wasn't as if they could go back to what they'd had. She was just feeling sad and a bit lonely, longing for the comfort of being really close to someone. For the first time in ages, she wished she was still with Gary. Damn it, she couldn't hack this. She didn't like David and she didn't want to be at his party with all these people she didn't know.

'Lesley, I'm sorry, but I—'

'You want to go?' Lesley guessed.

Romy nodded, feeling like the worst flake. 'I'm really sorry. Do you mind?'

'No, I'm fine. Go on. I know I bamboozled you into coming in the first place.'

'Thanks,' Romy said with an apologetic smile that she realised Lesley couldn't see. At least Lesley knew this wasn't like her. Romy was somebody who saw things through, and she was usually completely dependable as a friend, sibling, daughter …

Shaking the thought away, she hugged her friend goodbye and started to make her way out. She was trying to squeeze past a large group of people by the door, deep in drunken shouty conversation and oblivious to her attempts to get through, when suddenly she felt someone grab her hand from behind. She spun around expecting to see Lesley, and instead found herself face to face – well, mask to mask – with Darth Vader.

'Where are you going?' he asked, his voice slightly muffled by his helmet.

She said nothing, shaking her hand out of his grasp.

'Are you okay?' he asked, bending his head closer to hers in a strangely intimate way. He took her hand again, his gloved fingers stroking hers.

'I – I'm fine.'

'You don't seem fine. You're upset.'

How could he tell? He couldn't even see her face.

'Are you angry with me?'

She suddenly realised that he was still holding her hand and she pulled it away. 'No! Of course not. Though you were staring.'

'I thought you'd never shake off that Oompa-Loompa.'

God, this guy was intense. Even though he was no longer holding her hand, she felt super-glued to the spot. She'd never noticed how sexy Darth Vader was before. Was she imagining the heat between them? She'd swear he was smouldering at her under that mask. She peered into his eyes, wondering if he was someone she knew.

'I have to get out of here,' she said, but she didn't move.

'I know,' he said, grabbing her hand again. 'Come on.'

She didn't resist as he pulled her towards the door, the crowd parting easily to let them through. But when he made for the staircase, she dug her heels in. 'No, I want to leave,' she said, pointing to the door.

'We can't leave,' he said. 'David will see us.'

Before she had a chance to protest that it was a party and David was hardly going to hold them hostage against their will, he had turned and was striding up the stairs two at a time, pulling her along behind him. She needed all her concentration to keep up without tripping. She had drunk too much champagne and eaten too few canapés. It didn't help that all she could think about was sex. There was something so urgent about his whole demeanour that made her think this *was leading to one thing. And for some reason she was fine with that – as long as she didn't think about it too much …*

When they got to the top of the stairs, he started opening doors off the landing, seemingly at random. The first three were occupied by writhing, panting couples, but the fourth was empty and he pulled her in, flicking on the light and closing the door swiftly behind them.

'Shit, there's no key,' he said, his fingers tracing over the lock. 'Do you know where there's a key?'

She shook her head. How would she know where there was a key?

He pulled off his gloves and tossed them on the floor. 'We'll just have to be quick – and block the door,' he said, turning her around and pushing her against the door. She heard movement behind her and something fell to the floor with a thud. Then his hands were on her waist, pulling her closer to him, and she felt the wet warmth of his lips on her neck, and knew he had removed his helmet. If she turned around now, she would see him, but she didn't want to. He might be really old or repulsive, and she didn't want to know, because she really wanted this to happen. Though he didn't sound old …

'This means I won't be able to go down on you,' he whispered as he nibbled her ear, 'and I wanted to do all your favourite things.'

The words barely penetrated her fuzzy brain as he started palming her breasts. How would he know what her favourite things were? But when she opened her mouth to say something, all that came out was a squeak as he pinched her nipples. Her breath caught in her throat as he bent to grab the hem of her dress, hiking it up slowly until it was around her waist. He obviously wasn't going to waste much time with the preliminaries, and she didn't care. At least David's idea of the masks acting as an icebreaker was working – though she doubted this was quite what he had in mind.

'Red, very appropriate,' he said, chuckling softly when he saw her knickers, which she had bought specially to go with her costume. Then he was sucking on her neck again while his fingers plunged inside her knickers, his other arm clamped around her waist pulling her back into his body as he began to stroke her.

God, it had been too long since a man had touched her, and she felt herself melt around his fingers. She should have made more of an effort to find a boyfriend after she broke up with Gary. Maybe then she would have been able to resist letting a masked stranger feel her up at a party.

'This is new,' he said, his breath hot in her ear as his fingers brushed lightly over her pubic hair. 'Does David like it like this? Or do you think you'll need it to keep you warm in Canada?'

'Wh— what?' She gulped. Oh, God, he thought she was— 'I don't ... I mean, I'm not—'

'Hey, I like it,' he said soothingly, slipping a finger inside her. 'It's sexy.'

'Oh, my God!' she gasped. 'You're – you're having an affair with David's wife!'

His fingers withdrew instantly and she felt the loss of his body heat as he jerked away from her, leaving her twitching with need. Resting her forehead against the door, she gritted her teeth and squeezed her eyes shut, and resisted the urge to bang her fists on the wood in frustration. Just a couple more seconds and she'd have—

'Jesus! You're not ... you're not Katie?' he stammered breathlessly behind her.

'No.'

'Oh my God! Fuck! Oh my God!'

'Um ... maybe you should put your helmet back on,' she said, without turning around.

'Oh! Yeah ... fuck!' She heard shuffling behind her, and

then slowly turned around to find him stumbling around the room clutching his head, wailing 'Oh, Jesus! Oh, Jesus!' and bumping into furniture. She couldn't help smiling to herself at how comical he looked – Darth Vader having a panic attack.

'Hey, don't freak out.' He stilled at the sound of her voice. 'I haven't seen your face. I don't know who you are, remember? Just ... keep your helmet on.' And your hair, she thought.

'But I said – and I put my – oh, Jesus! I'm so sorry.'

'It's okay,' she said. 'Why don't you sit down?' She waved at the bed. He nodded and did as she suggested, sinking down onto the counterpane. She sat down beside him, putting a tentative hand on his shoulder. He was still hyperventilating. 'Maybe you should put your head between your knees.'

Damn, why had she said anything? If she'd just kept her mouth shut, maybe he'd have put his head between her knees.

'Oh my God, I'm so sorry. I can't believe that I – you won't tell David, will you?'

'No, I won't. Besides, what would I tell him? I don't even know who you are.'

'You could find out.'

'I won't even try, I promise.'

'Well, you could still tell him Katie's having an affair.'

'I won't. I'm not even friends with David really.'

'Thank you.' His body relaxed a little and his breathing calmed.

'So ... that's why you were staring at me – because you thought I was Katie. And why you ...' she trailed off, nodding to the door.

'Um ... yeah. I'm so sorry about that. I don't usually go around attacking women I don't even know.'

'You only attack the ones you do know? You're a real prince.'

He laughed. 'Actually I'm a lord – a dark lord.'

'Anyway, you thought I was someone else. It was an honest mistake.' She was painfully aware that she had no such excuse. Thankfully, he seemed to be too wrapped up in his own mortification and remorse for it to occur to him that she had been perfectly willing to let a total stranger fuck her up against a door.

'Thanks for being so nice about it. And for not telling David. Or, you know, calling the cops on me.'

'Well, I wasn't exactly fighting you off.' She was grateful for the mask to hide her blushes, but it wasn't fair to let him go on beating himself up about it when she had been a willing participant. Besides, he had put his fingers inside her. If he thought about it for a second, he'd realise how up for it she had been. 'No harm done,' she said brightly. Except for giving me a hell of an itch that you're now not going to scratch.

'It's all David's fault really for insisting on these stupid masks.'

'Yeah,' she said, laughing. 'Let's blame David. So, what made you think I was Katie?'

'She told me she was going to be dressed as Little Red Riding Hood,' he said. 'Great costume, by the way.'

'Thanks. I made it myself.'

'You made it? Wow! Well, I saw you dressed like that, and you're about the same height and build as Katie. Though her hair is a little shorter, I guess, now that I see you up close ...'

'And non-existent in places, obviously,' Romy said. 'But, of course, you couldn't tell that from across the room and through my clothes.'

'Oh, Jesus,' he groaned, clutching his head in his hands. 'I'm so sorry about that. And about commenting on ... you know ...'

'That's okay,' she said, finding his discomfiture amusing. 'At least you were complimentary about it.'

'Yeah, phew! Because otherwise, you know, this could have been really embarrassing!'

Romy laughed.

'God, you must have thought I was a total weirdo – staring at you all night, and then dragging you up here and pawing you like that.'

'How long have you two been …'

'A couple of years, I suppose,' he said, shrugging, 'off and on. It's just casual, nothing serious. I'm not here much, but whenever I'm in Dublin we … get together.'

'Right.'

'David's a tosser, you know,' he said defensively.

'Yes,' she nodded. 'I do know.'

'Anyway, it's over now. They're going to Canada soon.'

'So tonight was to be your last hurrah?'

'Yeah, something like that.'

'Sorry I messed that up for you.'

'That's okay. I wasn't going to come here tonight, to be honest. I didn't really want to do it in their house, right under her husband's nose. It seemed too … disrespectful.'

'Unlike doing it behind his back?'

He laughed. 'Yeah, you got me.'

'Sorry, I don't mean to be judgemental.'

'No, you're right. Anyway, Katie got really upset when I said I wasn't going to come, so at the last minute I decided, what the hell, I'd surprise her.'

'Well, maybe you should go and find her now. It sounds like you had quite a treat planned.'

'No, the moment has passed. I think I've had enough excitement for one night. Besides, what if I got it wrong again? My next victim might not be so understanding.'

'Well,' she said, getting up off the bed and smoothing down her skirt, 'I suppose I should go.'

'Yeah, you probably want to get back to the party.'

'Not really. I was leaving, actually, when you – when I bumped into you.' She didn't want to go back to the party, but she didn't want to leave either and go home alone to her flat. She was quite happy here with this very tall, very dark stranger.

'Why don't you stay here and talk to me, then?' he said.

'I shouldn't,' she said automatically.

'What's the matter? Afraid I'll eat you all up?'

'Hey, I may be Red Riding Hood, but you're no wolf.'

'Maybe I am. How do you know what I am under this costume?'

'A wolf in Darth Vader clothing? I don't think so.'

'Then stay,' he said, taking her hand and pulling her back down on the bed beside him.

'What could we talk about? You can't say anything that would give me a clue about who you are.'

'Right. So nothing about jobs – or where we live.'

'Or anything about our families or where we went to school. Or how we know David.'

'Doesn't leave much, does it?' he said.

'Only the big stuff.'

He was silent for a while. 'So,' he said eventually, 'um … do you believe in God?'

'No. Do you?'

'No … I don't think so. I mean, sometimes when there's something I really, really want to happen I think, Please God. Does that count?'

'Hmm, I don't think so. Maybe you're undecided – like a floating voter. Do you think this stuff is going to happen because you think, Please God?'

'Not really, no. I guess that means I don't believe in Him, doesn't it?'

'You know, it could be a Her.'

He laughed. 'You mean, this being you don't believe exists could be female?'

'Yes. Just because I don't believe in God, that's no excuse for sexism.'

'Right, sorry.' He put his hands up contritely. 'I guess I don't believe in God really, but sometimes … I kind of wish I did, you know?'

'Yeah, I know what you mean. It must be nice to think everything makes sense. And the idea that there's someone watching over you all the time. It's kind of comforting.'

'Yeah.'

'So, what religion would you like to be true, if you could pick one?'

'Um … I don't know. Definitely not Catholicism – heaven and hell and purgatory and all that.'

'Ugh, no. I'd like one that had reincarnation. But only if I could come back as someone much cooler. I wouldn't want to come back as a snail or something.'

'You'd be fine. I'd say you've got great karma.'

'Thank you! That's a lovely thing to say.' She sighed, drawing patterns on the bed with a finger. 'I like this world. I wouldn't mind if there wasn't an afterlife – I'd just like more of this one.'

'This life can be great, if you're one of the lucky ones. But I see a lot of people who—' He broke off abruptly. 'I can't say that.'

'Something personal?'

'Yeah – I was going to say something to do with my work.'

They both fell silent. 'Okay, that's religion sorted,' Darth said finally. 'What's next?'

Romy thought. 'We could tell each other our deepest, darkest secrets,' she said.

'You've already discovered my deepest, darkest secret.'

'That you tried to kill your son? Not a secret, dude. George Lucas put it in a movie.'

'Bastard!'

She laughed. 'Seriously – you and Katie is your deepest, darkest secret?'

'That's the best I can do,' he shrugged. 'I think it's pretty heinous, don't you? How about you? Do you have a terrible secret?'

'Yes. I do.'

'Really? You don't seem like the secretive type to me.'

'I'm not ... usually. But I've never told anyone this.'

'Is it bad?'

'Yes. Very.'

'Worse than mine?'

She nodded. 'Much worse than yours, I think.'

'You don't have to tell me if you don't want to.'

'I do want to.'

'Okay. I'm listening.'

Once she started speaking, she couldn't stop, and she marvelled at how easy it was. There was something very liberating about not knowing who he was or what he looked like – like the dark anonymity of the confessional. She didn't know if it was the drink that had loosened her tongue or the fact that they were both wearing masks, but she found herself able to tell this stranger what she hadn't been able to speak of to anyone, even those closest to her. She wasn't even rushing through it. Her words were slow and measured. She told him that she hadn't been herself lately. She told him her father had died and it had left her feeling shaky, like there was nothing to hold on to – like nothing you did in life mattered in the end because it would all turn to ash in the blink of an eye. As she spoke, he took one of her hands in his and held it, his thumb stroking soothingly over her fingers – and the more he *touched her, the more she relaxed and the more she said. She told him about her father's long degenerative illness. And, at last, she told him about the night her father died, and what she had done. He didn't interrupt. He just listened in silence as the words spilled out of her like blood, leaving her feeling drained, but also strangely cleansed.*

She jumped when she heard people in the corridor outside and gripped his hand in panic. She didn't want to break the spell he had cast with his stroking fingers and his silent, masked presence. She wanted to stay here with him and him alone. She had purged and she felt weak and small now that it was all out, and she wanted him to lie down on this bed with her and wrap her up in his thick dark cloak and hold her to the heat of his body. She wanted him to make her feel safe and cared for and protected, and ... forgiven. She had told him the worst thing she had ever done, and now she wanted absolution.

As footsteps thundered towards the door, he grabbed her hand and pulled her across the room and into a large walk-in wardrobe. He was just pulling the door closed behind them as a man and woman burst into the room, shrieking with laughter. It was dark inside the wardrobe, and Romy automatically reached for the light switch, but he grabbed her arm, stopping her. His hand slid down her bare arm as he placed it back by her side, and she shivered. She turned to him and he shook his head, putting a finger to his lips. They stood in silence, listening to the sounds of fumbling in the outer room. Then the door banged and the voices drifted away.

'They've gone,' he whispered, reaching past her for the door handle, but she stopped him. She didn't want to go out into the light.

'I've got another secret,' she said.

'What's that?' he asked, turning back to her.

She took his hands, feeling the firm warmth of his fingers and wanting more of his touch. 'Earlier, when we were ... out there,' she nodded to the door. 'I didn't want you to stop.'

'You mean—?'

'I didn't want you to stop,' she said, kneading his fingers. She took his hand and held it over one of her breasts. 'I didn't want you to stop,' she whimpered pleadingly. She heard him gasp and she took her hand away, but his stayed where it was, and his thumb started to move, stroking lightly over her nipple. She sighed with relief and instinctively tilted her face up to his. 'I wish ...' her voice broke and she realised she was crying.

'Shh,' he whispered. 'It's okay. What do you want?'

'I wish I could kiss you.'

He took his hand away and she felt bereft, but then he reached behind her and pulled something from one of the rails. He held up a long, silky scarf in front of her, and though she couldn't see his face, she knew he was asking for permission, and she nodded.

'Turn around,' he said. When she had her back to him, he pulled off her mask and tied the scarf gently around her eyes. It was cool and silky, and smelled faintly of perfume.

'Does it feel okay?' he asked as he turned her around. She swayed slightly, disoriented by the total darkness, and nodded.

She heard shuffling as he removed his helmet, and then he pulled her into his arms and his lips were on hers. Their kisses started out soft and slow, but quickly became heated, tongues crashing together as their hands groped inside each other's clothes. Being blindfolded only heightened Romy's excitement, seeming to intensify the sensations of his cool, wet tongue on her skin, the softness of his hair on her thighs as he did one of Katie's favourite things to her, the sounds of his panting and groaning, even the sound of ripping foil as he opened a condom, and the hardness of his cock as he pushed inside her. It should have felt sordid, but it didn't. It just felt kind and *comforting and … forgiving. It felt like absolution. Later, they fell asleep on the floor of the wardrobe.*

When she woke up, she was alone in the darkness. She pushed open the door to discover that it was morning, the light hurting her eyes. She wandered downstairs as if in a dream. There were just a few stragglers left from the party. A short fat Spider-Man was making out with Snow White on the sofa, and the Grim Reaper was slumped on the floor in the kitchen, sharing a joint with a gorilla. There was no sign of Darth Vader. It was as if she had dreamed the whole thing, as if he had never existed. But she soon had proof that it was very real; and, nine months later, she held the living proof in her arms – all eight pounds, nine ounces of it. She named the baby Luke.

Chapter Two

Kit Masterson lay on his narrow single bed, his hands behind his head, staring disconsolately at the ceiling as he listened to fireworks and bangers exploding outside the window. How the hell had he ended up back here? Two years ago, he had been a successful trader on Wall Street with a penthouse apartment on Riverside Drive and a beautiful trophy girlfriend at his beck and call. He had spent his summers in rented mansions in the Hamptons and his nights in upscale landmark restaurants and ritzy bars where the cocktails cost fifty dollars apiece. Now, he was in his old bedroom in his parents' house, jobless and broke, the boxes full of the belongings he had brought with him when he had packed up his life in New York crammed into the tiny space so that there was barely room to move. He hadn't had the heart to sort them out in the two weeks since he moved home – two weeks that had been spent mostly lying on this bed in a state of numb shock, pondering the crap-heap that was his life. Where had it all gone so wrong?

Of course, he knew where it had gone wrong – where it had gone wrong for so many people. This bloody recession was fucking things up for everyone. He knew it wasn't just him, but he was taking it personally just the same. He was supposed to be the exception, damn it! Losing was something that happened to other people, not to him. Stocks could go up or down, but he had got used to his stock only rising. His stomach still churned when he thought of that day when he and his co-workers had been lined up to face the firing squad. They had known it was coming, but that hadn't stopped it being a massive shock when it finally happened. Up until that moment, it hadn't seemed real. Even then, he had still believed that there would be some loophole that would enable him to avoid what was happening to everyone else, a golden rope that would be pulled aside to let him slip through. But it had rolled through Wall Street like a tsunami, indiscriminately engulfing everyone.

Still, he had been so ludicrously overpaid that he might have been all right – if he hadn't invested so heavily in a friend's property business. He had held out for as long as he could in New York, trying to hold the pieces of his life together. He downsized, he retrenched, he cashed in what few assets he had and he tried to find another job. But when the property market went tits-up, it was the beginning of the end. Finally, he had to admit defeat and let go, watching helplessly as the uncontainable tide swept everything out of his reach. And now here he was, sleeping in his old bedroom, surrounded by the remnants of his teenage life, with his mom cooking his dinner and doing his washing, and his dad offering to give him money to go to the pub. He couldn't live like this, but what the fuck was he going to do? He was thirty-one years old and fit for nothing.

Dealing was all he knew – all he was good at. He had fallen on his feet when, drifting through a series of dead-end jobs, he had stumbled into a lowly office job at a Wall Street brokerage and found himself in an environment that suited his talents exactly. He had never been bright academically, but he was sharp, energetic and driven, and that combined with his street smarts and charm had taken him a long way – all the way to the frenzied dealing room, where he discovered an intuitive feel for reading the market that bordered on the psychic. He became a prince among dealers, a legend in the company he worked for. He had made them a lot of money, and he had been rewarded accordingly. But then it had all melted away almost overnight and he was back to square one. It was as if the intervening years had never happened. Nothing had changed – except him.

He looked around the room, and he didn't recognise himself in it. It was a time capsule, stuffed with memorabilia and frozen in time somewhere in the late 1990s, and the only connection he felt with the objects in it was a nostalgic one – the movie posters of *Clerks* and *Kids*, the pin-ups of Kurt Cobain and Chloë Sevigny, the piles of home-made mixed tapes that he knew would be full of stuff by obscure indie bands, the song titles painstakingly scrawled in his spidery script on the cassette casings. It was like it all belonged to someone else, someone he had known long ago and who he thought of now with a sort of avuncular fondness. But he couldn't go back to being that person again. He was no longer the boy he had been, and the man he had become couldn't live here. It was an alien environment to him, a planet with no oxygen.

His parents knew nothing about the life he had lived in New York. They'd only seen the bits of it he'd wanted them to see when they came to visit for a holiday. It had been easy to keep up the pretence short-term, to eradicate the traces of his real life for a week or two. But how could he live with them on a daily basis without them discovering he'd been lying to them for years? It was impossible. He just had to find some way to make enough money to get back to New York as soon as he could.

His self-pity fest was interrupted by a light tap on his door. 'Come in,' he called, sitting up and swinging his legs to the floor. His mother pushed open the door.

'I'm just making a cup of tea, honey. Would you like one?'

'No thanks.'

'Okay. Well …' She continued to hover uncertainly in the doorway, her eyes flitting around the room. 'You might want to start unpacking those boxes.'

'I will. I just haven't got around to it yet.'

'It's been almost three weeks,' she said tentatively.

'I know.' He took a deep breath, trying not to feel irritated. He knew she meant well, but she made him feel like a sulky teenager being told to tidy up his room.

'I could help?' she said. The question in her voice told him she was afraid of getting her head bitten off, and it made him feel guilty. He knew he'd been sulky and belligerent since he'd moved home, and that he'd generally behaved like an ungrateful sod. It wasn't fair. After all, it wasn't *her* fault that her son was such a loser.

'No, I'll do it myself – but thanks,' he said, making a concerted effort not to snap at her.

'You know, you can spread your stuff out in the house. You don't have to put it all in this room. And we can change the decor,' she said, moving into the room and sitting beside him on the bed. 'Why don't we go out at the weekend and you can pick out some things – our treat?'

'Thanks, Mom, but I don't want you to go to any expense.'

'Don't be a feckin' eejit,' she said, bumping her shoulder against his affectionately. He knew she just said it to make him laugh, and it worked. A native of Minnesota, his mother had lived in Ireland for over thirty years but had never lost her accent, and the many Irishisms she had picked up still sounded comically incongruous in her Midwestern twang.

'Anyway, it doesn't have to cost much. We can go to Ikea. This room is long overdue a makeover,' she said looking around. 'I've been meaning to do something with it for ages. Your being here will give me the kick in the butt I need to get on with it.'

'Really, Mom, don't do it on my account. It's just until I sort myself out ...'

She sighed. 'I know you think this is just temporary, honey – and it is,' she rushed on as he opened his mouth to protest, 'but maybe it's not as temporary as you think. It could take you a while to find a job—'

'I know that. And I'm going to start looking soon, I promise. It's just taking me a while to get my head around all this.' At least he had got out of New York before he had burned through all his savings, so he wasn't dependent on his parents just yet.

'Hey, I'm not trying to kick you out. I hate that this has happened to you, but I love having you home.'

'I know. And I like being here with you guys. It's not that—'

'I know it's difficult,' she said. 'You're a grown-up and you're used to having your own life. It's hard to go back to living at home. I get that.'

'It's nothing personal ...'

'I know. But it's just for a while, so why not just relax and make the best of it for now? You'll find your feet in no time, I'm sure. And maybe you'll change your mind about moving back to New York.'

'I doubt it.'

'Well, you never know,' she said brightly. 'I just want to see you happy.'

'I was happy in New York.'

'Were you?' She looked at him narrowly. She seemed to be asking out of genuine curiosity, and Kit was taken aback by her almost pitying expression.

'Yes, of course! Why would you think I wasn't?'

'I don't know. You just always seemed a bit … lonely. Like there was something missing.'

'Lonely? Really? But I had lots of friends there.'

'I know, but—'

'And I had Lauren.' His mother turned her head away a little, but he didn't miss the slightly exasperated look at the mention of his ex-girlfriend. His mother had done her best to hide it and had never been anything but her warm, friendly self on the few occasions they had met, but she had never been very good at disguising her feelings, and he knew she had never approved of Lauren. It didn't bother him – he hadn't particularly approved of her himself. 'I had a really good life in New York,' he persisted, rattled by her question. 'I had a fantastic job, a great social life—'

'I know, it's …' She trailed off, shaking her head. 'It was just an impression,' she said with a soothing smile, clearly afraid she had upset him. 'Maybe it's just wishful thinking because I hate you being so far away. I wish you could have settled down here.'

'Well, at least Ethan's moving back soon.'

'Yes, thank God!' A wave of anxiety passed over her face.

'I'm looking forward to having both my boys home for a while at least. It'll be nice for you to have Ethan back too.'

Outside a firework whizzed into the air with a shriek and they both turned to the window to watch as it exploded in a shower of green and red sparkles.

'It's Hallowe'en,' his mother said, squeezing his knee. 'Why don't you go out and meet up with some of your old friends?'

'I think I'll just stay here and chill out.' Kit loved his mother dearly, but she was treating him like he was six years old. Next, she'd suggest he go trick-or-treating. She was always trying to get him to reconnect with his old friends when he was home. That was how he had ended up at that God-awful party of David Kinsella's last year. He shuddered at the memory. If his mother only knew what he got up to when he tried to reconnect with old friends, she'd probably lock him in his room and swallow the key.

She looked like she wanted to say something more, but instead she got up off the bed and went to the door. He was relieved she wasn't going to push him. They were starting to revert to their old roles. She was back in full-on mom mode, and he was behaving like a stroppy teenager, and he didn't like it. He needed to reclaim his adult life. If he couldn't get back to New York for the moment, he at least needed to get out of this house before he forgot how to be a grown-up.

His mother paused in the doorway, her eyes drifting to the photo on the chest of drawers by the wall. It was a framed collage of photos of him and Romy. Romy had made it and given it to him the Christmas before he went to America. His lips automatically curled in a smile as he looked at the overlapping photos caught beneath the glass of the cheap clip-frame – Romy lying on the grass at Slane Castle the day of the Oasis concert; the pair of them wrapped up against the cold and holding hands on a windswept beach during a

trip to Galway; messing around in the sea at Brittas Bay …
In the centre was a close-up of the two of them laughing into
the camera. He looked thin and rowdy, his hair spiked and
sculpted this way and that, too short and too long all at once
– and he had forgotten about that ridiculous piercing. He
touched his brow where it had been.

'You should look up Romy,' his mother said.

'We haven't kept in touch,' he said, shrugging.

'I could get you her number. Elaine from down the road is
still in touch with her mother, I believe. She has a baby now,
apparently – Romy, I mean.'

'A baby? Really?' Kit looked over at the photomontage.
It was hard to imagine the laughing, carefree girl in those
pictures with a baby.

'Yes, but she's single,' his mother told him hastily.

Oh God, was she going to start trying to fix him up now?
That was all he needed. His mother had always had a soft spot
for Romy. She was probably still nursing her disappointment
that they hadn't ended up together. But she had no idea how
much his tastes had changed.

'I don't know what the story is,' his mother continued,
'but she's definitely not with the father.'

'Huh!' That didn't seem like Romy. Kit couldn't see the girl
he had known doing something so haphazard, so *disorganised*
as becoming a single mother. She'd always been so sensible
and pragmatic. She liked things done the right way and in the
correct order. But then it was a long time since he had known
her. No doubt she had changed, just as he had.

'Her father passed away last year,' his mother was saying
now. 'I'm sure she'd love to hear from you. Why don't you
look her up on Facebook?'

'I don't know. It's been a very long time …'

'Come to think of it,' his mother said, brightening as a

thought occurred to her, 'I have her address. I got it when her father passed so I could send her a sympathy card. Wait here,' she said, holding up a finger – as if he had any intention of going anywhere. She bustled off and came back a few minutes later with a piece of paper, which she pressed into his hand.

'Thanks,' Kit said, glancing down at the address.

'She's in property developing, you know. Apparently she's done very well for herself.'

'Really? Good for her.'

'Well, she always had a good head on her shoulders, didn't she?'

'Yeah,' he smiled, glancing back at the photo frame. 'She did.'

'And you never know – she might be able to help you find a good deal on an apartment.'

When his mother had left, Kit sat staring down at the piece of paper in his hand. Romy. He hadn't thought about her for a long time, but he was suddenly overcome with nostalgia. He stood and grabbed the photo frame from the dresser, sitting back on the bed and gazing down at it. God, he looked like a prat. He'd been so convinced of his own cool, so full of himself with no good reason. He saw now what a bedraggled idiot he had been – a waster, as the teachers used to call him. Then he looked at Romy's lovely, open face and wondered what on earth she had seen in him.

In his defence, at least he had known a good thing when he'd seen it. He may have been thick, but at least he had been able to see what a fantastic girl Romy was, which was more than could be said for some of his supposedly brighter peers. He felt quite proud of himself for that. She hadn't enjoyed the kind of status at school that he had. Romy was funny and loyal, but she wasn't cool and she had never tried to be.

She was kind and clever, but those qualities weren't strong currencies in the schoolyard, and she was overlooked in favour of the more obvious charms of bubbly girls like Tanya Lynch, with their long legs, short skirts and low standards. They all thought he was out of Romy's league, but he had always known it was the other way around.

Romy was more herself than anyone he had ever met – more her own person. Even back then, when everyone was contorting themselves into all kinds of shapes in a desperate effort to fit in, she didn't hide how smart she was or fake a cool she didn't possess. Kit had been used to girls moulding themselves to him, aping his habits and mirroring his taste. Romy was different, and he loved her for it. He'd had enough of himself, and it was refreshing to be with someone *else*, someone other. He liked that it had taken time to get to know her, that she wasn't all there on the surface. It made her all the more worthwhile to him, like those obscure, unappreciated bands he had been so fond of ferreting out.

He loved that she had the courage of her enthusiasms – her unabashed love of The Backstreet Boys; the way she would make him take off Depeche Mode and dance around the room with her to Madonna. He didn't much care for television, yet he was never happier than when he was curled up on this very bed with her watching her beloved *Friends*. It had become one of the highlights of his week. If she loved something, she wasn't afraid to let it show. She had loved him like that.

She was way smarter than him (not that that was saying much), but she had worn it lightly. She would help him with his school work under the guise of 'studying together', and she never made him feel stupid. On the contrary, she had let him dazzle her with his knowledge of alternative bands and independent film. God, he'd been a pretentious wanker! He wondered how she had put up with him. In defence of the asshole he had been then, he had at least appreciated how amazing she was. And he had adored her.

He put the montage back on the dresser and eyed the boxes with a sigh. His mother was right. He was probably going to be here for a while, so he may as well get used to the idea. As he bent resignedly to tear the packing tape off the first box, he thought about what his mother had said. Had he been lonely in New York? He had been so busy, maybe he hadn't stopped going long enough to realise that his life was quite empty. He worked hard and played hard with people who did the same. He was popular. He always had friends to go out with at night, and colleagues to drink with after a hard day in the dealing room. He had gorgeous women to take to dinners and openings, and he was never short of company for holidays. But where were they now? It wasn't that he felt they had ditched him when his circumstances changed. It was more that the lifestyle they had all shared was all they had in common and now that it was gone, so was their connection. He still missed the life he had in New York, and he doubted he would ever feel comfortable living as he wanted here. But now that he thought about it, there was no one from New York he really missed – and no one who had missed him, judging by the fact that none of his crowd had been in touch since he had got home. Maybe he *was* lonely, he thought.

His eyes once more drifted to the photos of Romy and he suddenly had an overwhelming urge to see her. But he wanted to see her as she was then, the laughing girl in those photographs. He wasn't sure if he wanted to meet the woman she had turned into. She had a baby now … and she was a property developer. He smiled, thinking how developing would satisfy her need to fix things up and put them right. He wasn't surprised she had made a success of it.

Suddenly, the thought of property reminded him of something. Galvanised into action by the spark of an idea, he abandoned the box he had just opened and looked instead for the one marked 'files'. He pulled it out from beneath a couple of others, tore off the sealing tape and began rummaging through its contents. He wasn't even sure what he was looking for would be in there. He had filed it away ages ago and forgotten about it, and when he moved he had simply dumped the contents of his filing cabinet into boxes without looking through them. He pulled file after file from the box, rifling through them quickly. He was almost down to the last one when he found what he was looking for, thrown in among miscellaneous legal documents and out-of-date share certificates – the copy of his aunt's will. It was in a plastic wallet together with an accompanying letter from his mother and the information about the dilapidated monstrosity of a house in the middle of nowhere that his aunt had seen fit to leave him. When he had received the news of the bequest, he had barely glanced over the details before shoving the lot into a drawer. He'd known he would make a killing by renovating it for sale, as his mother had suggested, but it had been too much hassle to arrange from New York and he hadn't had the time or energy to put into it. So he had put it on the back burner and eventually forgotten about it.

He paid more attention to it now, a glimmer of hope flickering to life in his chest. He read his mother's characteristically sweet accompanying letter, obviously anticipating his ingratitude and pleading for understanding on his aunt's behalf.

She set great store by land and property, she'd written, *and she was very fond of this house. It shows how much she thought of you that she would leave it to you ... I know it looks like a wreck, but in her day it was quite something, and I'm sure in her mind she still saw it in its former glory.*

He felt ashamed now that she had been correct in surmising what an ingrate he was. At the time, he had just been annoyed that his aunt hadn't left him a straightforward cash bequest, like she had Ethan and Hannah, instead of this albatross.

He read over the will again, taking in every word this time, and actually finding comfort in the formal solidity and clarity of the legal language. Finally, he took out the details of the house – the title deeds and photograph. The glimmer of hope he had been feeling sprouted wings and took flight when he looked at the photo. It was even worse than he remembered – except that it wasn't ugly. It wasn't pretty – it was practically a ruin – but it had grandeur and elegance, and it was actually rather beautiful, in the way that an old overgrown graveyard could be beautiful. He had no idea if he would be able to restore it to its former splendour without bankrupting himself – or whether or not it would even be worth doing. He couldn't afford to sink his paltry savings into renovating the house if he wasn't going to be able to sell it when it was finished. But if there was any chance that this could be his ticket back to New York ...

There was a light tap on the door and his mother pushed it open, balancing a laundry basket on her hip. 'I'm doing a white wash if you have anything to throw in,' she said.

'Oh, that's okay, thanks,' Kit said, sitting back on his haunches. 'I'll do my washing myself.'

'It's no bother,' she assured him with a cheery smile, glancing towards his overflowing linen basket.

Reluctantly, he got up and pulled out a couple of his best designer shirts, dumping them into her basket with a mumbled 'Thanks.'

'Sure. And the *X-Factor* is starting in a few minutes, if you're interested,' she said as she turned to leave.

Kit sighed and flopped down on the bed. He was a very long way from Riverside Drive.

Chapter Three

When she had packed up all the stuff Luke needed for an overnight stay and her mother had come to collect him, Romy went to shower and change for the party. Danny and Lesley were coming early for a debriefing and they would be arriving soon – because there was more to tonight's party than met the eye. As well as all the usual suspects, she had invited everyone she could think of who might have been at David Kinsella's party the previous year, and told them to bring anyone they wanted, in the hope that Luke's father might turn up – or 'return to the scene of the crime' as Lesley put it.

It had been Lesley's idea and, realistically, Romy didn't hold out much hope. It had been a year, and while she could round up the old crowd from school, she didn't know half the people who would have been at David's house that night. Nevertheless, she saw it as a new beginning because she had decided to use her party to draw a line under the whole thing. After this, she was going to forget about trying to find Luke's father and just get on with her life as a single mother.

True to her word, after the night at David's party, she hadn't made any attempt to discover the true identity of Darth Vader. Then, by the time she discovered she was pregnant, the trail had gone cold. David and Katie had moved to Canada, and the details of the party were hazy for those she spoke to, their memories dulled by the passage of time as well as the vast quantities of alcohol they had consumed on the night. She felt entitled to make oblique enquiries about him once she knew she was having his baby, but she had come to a dead end – no one seemed to know who Darth Vader was.

She hadn't made it any easier by not letting anyone else in on the secret of how Luke was conceived. She had kept her pregnancy to herself while she decided what she wanted to do, and then she had presented it to everyone as a fait accompli, making it clear that the father wasn't going to be involved and she didn't want to answer any questions about him. She had been touched by the way her friends and family had respected her wishes and backed off, even though she knew they were all dying to ask questions. She had let them draw their own conclusions, knowing that they assumed he was married or just didn't want to know. And she had been happy to let them assume that – until a couple of weeks earlier, when she had spilled the beans to her little brother and her best friend.

❈

Lesley and Danny were hanging out at her flat. They were all a little drunk, lying around on the sofa, stuffed full of nachos and in that giggly, semi-drowsy over-sharing mode brought on by too many margaritas. Danny had told them about the drunken night in Majorca when he and his boyfriend Paul had ended up in bed with all five members of a well-known boy band. Then Lesley had started to regale them with the horrors of her latest adventures in internet dating.

'He seemed quite nice,' she was saying about the accountant she had dated the previous week. 'So I went back to his place after dinner. But then he asked me if I wanted some wine, and when I said yes, he – get this – he poured himself a glass, took a mouthful, and then he told me to open my mouth, and he sort of dribbled it into my mouth.' She shuddered.

'Jesus!' Danny swore.

'Ecw!' Romy grimaced. 'That's gross.'

'I know. I think he thought it was romantic.'

'A sort of wine spritzer with drool instead of soda – very romantic!'

'I'd say he saw it in a film or something. Films are terrible for giving fellas ideas.' Lesley took a slug of her drink. 'So that was the end of him. Then on Wednesday I went out with Michael.'

'Oh, was he the one who was just out of a long relationship?' Romy asked, remembering the men she had helped Lesley to vet online. 'Graphic designer, thirty-five? He was nice looking.'

'Thirty-five my arse!' Lesley scoffed. 'He was more like a hundred. Turned out, the picture he'd posted was his son. I mean, did he think I wasn't going to *notice*?' she asked, while Danny and Romy shrieked with laughter.

'So what did you do?' Danny asked. 'Did you blow him off straight away?'

'There was no blowing of any kind, let me tell you. But I was brought up to respect the elderly, so I had a very nice early bird dinner with him, and I helped him across the street before I kicked him to touch.' Lesley knocked back the rest of her drink and poured herself another from the jug on the coffee table. 'Oh, and I'm going out with the son next week,' she added.

'What?' Romy spluttered.

'Turns out he actually *is* just out of a long-term relationship. I made Michael promise to introduce us – said I'd have him up for grooming me on the internet if he didn't.'

'Oh, you *have* to marry the son,' Danny said. 'Just think what a cool story you'd have about how you met.'

As they all laughed, Romy racked her brain for something she could contribute to the conversation, but she came up a blank. Was she really that dull? Where were *her* funny stories, her tales of indiscretion? She could only think of one, and she suddenly found herself wanting to tell them because it felt daring, and it was funny and would make them laugh, and what the hell did it matter now anyway.

'So, do you want to know who Luke's father is?' she asked teasingly, while they were still laughing.

Danny and Lesley seemed to sober up instantly. Their laughter ceased abruptly and they both suddenly sat up poker straight and literally on the edge of their seats. 'Yes!' they gasped in unison.

Romy smiled to herself, prolonging their agony for a moment. 'Me too!' she said finally, and burst into giggles. Lesley and Danny looked at her uncomprehendingly, and then frowned at each other in bewilderment.

'What – you mean you don't know?' Danny asked.

'Nope. Absolutely no idea.'

'But how – when—' Lesley spluttered.

'Well, remember David Kinsella's Hallowe'en party last year ...' And so she had confessed all. She told them about Darth Vader, the cupboard, everything.

'So,' Danny said, 'what you're saying is Luke's father is ... Darth Vader?'

'Yes.' She glanced at Danny warily, bracing herself for his reaction. To her amazement, a wide grin spread across his face.

'Cool,' he breathed.

She laughed in relief. 'Well that wasn't the reaction I was expecting.'

'That's why you called him Luke,' Lesley said.

'Yeah. It seemed the obvious choice.'

'You could have called him Darth, after his father,' Danny said.

'Was Darth his first name, though? Were his parents Mr and Mrs Vader?'

'Yep. If you married him, you'd be Mrs Vader.'

'Wouldn't I be Lady Vader? He's a lord, isn't he?'

'A Dark Lord.'

'I could be a Dark Lady, like in Shakespeare's sonnets.'

'I'm not sure if that would make you a lady. I don't know how the peerage works in the Galactic Empire.'

'I doubt *anything* can make you a lady after that,' Lesley said. 'And you won't be getting into any sonnets with that kind of behaviour.'

'Lady Vader,' Romy mused. 'It has a nice ring to it.'

'So that was why you were always asking about him. I wish you'd told me this sooner.'

'What difference would it have made? We've already asked everyone we know who was at the party. No one knew who he was.'

'Couldn't you have just asked David?'

'I did. He'd gone to Canada by the time I found out I was pregnant, but I friended him on Facebook, and asked him. He said he didn't know.'

What he had actually said was that he must have been a friend of Katie's. She thought about Katie sometimes. It was weird knowing there was someone out there in the world who could simply give her the name of her baby's father. But how could she ask? She didn't know Katie, and even if she didn't feel it would be breaking her promise to Darth Vader, how could she approach a virtual stranger and ask who she had been cheating on her husband with? She would probably deny the whole thing anyway.

'Still, you should have told us,' Lesley said. 'Maybe we could have helped.'

Danny sighed. 'Well, maybe we can help now. Let's go over it again. Tell us everything you know about him.'

Romy thought hard. What did she know about him? Very little. She knew he didn't believe in God, but he prayed sometimes in his head. And she knew he had been having an affair with David's wife, but she couldn't tell them that. 'He was tall,' she said eventually with a helpless shrug.

'Okay, good,' Danny nodded encouragingly. 'And he likes *Star Wars*, we know that.'

'I suppose.' Romy bit her lip. 'But he might not. I mean, what if that was the only costume he could get? He might have just picked it at random.'

'Okay, tall and possibly likes *Star Wars*,' Lesley put in. 'Any other clues?'

'Um … I think he could be asthmatic.'

'Really? What makes you think that?'

'Well … he was breathing really heavily the whole time. He sounded quite out of breath.'

'Romy,' Danny smiled pityingly, 'you were having it off.'

'You know I hate that expression.' She frowned.

'Okay, you were … *making love*, whatever.' Danny sniggered. 'You were making love in a wardrobe with a guy you couldn't pick out in a crowd—'

'Oh, shut up!' She grabbed a cushion and swatted him with it.

He laughed more, raising his hands to defend himself. 'Okay, okay. But y'know, everyone breathes deeply when they're in the throes. Plus you were in a wardrobe – it was probably pretty stuffy in there.'

'And on top of all that he was wearing a mask,' Lesley added.

'Yeah, I know.' Romy sighed. 'I'm just clutching at straws.'

'Besides,' Danny said, 'he might have just been getting into character – you know, if he thought the Vader thing was a turn-on for you. Did he say anything?'

'Ugh! I'm not giving you details.'

'I don't want details, thank you very much. I just mean did he say anything to make you think he was trying to fulfil your Darth Vader fantasies?'

'Like what?'

'Like, "Can you feel the force, baby?"' Danny boomed in a Vader-like voice. '"Get a load of my light sabre."' He collapsed in giggles.

Romy looked at him crossly.

'Sorry, sorry,' he said, trying to rein in his grin.

'If you're not going to take this seriously—'

'I am, honest. Sorry.' He reached out to her and pulled her against him, and she laid her head on his shoulder.

'I just think he should know he has a child, whoever he is,' she said. 'And Luke should have a chance to know who his father is.'

'Didn't you get any glimpse of what he looked like? Did he leave his mask on the whole time you were …' Lesley trailed off.

'It was very dark in the wardrobe,' Romy answered evasively. She closed her eyes, concentrating. 'He had good arms,' she said, remembering the feel of muscle and sinew beneath warm skin, how strong his arms had felt wrapped around her. 'He was slim, but well built – he had a broad chest.'

'Right. So – someone with arms and a chest,' Danny said. 'We'll have this cracked in no time.'

'I know,' Romy said despondently. 'He could be anybody.'

'There has to be some way of tracking him down,' Lesley said briskly. 'We just have to be more creative.'

'*How*?'

Lesley was silent for a while, thinking. 'We could hold a DNA party!' she said finally.

'A *what*?'

'A DNA party. We throw a party, right, and then we keep a glass or something that everyone's touched, so we have their DNA. We'll get a load of freezer bags and mark who each glass belongs to. Then we send them all to the lab—'

'What lab?'

'You know – the lab. The DNA testing lab. You've seen *Sea of Love*, right? They did that. They went on dates with all these women and—'

'They were cops. They had access to a lab.'

'Well, there are places that do DNA testing, aren't there? What about all those skanks who don't get on the telly? They must have somewhere to go to find out who the father of their baby is if they don't get picked for *The Jeremy Kyle Show*.'

'And what kind of skank would *I* look like, turning up at the baby-father clinic with a hundred-odd DNA samples? Even those ones on the telly usually have it narrowed down to three or four suspects. Anyway, I'm pretty sure you can't collect people's DNA without their permission.'

'Well, maybe he'll start to look like his father,' Danny said.

'Big shiny helmet?' Romy said, her lips twitching.

'Big shiny helmet … mouth breather,' Danny sniggered. 'Seriously though, maybe he'll turn into a dead ringer for someone we know.'

'You know, sometimes he does almost remind me of someone. But I can't put my finger on who.'

'Mr Potato Head,' Lesley said.

'Sorry?'

'Mr Potato Head – that's who he reminds you of. I've often thought that myself.'

'My son does *not* look like Mr Potato Head.'

'Hey, calm down. I'm talking about if you do the button nose and don't use the moustache.'

'He still doesn't look like Mr Potato Head, okay? Anyway, this guy was too tall for Mr Potato Head. *Way* too tall, and less … potatoey.'

Lesley sighed heavily. 'I guess we're back to square one then.'

'Maybe it's just as well,' Romy said. 'I mean, what if I found him and he turned out to be an asshole?'

They were all silent for a moment, contemplating this.

'Nah,' Danny said finally. 'Luke doesn't have any asshole in him.'

'I've an idea!' Lesley gasped. 'We could stage a re-enactment.'

'What? Shove me into a cupboard with a masked stranger and see if it jogs anyone's memory?'

'No, silly! Although—'

'Don't even think about it.'

'Okay, okay. What I meant was we should have a Hallowe'en party and invite all the people who were at David's last year – or as many as we can.'

✳

So, after she had sworn them to secrecy about Darth Vader – threatening Danny with dismemberment if he told their mother – they had planned this party. She didn't really believe it was going to work, but as she stood in front of the mirror putting on her make-up, she still felt a little shiver of anticipation at the possibility that Luke's father could turn up. Her excitement was tinged with fear because, much as she wanted Luke to have the chance to know his father, there was a tiny part of her that was happy not knowing. She thought very fondly of her mysterious stranger – not just because he had given her Luke, but because she had turned a corner after that night with him. It had freed her somehow, healed her – as if when she told him her secret he had taken it from her and carried it off, taking all the burden and weight of it. She wasn't normally a fanciful person, but sometimes she thought of him almost as an angel who had taken away her pain and given her instead her beloved son. There was a part of her that wanted to keep him in the realm of fantasy, afraid of discovering that her beautiful seraph had feet of clay or a heart of stone.

※

'Okay, this is it,' Romy said as she sat in the pre-party lull with Lesley and Danny. 'Tonight is make or break. If I don't find out who Luke's father is at this party, I'm giving up the search.'

Lesley and Danny looked uncertain, but they nodded agreement.

'Okay, you both know what you have to do?' Romy asked.

'If we see anyone who might have been at David's party last year, we ask them pertinent questions,' Lesley responded.

'Such as?'

Lesley pulled a small ring-bound notebook from her jeans pocket.

'You wrote them down?'

'I just made a few notes,' Lesley said, flipping the notebook open. 'Were you at David Kinsella's Hallowe'en party last year?' she read. 'If yes, what costume did you wear? Where were you between the hours of ten p.m. and two a.m. on the night of October thirty-first?'

'Right. You don't have to make it sound quite so ... *Columbo*, though.'

'God, I love *Columbo*,' Lesley said. 'Always gets his man – or woman. At least in this case we know it's a man.'

'Yeah, that narrows it right down,' Danny said dryly.

'Just don't make them feel like they're being interrogated,' Romy said to Lesley, who took a small pen from her back pocket.

'Not ... being ... interrogated,' she said as she wrote.

'Um ... you're not going to take notes, are you? When you talk to people later,' Romy asked.

'Well, I thought it'd help – with the investigation, like.'

'I told you, it's not an investigation.'

'God, I wish it *was* an investigation! That'd be brilliant, wouldn't it? We could set up one of those incident rooms.'

'Look, chances are there'll be hardly anyone from David's party here anyway. We don't exactly mix in the same circles.'

'And if we don't find him tonight, we can set up an incident room.'

'No, no incident room.'

'Please,' Lesley begged. 'Just a small one? I'll set it up in my house. You won't even have to be involved.'

'No,' Romy said firmly. 'Tonight is my last shot at finding out who he is. After this, I'm just going to put it behind me and get on with my life. I've been living in limbo for long enough.'

Lesley's face fell about half a mile. 'You're calling off the investigation? Just like that?'

'I told you – there *is* no investigation. I've tried everything, but the trail's gone cold. I need to move on.'

'It's like one of those cold cases – they get solved every day,' Lesley persisted.

'Lesley—'

'And you haven't tried everything. I think an incident room could really help. We just need to focus on the details, follow the trail … And there was the DNA testing,' she said. 'You haven't tried that. And I've got lots more ideas. I was thinking if we could get our hands on one of those computer programmes that shows you what someone will look like when they're older—'

'Lesley, give her a break,' Danny chided.

Lesley looked rebuked. 'Sorry, babe,' she said to Romy. 'You're right. You should move on. He'd probably turn out to be a gobshite anyway. You're better off without him.'

'Yeah, I'm just going to settle down to being a single mother, concentrate on Luke.'

'Feck that!' Lesley said. 'You want to find yourself a nice man to love both you and Luke.'

Romy didn't have time to argue as the doorbell rang, so she went to answer it. It was her tenants, all arriving in a clump. Glancing at the clock in the hall as they filed past, she saw that it was seven thirty on the dot, and she wondered if they had been waiting outside the door, timing their arrival to the second. May and Frank led the way, presenting Romy with a bottle of champagne and a tray of home-made muffins. They were followed by Sarah and Colm, the young couple from one of the basement flats, with Stefan, the gigantic Polish plumber from upstairs, bringing up the rear. He kissed her on both cheeks and pressed a bottle of vodka into her hands before heading straight for the table where she had laid out nibbles. Romy started handing out drinks, and introduced everyone to Lesley and Danny.

'Hi, May, how are you?' Lesley already knew May. She had helped her set up her blog, where she was currently writing about her and Frank's experiences working through a popular sex manual as an elderly couple. They were methodically trying out all the positions, assessing their suitability for those with high blood pressure, arthritis and prosthetic joints, and working out adjustments that could be made to accommodate the less agile. A one-time agony aunt and sex therapist, May was still regarded as a bit of an authority on the subject, and Lesley was now building her a website devoted to all aspects of sexuality. 'Still working through the dirty book with yer man?' she asked, nodding to Frank, who was chatting to Stefan.

'Yes, we had a very good day today,' May said, beaming. 'We got through three new positions, so I've lots to blog about. And I still had time to make muffins for Romy's party.'

'Fair play!' Lesley made a mental note to give the muffins a wide berth. 'It's important to have a hobby when you're retired, isn't it? My dad retired recently and he's driving my ma mental. She keeps trying to get him to take up golf, but no dice.'

'Well, golf's not very stimulating, in fairness to the man. No wonder men are terrified of retiring if that's all they have to look forward to. You should direct him to my blog. It might give him some ideas.'

'Oh, I don't think sex is really my dad's cup of tea. He'd be more of an Airfix person really.'

'Of course it is! He's a man, isn't he?'

'Well ... I suppose – for want of a better word.'

'We're all sexual beings, Lesley. It's part of the human

condition. You know, it's the thing most people say they regret in life – not having had more sex.'

'Really?'

'Yes. That's why I'm so keen to set up this website. It's so important to explore your sexuality to the full. I hope you're exploring your sexuality, dear?'

'Oh, you know … whenever I get the opportunity.'

'By the way, I have lots of new material for you to upload. I've written a new piece on Tantric sex, and I have some new photos for the section on bondage.'

Lesley gulped. 'Photos?'

'Oh, don't worry, they're not photos of me and Frank, and nothing too explicit either. I don't want it to be pornographic. Not that there's anything wrong with pornography per se, of course,' she added hastily. 'It serves a purpose. But I don't like the idea of young fellows I don't know from Adam jacking off to photos of me.'

Not much chance of that, Lesley thought, struggling to keep her eyebrows out of her hairline. 'Great! Well, you can give it all to me tonight, if you like, and I'll get working on it.'

'Lovely. Oh, and I'm starting a new section too devoted to toys and props. Which reminds me, there's something I want to ask Romy about. If you'll excuse me.'

As May went off to talk to Romy, Lesley joined Stefan, who was standing by the buffet table, steadily demolishing the food.

'Hi, Stefan. How are you?'

'Ah, Lesley. I am tired.' Stefan spoke like a Hammer Horror Dracula, lending everything he said a rather morose air. He still hadn't adapted to Irish ways sufficiently to recognise 'How are you?' as a greeting like 'hello' rather than an actual enquiry after his wellbeing.

'Yeah? Been working hard?'

'Yes, but it's not that. It's May and Frank – the noise they make!'

'Right. That'll be them exploring their sexuality, I suppose.'

'I ask Romy to talk to them, but nothink change. Beng, beng, beng, all night!'

'Ah sure, what harm are they doing?'

Stefan looked mournfully at her. 'They are too old to be havink all this sex. I tell May she should do knittink like other old ladies.'

'Wait until *you're* a hundred. I bet you won't want to pack it in yourself.'

'Is May a hundred?' Stefan asked seriously, looking across at the elderly lady. 'She looks good,' he admitted. He still couldn't tell when people were joking either.

'No, she's not really a hundred,' Lesley said, following his gaze. 'Though, God, she could be. I don't know what age she is.'

Lesley had been vaguely aware of the doorbell ringing and people streaming in while she chatted to Stefan, and she suddenly noticed that the room was filling up.

'Well, can't stand here chatting to you all night.' She stuffed a couple of tortilla chips into her mouth and brushed the crumbs from her hands. 'I've got some serious mingling to do,' she said, pulling a notebook from her back pocket as she walked away.

Chapter Four

Kit watched Romy's house from his vantage point in the tree opposite as darkness fell and the road became populated with bands of miniature witches, vampires, superheroes and assorted ghouls. He burrowed closer to the trunk, clinging to the shadows of the branches as a group of children pushed through the green gate and ran up to the door with an explosion of giggles and squeals. He didn't want to be seen, but he was glad of the opportunity to see Romy again when she came to answer the door. He watched her bend down, smiling brightly at the children as she held out a tray of treats. Her face was as warm and lovely as ever, and he felt happy to see her. Nevertheless, he was relieved when the children thundered off again, clanging the gate behind them, and he felt safe once more.

'There's a man up that tree!' squealed a high-pitched childish voice below him, making him jump and almost lose his balance. He looked down to see a tiny witch with a pointy hat and an elaborate cobweb painted on her face standing at the bottom of the tree and pointing up at him. Luckily, her fellow munchkins weren't paying any attention and had already beetled off to the next house, oblivious to her shrieking. She was looking right up at him now and he put a finger to his lips to shush her.

'What are you doing up there?' she called to him.

'Sssh,' he hissed, shaking his head at her.

'Are you stuck?'

'No, I'm not stuck,' he whispered. 'Go away!' He waved a hand, shooing her.

'Why are you up a tree?'

Bloody little busybody! Why wouldn't she just piss off? 'I'm hiding,' he told her. 'I'm … playing hide and seek.'

She looked around the road and then back up at him. 'Who are you playing with?'

'Shut up and go away. They'll find me.'

'Are you playing with your children?'

'I don't – yes!'

'Oh.' She looked up and down the road again. 'Where are they?'

'What?'

'Where are your children? I don't see anyone.'

For fuck's sake! 'They're looking for me. They're … here they come now,' he said, waving vaguely to the end of the road, where a gaggle of trick-or-treaters had just rounded the corner.

'Them?' she pointed, peering at them closely as they drew nearer.

'Yes,' he hissed urgently. 'That's them. Now go away or they'll find me.'

'That's Josh and Alice and Gordon and Pearse. They're in my class. You're not their dad. I've seen their dads at school.'

'Look, will you just—'

'Why did you say you're their dad when you're not?'

She was looking up at him expectantly and he had no idea what to say. Then she suddenly gasped and he heard her mutter something to herself. 'Stranger danger!' she yelped, before letting out a blood-curdling scream and taking off down the road as fast as her little legs would carry her.

Thank fuck for that, Kit thought, relaxing back against the tree to watch the comings and goings at Romy's party, grateful to have the darkness to himself again. He didn't know quite why he had decided to hide in a tree and spy on her from a distance, but he felt weird about just marching up to her door and ringing the bell after half a lifetime. Yeah, this was definitely the not-weird option, he thought wryly – stuck up a tree in the sodium haze of the streetlights with fireworks exploding around his head while he spied on his ex-girlfriend. There was nothing weird about that.

His mother had been surprised when he had appeared downstairs and announced that he'd decided to go out after all. But when he'd said he thought he might take her advice and look up Romy, she had looked so pleased that it made him feel guilty – guilty that he could make her happy so easily if he tried, guilty that he hadn't tried harder since coming home, and most of all, guilty because he knew she would read something into him looking up Romy that wasn't actually there.

He watched Romy move around the brightly lit room, pouring wine and passing around food, and felt a longing to be on the inside. And yet he couldn't bring himself to move. It was getting cold in the tree, but it looked so cosy and inviting where Romy was that it warmed him up just looking at her. At one point, she stood in the window with a plate in her hand, forking food into her mouth and gazing out at the night, and it was like she was looking right at him, as if somehow she knew he was there and they were sharing the moment.

Later, she got everyone playing old-fashioned Hallowe'en party games. Kit couldn't see everything from his position, but he could see they were playing snap-apple at one stage. Snap-apple – without a hint of irony, and Romy was laughing her head off! She seemed to be having the time of her life with the old fogeys and deadbeats she had assembled in her house. She looked so happy, he thought wonderingly. Christ, if that was her idea of a good time, she'd probably be overjoyed to have him back in her life. Still he hung back, waiting to make his move …

✳

He's not here, Romy thought as the party clattered and hummed around her. *He didn't come.* It was completely irrational since she had no idea who he was and sometimes when she passed strangers in the street she thought 'that could be him' – so there was no reason why he couldn't be standing in this room right now. But, somehow, she knew that he wasn't. She was dismayed at how hollow that made her feel, and she turned to the window to give herself a moment of privacy, gazing out into the night as she forked cake into her mouth. He was still out there somewhere, and she would probably never see him again. She had thought she would feel relieved more than anything, but she realised now how excited she had been deep down at the thought that he might turn up.

She didn't know why, but as soon as she opened the door to the first guest, she had experienced a sense of absolute certainty that he wasn't going to come, and she had felt instantly deflated – and knocked off balance by the crushing disappointment she'd felt. After all, she had always known the chances of him showing up were slim. But until that moment she hadn't realised how much she had allowed the idea to take hold in her imagination. It was only when she was taking coats and exchanging small talk as she ushered in a group of her old school friends that the reality settled on her like the cold that still clung to them from outside, and she realised how fanciful she was being. Things like that didn't happen in real life, to ordinary people like her.

'Great party, Romy.' She felt someone at her side and turned to find Derek Hanly standing beside her, a bottle of beer in his hand. Derek had been in her class at school. Tall and gangly, with an unkempt tangle of dark auburn hair and pale freckled skin, he still looked about twelve.

'Hi, Derek,' she smiled at him, shaking herself back to the present. 'Glad you're enjoying it.' As she spoke, she saw Lesley in her peripheral vision, gesticulating at her wildly, alternating between pointing at Derek behind his back and waving her notebook.

Romy sighed. Even though she felt it was futile, she should probably go through the motions just to keep Lesley happy. 'Were you at David's party last year?' she asked him.

'Yeah, I was, but this one's a lot more fun. All that crap with wearing masks.'

'Hmm. What did you go as?'

Derek chuckled and took a sip of his beer before answering. 'Darth Vader,' he said, grinning at her. 'Yeah, really shot myself in the foot with that one … bloody helmet …'

Romy was aware that he was still speaking, but she had no idea what he was saying. It was as if the room and everything in it had faded into the background and all she could hear was the beat of her heart and the rush of blood in her veins.

'Romy?' He was looking at her with concern now. 'You okay?'

'What? Oh yeah,' she said faintly, 'I'm fine.' She looked

closely at him. He had a nice face, she thought – cute rather than handsome, but open and friendly. As far as she knew, he was a nice person. She hadn't seen him properly in years, but she had always liked him at school. He had loaned her a tennis racket once when she'd broken hers. And he had bought her chips one lunch-time when she didn't have any money. That was about the sum total of what she knew of him. Could he really be Luke's father? It didn't seem possible. And what was she supposed to do now that she'd found him? She couldn't just say, 'Oh, by the way, we have a child together.'

'What are you up to these days?' she asked, her voice sounding far away to her ears.

'Nothing much. Still working for my dad.'

'Computers, isn't it?'

'Yep. And I'm engaged! Orla and I are tying the knot next year,' he said, nodding across the room at a girl who was chatting to a group of their old school friends.

'Oh, that's exciting! Congratulations!'

'Thanks,' he said, grinning.

God, this was going to be even more complicated than she'd thought. She glanced back at Orla. She looked so happy – they both did – and they were about to get married. How could she barge into their happy uncomplicated lives with a baby? She wasn't sure she even wanted to. How good would it be for Luke having a father who was married to someone else, who would probably have children with someone else – a father who wouldn't have much time for him and might not even want to know him?

'Do you ever hear from David now? Or Katie?' she asked mechanically.

'No, not a sausage. But I was never really friends with David anyway. He only asked us lot to his parties to show off. And I didn't know Katie at all.'

'You didn't?' She watched him carefully, but there was nothing in his expression to suggest he was lying.

'No. Anyway, it's really nice to see you again, Romy. Thanks for inviting me. It's nice to catch up with the old crowd. We never see each other anymore. We should do it more often.'

She took a deep breath, steeling herself to speak. If she didn't say something now, she never would. 'I met you last year at David's party.'

'You did?' he frowned. 'I don't think so.'

'You were Darth Vader?'

'Yep.'

'We … talked. I was dressed as Red Riding Hood.'

'Doesn't ring a bell,' he said. 'But I was pretty pissed that night.'

'We went upstairs. We didn't take our masks off.'

'Nope, definitely not me.' She watched his face, but there wasn't a flicker. Maybe he genuinely didn't remember. But he hadn't seemed that drunk.

'It must have been the other Darth Vader,' he said.

'There was another one? Do you know who he was?'

'No, sorry – don't have a clue. He had a much fancier costume than mine – probably one of David's knobhead friends.'

'Oh. Right.' And there it was – the relief she had expected to feel earlier was seeping through her now like analgesic, softening and relaxing.

'Come over and I'll introduce you to Orla,' he said.

'Romy, sorry to interrupt,' May said, approaching her as she let Derek lead her away, 'but whenever you're ready, could I have a word with you about the swing?'

'Sure, May – I'll be with you in a sec.'

'One of my tenants,' she explained to Derek when May had retreated to a safe distance. 'She wants my permission to set up this swing she wants to buy.'

Derek looked across at May. 'She looks a bit old for a swing,' he said.

'You don't know the half of it,' Romy said, rolling her eyes.

She felt light-hearted as she joined the group around Orla, as if a weight had been lifted from her. She had caught a glimpse of what it might be like to find Luke's father – all the complications and problems it could cause. Just as she had realised she might be better off not knowing, she had been given a reprieve.

'Well, I've come up a blank,' Lesley said to her later. 'How about you? Did you question Derek?'

'Yeah, it wasn't him.'

Lesley sighed. 'That's it, then. He's not here.'

'No,' Romy smiled. 'He's not here.'

❊

Kit watched as the door opened and a flood of light illuminated the garden as another group of people hurried down the steps, waved off by Romy. He watched as they walked down the street and out of sight. When he turned back to the house, the door was closed again, the garden in darkness once more. He had made up his mind to go and knock on the door several times, but he had hesitated and started dithering again, and the moment had passed. Now the party seemed to be finally breaking up. Romy had been to the door several times, seeing people off, and now she was moving around the room, gathering things up. He lost sight of her for a while, and then a light came on at the other side of the house and she appeared in the window. It looked like she was cleaning up. He decided it was now or never.

He pulled the mask he'd bought from his jacket pocket.

He'd decided he would make an entrance – go up to her door in a mask and say 'trick or treat'. On the way here, he had slipped into a newsagent's and bought the first mask he could find – a cheap plastic one that made his face sweat, which was why he'd waited until the last moment to put it on.

Silly, it is, he thought wryly, looking at the wise old face of Yoda. Still, he had felt it would be easier to approach Romy with the mask as a shield – it also meant he could still run away if he changed his mind and she need never know it was him. He pulled the mask over his face, the thin elastic tight on his ears. He was about to climb down from the tree when Romy came to the door again and he paused. She stood at the top of the steps making that 'pshwsh' sound people make to call cats and calling 'Bumble' softly.

Kit looked down and saw a fat ginger cat rubbing himself on the bark of the tree – his tree! He tried to hiss at it really quietly, so Romy wouldn't hear, desperately willing it to go away. But it was too late. Romy spotted the cat and came bounding down the steps and out the gate. Kit froze on the spot, looking down at the top of her dark head and trying not even to breathe as she bent to the cat.

'There you are,' she cooed, crouching down in front of him and stroking his fur. 'Were you scared of the fireworks? Poor little fella.'

She was reaching to pick him up when a firework screeched into the sky and exploded with a loud bang. The cat yowled and scrabbled up the tree, landing right in Kit's lap, simultaneously sinking its claws into his crotch and its teeth into his hand. Already balanced precariously on a branch, Kit got such a fright he yelped and instinctively pulled away. Losing his balance, he came crashing out of the tree and landed with a thud right at Romy's feet.

'Ugh!' he groaned as he sat up. 'Nice one, Ginger!' He

scowled at the cat as it executed a perfect landing beside him seconds later and stalked over to Romy, its tail in the air.

'Oh!' Romy was looking down at him with a startled expression, and he jumped up quickly, brushing bits of twig and leaf from his clothes, aware that he must look like … well, like he'd literally been dragged through a tree backwards.

'Hello!' he said, giving her a big friendly grin, trying to look reassuringly normal, despite the fact that he had just come hurtling out of a tree.

'Hello.' She didn't smile back, looking at him sketchily as she bent to pick up the cat, as if afraid he would pounce on her if she let her guard down for a second. She held the cat to her chest, stroking its fur. 'Did you get a fright?' she whispered, frowning crossly at Kit as if it was his fault – as if he'd done something to hurt the bloody animal, when in reality it was the other way around. She looked the cat over, checking for injuries.

Kit waited for her to recognise him. He was surprised it was taking her this long, but then it was dark and it had been a very long time. Still, he didn't think he'd changed that much. He reached a hand up to run his fingers through his hair and rake out any bits of tree, and his fingers met plastic. Of course! He'd forgotten he'd put the mask on, and somehow it had survived the fall. Maybe he could get out of this with his dignity intact after all. He could run away incognito and she would never know it was him. Then he could call to her house tomorrow like a normal person.

'So … what are you doing here?' she asked him.

'Oh, just …' He shrugged, playing it casual while desperately trying to think of something to say to convince her he wasn't a nutjob or a pervert. 'Just, you know … Hallowe'en.' Great! He was really on fire tonight.

'You were up a tree.'

'Um … yes. I was.'

'Aren't you a bit old for climbing trees and dressing up for Hallowe'en?'

'I'm very immature.' Brilliant! Where the fuck had that come from? Still, it got a little smile from her. She nodded slowly, looking at him for a long time, like she was trying to decide something – probably whether he was an axe murderer or not.

'Well, happy Hallowe'en,' she said, throwing him a dubious look as she turned to go.

'Happy Hallowe'en,' Kit called. When she was at the gate, he bent down to brush mud from his trousers. 'May the force be with you,' he mumbled to her back.

Romy spun around. 'What did you say?'

'Happy Hallowe'en.'

She shook her head. 'After that.'

'Um … may the force be with you?'

The cat wriggled out of her arms and padded back through the gate and up the steps, but Romy still stood there, looking at him strangely. 'Why did you say that?' She looked a bit freaked out – which he supposed made sense in the circumstances. But why now? She hadn't seemed fazed when he first landed at her feet.

'It's just an expression.' Kit shrugged. 'It's *Star Wars*.' Surely she knew *Star Wars*? He was sure he could remember watching it with her.

'Yes, I know it's *Star Wars*. It just … it seems an odd thing to say.'

'I guess I'm just in a *Star Wars* frame of mind,' he said, pointing at his mask.

'Do you like *Star Wars*?'

'What?'

'I said do you like *Star Wars*.'

'Sure,' he said, shrugging. 'Doesn't everyone?'

'Who's your favourite character?'

Christ, did she think he was five or something? Granted, he had just fallen out of a tree wearing a Hallowe'en mask, but even so … and why was she still standing out here engaging him in conversation anyway? Shouldn't she be inside ringing the police or something? He just wanted to get away, as quickly as possible. 'I can't say I've ever given it much thought. I guess R2D2 is pretty cool.'

'Oh.' Her face fell, and he got the impression his answer disappointed her somehow. He must be imagining it. Why would she care who he liked out of *Star Wars*?

'Disappointed, you seem.'

'What?'

'You know, Yoda,' he said, pointing to his mask again in explanation. 'Says everything backwards, doesn't he?'

'Oh. Yeah.'

'I mean, obviously I like him too. But y'know, they're all good,' he said, hoping to cheer her up. Stop babbling about *Star Wars* and get out of here, he chided himself.

Romy was looking up at the tree where he had been sitting and across at her windows, clearly putting two and two together. 'Were you watching my house?' she asked.

Jesus, why was she standing here confronting him about it? Didn't she have any self-preservation instincts? If he really was a mad stalker, she could be in serious danger right now.

'No,' he said. 'I wasn't.'

'Really?' She regarded him sceptically.

'Look, it's not what you think—' Before he had a chance to say any more, they were interrupted by a herd of children in Hallowe'en costumes swarming down the path and bursting between them like a loud, debris-strewn river, leaving Kit and Romy on opposite banks. Romy stepped back to her gate to let them pass, but while the rest of them streamed away, one child stopped dead in front of Kit.

'Stranger danger!' He heard a breathy gasp and looked down to see his nemesis gazing up at him – the little witch with the spider's web face. 'Scream, kick, run,' she was muttering under her breath, as if coaching herself, before doing just that. She shrieked loudly, administered a sharp kick to Kit's shin, then sprinted off down the road like a firework rocketing into the night, emitting a high-pitched squeal the whole way.

'Fu-uck!' Kit puffed, reaching down to rub his shin. 'Bloody hell! What do they teach kids in school these days?' He looked up at Romy, who had backed into the gate and was opening it behind her without taking her eyes off him.

'They teach them, "Scream, kick, run." I'd say she's a credit to her teacher,' she said, looking after the little girl, who had now disappeared.

'Jesus, Romy,' he gasped, still winded from the pain in his shin, 'I'm not—'

'How do you know my name?'

'What?' Oh fuck! 'Look, I'm not a perv—'

'You were watching my house and you know my name. Who are you?'

There was nothing else for it. He was just going to have to take off his mask and reveal himself as the idiot he was. He stepped out of the shadow of the tree so she could see him better.

'Don't come any closer,' she breathed, her glance shifting nervously between the end of the road and him.

He stood still where he was and pulled the mask off over his head.

'*Kit*!' she gasped.

Chapter Five

'Hi, Romy.' He smiled at her sheepishly.

She just stood staring at him, dumbstruck. What on earth?

Kit glanced nervously to the end of the road. 'Do you think she's coming back?' he asked her.

'Oh, most definitely,' she said, a smile tugging at her lips. 'With townsfolk.'

'Oh!'

'Yeah. Pitchforks, flaming torches, the whole shebang.'

'Right.'

Still she didn't move. She stood there watching him, just letting him sweat. They both turned when they heard voices at the end of the road and he saw the little girl coming back, this time with a couple of adults in tow. 'He was pretending to be someone's dad,' she was saying as they drew closer, 'but I knew he wasn't—'

'Come on, you'd better come in before the lynch mob gets here,' Romy said, grabbing Kit's hand and pulling him through the gate and up the garden path. They jogged up the steps to the house and she opened the door quickly, hustling him inside. Bumble snaked between their legs and slid through the door at the same time and took off down the hall.

'Thanks!' Kit puffed once the door closed behind them.

'No problem. Anyway, I still want to hear your explanation.'

Kit opened his mouth to speak, but she shushed him. 'Later,' she said. 'I have guests.'

'Oh, sorry – I thought all the guests had gone.' He realised his mistake as soon as the words were out of his mouth.

'So you *were* watching the house.' She gave him a stern look.

'I can explain—'

'Later,' she said again, leading him through an inner door and into a large cosy living room.

There were only a few stragglers left – a pair of crumblies were wrapped around each other on the sofa and a huge guy stood by the buffet shovelling food into his mouth. A young couple sat at the other end of the sofa, their heads bent in conversation. They all looked up at the sight of fresh meat.

'Look who I found outside!' Romy said, pulling him over to the sofa. The old pair broke out of their embrace to look up at him. 'This is Kit,' she told them. 'He's an old friend. Kit, this is May and Frank. They live upstairs.'

'Very nice to meet you, Kit,' the woman said, shaking his hand. He got the feeling he was being thoroughly inspected.

Romy introduced him to the rest of the people in the room – Colm and Sarah from the basement, and Stefan, who lived upstairs – and he gave them an awkward wave.

'Right, come on, you lot,' May said, getting up from the sofa. 'Let's leave Romy and her friend in peace. Thank you for a lovely party, dear,' she said, kissing Romy's cheek on her way out. The others followed her lead and trooped out after her.

'Would you like something to drink?' Romy asked Kit when she had closed the door behind them. 'Wine? Coffee? Tea?'

'I'd love a coffee.' He still felt the chill of outside.

'Sure! Coming right up,' she said, gathering some empty plates from the buffet table.

'Can I help you clear up?' he asked.

'Thanks. You could help me bring this stuff out to the kitchen,' she said as she began to gather up plates and glasses. 'Would you like something to eat?'

Now that he thought about it, Kit realised he was ravenous. He glanced at the ravaged buffet as he collected cutlery and crumpled napkins. 'I don't want you to go to any trouble.'

'Hungry?'

'Starving!' Kit admitted with a guilty smile. 'I sort of missed dinner.'

'Well, that's what you get for spending the night up a tree.'

Kit laughed. 'Yeah, unfortunately, you need an address to get a takeaway delivered.'

'There's not much left,' Romy said, biting her lip, 'but there's still some cake. Or I could make you a sandwich.'

'A sandwich would be great,' Kit said as he followed Romy to the kitchen.

Romy deposited the stuff on the worktop and indicated to Kit to do the same. 'Cheese toastie?' she asked as she loaded the dishwasher.

'Perfect!'

'Okay, have a seat.' She nodded towards the little table.

'It's very nice of you to invite all your neighbours to your party,' Kit said, sitting down while Romy busied herself with the coffee machine.

'Oh, they're not just neighbours,' she said as she spooned coffee into the filter and switched on the machine. 'They're my tenants.'

'Really? So you own this whole house?'

'Yes.'

'Wow! It's a great house.'

'It is, isn't it?' Romy said as she sliced cheese and cut bread. 'I fell in love with it the minute I saw it.' She made a sandwich and buttered the outsides, then slid it into a pan. The smell of hot butter filled the air. 'Of course, I'd originally intended to have sold it on by now, but then the property market went into freefall. But I'm kind of glad now the way things turned out. It means I get to live in it – and own it for a bit longer.'

'Well, it's very impressive. Mom told me you'd done really well for yourself.'

'Not as well as you by all accounts,' she said, flipping the sandwich over and pressing it down so it hissed. 'I've heard you're taking Wall Street by storm.'

'Not anymore.'

'Oh, sorry to hear that.' She slid the sandwich onto a plate and handed it to him with a mug of steaming coffee.

Kit shrugged, biting into his sandwich hungrily as Romy sat down opposite him with a coffee.

'So what happened?' she asked, looking at him over the rim of her mug, which she cupped in both hands.

'Recession. The company I worked for went under.'

'I'm sorry. I should have thought. I hate this bloody recession.'

'Me too.' Kit sighed. 'I lost everything – my job, my

apartment in Manhattan, the lot. I had some savings, but I was burning through them so fast, it was scary. Eventually, I had no choice but to move back.'

'So you've come back here to live?'

'For the time being anyway,' he nodded. 'I've moved back in with my parents.'

'I can see that.' She smiled, nodding at his shirt, which was a pale washed-out pink.

'Yeah. Mom still hasn't got the hang of the laundry.'

Kit's mother was a domestic goddess of sorts – a goddess of destruction. Kit's regulation white school shirts had always ended up pale shades of pink, blue and green, depending on what colour had run in the wash that week.

'I used to think it was cool the way your whole family always dressed in the same colours – like a team uniform or something.'

Kit looked balefully down at his shirt. 'I wouldn't mind, but this is Armani.'

'So what are you going to do now?'

'Well … that's kind of why I came to see you.'

'By coming to see me, you mean hiding in a tree outside my house and spying on me?'

'Yeah.' He gave a nervous laugh. 'Sorry about that.'

'And in a mask too!'

'Yeah, well, I had planned to surprise you. I was going to call to the door and say, "Trick or treat?"'

'That would have been cute.'

'Yeah?'

'Cuter than the whole Peeping Tom routine anyway.'

'Right.' He looked at her warily. 'Anyway, when I got here and saw that you were having a party, I kind of lost my nerve. So I decided to hide out until I got up the courage to call, but I didn't want to loiter around the street like a weirdo, so—'

'Yeah, you avoided that pitfall,' she said dryly.

'I know, dumb move. It seemed like a good idea at the time. I'd have got away with it, though, if I hadn't been rumbled by your bloody cat.'

Romy smirked. 'He's not my cat. I'm just minding him for my tenant across the hall while she's away.'

'Just my luck!' Kit pouted.

'So there was some particular reason you wanted to see me?' she prompted. 'You weren't just suddenly overcome by nostalgia?'

'Well, that too. Being back in my old bedroom at home … there are so many reminders of you. I really wanted to see you again.' He smiled at her fondly. 'I'm sorry we lost touch.'

'Me too.' She smiled back at him. 'So what was the other thing that made you come here?'

'It was what Mom said, about you being a property developer. It gave me an idea, and I wanted to ask your opinion on something.'

'Okay,' Romy said warily, her heart sinking a little. She knew all too well that property developing was something everyone seemed to think they could turn their hand to when they wanted to make some quick money. During the property-buying frenzy of the Celtic Tiger she had lost count of the number of people who had asked her for help with projects, expecting her to act as consultant, site manager and interior decorator as a favour and getting very put out when she explained as nicely as she could that property development was how she earned a living and she couldn't afford to put the time and effort into doing freebies. She really hoped Kit hadn't come here after all this time to ask her for that.

'I was hoping you could advise me,' Kit said, pulling some papers from his jacket on the back of his chair. 'I have this house that I inherited years ago from my aunt and I never did anything with it. I was thinking maybe I could renovate it now – as a way to make some money. I don't have a clue about this stuff, so I thought maybe you'd be able to tell me whether it'd be worth doing, or if I'd just be wasting my time and money.'

Romy sighed. 'You know, developing's not as easy as it looks.' She began the speech she had made countless times to hopeful amateurs.

'I know that.'

'And the property market is abysmal right now.'

'Tell me about it. But you seem to be doing okay,' he said hopefully.

'I did well in the boom,' she said. 'And I was careful.' She had been told she was *too* careful, that she should get more mortgages, buy more properties, take on more debt, do whatever it took to capitalise on the opportunity of an out-of-control property market. It was like they were all in this glorious casino where no one ever lost. It didn't matter where you placed your bet – as long as it was on the table, you would win. The only losers were those who were too afraid to put their chips down. 'You can't lose,' everyone had told her. Sometimes she had thought they were right. She knew there had been times when she could have made more money, and she had turned her back on some potentially lucrative opportunities, but she had never regretted it because she had always known her limits. There was only a certain level of debt that she could cope with, and she was not prepared to go beyond that. She preferred to sleep at night.

'And what about now?' Kit broke into her thoughts.

'I'm okay. I own this house, I have no mortgage.' She sighed. 'I'm lucky. I can ride it out, live on rental income until things pick up again. But I'm not doing any new projects because the market's so bad. It's just not worth it.'

'I know things are bad, and it would be hard to get a return on your investment. But the thing is, I own this house outright. So it would only cost whatever it would take to renovate it – after that, the rest would be pure profit.'

'If you managed to sell it.'

Kit's face fell a little at this, but she knew she had to be brutally honest. There was no point in giving him unrealistic hopes.

'Well, yeah – that's why I need your advice. It does need a hell of a lot of work. I still have some savings, but I have no idea if I can afford to do it – or even if it'd be worth doing. I might end up spending more than I could possibly get for it.'

'How bad is it exactly?'

'Well, I haven't been down there in years – not since we were kids and Aunt Lillian lived there, and it wasn't great even then. I have a photo,' he said, pulling it from the papers and pushing it across the table to her along with the estate agent's details.

'It looks pretty neglected,' Romy said, staring down at the photo.

'Yeah, and that was taken about eight years ago, so it's probably a lot worse now. It's been empty since Aunt Lillian died.'

'Well, on the surface it looks like a classic money pit and my instinct would be to tell you to stay well away from it. But it's hard to tell much from a photo. I'd need to see it in person to properly assess what kind of condition it's in and what sort of money you'd need to spend.'

'Would you do that?' Kit said, brightening. 'Come down and have a look at it?'

'Sure.' What had she got to lose? She loved looking around houses, imagining what she could do with them. She already knew from what Kit had told her about the house and what she knew of the current market that her instinct to advise him not to touch it was unlikely to change. But there was no harm in looking – and she could at least give him a realistic assessment of what it would cost to renovate, so he could make his own decision. It was a beautiful house, though … 'Where is it?'

'In Wicklow. A stunning location in the arsehole of nowhere,' he said, laughing wryly.

'It's big, isn't it?' she said thoughtfully, looking at the spec.

'Huge.'

'And it's got a lot of land around it, which is a good thing.'

'If you did think it was worth doing, would you be able to … help?'

Here it comes, she thought. 'Help how?'

'I'm completely clueless about developing. I don't even know where to start. And it'd be so obvious I didn't know what I was doing, I'd probably get fleeced. Plus you'd have all the contacts with builders and so on. I thought maybe you could project manage it for me.'

'I don't know, Kit—'

'You said you don't have any projects on the go at the moment.'

'I don't, but—'

'And I can't imagine being a landlady takes up a lot of your time.'

'No, it doesn't.' That was an understatement. She was so bored of sitting on her arse collecting rent. She really missed developing.

'Well, think about it anyway,' Kit said. 'And factor in your fees when you're calculating what I'd need to spend. If you're not doing it, I'd need to get someone to manage it anyway – someone who knew what they were doing.'

She smiled, relieved that he wouldn't expect her to project

manage the renovation as a favour. She looked at the photo again and started to feel the stirrings of the old excitement. It had been a long time, and it would be lovely to have the challenge of a new project. 'I don't need to think about it. If I think it's viable, I'll be your project manager,' she told him.

'Brilliant!' He grinned.

'But I can't promise anything until I've seen it.'

'Understood.'

'Would you like more coffee?' she asked, standing and taking his empty plate. 'Or some wine?'

'Thanks, but I should be getting home,' he said, glancing at his watch. 'Wow, I didn't realise it was so late. We've hardly even had a chance to talk. I guess I should call a cab.'

'You can stay here if you like. I have a pretty decent sofa-bed.'

'Well, I'd love to stay and chat – we have a lot of catching up to do. Unless you want to go to bed?'

'No, I'd love you to stay. It's so amazing to see you, Kit.'

'You too. Okay then, the sofa it is – and wine, please.'

She opened a bottle and they retreated to the living room, sitting amidst the detritus of the party.

'I was sorry to hear about your father,' Kit said.

'Thanks. It was merciful really – he was in a lot of pain.'

'And Mom tells me you have a baby now?'

'Yeah.' She smiled reflexively at the mention of Luke. 'He's staying with Mum tonight – she took him so I could have this party.'

'How old is he?'

'Three months.'

'And his father?'

'Not on the scene.'

Kit just nodded when she didn't elaborate, and she was grateful he didn't ask more questions.

'So, is there anyone … else?'

'Are you asking me if I've got a boyfriend?' She smiled.

'Yeah, I guess I am.'

'No. No one since I broke up with Gary. That was about …' she thought, 'gosh, almost two years ago. I can't believe it's been that long!'

'Well, I suppose having a baby is a bit of a distraction.'

'Yeah,' she laughed. 'To put it mildly.'

'Were you with Gary long?'

'Almost three years.'

'So what happened?'

'He met someone else.'

'Oh, sorry.'

'It's okay. It was fine, actually.' Her friends had dutifully lined up to call Gary a bastard, but the fact was there were no hard feelings. 'He fell in love, and I guess he realised he'd never felt that way about me.'

'He sounds like a tosser!'

Romy smiled. 'He's not. I don't think I was ever in love with him either. We were good friends more than anything.'

'You weren't even the tiniest bit jealous?'

'I was a bit, but it was a dog-in-the-manger kind of jealousy. I was jealous that it wasn't me he'd fallen in love with, even though I knew I wasn't in love with him. And I envied him, falling in love – the excitement of it.' She hadn't been in love with Gary, but she knew what it felt like because she had been in love with Kit. She knew now that she didn't fall in love easily or often, and she wondered sometimes if she ever would again.

'Wow, you're so … adult!'

'I'm all grown up,' she quipped. 'I was sad about the break-up, of course. We were such good friends – we really liked each other, we had fun. But we were just drifting along really.'

She sometimes wondered how much longer they'd have drifted along happily if Gary hadn't had his thunderbolt. Maybe they would have been together when her father died. She would most likely never have met Darth Vader. She wouldn't have Luke … 'I think it all turned out for the best.'

Romy poured wine as they talked and talked, and when they got to the end of the bottle, she opened another.

'So, how about you?' she asked him when they were deep into the second bottle and everything was getting a little fuzzy around the edges. 'Do you have a girlfriend?'

'I had,' Kit said, 'but she was sort of another casualty of the recession.'

'Huh?' Romy wondered if she'd heard him correctly. Maybe she'd had too much wine. 'How can you lose your girlfriend in the recession? You don't mean she was just with you for your money?' She searched Kit's face for some clue as to how he felt about this, but his expression was blank. She had heard of it happening – trophy wives and girlfriends flying the coop when their partner's money ran out. But she had always assumed it only happened to ogres – ugly, dull or plain nasty men who had nothing else going for them besides their money – not to someone like Kit.

'It's complicated. But I suppose money was a factor. I mean, if you're successful and wealthy, that's part of who you are, isn't it? You have a completely different sort of life. She hadn't signed up for a broke loser.'

'You're not a broke loser!' Romy said, shocked.

'It's fine,' he said, and there was no bitterness in his tone. He really didn't seem to mind that this woman had abandoned him as soon as he was down on his luck. 'We had a certain lifestyle, and I didn't expect her to stick around when I couldn't keep up my end of the deal. Besides, I knew she'd never leave New York.'

'But … what was *her* end of the deal? I mean, if you didn't love each other …' She suddenly felt very naive talking about love. But she couldn't understand why Kit would settle for someone who only seemed interested in him for his money. It didn't make sense.

He shrugged. 'Look beautiful, accompany me to business functions, host dinner parties, impress clients. Be beautiful and charming – and discreet.'

She sounded like a classic trophy girlfriend. Romy frowned, struggling to get her head around what Kit was telling her. No doubt the woman had been stunning, but so was Kit – surely, he wouldn't have any problem getting a woman who could do all that stuff and who would care about him into the bargain. Still, we never really understand what goes on in other people's relationships, she thought.

'It's hard to explain,' he said as she looked at him uncomprehendingly. 'We had a … particular sort of relationship. It's a bit like you and your bloke, I suppose – we weren't in love.'

Romy didn't think it was anything like her and Gary. They may not have been in love, but they did care deeply about each other. She would never have left him over money.

'I led a very different life in New York. I had a certain image to maintain. Lauren understood that and she fitted into my world. The arrangement suited us both.'

Romy wondered about this lifestyle Kit alluded to that required discretion but not love, and all sorts of scenarios flashed through her mind. Perhaps they were swingers, or maybe they were involved in some kind of sadomasochistic relationship. Did he give her the use of his money in return for her letting him indulge his dark fantasies with her and keeping quiet about it? Or maybe Kit just wanted no-strings sex without the hassles of a relationship and this woman was willing to trade that for the ritzy lifestyle he could provide. Perhaps he had inhabited such a vacuous, superficial world that all he cared about was having a beautiful girl on his arm to show off like a flash car or a fabulous apartment – someone to impress his friends and colleagues.

'There were no hard feelings,' Kit said.

'So you're not sad about breaking up with her? You don't miss her at all?'

'Not really. Though, God, I wish she was here now,' Kit said, 'with Hannah's wedding coming up.'

'Hannah's getting married?' Hannah was Kit's younger sister.

'Yeah, at the beginning of December. She's marrying a friend of our cousin Wedgie – I can't believe it!' Kit pouted.

'Can he not pronounce his 'Rs'?'

'What?'

'Your cousin Reggie.'

'Oh no, his name's not Reggie – it's John.'

'Then why …?'

'Wedgie is his nickname, because he's famous for giving wedgies. Used to make my life a misery whenever we went down to Galway for the holidays. I'm dreading this wedding. Wedgie's going to be best man. I'm wondering if I can get away with wearing a kilt.'

'No,' Romy said flatly.

'What?'

'No, you can't get away with wearing a kilt.'

He raised an eyebrow haughtily. 'I have very good legs, I'll have you know. I think I could look pretty spectacular in a kilt.'

'No. You're not Scottish, so you'd just look like a wanker. Anyway, there's no need for that. You're all grown up now. He's hardly going to give you a wedgie at the wedding, is he?'

'I don't know. He gave me one the last time I met him.'

'Yes, but when was that?'

'That would have been last year at my father's sixtieth birthday.'

'Oh.'

'Yes. Oh.'

Romy giggled. 'Right, I have to go and pee,' she said, getting up. 'When I come back, I want to hear all about this lifestyle of yours in New York.'

They talked and talked, until eventually Romy's eyes started to droop and they were both yawning more than they were speaking. Romy made up the sofa bed for Kit and went to bed to ponder the magic of Hallowe'en. What was it with her and this holiday? Last year it had brought her Luke, and now Kit.

Chapter Six

Despite the fact that she had got to bed in the early hours, Romy woke at five the following morning feeling vaguely excited, and couldn't go back to sleep. She knew there was something at the edge of her consciousness that would account for the jittery feeling in her stomach, but in the first few moments of wakefulness it eluded her. And then last night came back to her, like a picture slowly coming into focus, and there in the centre of it was Kit Masterson. Kit, her first love, was at this very moment lying on the sofa in her living room, probably fast asleep. She hadn't really thought about him in years, and yet knowing he was here brought back all the edgy excitement she used to feel when they were together.

He had been the sun around which her teenage world had revolved – and the best part of it had been knowing he felt the same. She hadn't gone through any of the angst and insecurity that she had seen her friends suffer with boys, and had never doubted for a moment that he adored her. They had been completely crazy about each other, a perfect match – even if no one else thought so.

She had known that no one understood or approved – not the popular girls who had thought Kit was out of her league and rightfully belonged with one of them; not her parents and teachers who had feared Kit would lead her astray. Her friends had thought Kit was trouble and were even a little afraid of him – like a sleek tiger, beautiful but wild and dangerous, only to be admired from a safe distance – while the painfully cool crowd that hung around Kit had dismissed Romy as too dull and quiet to be of interest. To onlookers, they had resembled some freakish fairytale coupling – a girl and a wolf, a prince and a frog. Who was getting the better end of the bargain depended on your point of view. Some people had sided with Romy, others with Kit. No one had been on the side of Kit-and-Romy.

She had to admit they had a point. Any way you looked at it, they hadn't been an obvious match. She had been a straight-A student who hadn't even customised her school uniform. He had worn eyeliner and earrings, and bunked off school on a regular basis. But eventually it had become clear to everyone that they were a couple, a unit – Kit and Romy; Romy and Kit. However odd they might have looked roaming around hand in hand – her in her pristine regulation uniform and neat ponytail, he with his grungy clothes and spiky hair – they had been inseparable and there wasn't much anyone could have done about it. Despite the fact that no one else had been able to see it, she had known they made perfect sense together.

Where he had been weak, she had been strong, and vice versa – they complemented each other perfectly. She hadn't minded that Kit wasn't as bright as she was. She had been happy to help him with school work, glad that there was something she could do for him. And he had taught her things too. He had life skills to pass on, mysteries she would never have been able to penetrate on her own. He had shown her how to smoke a joint and had taken her to see bands no one else had heard of. And, shallow though it was, she had enjoyed the prestige that came with being his girlfriend. She had liked the fact that people looked at her differently when she was with him – boys with admiration; girls with envy. But more than all that, she had felt like Kit was the only person who really understood her. He had seen beyond the 'good girl' conformity to the person who was exactly like him – the person who felt just as out of place at school as he did and was simply taking the line of least resistance – keeping her head down and biding her time until she could take possession of her own life.

Looking back, she didn't think she had ever quite got over Kit. She knew she had never felt the same way about anyone else. Perhaps it was simply the intensity of first love that could never be matched. Maybe it was like that for everyone. But she couldn't help longing to feel that way again. It wasn't that she imagined herself still in love with him. He hadn't been a part of her life for a very long time and she didn't even know him anymore. She hadn't spent the intervening years hankering after him, but she had hankered after someone *like* him – someone who would 'see' her like he had. She was a slow burn – she had come to realise that about herself. She wasn't bubbly and vivacious, and easy to know – it took time and effort. But Kit had got her straight away, and had seen her as someone fun, interesting and worthwhile. There had never been anyone like him. And now he was downstairs on her sofa.

By six o'clock she was too restless to stay in bed any longer. She got up, pulled on an oversized cardigan and her boot slippers, and crept downstairs quietly so as not to wake Kit. She tiptoed into the living room and found him still fast asleep on the sofa-bed. She stood there for a moment, watching him. God, she'd had good taste back then. He had a fierce, striking kind of beauty. The sharp points and smooth planes of his face could have been chiselled from marble. He wore his hair very short now, and it accentuated the strong definition of his features.

It seemed surreal that he was here in her house after all these years. It was hard to believe now that they had once been inseparable – her and this virtual stranger. They had been joined at the mouth for the whole of the final year of school, spending hours on end snogging. She looked at him wonderingly, remembering long summer days, the warmth of sun-baked red brick at her back, the heat of Kit's body pressed against hers, and frosty winter nights under the orange glow of street lights, their breath mingling in the air between them. It all seemed so sweetly innocent now.

As it didn't look like he was going to wake up anytime soon, she finally dragged herself away and went to have a shower and get ready for the day.

❉

'Good morning.' Romy was sitting in the kitchen, having coffee and leftover cake, and reading a magazine. She looked up to see Kit standing in the doorway, looking sleepy and dishevelled. He was wearing his jeans and his shirt was hanging open over them.

'Hi! Would you like some coffee?' she asked, jumping up from the table and moving over to the counter to grab the pot.

'Yes, please,' he said, buttoning up his shirt as he moved into the room.

Romy busied herself with making fresh coffee and setting a place for him at the table. She felt unbelievably skittish and was grateful to have something to do to distract her.

'Did you sleep all right?' she asked him.

'Yeah, I slept great, thanks.' She noticed him wince slightly as he sat down at the table.

'Is your head okay?' She poured him a glass of orange juice and put it on the table in front of him. 'Do you want some paracetamol?'

'No thanks. It'll be fine after some food.' He grabbed the glass of juice, draining it in one go. 'God, how much wine did we put away last night?'

'Quite a lot in the end – at least a bottle each.'

'Ouch! I think I'm out of practice. You look very bright-eyed.'

'Well, I probably had more to eat last night than you did. So, what would you like for breakfast? I could make you a fry-up, if you like.'

'No thanks. I'll just have what you're having. This looks very decadent,' he grinned, indicating Romy's half-eaten slice of cake. 'Do you generally have cake for breakfast?'

'Just on special occasions.' She placed the fresh pot of coffee on the table.

'So what's today's occasion?' he asked, pouring himself coffee as she sat down opposite him.

'It's … the day after Hallowe'en. The first of November!'

'Well, happy first of November!' he said, clinking his mug against hers.

'I have normal breakfast foods if you'd prefer. There's muesli, or I could make you toast?'

'No, this is great,' he said, as Romy cut him a huge wedge of cake. 'It's a treat. Mom doesn't let me have cake for breakfast.'

'Right, I forgot. Does she make you eat up your vegetables at dinner too?'

'Yep. I have to clear my plate or I'm not allowed any TV.'

Romy giggled. 'It must be quite hard living at home at this stage.'

'Yeah,' he sighed. 'I mean Mom and Dad are great, but it's not easy. Still, hopefully it won't be for long.'

The microwave pinged and Romy got up and retrieved a small jug. 'There's butterscotch sauce to go with the cake if you want,' she said, holding it out to Kit as she sat down again.

'Yes please.' He took the jug from her and poured a generous dollop of sauce over his cake. 'Wow, this is the best breakfast ever. It's what you dream being a grown-up will be like when you're a kid – cake for breakfast, ice cream for dinner ...'

'Yeah, and then when you finally do grow up and you're old enough to do whatever you want, you're too sensible and you don't want to do that stuff anymore.'

'Sad, isn't it?'

'Adulthood is wasted on adults,' she sighed.

Just then her mobile buzzed, vibrating on the table, and she picked it up, checking the message. It was her mother, saying she was on her way over with Luke and would be there in about ten minutes. She closed the message and tossed the phone back on the table. Then suddenly realisation hit her. She gasped and rose to her feet, clapping a hand to her mouth. 'Oh my God, Mum's on her way over!'

Kit looked up at her uncomprehendingly. 'Well ... that's okay, isn't it?'

'No, it's not! You can't be here!'

'What?' He laughed in surprise. 'Oh, are you afraid she'll think we shacked up last night? Just tell her I slept on the sofa. It has the advantage of being true.' He shrugged unconcernedly and went back to his cake.

'No!' Romy whisked the plate away, leaving his fork hovering in midair. 'It's not that. 'You just … you seriously can't be here when she comes.'

'Why not?' He frowned.

'She – she doesn't like you.'

'Oh, come on,' he said, reaching to take the plate from her hand. Romy moved it farther away, extending her arm fully to hold it out of his reach. 'That was ages ago. Let me stay and meet her and she'll see how well I turned out.'

'No, you have to go!' Romy said urgently.

'But that's ridiculous. I'm sure you're overreacting. I mean, it's not as if I'm trying to defile her only daughter anymore, is it?'

'Well … about that …' Romy chewed her thumb, breathing shallowly.

'What?'

'Look, I'll explain later,' she said, tugging at his arm to pull him out of the chair. Fortunately, he helped her by standing up. She grabbed his jacket from the back of the chair, stuffed it into his hand and started guiding him towards the door. But it was too late. She heard a key in the door and her mother's light step in the hallway.

'Shit! You'll have to hide.' She turned Kit around and started shoving him towards her bedroom. It was like trying to push a tractor.

'Romy?' She spun around to see her mother standing in the doorway, carrying a sleeping Luke in his car seat. Damn!

She sighed, her arms going limp, releasing Kit. 'Hi, Mum,' she said defeatedly.

Her mother's eyes were popping out of her head as she took in Kit and the breakfast things on the table. 'Well, well, well – Kit Masterson!'

'Hello, Mrs Fitzgerald.' He smiled, giving her a little wave.

She stood there, looking between Romy and Kit with a look of wonderment until her attention was drawn by Luke gurgling and stirring in his seat.

'Well, I'm very glad to see you, Kit,' she said, placing the car seat on the floor and bending to unstrap Luke and lift him out. 'Better late than never, right?' She smiled down at the wriggling baby in her arms and then walked straight up to Kit. 'Why don't you sit down and I'll give him to you to hold?'

'Oh, no, that's not – I mean I'm not very—'

'Go on, he won't bite. You'll be fine. It's about time you two got acquainted.' She continued to advance towards Kit, nudging him towards the chair until he had no choice but to flop down into it.

'Oh well, all right then. Just for a minute …' Kit looked so terrified as her mother carefully handed Luke to him that Romy was almost tempted to giggle – except this situation wasn't funny.

'There!' Her mother straightened, smiling down warmly at Kit and Luke. 'You're a natural,' she said encouragingly, despite the fact that Kit was holding Luke like he was a ticking bomb about to go off any second. 'You know, he's the spit of you,' she continued, looking down at Kit, who thankfully had his head bent.

'Yes, I know!' Romy said brightly. 'He's the image of me.' Kit shot her a quizzical look – probably wondering why she was behaving like a nutcase.

'I didn't mean—'

'I know what you meant, Mum. But look at the time! Thanks for minding Luke, but you don't have to hang around here with us. Aren't you meant to be meeting Maeve for coffee?'

'Oh, I've plenty of time,' she said, waving away Romy's protests. 'She's always late anyway. So, are you home for a holiday?' she asked Kit.

'No, I've moved back – for the moment anyway.'

'Oh, that's great! I'm really glad to hear it.'

Romy was aware of Kit looking nervously down at Luke as if waiting for instructions about what he should do next. 'Here, let me take him,' she said, bending towards him, but her mother held her back.

'Romy, you have to give Kit and Luke a chance to bond. You've had him to yourself for three months. Kit's only seeing him for the first time today. You just have to give them time.' She folded her arms, looking down fondly at Kit and Luke. 'He's great, isn't he?' she said to Kit.

'Brilliant!' Kit, feeling the weight of Mrs Fitzgerald's gaze and clearly feeling something was expected of him, pulled Luke up towards his face. 'Um … say Mama,' he quavered uncertainly to Luke, who rolled his head around a little and gurgled, his tongue rolling out of his mouth.

'Ma-ma,' Kit tried again, enunciating each syllable clearly.

'He's only three months old, Kit,' Romy's mother said.

'He's not talking yet,' Romy clarified.

'Oh, is that … I mean is he … okay?'

'Yes, it's perfectly normal,' Romy told him, bending and scooping Luke out of his arms, to his obvious relief.

'I'm sorry, I don't know much about babies,' Kit addressed Romy's mother.

'Ah well, you've plenty of time to learn,' she said. 'You've just got some time to make up with him.'

'But I wasn't—'

Mrs Fitzgerald put up a hand to silence him. 'Don't worry,

Kit, there'll be no recriminations from me. I know there was a pair of you in it. I'm just glad you're here now. I'd never say anything, but I always hoped ...' she trailed off, smiling at Romy. 'I think it'll be the best thing for Luke, having you here.'

'Mrs Fitzgerald, I—'

'Call me Marian. We're going to be seeing a lot of each other from now on, aren't we? Okay,' she said with a sigh, glancing at her watch, 'I really should get going. Sorry I can't stay longer, but I'm sure we'll see each other again soon.' She bent and gave a startled Kit a kiss on the forehead, kissed her daughter and grandson goodbye with a quick 'talk later' to Romy and strode out.

The stunned silence that followed was broken only by Luke's intermittent gurgles.

'What the hell was that all about?' Kit said finally. 'I thought you said she didn't like me! She *kissed* me!'

'I know. That was a bit weird.'

'And why did she want me to hold ... Whatsisface?' he asked, waving towards Luke. 'Why would she want me to bond with your baby?'

So many questions, and only one answer. There was nothing else for it – she was just going to have to tell him the truth.

'Yeah, sorry about that,' she said, holding Luke in one arm while she pulled out a chair with the other and sat down opposite Kit. 'I have to tell you something ... and you're going to go apeshit, which is perfectly understandable.'

Kit looked freaked out. 'Oh Christ, you're not dying and leaving the baby to me, are you?'

'What?' Romy spluttered with laughter. 'No! God ... of course not, you dope.'

'Good. Phew! That's a relief.'

'That I'm not dying or that you're not getting the baby in my will?'

'Both,' he grinned.

'Not that you wouldn't be the obvious choice, of course. If I was dying and looking to leave Luke with someone, the first person who'd spring to mind would be that bloke I went out with in school who I haven't seen in yonks.'

'Okay, okay. I just panicked. So …?' He looked at her expectantly.

She took a deep breath. 'The thing is … it's just – Mum thinks … shethinksyou'reLuke'sfather.' She thought if she said it really fast it might go better, like ripping off leg wax.

'She … *what*? Why on earth would she think that?'

'Um, because … I kind of told her you were.' She winced, waiting for him to go ballistic on her. 'But before you say anything,' she rushed on when he remained silent, 'don't worry. I'm going to straighten her out.'

'But – but –' Kit stammered, struggling to find words. 'Why would you tell her that?'

'Because … I didn't want to tell her the truth – which is that I don't know who Luke's father is.'

'You don't?'

She shook her head. 'No. No idea.' She watched his face, trying to read his expression. 'Are you shocked?'

'Well,' he frowned, 'not shocked exactly, but … yeah, actually, I am kind of shocked. It just doesn't seem like … *you*.'

'It's not like me. Honest!' She smiled. 'I haven't turned into some heinous über-slut since you left. It was just this one time. I was all over the place—'

'Hang on. If it was just one time, then how come you don't know who it was?'

'Oh, it was at this party where everyone was wearing masks – and then later I was blindfolded—' she trailed off, blushing.

'Long story,' she said with a dismissive wave of her hand. 'Anyway, it happened and I got pregnant, and I just couldn't face telling Mum that I hadn't a clue who the father was. I couldn't bear to disappoint her like that.'

Her mother had characteristically respected Romy's wishes and not asked any questions – until one day she had broken down and admitted that Romy's silence on the subject had led her to imagine the worst. She didn't want a name or details, she just wanted to know that Romy hadn't been raped. So, horrified that she had been unknowingly causing her mother such anxiety, Romy had told her a lie to reassure her. She told her Luke's father was someone she had known for a long time, someone she had loved, who now lived abroad …

'I didn't *exactly* tell her it was you, but I led her in that direction and let her come to that conclusion.'

'But why did you pick me?'

'Because you were safely out of the way – or so I thought,' she added, flashing him an accusing look. 'You weren't supposed to come back here – ever.'

'Tell me about it,' Kit said glumly. 'But how could she have believed that? I mean we haven't seen each other in years. I live in New York; you live in Dublin. She does know how babies are made?'

Romy sighed. 'She knew you were home last Hallowe'en for your dad's sixtieth. She heard it on some ladies-who-lunch grapevine or whatever. Anyway, she was on my case to look you up – kept telling me how well you'd done for yourself, what a catch you'd be,' she smiled at him teasingly. 'So I pretended I had – looked you up. Well, not exactly looked you up – I wouldn't want to look desperate, after all. But I pretended I bumped into you, and coupled with the other things I'd said about Luke's father … well, she kind of put two and two together. And I let her.'

'So does everyone think I'm his father?'

'No, I only told my mother – and I swore her to secrecy.'

'And you trust her?'

'Yes, absolutely. She's very honourable like that. As far as she's concerned, it's my secret to tell.'

'So why didn't you – look me up?' Kit asked.

Romy shrugged. 'I figured if you wanted to see me you knew where I was. You could have called.'

'Right back at you,' he said, cocking an eyebrow challengingly.

'But you were the one coming and going. I was here all the time.' She tried not to show that she had been hurt that he had never bothered to contact her when he had been home. It would have been nice to see him now and then. 'How was I to know when you were home?'

'I don't know – through your mother's ladies-who-lunch grapevine?'

She laughed, relaxing. 'Touché.'

'I wish I *had* kept in touch. I did think about calling you sometimes, when I was home. But I guess I was afraid.'

'Of?'

He shrugged. 'That it wouldn't be the same.'

'Afraid you wouldn't like me anymore?'

He smiled, shaking his head. 'Maybe afraid *you* wouldn't like *me*.'

They were interrupted by Luke, who started to cry, his small whimpers building up to a deafening crescendo as he squirmed in Romy's arms.

'I think he's hungry,' Romy said.

'Oh!' Kit's eyes darted around in panic. 'You're not going to—'

'What?'

'You know – feed him?'

94

'Of course I'm going to feed him.' She got up and went to the fridge, taking out a bottle she had made up that morning.

'Oh, right,' Kit sighed in relief as she put the bottle in the microwave. 'For a minute there, I thought you were going to whip out your tit.'

'And how do you think my mother fed him last night? Actually, don't tell me – I don't want to know. Or did you just think I'd let him starve for the night so I could have a party?'

'I didn't think. I mean, jeez, I don't know how babies work.'

'Well, maybe you'd better find out in case someone decides to leave you one in their will.'

'Yeah, yeah, laugh it up. Anyway, you could have used one of those milking machines.'

Romy rolled her eyes. 'Cows have milking machines. Human beings have breast pumps.'

'Potato, pot-ah-to.'

Luke was sucking contentedly on the bottle, and Romy sat down again. 'Anyway,' she said, 'I'm sorry I pretended you were the father.'

'So I'm a shit who abandoned you when you were pregnant! No wonder your mother doesn't like me.'

'No, not at all. You didn't know. I never told you about Luke.'

'God, that's a bit cold, isn't it?'

'No, it's just … sensible. It made sense. There wasn't really anything between us, and I didn't want to trap you. I didn't want you to be with us just because of a split condom. You had a life abroad and I was happy to raise Luke on my own.'

'Weren't you ever going to tell me?'

'No,' she admitted. 'Mum thought I should, but …' She shrugged. 'I decided it was for the best if you didn't know.

'Huh!' Kit appeared well and truly flabbergasted. 'You should write movies or something. You've really thought of everything.'

'Mmm. Except you moving home.' She smiled wryly at him, chewing her lip. 'But, like I said, don't worry about it. I'll come clean.' Luke had guzzled the whole bottle, and his eyes were drooping as she pulled it from his mouth and wiped his face with his bib. 'I'll tell Mum everything the next time I see her.'

'But won't she think you're a heinous über-slut?'

'That's my problem,' she said, trying to sound tougher than she felt. 'Besides, I don't have to tell her the whole truth. I can just tell her she got the wrong end of the stick about you. I only ever hinted that it was you anyway.' She got up and laid Luke gently in his Moses basket.

'You know, maybe you don't have to tell her anything.'

She spun around. 'But I can't let her go on thinking you're Luke's father.'

'I don't mind.'

'You don't?' She looked at him in amazement as she sat down opposite him again. He really did seem remarkably calm. She had expected her revelation to unleash a shit-storm; instead, Kit looked perfectly relaxed, leaning back in his chair, smiling at her, his hands crossed behind his head.

'It's the least I can do,' he said, smiling. 'I mean, I landed you in it by coming home.'

'Don't be silly. You have a perfect right to move home. You weren't to know I was making up slanderous stories about you. No,' she said firmly, 'I got myself into this mess and I'll get myself – and you – out of it.'

'Well, it's up to you. But if you want to let your mother go on thinking I'm the father, that's fine by me.'

'But it's not just my mum. Now that you're home, it would

seem weird if your family didn't know, and if you weren't involved with Luke.'

'So we could tell my family,' he said calmly. 'And I could be involved.'

'We couldn't lie to your parents like that – let them think Luke is their grandchild when he's not.'

'Would it really be so bad? It'd make them really happy, and they'd love … Whatsisface.'

'Still, it's not right.'

'Honestly, Mom would be delighted. She's always on at me to find a nice girl and settle down, start a family. And it'd take the heat off me if she thought I already had.'

'It's a bit drastic, isn't it? Pretending you have a baby just because your mother's on your case a bit about settling down. Besides, what if I find Luke's real father?'

'Is that likely?'

She knew it wasn't at all likely, and she had, just last night, resolved to give up on the idea for good.

'I could do the dad part for real,' Kit said earnestly.

'You really think you could do that?'

'Yeah, sure. It'd be fun.'

'You'd have to stop calling him "Whatsisface" for a start.'

'Well, of course, I'd learn his name – it *is* a boy, right?'

'Yes. Luke. The name's a bit of a giveaway.'

'Sorry. I'm not very good with names. Better with faces. Although not with babies because they all look the same, don't they?'

'No.'

'Well, anyway, I could buy him presents and take him to his football matches or whatever, and go to his school concerts …'

'Yeah, well, that's all down the road a bit,' Romy said, smiling. 'But what about when you move back to New York?'

'Then we could go back to your story that we're not

into each other and don't want to stay together for the sake of wh – um …'

'Luke.'

'Right. And I could be a long-distance dad. It happens.'

That was true. Plenty of children grew up rarely seeing their fathers. And she could tell Luke the truth when he was older and explain that Kit was a sort of step-dad.

'He'd still have more of a father than he does now,' Kit said, and Romy felt a tug of temptation. Kit's idea would give Luke some sort of father figure – not to mention another extended family. And it would be nice not to have to tell her mother the truth …

'I don't know, Kit …' She was touched that he had made the offer, but it was a crazy idea and she didn't see how it could possibly work. Just trying to think through all the implications was already making her brain ache.

'Well, think about it. And *please* come to Hannah's wedding with me anyway – as my date. I need someone to protect me from my nosy relations – not to mention Wedgie.'

'I have no problem going to Hannah's wedding with you. Besides, I kind of owe you for letting Mum think you're Luke's father.'

'You can have that one on me,' he said, smiling.

'Thanks. Do you want some more coffee?' she asked.

'No, thanks. I'd better get home,' he said, standing and stretching. 'Mom will be wondering where I got to.'

'I hope you don't get grounded for staying out all night.'

He smiled. 'Thanks for the bed, Romy. It was really good to see you again.'

'Yeah, you too.'

She saw him to the door and they made arrangements to go and look at Kit's house the following week.

Romy leaned against the door after she had closed it

behind him. She felt like she had been run over by a train. Her head was spinning from everything that had happened in the past twenty-four hours – Kit turning up on her doorstep, his amazing offer to pretend Luke was his – she couldn't keep up with it all. She didn't know what to make of Kit's bizarre offer, but she was touched that he had made it. No doubt when she thought it through she would realise that it couldn't possibly work. It was already making her brain ache.

Pushing herself away from the door, she galvanised herself into action. Going into the kitchen, she took Luke from his Moses basket, careful not to wake him, and put him in his car seat, then packed a bag with bottles and nappies.

'Come on,' she whispered to him. 'We're going to see your Auntie Lesley.'

Chapter Seven

It was only when she pulled up outside Lesley's house that Romy remembered that today was a Tuesday and Lesley would probably be working. She looked at her watch – it was only eleven thirty. Maybe she should have called and suggested meeting up for lunch. Still, she was sure Lesley wouldn't mind the interruption – especially when she heard what Romy had to tell her. Lesley worked from home now, but Romy knew she found it a bit isolating and was always grateful for a distraction. She could have a mid-morning break. Luke was still asleep, so she lifted his car seat out gently and walked up the path.

'Romy! Lesley greeted her with a big smile when she opened the door. 'Boy, am I glad to see you. Come on in.' She led Romy down the narrow hall towards the kitchen.

'I hope I'm not interrupting your work,' Romy said as she followed her.

'Believe me, I was gasping for an interruption. This site I'm working on is doing my head in. The client's a nightmare – vetoes everything I come up with, and then complains that it's taking me too long and accuses me of spinning it out so I can charge her more. I can't wait to get the stupid wagon off my back.'

'Can I just leave Luke in here?' Romy asked quietly, stopping outside Lesley's study.

'Yes, of course.'

As she pushed the door open farther, something on the far wall caught Romy's eye. 'Is that—' She turned to Lesley. 'Have you set up an incident room in here?' she asked, pointing to the study.

'No! Don't be daft,' Lesley said, trying to pull the door shut, but Romy put Luke down and pushed past her into the room. In the far corner hung a large whiteboard with a picture of Darth Vader in the middle surrounded by lots of magic marker arrows and scribbles, and flanked by other, smaller pictures. Romy marched straight up to the board to examine it. Underneath the picture of Darth, a list read:

Tall
Possibly asthmatic
Likes Star Wars??

On either side of Darth Vader, under the heading 'Suspects' were photos of various of their old friends who had been at

Romy's party the previous evening. Each picture had a red cross through it. There was even a picture of Mr Potato Head, who also appeared to have been eliminated.

'It looks like an incident room to me,' Romy said, turning to her friend.

'Don't be silly! What gave you that idea?'

'Oh, I don't know,' Romy said, looking at the board, 'maybe it's the suspects list with pictures of all the guys who were at the party last night.'

'Oh, that's just a bit of doodling I did when I was bored.'

'Where did you get these by the way?' Romy asked, fingering one of the photos.

'I downloaded them from Facebook.'

'That's a very good one of Neil.'

'I know, isn't it? It's from his holidays in Greece last year. That's why he looks so tanned.'

Romy realised they were getting away from the subject. 'Lesley, I told you I didn't want an incident room.'

'But it's only small. Look – it's tiny,' she said, waving at the board. 'It's more of an incident *nook*, if anything.'

'An incident nook?' Romy couldn't help smiling. 'Every home should have one.'

'God, they should! I bet a lot of women could save themselves a fortune in private detectives if they got one of these. It's just a matter of following the clues.'

'You know, you totally missed your calling. You should have been a detective.'

'I know,' Lesley sighed wistfully.

Romy looked back at the board. 'Apart from ruling out everyone who was at the party last night, and Mr Potato Head, it doesn't look like you've got very far.'

'No, I've hit a bit of a dead end. I know Mr Potato Head was never really in the frame, but I thought I'd put him up there anyway for the sake of completeness. No stone unturned and all that.'

'Oh well, just file it under unsolved, I guess.'

'No! I'm not giving up. The investigation is only just starting to build up a head of steam. I've loads more ideas. Look,' she pulled a thick sheaf of A4 pages stapled together off the top of her desk and laid it down in front of Romy. 'This is what I'm working on at the moment.'

Romy flicked through the document, which seemed to be pages and pages of printouts of status updates from Facebook. 'What is it?'

'I downloaded mug shots of all David's friends on Facebook. Then I went back to last October on his page and printed out any photos he had of the party, see?' She flicked to the back of the bundle and pointed to a page of photographs. 'Then I looked at anyone who was tagged in the photos and cross-referenced them with their profile pictures. See, this Dracula, for instance, is tagged as one Stephen Lawlor,' she said, flipping the pages and pointing to a picture of a spectacularly unattractive pasty-faced man with thinning ginger hair. 'So I was able to rule him out.'

'Right. Well, I've never seen him before, but I'm glad he's been ruled out all the same.'

'I know. Brutal, isn't he? I also looked through comments about the party and was able to rule out a few more who mentioned what they went as.'

'Wow. I'm impressed.'

'Like you said, I missed my calling.'

'You did. You're really good at this. You could actually end up finding him.' Romy was still ambivalent as to how she felt about that.

'So you'll let me keep it?'

'Keep what?'

'The incident r— nook. Please? You don't have to be involved. I'll only tell you if I come up with something.'

'Well, it's in your house. I can hardly stop you.'

'I know. But if it really freaks you out, I'll dismantle it. Just say the word.'

'No, it's fine. Far be it from me to deprive you of hours of pleasure. But do you ever get any work done?'

Lesley looked guilty. 'I have been skiving off a lot lately. It's an even bigger distraction than Twitter or Facebook.'

'Blimey!' Lesley was completely addicted to Twitter since she had started working from home. 'Anyway, I didn't come here to argue with you about your incident r— er, nook. I've got loads to tell you.'

'Ooh, great! Come on, then. You can leave Luke in here.'

Romy carried Luke's car seat into the office and hooked up the baby monitor before following Lesley into the kitchen.

'Coffee?' Lesley offered.

'Yes, please. Though, God, what I really need is a drink.'

'This sounds interesting.'

'Interesting doesn't even begin to describe it,' Romy said, taking a seat at the kitchen table. 'You'll never guess who turned up last night.'

'Who?' Lesley asked as she spooned coffee into the filter.

'Kit.'

Lesley froze, the coffee spoon suspended in midair. '*Kit Masterson*?'

'Yeah.'

'Oh my God! When did this happen?'

'Not long after you left.' Romy gave Lesley a brief rundown of what had happened the previous night.

'So what's the story? Has he come back here to live?'

'Yeah, apparently. He lost his job in New York, his apartment – everything. He's back living with his parents.'

'God, poor him,' Lesley said, handing Romy a mug of coffee and sitting down opposite her. 'What was it like seeing him again? Did you feel any stirrings of the old magic?'

'No, not really,' Romy said, shaking her head. 'But it was … nice, you know?' She smiled. 'It was lovely to see him again. I felt stirrings of the old friendship.'

'Well, you never know. It'll be nice for you to have him around again anyway.'

Romy groaned, resting her head on the table momentarily. 'It makes things very complicated,' she said, lifting her head again.

'How so?'

Romy took a deep breath. 'Mum thinks he's Luke's father. I sort of told her he is.'

'*What*? Why on earth would you – wait, *is* he?'

'No. Of course not.'

'Then why—'

'Mum was very good, not asking me anything about Luke's father. But then one day she said something and I realised she thought maybe I'd been attacked or something and that was why I didn't want to talk about it. She'd been worrying about it all that time and said nothing.'

'God!'

'I know. I felt terrible. So I told her it was fine and it was all consensual and everything. But I was worried she still wasn't convinced, so I threw in some details to put her mind at rest.'

'And the details you gave her led to Kit?'

'Yes. I knew they would. I told her it was a friend, someone I used to know who now lived abroad, and I said I'd bumped into him at David Kinsella's party. Kit fit the bill, and she knew he was home that weekend.'

'He was?'

'Yeah, she'd heard they were having a big party for his

father's sixtieth birthday and Kit was back for it. No names were ever mentioned, but we both understood it was Kit we were talking about.'

'Shit! What are you going to do when she finds out he's back?'

'Oh, that's already taken care of,' Romy said. 'She met him this morning when she came to drop off Luke.'

'You mean he was still there? He spent the *night*?'

'Yes.'

'Fair play to you!' Lesley raised her coffee mug in salute. 'That was fast work.'

'It wasn't like that. He slept on the couch.'

'Hey, I'm not judging you.'

'Seriously – we just stayed up till all hours talking, and then it was so late, there was no point in him going home.'

'Okay, now I am judging you. You stayed up all night *talking*? What are you, sixteen?'

'Well, we had a lot of catching up to do.' Romy smiled fondly at the memory of the previous night. It *had* almost been like being sixteen again. They hadn't seen each other for so long, it was like they were discovering each other all over again. There was that excitement of meeting a kindred spirit, a soul mate – because, despite the very different courses their lives had taken, they were still on the same wavelength, and it was like they had never been apart. It had taken a long time to catch up on all their news, but it had taken no time at all to catch up on the connection they used to have. It was easy and familiar and comfortable, like pulling on a favourite old jumper. They were instantly friends again, and she realised that was what she had missed most about Kit – his friendship. They had been great allies.

'So, what happened with your mother?' Lesley asked. 'Did she go ballistic when she saw Kit?'

'No, she was really nice to him – a welcome-to-the-family sort of thing.'

'Jaysus! What did Kit make of that? Did he freak out? Did he know he was supposed to be Luke's father?'

'No. But Mum was acting so weird, of course he wondered what was going on. She made him hold Luke. You should have seen his face!' She laughed. 'I thought he was going to piss himself with the fright. And then she was going on about the two of them needing to bond, and how Luke was the spitting image of Kit. It's amazing what the power of suggestion can do,' she said, rolling her eyes. 'He must have thought he was on one of those secret camera shows or something. So after that performance I had to tell him.'

'And how did he take it?'

'That's the really weird thing. He was really cool about it – not bothered at all. He actually seemed quite pleased after he'd let it sink in.'

'Pleased?'

'Yeah, and this is what I really wanted to talk to you about. He said I could go on pretending he's the father if I want.'

'Really! Well, that was very nice of him.'

'It was. Though he said it would have advantages for him if his mother thought he was … in a relationship.'

'Do you think he wants to be "in a relationship" with you?'

'I don't know. He did ask me to go to his sister's wedding with him. But I got the feeling he's more interested in having an alibi, so his mother doesn't pry into his private life.'

'An international man of mystery, eh? Romy, do you have any photos of Kit?'

'I suppose I have some old photos around somewhere. Why would you – is this for your incident nook?'

Lesley looked sheepish. 'Well …'

'No. No way,' Romy said flatly. 'It couldn't have been him.'

'Why not?'

'I'd have recognised him, wouldn't I?'

'Would you? In a Darth Vader helmet? After all this time?'

Romy thought back to the previous night. She hadn't recognised him in that Yoda mask. 'No, it's not possible.'

'Romy, look at the facts. He's tall,' she began, counting her points out on her fingers, 'he was in town on the night in question, your mother thinks Luke is the spitting image of him, you've always thought Luke looks like someone familiar and … you like each other,' she said, finishing with her thumb.

'That's all just … circumstantial.' God, she was starting to talk like Lesley now.

'I agree we need more to go on. But I would definitely have to include him as a suspect.'

'You watch way too much TV.'

'Well, now it's finally going to pay off,' Lesley said cheerfully. 'Do you know if he was at David's party?'

'No, I didn't ask him. But he wouldn't have been. He never got in touch with any of us when he was home, did he?'

'Well, maybe he did this time. You have to ask him.'

'Okay, I'll ask him. But even if he *was* there, there were hundreds of people at David's party. My mother just sees a resemblance with Luke because she thinks he's the father – like I said, the power of suggestion. And yes, he's tall – but so are lots of people.'

'Well, I'm treating him as the prime suspect until we get evidence to the contrary.'

Romy sighed. 'Suit yourself. Anyway, I came here to talk about Kit, not Vader.'

'Maybe they're one and the same.'

'They're not.'

'But have you ever seen the two of them in a room together?' Lesley said quickly, collapsing in giggles at her own joke.

Romy rolled her eyes exasperatedly at her.

'Just saying,' Lesley said, holding her hands up defensively. 'It's something to think about.'

'Thank you, Sherlock. Anyway, what I really wanted to talk to you about was this idea of Kit pretending he's Luke's father. What do you think I should do?'

'God, I don't know. What do you want to do?'

'I haven't a clue!' Romy wailed, clutching her head. 'I mean, it would simplify things in the short term – I'd get out of having to tell Mum I'm a candidate for *The Jeremy Kyle Show*. But in the long term … I can't see how it would work. There's Luke to consider – I'd have to tell him the truth at some stage. And it would mean involving Kit's family as well. Plus, I hate lying to Mum.'

'Well, maybe you should tell her the truth. Your mum's cool. I'm sure she'd be fine about it.'

'I know she would – only now I'm afraid she'd be upset that I didn't tell her in the first place. It's like I didn't trust her or something. God, what a mess! Why did I ever tell that stupid lie? Whoever said that thing about the tangled web wasn't kidding.'

'It sounds like Kit has a few secrets of his own. I mean, who needs a decoy girlfriend?'

'Hmm,' Romy murmured thoughtfully. 'He does seem to be very secretive about his private life.'

'I'd like to get to the bottom of that. What's he hiding? You don't want to get involved with him again and find out too late that he's turned into a total weirdo.'

'Actually, I wouldn't mind finding out more about that myself. I'm sure it's not anything dodgy, but still …'

'I might have to expand the incident nook!' Lesley said, her eyes lighting up. 'Did he give you any clues?'

'No, not really.'

'Tell me everything he said.'

Romy could tell Lesley was itching to get out her notebook. She raked through everything she could remember of the conversation she'd had with Kit. She had the feeling that the later it had got and the more they'd had to drink, the more indiscreet Kit had become. Unfortunately, she'd been drinking too, and some of the details were fuzzy, coming back to her in bite-sized snippets.

'He had a girlfriend in New York and he said that their relationship hadn't been what it appeared on the surface. It sounded like – almost like a business arrangement. He gave her money and she acted as his girlfriend in public.'

'And in private?'

'I don't know. He mentioned "specialist interests" or "special tastes" or something, and he kept talking about this "lifestyle" he had there, and he said something about being part of a community … It's a bit hazy,' she said frowning.

'Oh my God, I think I know what it is!' Lesley gasped, pulling herself up straight.

'What?'

'BDSM,' she said, slapping the table for emphasis.

'Beady *what*?'

'B – D – S – M,' she said, enunciating the letters clearly. 'It's like S&M only … with knobs on. Wait, I'll show you.' She jumped up and left the room, appearing back moments later carrying a laptop, which she put on the table in front of Romy. 'It stands for bondage and discipline, domination and submission, and sadism and masochism. I've been reading all about it lately thanks to May. She's devoting a section of her website to it.'

'You've been spending too much time around May and her sex obsession. I'm sure that's not it.'

'I bet it is. Kit has a cruel mouth. I can see him with a whip.'

'He does not have a cruel mouth!'

'They use the same language as he was using – "lifestyle", "community" – look.' She typed BDSM into the search engine and clicked on the first link, opening a Wikipedia entry.

Romy scanned the introductory paragraph and scrolled down through the page, skim-reading fragments and looking at the photographs of men and women in collars and bondage gear, strapped to various kinds of equipment.

'I bet Kit's girlfriend in New York was really his submissive,' Lesley said as Romy clicked on more links.

The photographs were all similar – whips, chains, collars and leather gear – and the articles all referred to the 'lifestyle' and the 'BDSM community'. They even talked about being in the closet and coming out, in the same way that gay people did.

'You know, maybe the reason he doesn't want to have a relationship with you is because he thinks you wouldn't be into it,' Lesley said.

'Well, maybe he'd be right.'

'Hey, don't knock it until you've tried it.'

'Have you … tried it?' Romy asked, her eyes widening in shock.

'Me? Christ, no! You know me, I'm all talk. If someone tried to whip me, I wouldn't even have time to cut his balls off, I'd be legging it so fast. I like it in bed under a nice warm duvet – preferably with the lights out. I'm a terrible disappointment to May. She makes me feel like a right duffer in the sex department. She keeps telling me I should experiment more.'

'She's too bloody adventurous for her own good. I'm terrified of going up there one day and finding the pair of them dead and naked, knotted around each other after having a simultaneous heart attack.'

'Well, at least they'd go out with a bang!' Lesley laughed.

'And now she wants to set up this swing.'

'A swing?'

'Yeah, a sex swing. She has to drill holes in the ceiling for it, so she had to ask me about it. I wish she wasn't such a conscientious tenant and would just put the thing up without having to discuss it with me.'

'Well, if you want to find out about BDSM, she's your woman.'

'Eww, I don't think I want to chat to my OAP tenant about … this!' Romy said, waving at the screen.

'What about me? I'm going to have to listen to her going on about it for weeks while I'm building her website – and God knows what else.'

'Well, maybe you'll learn something – become more adventurous,' Romy grinned.

'I don't think I could do this S&M stuff, do you?' Lesley asked, nodding to the laptop screen, which was frozen on a photograph of a young woman, gagged and strapped to a cross, wearing what looked like a leather swimsuit. 'You'd feel like such an eejit.'

'Unless you were the dominant one. That wouldn't be so bad.' Romy scrolled down again, stopping on an image of a leather-clad young woman brandishing a whip and leading a man in a gimp mask on a dog leash. 'Those boots are great,' she said.

'Might be nice to have a boyfriend you could put on a leash,' Lesley said dreamily. 'At least you'd always know where he was.'

'But I don't think I could respect a man who'd want me to do that to him.'

'I don't think you need worry. I can't see Kit being a submissive.'

'I can't see him being into this stuff at all. You've just got kinky sex on the brain because you've been spending too much time with May.'

'Well, it'd probably be quite easy to find out – easier than finding Luke's father anyway.'

'How?'

'I could put a tail on him for a start—'

'You do know you're not *really* a detective, right?'

'Doesn't mean I don't know how to conduct surveillance. It wouldn't be the first time.'

'I remember.' Lesley had once done a series of stakeouts on her little sister's boyfriend and outed him as a cheater. 'But I don't think we should be snooping into Kit's life anyway. He's entitled to have his secrets. Even if he *is* into this, there's no harm in it – as long as he's not hurting anyone.'

'Anyone who doesn't want to be hurt,' Lesley added, and they both laughed.

They were interrupted by Luke's cries on the baby monitor as he woke up, and Romy went to get him. She chatted to Lesley some more while she fed and changed Luke, and packed up to go.

'Don't forget to ask Kit about David's party,' Lesley said at the door.

As she drove away, Romy felt more confused than ever. It had been good to talk things over with Lesley, but she was no nearer making a decision – and now her head was full of images of Kit in all sorts of S&M scenarios, wielding whips and floggers on women in strange leather outfits and tying them up to bizarre contraptions.

'What are we going to do?' she whispered to Luke. 'What the hell are we going to do?'

Chapter Eight

On Sunday, Romy arrived at her mother's house for lunch, having made up her mind to tell her the truth. It was the only way. The alternative was way too complicated. She would just say it and get it over with, and it might be horrible for a few minutes, but then they would get past it and move on. In a week or two, everything would be back to normal – only better because she would be free of the awful lying. She wouldn't have to feel guilty every time she spoke to her mother.

After her father's death, Romy's mother had sold the large family home in Ranelagh and moved to a little cottage near the sea in Sandymount. Romy got out of the taxi, carrying Luke in his car seat, wrapped up against the cold in a thick winter jacket and layers of blankets. When she had paid the driver and the taxi had pulled away, she stood for a moment surveying the house critically, noticing that the railings needed painting and a section of gutter was sagging. She would come over during the week and do some jobs on the house, she decided as she walked up the short path to the door. The garden, however, was neat and well maintained, the little flowerbed planted with winter shrubs, the dark soil free of weeds and the grass neatly clipped. The rain earlier had brought out the smell of clean, freshly turned earth. Danny must have done it recently, Romy thought. Their mother was oblivious to such things, and if it weren't for her and Danny, she would have let the house fall into disrepair without even noticing.

'Hello, pet,' her mother greeted her, kissing her on the cheek. 'Oh, you shouldn't have bothered,' she said as Romy handed her a bottle of wine, 'but thanks.'

Romy took off her coat and hung it up on a peg in the hallway, then unstrapped Luke from his car seat and lifted him out, following her mother into the kitchen. The house was deliciously warm and toasty after the cold outside.

When she had put the bottle of wine on the worktop, Marian held her arms out for Luke and Romy handed him to her.

'Hello, you,' Marian beamed at him, cuddling him to her. Watching her mother stroking Luke's face and playing with his grasping fingers, Romy wondered if she should say her piece now and get it over with. When she saw her mother looking at Luke with such joy and adoration, she knew nothing would make her love him less – and nothing would make her love Romy less either. She suddenly felt very sure of that. On the other hand, maybe when she was holding Luke wouldn't be the best time to deliver her bombshell – what if her mother dropped him in shock? Romy opened her mouth to speak, but Marian beat her to it.

'Why don't you go and see if you can cheer your Uncle Danny up,' she cooed to Luke, handing him over to Romy.

'Oh, Danny and Paul are already here?'

'Just Danny,' Marian said in a low voice, nodding towards the living room. She was no longer smiling. 'He's been dumped,' she mouthed to Romy, her expression grim.

'*What*?' Romy breathed. 'I don't believe it! When did this happen?'

'Just last night.'

'Oh my God!' Romy frowned uncomprehendingly.

'I know. I'm glad you got a taxi. We're going to need a lot of this today,' she said, tapping the wine bottle.

'Jesus!' Romy was so floored by this news she couldn't think of anything coherent to say.

'Go on,' Marian said, nodding towards the door. 'I'll just finish lunch. It'll be ready in about ten minutes.'

Romy carried Luke into the living room, where she found Danny slumped on the sofa in front of the fire, watching TV. She glanced at the screen. It was an old movie with Tony Randall, Rock Hudson and Doris Day. 'Hi,' she said softly. Her breath caught in her throat as her brother looked up at her. He looked pale and washed out, and had obviously been crying, his face puffy and his eyelids swollen.

'Hi,' he said, mustering a smile. He pointed the remote control at the TV and muted the sound.

'You look like you need a go of the magic baby,' she said, holding Luke out to him.

Danny took him, a smile softening his features as he settled Luke on his lap.

Romy flopped onto the sofa beside them. 'Mum told me – about you and Paul,' she said, putting an arm around his shoulders and hugging him to her. 'You okay?'

'I've been better,' he shrugged, his eyes welling up. He

cleared his throat. 'The magic baby helps,' he said, bouncing Luke on his knee.

'He's a cure for all known ills.' Romy smiled fondly, stroking Luke's downy hair. 'I just hope he doesn't grow up to be a bastard like – are we saying his name?'

'Which one? Tool, dickhead, arsehole? He has many names.'

'Like Satan. What happened anyway? I mean, he was here just last week. You were planning your holiday. You seemed fine.' She couldn't get her head around it. Last week, they had chatted and laughed and drunk wine together. She had given Paul advice on his rising damp, he had tossed Luke in the air and made him laugh. Last week, Paul had been one of the family. How could he vanish from their lives just like that? How could that all get cancelled out so suddenly? It didn't make sense.

'He just said he didn't love me anymore. But I think he's seeing someone else.' Danny's voice was hoarse and shaky, and Romy felt her eyes well up. That made the least sense of all. How could anyone stop loving her beautiful brother? He was the easiest person in the world to love.

'Bastard!' she said. 'Bloody men, eh?'

'Bloody men,' Danny said miserably.

'Well, he doesn't deserve you. You're better off without him. And other clichés,' she said, smiling ruefully. 'Sorry I can't come up with anything more original, but it's very short notice.'

'That's okay. The oldies are the best.'

'Speaking of which, what's the movie?' she asked, nodding towards the TV as she rested her head on Danny's shoulder. Doris Day was now engaged in a very heated exchange with Rock Hudson. Even with the sound off, you could tell Doris was fuming.

'I don't know. Some Doris Day movie where she tricks Rock Hudson into marrying her with a cunning plan.'

'Oh, *Pillow Talk*! I love that movie.'

'How the hell do you tell them apart? I just described the plot of every Doris Day film ever made.'

'Hey, not fair to Doris.'

'Really?' Danny gave her a sceptical look.

'No. There's *That Touch of Mink*, for instance.'

'What happens in that one?'

'She tricks Cary Grant into marrying her – with her most elaborate cunning plan ever.'

'Ah, I take it all back.'

'And *Calamity Jane*. She didn't even *have* a cunning plan to get someone to marry her.'

'Well, she had a gun. She didn't need one.'

'True.' Romy sighed. 'God, I wish *I* had a gun,' she said, thinking of Paul.

'Lunch is ready,' Marian said, popping her head around the door. Danny switched off the TV and they all trooped into the kitchen. Romy took Luke from Danny and strapped him into the swing chair that her mother kept for him, while Danny poured wine. She positioned the chair so that Luke could see everyone and set it swinging gently.

'This looks fantastic, Mum,' Romy said as she sat down. Marian was a superb cook when she made an effort, which she hadn't that often since their father had died, but she still always pushed the boat out for family Sunday lunch.

'There's an extra lamb shank, if anyone wants more,' Marian said with a wary glance at Danny as she began passing around dishes, and Romy guessed that she had been expecting Paul to join them as usual.

'Well, here's to us,' Marian said when they had all helped themselves, and they clinked glasses.

Romy groaned in appreciation as she dug into meltingly tender lamb shanks with gravy, creamy mashed potato and roast vegetables. 'This is amazing, Mum.'

'Mmm,' Danny grunted in agreement, his mouth full.

'So how was the Hallowe'en party the other night?' Marian asked. 'I never really heard about it properly. Who was there?'

Romy and her mother chatted about who had been at her party, what her old school friends were doing now, which of them had got married or had children. Danny was subdued, his head bent over his plate, and Romy and her mother exchanged worried glances when he wasn't looking. They all fell silent eventually, the silence only broken by Luke's gurgles and the jangle of the rattle he clutched in his fist.

'You know, I never liked Paul,' Marian piped up eventually.

Romy looked at her mother in astonishment. She had adored Paul. He had come to Sunday lunch with them almost every week for the past two years and she had doted on him. She had even started making hints about a wedding from the moment civil partnerships had become legal in Ireland. 'Mum, you did like him. We all did.'

'Well, okay, maybe I was taken in by his charm. But there was something sly about him. I never thought he was good enough for you,' she said to Danny.

'Thanks, Mum,' Danny said simply, seemingly touched by her show of support.

'It's just the truth. I didn't think he appreciated you enough. And he was charming on the surface, but when you got down to it, he was always a bit aloof. It was hard to get to know him really.'

'Yeah, I found *that* out,' Danny said with a bitter laugh.

'He was good-looking,' Marian continued, 'but you could tell he was going to be paunchy and bald in middle age. He was already starting to lose his hair.'

'And his waistline,' Romy added.

'He pronounced "tissue" as "tiss-ew",' Marian said.

'And he had that terrible unibrow,' Romy said, getting a small smile from Danny.

'Yes,' Marian said, 'and you know what they say – "Beware of those whose eyebrows meet."'

'He had shit taste in music,' Danny said quietly.

'And he was scared of babies,' Romy said. 'He tried to cover it up by being all hearty, but he always tensed up around Luke.'

'He left skid marks in the loo.'

'Danny, we're eating!' Marian protested, but she looked pleased.

'He kept calling Luke, "little man".' Romy shuddered.

'He never helped out when he came over for lunch.'

'He had back hair.'

'And ear hair.'

'And nose hair.'

'Shit! He was the missing link!' Danny said, and now he was laughing.

Soon they were all happily trying to outdo each other in tearing Paul to shreds. By the time Marian brought in the banoffee pie for dessert, the tension had dissipated and it was a normal, convivial Sunday lunch.

'Anyway, I haven't asked you about Kit,' Marian said to Romy as she sat down after handing around plates. 'Bloody Paul has put everything else out of my head. I couldn't believe it when I saw him the other day.'

Danny looked up. 'Kit Masterson?'

'Yes. Didn't Romy tell you?'

'No. Tell me what?' He looked at Romy questioningly.

'Just that he's back,' Romy said quickly, shooting her mother a warning look. Marian gave her a slight nod, indicating that she had taken the hint, but she looked puzzled. 'He's come back here to live. He called over the other night – on Hallowe'en.'

'You didn't see him at the party?' Marian asked Danny.

'It was after Danny had left,' Romy explained.

'I met him when I was dropping Luke home the next morning,' Marian said.

'He spent the night?' Danny's eyes widened.

'On the couch.'

'Wow! You haven't seen him in years, have you? I wonder what made him look you up suddenly after all this time.'

Romy shrugged. 'Just feeling nostalgic, I guess. And he wanted to get my advice on this house he's inherited that he's thinking of renovating. I might be helping him with it, if I think it's worth doing. He'd be paying me, of course,' she added when Danny bristled visibly.

'Well, I think it'll be lovely for you having him back. I always liked Kit,' Marian said, smiling fondly.

Romy laughed. 'Mum, you did not! You hated me going out with him. You were always hoping we'd break up and trying to fix me up with other boys.'

'Was I? Oh well, you shouldn't go by me. I liked Paul. I married your father.'

An awkward silence fell over the table. Marian busied herself cutting the pie and handing it around, and Romy looked at her in confusion, trying to read her expression. She and Danny exchanged bewildered glances across the table. What had her mother meant by that? Had they not been happy together? She had never heard her mother say anything critical or disloyal about her father before.

Finally, Marian looked up, catching Romy's puzzled expression. 'Look, I know you shouldn't speak ill of the dead, and I'm not really saying anything bad about him, but your father could be very … difficult.'

'He was in a lot of pain,' Romy said quietly, not meeting her mother's eye. She felt the icy-cold dread wash over her as the memories crowded in, threatening to overwhelm her.

'I don't mean just at the end, Romy. He was always difficult. You must have seen that. He was always so hard on you two – so demanding. Romy, I know you and your father had a … special bond …,' she began, choosing her words carefully. Then she sighed and said, 'Look, I know you're not supposed to say this out loud, but we all know you were his favourite.'

'Gee, thanks, Mum,' Danny said, but he was smiling and didn't appear at all hurt, or even surprised.

'I include myself in that, Danny, if it's any consolation,' Marian said, squeezing Danny's arm.

'Mum, I'm sure that's not—'

'It's true, Romy, and it's fine. I was over him years ago,' she said with a wry smile.

Now that Romy thought about it, her mother had been different since her father died – more light-hearted and relaxed, as if some invisible constraint had been removed. It was nothing dramatic, just a subtle letting go, the gentle expiration of someone who hadn't even been aware she was holding her breath. Everything about her was softer, easier. She had stopped trying to tame the uncontrollable frizz of her hair. She looked messier, and happier. Her house, too, was scruffier, but more cosy and homely. Every surface was covered in a jumble of bits and pieces, and setting the table always first necessitated shifting the piles of paperwork that constantly littered it. The shelves and bookcases were full to bursting, and when space ran out, books were stacked in high piles on the floor, forming teetering skyscrapers.

She had never thought of her mother as downtrodden, but now Romy wondered if it had been necessary for her to suppress some part of herself in order to be with the dynamic, forceful presence her father had been. She hadn't given much thought to her parents' relationship before. She had been aware that they were very different people, but they had seemed to suit each other. They were both journalists, and both highly respected in their fields – him for hard news and her for 'soft' features, categories which Romy thought typified them both perfectly. Her father could be stern, austere and intimidating, while her mother was never anything but warm, gentle and compassionate. Fiercely intellectual and politically astute, Frank Fitzgerald had been widely admired for his rigorous pursuit of the truth and his commitment to a liberal agenda. When he died, the nation had mourned the loss of one of its most valued political commentators. But while her father was revered, her mother was loved. He made people think, but she made them *feel*. Romy loved her mother's writing. Her humanity and warmth shone through in everything she wrote, and her regular column in a national newspaper had won her many devoted fans. People would write to tell her how one of her pieces had touched their lives, and complete strangers approached her in the street, treating her like an old and trusted friend.

'I loved him to bits, don't get me wrong,' Marian said now. 'He was the love of my life and I got to be with this person whom I was totally crazy about. If I could go back and do it all again, I wouldn't change a thing.' She sighed. 'That kind of love fades,' she continued, 'and it's not always what makes you happiest in the long run, but that doesn't mean you shouldn't grab it when you find it. Sometimes, the things that make you unhappiest are also the things that bring you the most joy.'

'What are you saying?' Romy asked.

'I'm just saying I wouldn't necessarily be the best person to decide what's right for you. You've always been the best judge of that yourself.'

'You think Kit could be the love of my life?'

'You certainly thought so when you were going out with him. I remember how distraught you were when he disappeared off to America and didn't come back,' Marian said.

'But Mum, that was a lifetime ago. We were just kids.'

'I'm just saying it's possible,' Marian said. 'You've always known what you wanted, Romy, and you've followed your heart no matter what anyone has said. And you've shown better judgement than any of us most of the time. But lately it's like you've started to doubt yourself. I'm just saying don't close yourself off to the possibility.'

'You think I'm closed off?'

'You haven't been out with anyone since Gary. I'm not saying having a boyfriend is the be all and end all, but I just don't want you to miss out.'

'Well, I've been a bit busy. I've had Luke to take care of. And it's not that easy finding a boyfriend when you have a baby.'

'But it's not just that, is it?' her mother said gently. 'I think you're hiding behind Luke a bit, using him as an excuse. Even before you had Luke – in fact, ever since your father died, you've changed. I know you've had a hard time getting over his death. But we all lost him, and we all miss him in our own ways. It's been over a year now. Life goes on.'

'I know, Mum.' She felt tears burning the back of her throat and she clenched her hands under the table. 'It's just – I feel …'

'What, love?'

'I just feel what's the point? What's the point of loving someone and doing everything you can to make them love you back, when they can just turn around one day and say that's it, they don't love you anymore? Why put yourself through it when they can just cut you off like that? Like Dad. Like

Danny and Paul,' she wailed, waving at her brother. Tears were welling up in her eyes now and she brushed them away with the back of her hand. 'I mean, why bother when it all means nothing in the end?'

'But that's just life, Romy. People die … and split up. Besides, your father dying is nothing like Danny and Paul. He died – he never stopped loving you.'

If only she knew! Romy thought about telling her mother the truth now about how she had got Luke. If she told her, she would understand. She would tell her how she hadn't been herself when she went out and fucked a stranger in a cupboard, and her mother would understand why nothing had seemed to matter to her then – why a connection with someone she had just met had seemed at once as precious and meaningless as a relationship with someone she had known her entire life. Because they could both turn to dust in seconds. It would be a relief to finally have it all out in the open. She took a deep breath, steeling herself to do it, but once again she couldn't bring herself to say the words. She looked at her mother's kind, loving face and her courage deserted her. Because what if she didn't understand? What if she looked at her the way her father had that night – with such hurt and disappointment, such anger and … hatred. She shuddered inwardly at the word.

'Just don't be afraid to grab whatever life offers, Romy. You never were before. It used to worry me sometimes how you threw yourself full-tilt into everything you did and gave so much of yourself to people. But that's you, and now I miss it.'

Romy nodded, sniffing and wiping her eyes with the back of her hand.

'Sorry, I didn't mean to upset you,' her mother said, patting her hand. 'And this won't be cheering Danny up,' she added with an apologetic look at her son.

'Actually, I was just wondering if I could tie all the napkins together and fashion a noose for myself,' Danny said.

'Okay, change of subject. Let's talk about celebrity gossip and trashy TV,' Marian said gleefully, and both her children smiled. 'There's no one to disapprove of us now.'

She felt disloyal even thinking it, but Romy had to admit Sunday lunches were a lot more light-hearted now than they had been when her father was alive. He had always dominated the conversation, and they had discussed politics and current affairs, debating the big issues of the day. He would expound on the background behind the headlines – the stories about corrupt governments, foreign wars and economic crises that he covered. She hadn't resented it. He knew how to tell a story, and he had lots of stories to tell. It was always interesting and stimulating. But lunch with her mother was different – it was *fun*.

Maybe they were all more relaxed now, she thought, looking at Danny. Their father had been charming and charismatic, but he had also been something of a bully. He had always claimed to value independent thought, and encouraged his children to express their opinions, but Romy had seen the harangues that Danny and her mother were subjected to when they disagreed with him or put up a stubborn, emotional resistance to his rational, analytical arguments. Romy had always been on the same side as him. She questioned now if she had actually agreed with him or if she had been subconsciously trying to win his approval. It had made her feel special to be allied with her brilliant, incisive father. But now she wondered had he been coaching her all along, priming her to go along with whatever he wanted, whatever he thought was right – to trust his judgement and never question or defy him. Had he been training her to be his co-conspirator?

No, she mustn't think that. She would drive herself crazy.

She was being paranoid. He couldn't possibly have known it would come to *that*. Her father wasn't a monster – she shouldn't make him into one now that he was dead.

She felt even more disloyal for her thoughts in light of what her mother had said about Romy being his favourite. She wondered if it was true. He hadn't always been happy with her choices, but like all bullies, he perversely had more respect for people who stood up to him, and she had always been less cowed by him than Danny. He had been disappointed – disapproving even – when she didn't follow in his footsteps and go to university, but she had never had academic aspirations. She preferred doing practical things, and she didn't want to study law or medicine just because she could, because she had the grades. He had reproached her for wasting her brains and doing what he had called 'navvy work'. But she had stuck to her guns, and in the end he had come round. He had admired her energy and work ethic, and had respected her integrity and independence. She was glad that he had come to be proud of her for making a success of her chosen career, and glad too that she had stood her ground, not just for her own sake, but for Danny's. Without her paving the way, Danny might never have had the courage to pursue his dream of becoming a landscape gardener, and could have allowed himself to be pushed into some line of work where he would have been miserable, his real talents wasted.

'Jeez, does no one have any scandal?' Danny said suddenly, shaking her out of her contemplative silence.

'I don't know who Luke's father is,' Romy said, looking at her mother. She hadn't meant to blurt it out like that – she hadn't planned to say it *at all*. It had just popped out. She felt her skin get hot.

Danny turned to her with a 'what the fuck?' look. 'I was thinking of something more along the lines of who's Jennifer

Aniston's latest squeeze. Is Lindsay Lohan back in rehab? That sort of thing.'

'I just need to say this,' she said to him apologetically. Her mother was looking at her confusedly.

'But what about—'

'It's not Kit.'

'*Kit*?' Danny turned to her, his eyes theatrically wide, mouth hanging open.

'I'll explain later,' she mumbled to him.

'But …' her mother began, her brow furrowed, 'Luke is the image of him.'

'You just think that because you thought he was the father.'

'You're not just saying this because he's come home now and doesn't want to be involved?'

'No. It really isn't him.'

'But you told me it was an old friend …'

'I know – because I knew you were worried about me, and I didn't want to tell you the truth.' She took a deep breath. 'The fact is I don't know who his father is. It was a one-night stand – with a total stranger. I don't even know his name.'

There, she'd said it. It was done. Her mother was looking at her in silence, and Romy wished she knew what she was thinking.

'That's not like you, Romy,' she said finally. There was no judgement in her tone – it was just a statement of fact.

'No, it's not like me. But it happened. And it's okay.' She looked at her mother steadily, trying to convey reassurance with her eyes.

Her mother nodded silently. Then suddenly she gasped, her hand flying to her mouth. 'Oh my God, the other day at your house! Poor Kit must have thought I was some kind of loon!'

'What did you do?' Danny asked.

'I was – oh God.' She put a hand to her forehead. 'I gave

him Luke to hold, and I was going on about them needing to spend time together to bond.'

'It's okay, Mum – I told him why you were acting like that. You've nothing to be embarrassed about. It was all my fault.'

'Did he go apeshit?' Danny asked.

'No.' Romy smiled. 'He was really nice about it, actually.'

'See, I told you I liked that boy,' Marian said, smiling at her.

'Okay, *now* can we dish the dirt on Cheryl Cole and Victoria Beckham?' Danny asked, and they all laughed.

'I was at the hairdresser's this week, so I'm all stocked up on celebrity gossip,' Marian said, topping up all their glasses. 'Ask me anything.'

And just like that, everything was back to normal.

❋

'Do you think Mum seems different these days?' Romy asked Danny later as they shared a taxi home, Luke asleep in his car seat beside her. She felt mellow from the wine and boneless with the relief of having finally told her mother the truth.

'Happier, you mean?'

'Well … yeah,' she admitted reluctantly. It seemed wrong to say it.

'Yeah, I think she is – some of the time anyway. It doesn't mean she wasn't happy then. She just has a different sort of happiness now.'

'You know what she said …' she hesitated.

'About you being Dad's favourite?'

'It wasn't true, you know. At least not—'

'Hey, it's not your fault. You couldn't help being perfect.' He grinned at her.

Romy gave a little moue of dissatisfaction. 'I wasn't perfect. That's a horrible thing to say.'

'Anyway, you weren't *always* his favourite.'

'No?'

'No. I had my moment in the spotlight. There was the time I came out, don't forget. I was his favourite for at least a month after that.'

'Oh, at least,' Romy said, giggling. Her father had revelled in the cachet of having a gay son, wearing it like a badge of pride, further testimony to his liberal credentials.

'Most of my gay friends put off coming out to their parents because they were afraid of how they'd react. I just didn't want to give Dad the satisfaction.'

'You brat! No wonder I was his favourite.'

'I knew he'd be unbearable about it,' Danny said, rolling his eyes. 'And he was. Anyone would think it was all his idea.'

Romy smiled fondly. 'Pity he missed me becoming a single mum.'

'He'd have been so proud.'

'He really would.' She sniffed. 'He'd want to kill Paul.'

'I know.' Danny's smile faded and he looked out the window.

'*I* want to kill Paul.'

'Mum wants to kill Paul,' Danny mumbled without turning around.

'We *all* want to kill Paul.'

'I miss him.' Danny turned to her, his eyes shining with tears.

'Paul?'

He shook his head. 'Dad. I still miss him so much sometimes.'

'I know.' Romy put her hand over his. 'Me too.'

'And then sometimes I don't,' Danny said, 'and that's worse. Sometimes, I'm kind of glad he's not there, and I feel so …'

'Guilty,' Romy finished.

'Yeah.' Danny sighed.

'I think it's the same for Mum. I know she misses him. But she seems … more relaxed. More herself or something.'

'Freer,' Danny said.

'Yeah, freer,' Romy said, almost to herself.

Romy sighed and looked out past her reflection in the car window into the darkness of the night. That was how she felt too, now that the truth was out. Free and ready for a new start – no more lies. Her mother was right: she had shut herself off from life for too long. Maybe this secret had been holding her back and now she would be able to move forward again. She already felt that life was opening up, full of possibilities. Suddenly, she felt like anything could happen.

Chapter Nine

Romy had arranged to drive down to Wicklow with Kit to look at his house the following day. It was a cold, wet day, rain coming down in slanting sheets. She had already been out and left Luke with her mother when Kit called at ten o'clock.

'Do you want a cup of coffee before we go?' she asked as he shook himself in the hallway like a wet dog. 'I just have something I want to finish first.'

'Yes, please. That'd be good.' He took off his coat and hung it on the coat-stand in the hallway, and followed her into the kitchen. Romy already had a mug of coffee sitting on the little table alongside her laptop. She poured Kit a mug from the coffee pot and he sat down opposite her.

'Sorry, I just want to get this done,' she said, clicking the mouse. 'It'll only take a few minutes.'

'What is it?' Kit peered at the laptop.

'I'm trying to word an ad for the flat downstairs. I want to get it up on Daft this morning.'

'You have a flat to let?'

'Yes,' she said absently, as she started to type. 'One of the basements.'

'Um, Romy ...'

'Yes?' she said, without looking up.

'Well ... I'm sort of looking for somewhere ...'

'Oh.' Romy raised her head, catching the hopeful tone in his voice. He was looking at her expectantly and her heart sank. 'The thing is, the rent on that flat is really cheap—'

'That wouldn't be a problem,' he said, smiling.

'Well, yes, but the reason it's cheap—'

'Is it a bit of a dump?' he interrupted eagerly. 'I don't mind. It'd be better than living at home in my bedroom like a bloody teenager.'

'No, it's not a dump. It's very nice. But the reason the rent's so cheap is because I want to let it to a handyman – someone who can do maintenance work around the place. I'm offering the flat in lieu of part of the rent – most of it, in fact.' She smiled ruefully. 'It's a really good deal. So if you know anyone who can do odd jobs ...'

'*I* can do odd jobs.'

'*You?*' She looked at him sceptically.

'I'm not as useless as I look, you know.'

'I'm not saying you're useless. There are plenty of very clever, talented people who can't do any DIY.'

'Well, I'm not one of them,' he said.

'I'm sure you're brilliant at what you do, but—'

'I didn't start out in a dealing room on Wall Street, you

know. I had a few other jobs when I first moved to New York. You'd be surprised, some of the skills I've acquired.' He raised an eyebrow at her.

'Really? What other jobs did you have?'

'Oh, let's see. I worked construction—'

Romy raised her eyebrows in surprise. She really couldn't see Kit on a building site – though he did have very good muscles. She'd seen him with his shirt off. Maybe they hadn't all been acquired in an expensive gym.

'I was a short order cook for a while. I did a stint in a juice bar, I delivered flowers, waited tables, I worked behind a perfume counter in Saks – you name it. And I lived in shitty apartments for about the first five years. I *can* fix things.'

'Well …'

'Please, Romy. Living with my folks is impossible, and anywhere I can afford is too grotty for words. This would be perfect. Plus it'd be handy for us to be living close if we're going to be doing this project together.'

'You can put up shelves? Do basic plumbing?'

'Yes, absolutely. I have my own tools and everything.'

Romy really couldn't see Kit in handyman mode, but she didn't have the heart to say no to him when he was so down on his luck. So she decided to give him the benefit of the doubt. She didn't want to think about how much she was motivated by the idea of having him living in her house. Anyway, even if that *was* part of the reason, so what? She was opening herself up to possibility, as her mother had said she should – she was letting life in, giving things a chance to happen.

'I should show you the apartment,' she said. 'It's a basement, but I've maximised on the light and it's not gloomy at all.'

'Are you saying …'

'It's yours, if you want it.' She clicked out of the screen, then turned off the laptop and closed the lid.

Kit grinned. 'I want it. I don't need to see it – I trust you. Thanks, Romy. You won't regret it. I'll be a model tenant. I'll even throw in some babysitting, if you like.'

'I'm not so sure about that. You don't know how babies work, remember?'

'Well, I can learn. If I'm going to be his dad—'

'Oh, you're not. Sorry, I should have said. I told Mum it's not you, so you're off the hook. You can consider your brief stint of fatherhood over.'

'Oh.' His face fell. 'Probably just as well,' he said, but he didn't sound convinced.

'But I'll still be your date for Hannah's wedding, if that's what you're worried about.'

'You'll come as my girlfriend?' he asked, brightening.

'Sure, if you want me to.'

'I do. You know what people get like at weddings. All my relations will be trying to fix me up with someone if they think I'm not partnered up.'

'So you want me to be a sort of smokescreen? Is that what your girlfriend in New York was?'

Kit shifted, looking at her warily. 'How much did I say about that the other night?'

'Oh, don't you remember? You told me all your deepest, darkest secrets,' Romy smirked.

'Really?' Kit's eyes widened.

'Yep. You're quite the dark horse, aren't you?'

'Look, Romy, I was a bit drunk, and I may have said some things—'

'Calm down,' she said, relenting. 'I'm just winding you up. You didn't tell me all that much – just that you had this show-pony girlfriend who you weren't in love with.'

'That's all?'

'Pretty much. I don't get why you'd basically pay someone to be your arm candy—'

'It just made life easier,' Kit said, shrugging. 'I like to keep my private life private, and it stopped people prying.'

Romy still felt she was missing something, but she decided to drop it. 'So, when do you want to move in?'

'The sooner, the better.'

'Okay, well, it's ready whenever you like.'

'Um, Romy … you know the way you have a van?'

She smiled resignedly. 'Okay, I'll help you move. I can't do it tomorrow, but how about Wednesday? I'll ask Danny to mind Luke.' Danny had told her he didn't have much work this week, and he would probably be glad of the distraction. He was still feeling a bit lost after the break-up with Paul and she knew that he needed to keep busy so he didn't have time to brood.

✳

When they had finished their coffee, Romy changed into Wellingtons and pulled on her big parka jacket.

'You're coat's still soaking,' she said, pulling it off the hook and handing it to him. It was thick wool and very expensive-looking, but completely inappropriate for the weather. It was sopping wet and weighed a ton.

Kit just shrugged and put it on. Romy pulled up her hood and they made a dash for it. They still got soaked in the short hop from the door to the van.

'Okay, show me the address again,' Romy said as she put on her seat belt, shaking dripping tendrils of hair from her face.

Kit passed her the paper with the estate agent details and she punched the address into her GPS. 'Right, let's go.'

Rain pelted the windows the whole way, the windshield wipers sloshing it away as fast as they could, but not able to keep up with the onslaught. They left behind open carriageways and wide fields, and drove through narrow twisting roads where the trees formed dark, verdant tunnels. Fat water-bombs dropped from the leafy branches that canopied the road and burst on the van roof.

'We could have picked a better day,' she said to Kit, who smiled at her resignedly. But despite the weather, she was enjoying the drive. It was nice to get out of Dublin, and the countryside was at its most lush and green. Besides, she was excited to be going to look at a prospective new project, and she felt mounting anticipation as they neared their destination.

Finally, the disembodied robotic voice of the GPS directed her to turn left and they passed through a set of gates into a narrow laneway. A small, stone cottage nestled just inside the entrance. Romy manoeuvred the van carefully along the muddy track, shrubbery brushing the sides as they passed, like a natural carwash. At the end of the bumpy, twisty lane, they emerged onto an unkempt gravel patch, and there was the house in all its … well, former glory. An imposing double-fronted building with stone steps leading up to the front door, it faced onto sweeping grounds, surrounded by a dilapidated fence that was broken in places. She bent down and peered up at the house through the windscreen, then checked the estate agent's details again.

'Yep, this is it,' she said, trying to sound cheerful as she cut the engine, though the house was in even worse repair than it had been when the photograph was taken. 'Let's go take a look,' she said to Kit, who already appeared despondent. 'Here, take this.' She grabbed a large umbrella from the back seat and handed it to him. She pulled up her hood, got out of the car and stood surveying the house and the surrounding land. When she looked back at Kit and found him watching her intently, she tried to perk her expression up a bit.

'I guess it's not looking its best today,' he said. 'The rain and everything …'

'Right.' Yeah, the rain – *that* was the problem. Kit stood, looking forlornly up at the house, his thick wool coat soaking up water like a sponge, his expensive-looking brogues already caked in mud. 'Your shoes will get ruined,' she said, pointing at his feet.

Kit just shrugged wearily.

'Come on, let's look around.' She led the way around the back of the house, examining pipes and gutters as she went. Kit hopped after her, trying to pick his way over puddles, but his feet inevitably sank into the mud, making a great sucking sound as he pulled them out again. At the back of the house, they stood ankle-deep in muck and Romy surveyed the roof. From what she could see, its condition suggested that it wouldn't be much drier inside the house than it was out.

'God, it's a shithole, isn't it?' Kit said beside her. 'I'm sorry I've wasted your time.'

'Well, it doesn't look great, I admit. But if it's structurally sound … Have you got the keys?'

Kit pulled a set of keys from his pocket and jangled them.

'Right, let's go and look inside.'

They walked up the wide granite steps that led to the front door, which Kit managed to open after a lot of fiddling. As they stepped inside, the smell of damp and decay was overwhelming.

'Jesus!' Kit swore, looking around in disgust.

Romy flicked a light switch, more in hope than expectation, but there was no electricity. It was only mid-morning, but it was such a grey, overcast day that it was still frustratingly dim inside. 'Wow,' she said as she looked around the vast entrance hall.

'I know, what a dump!' Kit said. 'Why don't we cut our losses, go down the local pub and get wrecked instead?'

Romy turned and smiled at him. 'I'm driving, remember? Anyway, I meant that "wow" in a good way.'

'Seriously?' Kit looked at her disbelievingly.

'Yes, totally,' she said distractedly as she took her torch from her pocket and turned it on, shining it on the ceiling and lighting up the ornate plasterwork and ceiling roses. 'This is an amazing house!' she breathed. 'Well, it was once …'

She looked at Kit's sceptical expression and realised that of course he couldn't see it as she did. He only saw how it was now – the crumbling floorboards, the damp dripping down the walls, the broken plasterwork and peeling paint. But she saw its potential. She saw how beautiful it had been once and could be again. Already her imagination was running riot with ideas and plans, and they were only in the hall. Okay, rein it in, she told herself. Don't get carried away by the excitement of it all. She knew the thrill and satisfaction she would get from turning this crumbling scrapheap into something truly amazing. But it probably wasn't viable, and she had to be sensible about it for Kit's sake.

She wandered from room to room downstairs, shining her torch on walls to examine wires, pipes, cracks in the walls and rotting woodwork, while Kit trailed behind her. Back in the hall, she placed a foot gingerly on the bottom step of the stairs, holding on firmly to the banisters.

'Are you sure you want to chance that?' Kit asked. 'They might collapse.'

Treading lightly, she made it to the first landing. 'Come on,' she said, turning and smiling down at him. 'They're perfectly safe.'

Kit followed her, and for the next hour they explored the house, the huge, high-ceilinged rooms echoing with emptiness.

There were still some odd pieces of old furniture around the place, chairs and sofas covered in threadbare brocade, a gigantic monster of a four-poster bed in one room, heavy velvet curtains tied back by thick twisted rope in another. Romy made notes as she went.

'This must have been an amazing house,' she said, sitting down on a window seat in an upstairs bedroom. 'Do you remember coming here when your aunt was alive?'

'Barely,' he said. He picked up an old birdcage from where it lay on the floor, examined it and tossed it onto the couch. 'Even then it was a dump. For as long as I can remember, she just lived in the basement. The rest of the house was derelict. Ethan, Hannah and I used to play up here.'

'What about the gate lodge?'

'I think a caretaker bloke used to live there back in the day, but he was long gone when we were kids. My aunt used to rent it out a bit.'

'Really? It doesn't strike me as a great holiday spot.'

'She knew a bunch of writers and artists – they used it when they wanted to get away from it all.'

'It's such a shame,' Romy said wistfully, looking out to the garden below. The glass in the large sash window was cracked and grubby. 'I don't know why people let houses fall into such disrepair.'

'So,' Kit said, sitting down beside her. 'Do you think there's any hope for it?'

Romy sighed. 'Well, normally I'd say your best bet would be to tear it down and start again – build something new from scratch. But it's such a beautiful house …'

'If you say so,' Kit smiled.

'It does need an awful lot of work – maybe more than you can afford. It will need a new roof for starters,' she said, consulting her notebook, 'new plumbing, rewiring, replastering, there's dry rot that will have to be dealt with …' She trailed off. 'Look, leave it with me. I'll work up some figures when I get home and give you an estimate.'

'Can you give me an estimate for building from scratch too?'

'Yes, I can. The only problem with that is, I'm not sure you'd be able to build something special enough to get the price you'd need – not with the market the way it is at the moment.'

'But you think I could maybe make the money back if we did up *this* house?'

'Possibly. I'll have to go into the figures, but if we did the right thing with it … It would make a fantastic country house hotel.'

'Oh, I never thought of that.'

'It could be great. I can put out some feelers, see if anyone's looking for a property like this.'

'Thanks, Romy,' he said. 'I don't know what I'd do without you.'

'Don't thank me yet,' she grinned. 'You might run screaming when you see the figures.'

❊

The rain eased up on the drive back to Dublin. Romy drove Kit back to his house first. Kit's parents still lived on the road where she and Kit had grown up, and she was overcome with nostalgia as she turned into the tree-lined cul de sac. She had lived just four doors down on the opposite side from Kit. As she backed into the driveway, she glanced towards her childhood home. There were two children, a boy and a girl, playing ball in the front garden. It felt weird to think of someone else sleeping in her bedroom. Cutting the engine, she looked at Kit's house in her rear-view mirror. It harboured almost as many memories as her own. She had spent so much time here when she was with Kit, it had been like a second home to her. It was strange to be back. Everything looked the same, yet different.

'You okay?' Kit asked her.

'Yeah. I just haven't been around here in so long. It's kind of weird. It all looks so much *smaller*.'

'I know, doesn't it? I'm glad you said that. If *I* say it, I get accused of being all up myself and Americanised.'

'Well, your mum can hardly hold that against you.'

'Don't be so sure.' Kit removed his seat belt and made to open his door. 'Are you going to come in? Mom would love to see you.'

Romy glanced at her watch. 'I'd better not. I need to pick Luke up from my mum's. But I'll see her when I come to help you move. Do you think you'll be able to get your stuff packed up by Wednesday?'

'Um … yeah,' Kit said with a little smile. 'That's not a problem.'

'Don't tell me – you haven't unpacked yet, have you?'

'Er … no, not really,' he mumbled guiltily.

Romy laughed. 'Okay, well, I'll see if I can get Danny to babysit and I'll give you a ring later to sort it out.'

❋

Kit found his mother in the kitchen, standing over what appeared to be a large chocolate puddle that was oozing and spreading across the table before his eyes.

'Kit, thank goodness!' Laura said, looking up at him. She appeared to be using a palette knife as a dam to contain the tide of chocolate before it reached the edge of the table.

Kit was about to ask what it was when his father came in from the garden.

'Colm, great! I need you two to give me a hand with this.'

Kit and his father approached the table cautiously from opposite directions.

'Hold this,' she said to Kit, nodding to the palette knife. When Kit had taken hold of it, she let go. 'Don't let it get away,' she said, nodding to the encroaching chocolate before turning to rummage in the drawers.

Kit and his father exchanged puzzled looks.

'Here,' she said, turning back and handing a spatula to her husband. 'I need to find a tin to put it in. I think there's one in the cupboard under the stairs. If you could just ...*contain* it until I get back.' She bustled off and Kit and his father looked at each other in bewilderment.

'What is it?' Kit's father hissed as soon as she was out of earshot.

'Haven't a clue.'

'You don't know?' His father looked panicked.

Kit shook his head. 'I was going to ask you.'

'How would *I* know?'

'You're the one who lives here.'

'What's that got to do with anything?'

'Well, I thought maybe you'd ... had it before.'

'I've never seen it before in my life.'

'Hey, you're letting it escape.' Kit nodded to where the mixture was oozing around the sides of his knife towards the edge of the table. Colm started batting it back with his spatula.

'Could it be some class of trifle gone wrong? Or a mousse?' Colm hissed frantically.

'No, it's warm,' Kit said, indicating the steam gently rising from the chocolate. It looked like an evil swamp from a children's story.

'So it's something you cook,' Colm said thoughtfully, as if trying to solve a crossword clue. 'Chocolate … *soup*? We had chocolate soup in that fancy restaurant you took us to in New York, remember?'

'But you wouldn't put chocolate soup on the table, would you?'

'Well, I don't think this is deliberate, in fairness. Something's gone horribly wrong.'

'It looks like a gigantic cowpat,' Kit sniggered.

'It's not funny,' his father reprimanded. 'Anyway, you don't cook a cowpat. Come on, think. We have to figure it out before she gets back,' he said, looking anxiously towards the door.

Kit looked around for clues. 'There's a cookbook open on the counter,' he said, twisting his neck to see it.

'Great. You hold the fort here and I'll go and have a look.' After pushing the chocolate mixture well back on both sides, he abandoned his spatula and hopped over to the counter.

'Well?' Kit turned to look at his father. He was holding the book in his arms, frowning down at it.

'It's a cake,' he announced.

'A *cake*? Are you sure?'

'It's a cake, I'm telling you. Look.' Colm brought the book over to Kit and pointed to a picture of a tall, two-tiered chocolate cake, covered in thick luscious icing, sitting on a cake stand. The page was covered in flour and grease stains.

'Is that it?' Kit asked, looking between the photograph and the mess on the table.

His father just nodded, apparently dumbstruck.

Kit prodded the lake with a finger. 'I think there *is* something solid under there.'

When they heard Laura coming back towards the kitchen, Colm ducked back to the counter and replaced the book, and resumed his position with the spatula.

'Phew! I need to clear out that cupboard,' Laura said, coming back into the room bearing a tin.

'Smashing-looking cake,' Colm said, smiling at her.

'Oh dear,' Laura said, 'it was supposed to be a welcome home cake for Ethan, but it hasn't turned out quite right.'

'Not at all, it looks great,' Colm said. 'Lovely and moist. Isn't that right, Kit?'

'Oh, um, yeah. It looks really … *wow*.'

'Nothing worse than a dry cake,' his father continued, gamely batting the mixture back.

'Well, I thought maybe if I could get it all into a tin, it might set in the fridge.'

'Good idea. Right,' Colm said, 'all hands on deck.'

When they had wrestled the two flat discs of sponge into the tin with an assortment of spatulas and fish slices, they scooped the icing up and poured it in on top.

'I wanted it to look so pretty,' Laura said sadly, surveying the slurry of chocolate in the tin. 'It doesn't look anything like the picture in the book. I don't know what went wrong.'

'Maybe you should have let it cool before you put the icing on,' Kit said.

'Ah, you can't trust those cookbooks,' Colm said. 'They use trick photography and all sorts of things. I bet there's a mistake in the recipe. You should throw that book out.'

Kit mentally rolled his eyes, but said nothing. 'So, when's Ethan coming home?' he asked as his mother put the tin in the fridge.

'He called from the airport,' Laura said. 'He'll be home tonight – or in the early hours of tomorrow, actually.'

'Right, well, I have to get on with clearing out the back bedroom for him,' Colm said, wiping his hands on his jeans. 'I'll leave you to it.'

When he had left, Kit started helping his mother to clear up.

'You look very chipper, sweetheart,' she said, smiling at him curiously.

'Yeah, well, you know I told you I met up with Romy the other night? Well, we've been hanging out together a bit and … I'm moving out.'

'Oh!' His mother looked pleased and concerned in equal measure. 'That's fast work, isn't it? I mean you've only just met her again—'

'Oh no! I'm not moving in with her. She has a flat she's going to rent cheap to me. It's in her house, but we're not going to be living together as such.'

'Oh, well that's great, honey,' she said, smiling. She seemed reassured, but Kit could see she was a little deflated at the same time.

'It's so great to be with Romy again, though,' he said. 'I'm really glad you suggested I look her up.'

'Well, I'm happy you're friends again. You know I was always very fond of Romy. You two made a great pair,' Laura said.

Kit couldn't stop smiling as he loaded the dishwasher. Being with Romy again was so comfortable and easy, and he realised he hadn't felt that relaxed in a long time. Romy had always been able to make him feel that everything would be all right, and he felt more secure already knowing he had her in his corner again. He was even beginning to think that he might be able to have a life here after all. Perhaps he could even have the sort of life his parents wanted for him – the sort of life he wanted for himself. He was so tired of hiding and living in fear of exposure. He might be deluding himself, but he had loved Romy once. Maybe he could again …

❋

After she had collected Luke, fed him and put him down for his nap, Romy sat down at her computer and opened up a new spreadsheet to work on the figures for Kit's house. No matter what way she crunched them, they were coming out looking pretty daunting. She really wanted to make it work, but she tried to be detached and dispassionate about it and not to allow her enthusiasm for the project, or her desire to help Kit, influence her calculations. After all, that was why she was good at property developing. She made decisions based on sound business sense, and didn't allow herself to get emotionally involved in her projects. However, since Kit already owned the house outright, she thought there was a chance she could make it work. It would be tight, but might just be feasible – particularly if she could find a potential buyer before they started. She searched the internet for comparable properties to get a feel for the market, then she sent a couple of emails to some upscale estate agents she dealt with, asking if they had any clients currently looking for a house like Kit's. Then she rang Danny.

'Hi,' she said when he answered the phone. 'How are you doing?'

'I'm okay. Keeping busy, you know.'

'I was wondering if you'd be able to come round and babysit on Wednesday?'

'Huh! Taking advantage of my single status already? Have you got a hot date?'

'Hardly. Where would I find a hot date? Anyway, I meant during the day.'

'Sure, no problem. What are you up to?'

'I'm just helping … um … someone,' she said vaguely. 'I got a tenant for the basement flat and I'm helping him move his stuff in.'

Danny sighed heavily. 'Romy, when are you going to realise they're your tenants, not your friends. You should keep your distance – keep the relationship strictly professional.'

'I know, I know.' She had already anticipated his disapproval. Despite the fact that he was a complete pushover himself, Danny was very protective of her if he thought someone was taking advantage of her helpful nature. 'But you know I'm no good at staying out of it. He doesn't have any transport and I've got the van—'

'That's what removal companies are for. Let him get his own van. It shouldn't be your problem.'

'It's just, he's a bit strapped for cash—' She stopped herself, realising that would only make it worse.

'All the more reason, then. You need to start off on the right foot or he'll have you down as a soft touch.'

'Well, the thing is, he's not just a tenant. He's … an old friend.'

'Who?'

'Look, um … I think Luke's waking up. I've got to go. I'll see you on Wednesday, okay?' She knew Danny would go ballistic if she told him it was Kit, and she wasn't in the mood right now. Time enough for him to find out on Wednesday.

'Romy—'

'Really, I've got to go.'

'What time?'

'Oh! Whenever suits you. Early in the morning would be best, but it probably won't take too long. I don't think he has much stuff.'

'Okay, I'll be there around ten. And Romy—'

'Great, thanks. See you then. Bye.'

Chapter Ten

On Wednesday morning, Danny arrived at Romy's house early. He sat and had coffee with her, taking Luke on his lap and keeping him amused while she ate her breakfast.

'So who's this new tenant, then?' he asked.

Romy sighed. There was no point in putting off telling him any longer. Kit would be here soon and he'd find out then anyway. 'It's Kit.'

Danny gave her a meaningful look.

'What?' she said defensively. 'He was looking for a place, I have a place – it suits us both. Saves me putting in an ad and vetting all-comers.'

'I thought you wanted to get a handyman for that flat.'

'Kit's going to be the handyman.'

Danny just rolled his eyes. 'So, first he has you project managing his house, and now you're letting him move in.'

'As a tenant. He'll be paying rent. And I told you he's going to pay me *if* I decide to help him renovate the house.'

'Just don't come crying to me when he has you washing his jocks.'

'Noted. So, any plans for the weekend?' she asked to change the subject.

'No,' he sighed. 'Plenty of offers. Everyone's trying to get me to go out, but …'

'Not ready to get back in the game yet?'

'Nah. You know I was always rubbish at that whole scene anyway.'

'Well, it's only been a couple of weeks. You've plenty of time before you end up on the shelf like me. Why don't you come over tonight? We'll have a quiet night in – you, me and Lesley.'

'All the single ladies?' He grinned.

'Hey, don't knock it. Being a spinster gets a bad rap. It's fun. Did all those years of watching *Sex and the City* teach you nothing?'

'I'm not knocking it. Count me in.'

'Cool. We'll help you embrace your spinsterhood.'

'I can't wait.'

The doorbell rang. 'That'll be Kit,' Romy said, going to answer it. 'You remember Danny?' she said, as she led Kit back into the kitchen.

'Yes! Hi. Nice to see you again.'

'Hi,' Danny said, his tone not entirely friendly. 'So you're the new handyman?' He eyed Kit up warily.

'Um, yeah. Seems so.'

'Danny's babysitting so I can help you with your stuff.'

'Oh great! Thanks.'

Danny threw Kit a look that said he wasn't doing it for *his* sake.

'Okay, let's go,' Romy said, not wanting to leave Danny and Kit together for too long. Danny's protectiveness of her was touching, but his hostility was starting to get embarrassing. 'The sooner we start, the sooner we'll finish,' she said idiotically.

'Take your time,' Danny said. 'I've nothing on today.'

'Okay, thanks. See you later.'

❋

'Sorry if Danny was a bit ... off,' she said to Kit once they were outside. 'He's not in a great mood these days. He's just been dumped.'

'Oh, right. I thought he seemed a bit grumpy. I'd have thought it was something I said, but all I said was hello.'

'Well, it doesn't take much at the moment,' Romy said as they got into her van. 'He's pretty devastated.'

'Poor guy. Had they been together long?'

'Over two years. Danny thought this was "the one". We all did.'

'So did she go off with someone else, or—'

'He. Paul,' Romy said as she backed out of the driveway. 'And Danny doesn't know for sure, but yes, he thinks there was someone else.'

'Oh, so Danny's ...'

'Gay, yes.'

'I didn't know.'

'Why would you? The last time you'd have seen him he'd have been, what – twelve? I don't think he knew himself at that stage.'

'So when did he … come out?'

'When he was sixteen.'

'And your parents were cool about it?'

'Oh, yeah, absolutely. You know what Dad was like – always looking for an opportunity to nail his colours to the mast.' She smiled. 'Danny actually put off telling them because he didn't want to be some kind of mascot for one of Dad's crusades.'

'Wow! I've never heard of anyone not coming out because they're afraid their parents will be *too* supportive.'

'I know. Anyway, sorry you didn't see him at his best today. He's usually a total sweetie.'

'God, I don't blame him,' Kit said, sighing. 'Still, it's nice to know it wasn't anything to do with me personally.'

Romy glanced over at him. 'It was a *little bit* to do with you,' she said, smiling mischievously. 'He thinks you're taking advantage of me.'

'Oh! Am I?' He looked at her anxiously.

'I don't know. But don't worry – I've decided to let you,' she said, grinning at him.

❊

When they got to Kit's house he led her straight to the kitchen, where they found his mother folding laundry.

'Mom, you remember—'

'Romy!' she said, dropping the pale pink sheet she was holding back into the laundry basket and rushing forward to envelop Romy in an enthusiastic hug. 'Oh my goodness, it's so good to see you,' she said, pulling back. 'It's been such a long time.'

'It's really nice to see you too, Mrs Masterson.' Romy had forgotten how fond she had been of Kit's mum, but one look at her plump, friendly face brought it all back.

'Call me Laura. You're too old now for that "Mrs Masterson" stuff. Would you like a cup of coffee?'

'Actually,' Kit said, 'we're just going to go up to my bedroom first – start sorting out my stuff.'

'Oh, okay.' Her smile faltered, and Romy wondered for a moment if she was going to automatically object to the two of them going to Kit's bedroom together, or tell them to leave the door open and not stay up there too long, like she would have done when they were teens. 'Just try not to make too much noise,' she said. 'Ethan's still sleeping.'

'We won't. I still have some stuff to pack up first anyway.'

'I'm not in any rush,' Romy said. 'We don't have to start moving stuff right away.'

'Well, come down for a coffee when you're done. Your dad will help you with the boxes when you're ready. He's out in the shed.'

'Okay. Come on,' Kit said, nudging Romy's hand, 'better get started.'

He led her upstairs, taking them two at a time in long strides. Once again, she had that weird sensation of everything being smaller as he led her along the landing to his bedroom. The room was stuffed full of packing boxes, but otherwise it was pretty much as she remembered it – the same blue wallpaper, the same mismatching pale pink net curtains (though she could remember when they had been white), the same narrow single bed, the same posters on the walls. It was like no time had passed at all and, as if in response, she felt a squirming excitement in her stomach that brought her right back to her teenage self.

'Wow, this brings back some memories,' she said, looking around, letting the nostalgia wash over her. She could practically feel the teenage hormones hanging in the air like perfume. They had spent hours together in this room. Quite a few of those hours had been spent sitting on Kit's bed pretending to do homework, their books spread out between them for camouflage, while they kissed and kissed, only breaking apart if they heard a step on the stairs. By the time Kit's mother would look in to check on them, they would be sitting cross-legged opposite each other, their heads bent studiously over their books.

'It does, doesn't it?' Kit threw himself onto the bed, lying on it at full stretch. He edged to one side and patted the space beside him, looking up invitingly at Romy.

She lay down on the narrow bed, facing him, so close they were almost touching, and wondered if he was remembering the same things. She pictured him as he had been then, with his spiky hair and his eyebrow piercing, trying to look dangerous. He looked more dangerous now, his fair hair cut so close to his head giving a brutal thuggishness to his features.

'I spent many happy hours up here cogging your homework,' he said.

'Well, that wasn't all we did,' she said, grinning, her gaze flicking to his mouth. She remembered those kisses as the best of her life – but maybe that was just because they were her first real kisses. Or perhaps it was because that was pretty much all they did. The kissing wasn't just a preliminary to be rushed through so they could get on to the next thing – it was the main event. She looked again at his beautiful mouth and wondered if he was as good a kisser as she remembered. If they kissed now, would it live up to her memories?

'Yeah,' he said, laughing. 'There was a lot of snogging too, wasn't there?'

'A lot. Hours and hours of snogging. It's a wonder either of us ever passed an exam.'

'It's only thanks to you that I ever did.'

'Well, you taught me stuff too. You completed my musical education.'

'That's true. If it wasn't for me, you'd probably still be listening to The Backstreet Boys.'

'Well, about that …' she said, giving him a sheepish smile.

'Oh my God, don't tell me – you *are* still listening to The Backstreet Boys?'

'Not exactly, but …'

'Come on – out with it.'

'Well, last summer I went to see Take That.'

'Take That? For fuck's sake – the minute my back is turned!'

'And they were *brilliant*!'

'Please. They were *not* brilliant.'

'They were. You weren't there. They were completely amazing! It was the best concert I'd ever been to.'

'*What*?'

'Oh, apart from that one you took me to in Belfast, obviously – what were they called? Something about Dirt Bikes?'

'Dirt Bikes for the Elderly?'

'That's it. They were *amazing*,' she said, not hiding her grin.

He pouted. 'They were seriously underrated.'

'Well, maybe you should have formed a fan club, spread the word – you and those other two guys in the audience.' She giggled.

'Oh, that's so unfair! There were way more people than that there. There were at least … five,' he conceded, laughing. 'And that's not even including you and me.'

'Wow, next stop the O$_2$! Sorry. I'm a hopeless case. That music-to-slash-your-wrists-by just never did it for me.'

'Just don't tell me about going to Take That concerts. It upsets me.'

Romy looked around the room. The wardrobe doors were open and it was empty, and apart from a few knick-knacks it seemed completely bare.

'Is this all there is?' she asked Kit, waving around at the boxes and suitcases stacked on the floor.

'Yeah, that's everything.'

'We should be able to do it in one trip, then. What about the stuff you said you still had to pack?'

Kit smiled guiltily. 'There isn't anything. I just wanted to lure you up here to my room.'

'Oh.' Romy's heart beat faster. Maybe she wasn't the only one thinking it might be nice to re-enact one of their make-out sessions.

'Well, I wanted Mom to *see* me lure you up to my room, actually.'

'Oh.' The little flame of excitement that had flickered to life inside her was doused. 'You want her to think we're up here … canoodling or something?'

Kit laughed. 'Canoodling! Sometimes, you talk like you're from the fifties.' He pulled her into a hug. 'Well, you know, since you're going to be my fake girlfriend for this wedding, I thought we should start to lay the groundwork for that.'

'Right.' She tried to hide her disappointment.

'Oh, by the way, Mom said to ask you to dinner tomorrow.'

'Tomorrow?'

'It's Thanksgiving.'

'It is? Already?'

'Well, it's not really Thanksgiving for another two weeks, but we're having it tomorrow because everyone will be too busy getting ready for Hannah's wedding by then. And it's sort of a homecoming dinner for Ethan too – we're killing the fatted turkey.'

'Oh, right. I'll have to see if I can get a babysitter.'

'You don't have to come, you know.'

'I'd like to. I mean, if you want me to …'

'Yeah, I'd love you to come. But Mom will be cooking, so—'

'I love your mother's dinners.'

Kit gave her a sceptical look.

'What? I do! I used to love when I'd get asked to stay to dinner here.' She meant it. Granted, Kit's mother was a pretty awful cook, but she did everything with such warmth and love that somehow she managed to achieve an overall effect of comfort and cheer.

'Well, on your head be it,' Kit said, getting up off the bed. 'I'm just going to the loo. Back in a sec.'

When he was gone, Romy sprang off the bed and looked around the room. Her eyes drifted to the packing boxes. There was one by the door still open and she spotted the framed photomontage she had made for Kit lying on the top. She picked it up and examined it, smiling at the memories it conjured up. As she placed it back in the box, something else caught her eye that caused her heart to start racing. Through the heap of jumbled bits and pieces, she could see a long black glove. It was a gauntlet-type glove … the kind of glove that Darth Vader wore … the kind of glove she had seen lying on the floor of David's bedroom last Hallowe'en. She never did ask Kit if he was at David's party, she thought.

Darth Vader had said he wasn't in Ireland often … and though she didn't like to admit it, even to herself, there really was a superficial resemblance between Kit and Luke. She knelt and delved into the box, reaching for the glove so she could get a better look at it. But as she pulled other things out of the way, she found herself holding a box with a picture of an oddly shaped red object on the cover under the word 'Rascal'. She glanced towards the door guiltily before pulling it out, then knelt back on her heels, staring mutely at the box in her hands. She knew what it was – she had seen enough of them recently on those BDSM websites Lesley had shown her. Even before she saw it was made by a company called Bum Rush or read the product description on the back with its promises of easy insertion and safety during play, she knew it was a butt plug. That word 'play' leapt out at her, her eyes widening. She had seen it countless times on those websites too. It was how people in the BDSM community referred to their … activities. Lesley was right, she thought, feeling deflated. Kit really was into all this kinky stuff.

She heard his footsteps coming back across the landing and hastily shoved the Rascal to the bottom of the box, spotting the forgotten glove. She picked up the photomontage and had it on her knee when Kit came back into the room.

'I was just looking at this,' she said, smiling up at him.

'Oh yeah,' he grinned, taking it from her and studying it. 'God, I looked like such a thug. What did you see in me?'

'You were the coolest boy in school. You were the one everyone wanted. Didn't you know that?'

'I guess,' he said, shrugging casually. He tossed the frame back into the box. 'Come on, I'll go and get Dad to help me take this stuff out to the car.' He held his hand out to her and pulled her up. Romy followed him somewhat reluctantly, wishing she could stay behind in his room on her own for a while. Maybe if she could have a couple of hours alone with those boxes, she would be able to find out all Kit's secrets.

✳

When they got downstairs, Laura put the kettle on and Kit went out to find his father.

'Romy!' Mr Masterson beamed at her as they came in

through the garden door, his round cheerful face lighting up as he reached for her hand. 'It's great to see you again.'

'Lovely to see you too,' she said, smiling as she shook his hand. 'You look well.'

'I'm embracing my feminine side,' he said, pointing to his shirt, which was the most delicate shade of pink.

Laura tutted. 'That was your last white shirt,' she said sadly.

'Ah, sure, what would I want with a white shirt?' Mr Masterson said, turning to her. 'White doesn't work well with the Irish complexion. Isn't that right, Romy?' he said, looking to her for affirmation.

'Yes, the pink really warms up your skin tones. It's very fetching.'

'You see?' he said, smiling around at them all. 'Romy knows her stuff.' He gave her a friendly wink. 'Right, son, let's get you sorted,' he said to Kit, rubbing his hands.

Romy handed Kit the keys to her van.

'Come and join us for coffee when you're done,' Laura called after them as they left the kitchen. 'Have a seat, Romy.'

Romy sat at the large wooden kitchen table while Laura busied herself making coffee. 'Did Kit ask you to Thanksgiving dinner tomorrow night?' she asked.

'Yes. I'd love to come – as long as I can get a babysitter.'

'Well, I hope you can make it. How old is your baby now? It's a boy, isn't it?'

'Yes, Luke. He's three months.' Romy smiled.

When Laura had joined her at the table and they were both clutching mugs of coffee, Romy took out her phone and showed her the picture of Luke that was her screensaver. 'That's him.'

'Oh, he's just adorable!' Laura said, smiling down at the image. She handed the phone back to Romy.

'He is, he's great. And he's really good, sleeps really well and everything. I'm so lucky.'

'It's so good to see you again, Romy,' Laura said. 'It's been such a long time, and you were like part of the family at one stage. I was so sorry to hear about your father passing,' she said, touching Romy's hand gently.

'I got your card – thanks. It was good of you to think of me.'

'And how's your mother?'

'She's fine – getting on with things.'

'I'm so pleased Kit got in touch with you again. You know, I think this redundancy could end up being the best thing that ever happened to him. I'd love to see him settle here. I don't think he was happy in New York – not really.'

'Oh? He seems pretty keen to get back.'

'He had a lot going for him there on the surface – a great job, a lovely apartment. But he seemed a bit … lost. And that girl he was with – Lauren – wasn't right for him.'

Lauren – that was the girl he had mentioned to her, his just-for-show girlfriend. Clearly they hadn't done as good a job of fooling everyone as Kit liked to think.

'She was perfectly nice in her way,' Laura continued. 'Very polite and proper – and so beautiful. Stunning actually. But she was sort of cold, and I never felt they really cared about each other. It was the same with all the girls he went out with over there. They were all the same type – almost interchangeable, in fact.'

Maybe they were interchangeable, Romy thought, the discovery she had made in Kit's room to the forefront of her mind. Perhaps Kit's 'girlfriends' were really a succession of submissives, trained to look and behave a certain way – to be polite and respectful, deferential and *discreet*. Perhaps Kit and these women didn't care about each other at all and were only together because they liked doing the same things – things that involved whips and anal plugs … She shook herself. She shouldn't be thinking about Kit doing things like that while sitting across the table from his mother.

'I still think he has his heart set on going back to New York,' Romy said.

'Well, we'll have to see what we can do to change his mind about that, won't we?' Laura said, with a twinkle in her eye.

Romy smiled weakly. An hour ago, she'd have been receptive to Laura's implication that she and Kit should get back together. Now, she wasn't so sure. Not if it involved letting him use a butt plug on her …

A loud buzzing from the far corner of the kitchen startled her out of her thoughts.

'That'll be my pastry. I'm making pecan pie for tomorrow's dinner. Excuse me a moment, dear,' Laura said, getting up from the table and crossing the kitchen. As she bent to open the oven, she was obscured from view by the large kitchen island.

'Hi,' someone said from behind Romy. She turned in the direction of the voice to see a tall, gangly guy leaning against the door-jamb, arms folded, looking at her. He was barefoot, dressed in a white T-shirt and a pair of soft grey jogging bottoms, and was clearly just out of bed.

'Oh, you're up,' Laura said, straightening up as she took a tray from the oven and placed it on the counter. 'You remember Ethan, Romy?'

'Ethan?' Romy gulped as he nodded hello to her. She did remember Ethan, Kit's little brother, but she didn't remember him like *this*. The last time she had seen Ethan he was probably eleven years old. He had been a shy but friendly boy, a cute kid who had always been very sweet to her. Now he was … *hot* with a capital H O T. Everything about him seemed exaggerated – his enormous blue eyes with their long sweeping lashes, his full red lips and strong jaw, and most of all his wild thatch of light brown hair that swept and swirled around his head in all directions, like whipped ice-cream. He was implausibly beautiful, like he had been drawn by a Manga artist.

He rubbed his eyes with the heels of his hands and blinked at her.

'Hi, Romy,' he said, and he smiled at her, which just made his face even more beautiful.

It was on the tip of her tongue to say something completely inane and idiotic like 'my, how you've grown', but she stopped herself in time. 'I'd hardly have recognised you,' she said instead.

She watched as he peeled himself away from the door and moved around the kitchen, pulling stuff from cupboards, shaking cereal into a bowl, pouring milk.

'I hope Kit and Dad didn't wake you,' Laura was saying from her position over by the island.

'Nah, I was awake anyway,' he said, his voice still thick with sleep. He pulled out a chair, placed his bowl of cereal and spoon on the table and sat down opposite her. 'Wow, Romy! This is surreal. I can't believe you're here,' he said, beaming at her. 'I feel like I've gone through a time portal.'

'I know what you mean.'

'It's really nice to see you again.' He leaned back against the chair, running a hand through his already messy hair, his frank scrutiny of her unnerving. 'God, I used to have such a crush on you,' he said with a crooked smile. Then he bent forward and began shovelling cereal into his mouth.

Romy laughed in astonishment at his frank admission. 'I know,' she said, smiling back at him.

'Really?' He looked up at her from beneath his lashes.

'You knew? That's a bit embarrassing.' But he didn't look embarrassed.

Romy shrugged. 'Well, it sort of comes as standard, doesn't it – a crush on your older brother's girlfriend?'

'Hmm, I guess. It's still embarrassing.' He gave a huge yawn, laying his head on the table momentarily before lifting it again. 'Sorry, knackered.'

'Ah, you finally woke up, Rip van Bollocks,' Kit said, striding back into the kitchen. He poured himself a mug of coffee from the pot on the worktop and sat down beside Romy. 'Dad's just rearranging the stuff in the van,' he said to Romy. 'He has a system. I was just getting in the way. I hope my little brother hasn't been pestering you.'

'No, he's being very charming.'

'You want to watch him. He'll charm the pants off you. It's his thing.'

'Yeah, no woman can resist my thing,' Ethan said, laughing.

Boys! Romy thought, rolling her eyes. 'So, what are you up to these days?' she asked Ethan. 'Apart from wowing the ladies with your thing. Last time I saw you, you wanted to play for Manchester United.'

'Ah, well, that didn't work out, unfortunately.'

'Never got the call?'

'Nope. So I had to settle for Plan B.'

'What's that?' Underwear model seemed the most likely option. Maybe he had been away somewhere exotic shooting a catalogue.

'Medicine.'

'Oh, you're a doctor?'

'Yep.' He nodded.

'Ethan's been working for Médecins Sans Frontières,' Laura put in, pride evident in her voice. 'He's spent the past year in Haiti.'

Ethan squirmed uncomfortably.

'Wow, that's—'

'Oh, don't pay any attention to him,' Kit said. 'He just does it to get laid.'

'That's true, actually,' Ethan said, grinning. 'It's much better than being a footballer in that way. Doesn't pay as much, though.'

'All the girls love a do-gooder. Jammy bastard!' Kit put an arm around Romy's shoulders, a proprietary gesture that she found amusing. Was he feeling threatened by his little brother?

'I can't help it if I have an awesome bedside manner,' Ethan said. 'Actually, that's all down to you,' he said to Romy. 'You were my first.'

'What?' Romy gulped. 'I was?'

He nodded. 'You were an excellent patient.'

'Oh! That,' she said, remembering. Ethan had been doing a first aid course and she had let him practise on her. He was studying for his certificate, and he had taken it very seriously. She still remembered his enthusiasm, the solemn intensity with which he had worked, and the gentleness of his touch as he ran his hands over her, checking for phantom injuries. 'You bandaged my arm,' she said.

'And you let me put you in the recovery position.'

You could put me in any position you like now, Romy thought as images flashed through her head of him laying her down on the floor, arranging her limbs to his satisfaction while she lay passive beneath his expert hands. *Hang on – I didn't just think that, did I? Not about Ethan!* He was Kit's little brother. He was twelve, for Christ's sake! Well, not now … obviously. But still – he was twelve once. She shouldn't be having those kinds of thoughts about someone who used to be twelve.

'You did a very good fainting victim,' he said. 'You didn't give it up too quickly – really made me work to bring you round.'

'Well, you were very dedicated to getting me back on my feet. And you *did* have a lovely bedside manner,' she said. She smiled, remembering. He had been slightly shy and awkward about touching her, blushing as he explained that he was supposed to loosen her clothing, and offering to let her do it herself. But she said it wouldn't be authentic and insisted he should do it.

'Huh!' Kit said, pouting. 'Where do you get off practising your bedside manner on my girlfriend?'

Oh God, Romy thought guiltily, had she just been flirting with Ethan?

She couldn't do that. She was supposed to be starting to clock in as Kit's girlfriend. She had to try and remember that. She couldn't flirt with his brother right in front of him.

Just then Mr Masterson came back in. 'Ethan, you got back,' he said, as casually as though Ethan had just been away for the weekend.

'Hi, Dad,' Ethan said, smiling as his father ruffled his hair affectionately, as if he was five years old.

'Everything's packed up, ready to go,' Colm said to Kit.

'Thanks, Dad. I guess we'd better get going,' Kit said to Romy as he stood.

'Okay,' Romy joined him. 'It was lovely to see you all again.'

'You too, honey,' Laura said to her. 'And hopefully we'll see you again tomorrow for Thanksgiving.'

✳

Seeing Ethan had taken Romy's mind off everything she had discovered in Kit's room, but as soon as she sat into the van with him it all came flooding back. She put the key in the ignition, but didn't start the engine, turning instead to Kit.

'You were over here last Hallowe'en, weren't you?' she asked him.

'Yeah, I was over for Dad's sixtieth around then.'

'You didn't … you weren't by any chance at David Kinsella's party, were you?'

He gave her an odd look. 'Why do you ask that?' He frowned.

She shrugged. 'Just … curious.' She had expected him to just say that he hadn't been there. Instead he was acting shifty – almost as if he had something to hide. 'So … were you?'

'Um … yeah, I was, actually.'

'Really?' she gasped, her heart hammering. 'So was I.'

'Oh. Pity we didn't bump into each other.'

'Well … maybe we did,' she said breathlessly. 'I met someone … it was dark and I never saw his face, but …'

Kit's eyes widened. He looked startled, panicked almost.

'I was dressed as Little Red Riding Hood.'

'Oh, Christ!' Kit hung his head. 'That was *you*?'

Romy nodded. She couldn't find the breath to speak.

'Oh, God – I didn't know.'

'Well, how could you? The masks …'

'God, I'm so sorry – about what happened. I don't usually—'

'I know,' she nodded. 'Me neither.'

'Honestly, I've never done that before—'

'What?' She frowned. 'Sex?'

'Well, obviously I've done *that* before,' he stammered. 'But not, you know, like that …'

'No … well, it wasn't exactly in the mainstream,' she said with a giggle.

He turned and gazed out the window. 'Can we just …

166

not talk about it?' he gulped. 'I just want to forget it ever happened.'

'Oh … okay.' God, he couldn't even look at her. They would have to talk about it more at some stage, but she couldn't pursue it right now – not when he was obviously so horrified by the whole thing! Anyway, she needed some time to get used to the idea herself and decide how she felt about it. Right now, she was too stunned to think straight.

'I was really messed up that night. I mean, it's no excuse, but—'

'It's okay,' she said. 'Don't worry about it.' Strange, she thought *she* was the one who was messed up that night – he had seemed very together and grounded. Her hands were shaking as she started up the engine.

'Um, Romy?' Kit turned to her. 'Are you still coming to Hannah's wedding with me?'

'What?' She spun around to look at him. 'Yes, of course. Why wouldn't I?'

'I just thought maybe you wouldn't want to after …' he trailed off.

'Hey, it's no big deal,' she said, trying to give him a reassuring smile. But it was disconcerting that he was so freaked out about what had happened that night. How could she possibly bring the subject up again?

She could hardly concentrate on driving, there were so many thoughts swirling around in her head. So Kit *was* Luke's father. After all this time of wondering, suddenly she had the answer. But instead of bringing her closure, it just opened up all sorts of other dilemmas. How did she feel about it? How would he feel about it? And the hardest question of all – how in hell was she going to tell him?

Chapter Eleven

'So I take it you've agreed to be Kit's fake girlfriend, then, since you're off to have Thanksgiving dinner with his family?' Lesley asked Romy on Thursday evening. She was sitting on Romy's bed holding Luke, watching Romy put on her make-up.

'Well, I said I'd go to his sister's wedding with him as his girlfriend. He seems to be terrified of his matchmaking relations.'

'We've all been there. Have you asked him if he was at David's party?'

'Yes.' Romy leaned closer to the mirror as she applied mascara. 'And he was there.' In the mirror she saw Lesley's eyes widen.

'And?'

Romy sighed as she tossed the mascara onto the dressing-table and turned to face Lesley. 'If I tell you something, can you keep it to yourself?'

'If you asked Poirot that, he'd have a face on.'

'Well, I'm not asking Poirot, I'm asking you. Not that you aren't equally awesome,' Romy added hastily.

'Of course I can keep it to myself. If you watched more TV detectives, you'd know that discretion is the byword of the amateur sleuth.'

'Okay. Well ...' Romy took a deep breath. 'It was him. Kit is Luke's father.'

'Oh my God!' Lesley gasped. For a moment, she just stared at Romy in wide-eyed, open-mouthed silence.

'So you can ... close your file or whatever,' Romy said. 'Pack up the incident nook.'

'I told you!' Lesley said, despite the fact that she couldn't look more amazed. 'But I can't believe you're being so cool about it.'

'Believe me, I wasn't when I first found out. I've had some time to think about it.' She had thought of nothing else since yesterday and she had barely slept last night. But she had come to some conclusions. She had decided she was glad that it was Kit – someone she liked, someone she had loved once ... someone she could possibly see herself having a relationship with. She wanted Luke to know his father, and if she got the chance, she would try to make a go of it with Kit. They liked each other, they got on well – she felt they could be happy. Besides, what were the chances of her meeting someone else when she had a baby in tow?

'So what did he say when you told him?'

'I haven't told him ... not yet.'

'Why not?'

'Well ... it's not the easiest thing to just come out with.'

'I guess not.'

'Plus he seemed really freaked out about what happened that night.' Romy bit her lip, remembering Kit's reaction when they'd spoken about it. 'It was like he felt really ashamed about it.'

'Well, he was shagging a stranger in a cupboard. It probably wasn't his finest hour.'

'I suppose. And besides …'

'Yes?'

'Well, I want us to have a chance to get to know each other again first, you know? I mean, I'd like to know how Kit feels without this being a factor. Then if something happened between us …'

Lesley perked up. 'Do you think something's going to happen?' she asked eagerly.

Romy smiled. 'I think it's possible. I'd like it to, for Luke's sake. But if it does – I'd like to know that it's real and he really wants to be with us, and he's not just facing up to his responsibilities and doing right by me because he's Luke's father. I don't want him to feel trapped.'

'But you do intend to tell him eventually?'

'Of course. I just want to give things a chance first. Once I know how he feels, I'll tell him either way.'

'But what about you? Do you want to be with Kit for his sake or because he's Luke's father?'

Romy shrugged. 'I honestly don't know. The waters are already muddied for me. But I want to try, for Luke's sake. We like each other a lot, so that's a start. And he's attractive …'

'So, maybe your fake boyfriend will turn into the real thing,' Lesley said. 'You can fake it till you make it.'

'That's sort of what I was thinking.' Romy smiled at her.

'But are you sure you *want* to make it?' Lesley asked, her face falling. 'What about all the BDSM stuff?'

'We don't even know he's into that. You've built it up in your head based on a few random remarks. Although …' she bit her lip.

'What?'

'Well, I did find something in his room yesterday that kind of made me wonder.'

'*What*? God, don't make me shine a light in your eyes.'

Romy sighed. 'I found a butt plug.'

'Oh my God!' Lesley gasped, her eyes wide. 'Well, there you are, then.'

'Well, I thought that at first, but now I'm not so sure that's what it means.'

'Oh, come on. What more proof do you need? You had the evidence right there in your hands. Wait – you didn't *actually* have it in your hands, did you?' Lesley asked, screwing her face up.

'Eew! No!'

'I mean it's not like you don't know where it's been.'

'If only! No, it was in a box.'

'That will have made a nice change for it,' Lesley said, and they laughed.

'But I've been thinking about it,' Romy said, 'and lots of people have anal sex, don't they? It doesn't mean he has to be an out-and-out kinkster.'

'I suppose,' Lesley conceded reluctantly.

'He might just have tried it once or twice. We've no evidence he even tried it at all. Maybe he bought that thing and never used it. It *was* still in the box. Or it could have been a joke gift from a stag party or something.' The more she thought about it, the more convinced she was that there could be a perfectly innocent explanation for Kit owning a butt plug that didn't involve him being into a BDSM lifestyle. Well, maybe *innocent* wasn't the right word …

'Hmm,' Lesley said thoughtfully, sounding unconvinced.

'The thing is, though, lots of people have anal sex, but they don't think of themselves as a community, do they?'

'I guess not.'

'It's not like you join a club or something. It isn't a whole way of life. I mean do they even have a group on Facebook?'

'I don't know.'

'Although that's worth looking into,' Lesley gasped, struck by her own brilliance. 'You should look at Kit's Facebook, see if he's in any weird groups.'

'Maybe.' Romy turned back to the mirror to put on her earrings.

'And what if you find out that he *is* into BDSM? What will you do?'

'I can cross that bridge when I come to it – *if* I come to it. For now, I'm just going for a wholesome Thanksgiving dinner with his family.'

'Doris Day would be proud of you.'

'I know,' Romy said, turning around and beaming delightedly. Doris Day was her heroine. She went over to the bed and sat on the other side to Lesley, laying back against the headboard with Luke between them, and started tickling him, making him giggle. Then she bent her head and blew raspberries on his belly until he was a wriggling, gurgling ball. 'I don't need any other guy when I've got you,' she said to him, holding his tiny soft hands and peppering his face with butterfly kisses, loving his toothless smile, the adoring way his eyes fixed on her like she was the only person in the world. She could stay here and gaze at him all night. Who would have thought that just looking at someone, watching him sleep, touching his velvety skin could make you so happy and fulfilled? He really was very like Kit, she thought, as she gazed down at him. It was so glaringly obvious, she couldn't believe she hadn't seen it before.

'At least you have a boyfriend, even if he is fake,' Lesley said, breaking into her reverie. 'It's so unfair. All the effort I put into dating, and I have nothing better to do than babysit on Thanksgiving, when everyone else is out gallivanting.'

'Hardly,' Romy said. 'It's not really Thanksgiving, and even if it was, it's not exactly a major holiday in Ireland. And it's a family dinner, not a date.'

'So who else will be there, apart from Kit and his parents?'

'His sister Hannah – and presumably her boyfriend.' Romy sat up again. 'As they're getting married in a few weeks. And his younger brother, Ethan. He's just got back from Haiti. He works for Médecins Sans Frontières.'

'Ooh, what's all this?' Lesley said, perking up.

'What?'

'This brother – Ethan. Why are you telling me about him all of a sudden?'

'It's not all of a sudden. You asked me who was going to be there – I'm just telling you.'

'Yes, but you said it in that mention-y way, trying to be casual. And you should see your face. You look all goofy and smitten.'

'Don't be daft.'

'You like him, don't you?'

'No,' Romy said, frowning, but still hardly able to wipe the smile off her face. 'Don't be silly. I don't even know him.'

'Oh, come on! You don't have to know someone to fancy the pants off them. You don't *know* Bradley Cooper. Doesn't stop him turning up in your fantasies, though, does it?'

'Well, Bradley Cooper is one thing. Ethan is …' she paused, 'way sexier actually,' she said with a confiding grin.

'Oh my God! I knew it!'

'He's absolutely gorgeous, okay? Sex on legs. Satisfied?'

'Hardly. I'll be satisfied when you tell me you're going to do something about it.'

'You're going to be frustrated, then, because that's not going to happen.'

'Why not?'

'Well, for starters, he's my fake boyfriend's brother – not to mention Luke's uncle.'

'Oh yeah. That could be awkward.'

'And besides, I told you – he's knicker-droppingly gorgeous. Totally out of my league.'

'Hey, don't put yourself down.'

'I'm not. I'm just being realistic. People get together with people of the same level of attractiveness – they've done studies. Ethan's just on a different level to me. I know I'm attractive enough, but I'm no supermodel. And Ethan could get a supermodel.'

'I'm sure there are exceptions.'

'He's too young for me anyway,' Romy said.

'How old is he?'

'I guess he'd be … twenty-six, twenty-seven?'

'Well, that's not a huge age difference – four or five years. It doesn't exactly make you Demi Moore to his Ashton Kutcher.'

'It's not a big age gap now, but it is when you're sixteen. I guess in my head he's still this kid who plays Nintendo and giggles when someone farts.'

'I know some men in their thirties who still think farting is hilarious,' Lesley huffed.

'Anyway, he's out of bounds, and that's the end of it,' Romy said. 'I can't be unfaithful to the father of my child with his own brother.'

'It does sound like a bad soap opera.'

'So, do you have any plans for the weekend?' Romy asked, changing the subject. 'Any dates lined up?'

'Ugh, no. I'm taking the weekend off – just couldn't face it. It's like going to endless interviews and never getting the job – not only not getting the job, but discovering you don't even *want* the job when you get there.'

'Well, come over tomorrow night, then. We'll have a spinsters' night in. Danny's coming too. He needs cheering up.'

'Here's a tip. Inducting him into your spinsters' club might not be the best way to cheer him up.'

'It'll be fun.'

'I know it will. Believe me, it'll be a whole world more fun than going on another bloody date with some wanker from that website.'

Just then the intercom buzzed. 'That'll be Kit with the cab,' Romy said, standing up and smoothing down her dress. 'Be good for your Auntie Lesley,' she said, bending to kiss Luke. 'Have fun,' she said to Lesley.

'Oh, I will. This guy is the best date I've had in ages,' she said, picking Luke up and following Romy into the living room.

'Bye,' Romy said, giving Luke another kiss on the forehead, breathing in the delicious baby smell of him, before grabbing her coat and heading for the door.

'Happy Thanksgiving!' Lesley called after her.

✳

'Wow, you look great,' Kit sad when they were in the cab.

'Thanks.' Romy felt very nervous as the taxi pulled off and she was alone with Kit. She hadn't seen him properly since they had talked about what happened at David's party, and she felt awkward with him now. She looked at him wonderingly, trying to get her head around the idea that they had had sex, that he was Luke's father, but it all just seemed too amazing and unreal.

'So – ready for your first official outing as my girlfriend?' Kit asked her.

'We're on now, are we?'

'Well, I thought we should have a bit of a lead-up before the wedding – get everyone used to the idea.'

'Don't you think it's a bit sudden?'

'You swept me off my feet,' he said, grinning and putting an arm around her. 'What could I do?'

She smiled, snuggling into him as he pulled her closer, breathing in the sharp, citrusy tang of his aftershave.

'Won't your parents think it's a bit strange, though?'

'Not at all. They always thought I was crazy to let you get away. And maybe they were right.'

'And will they approve of you going out with a single mum?'

'Honestly, Mom will be thrilled. She's dying to be a grandmother, and this is about as close as she's going to come for quite a while. It'll take the heat off me – and the rest of us.'

'What about Ethan?' Romy asked, aware that she was fishing, but she couldn't help it.

Kit snorted. 'No chance! She'd have more luck with me.'

'Why? Is he gay or something?'

'No, definitely not. He's quite the vagina enthusiast. But he's far too busy shagging his way around the world, dazzling the female population with his good looks and his good works.'

'So he doesn't have any steady girlfriend?'

'No. Commitment isn't really his thing. He likes his freedom. And to give credit where it's due, he does make the most of it.'

'Well, what about Hannah? She's getting married soon …'

'No way.' Kit shook his head. 'Hannah and Tank have made it very clear that they intend to enjoy a good five years of coupledom before they get sprogged up.'

'*Tank?*' She pulled back to look at him. 'Your sister is marrying someone called *Tank?*'

'Well, that's not his real name, obviously. It's a nickname. He plays rugby,' Kit added, as if that explained everything.

'Why Tank?'

Kit shrugged. 'Built like a tank, behaves like one – take your pick. It suits him. You'll see.'

❋

The evocative smell of roasting turkey hit Romy's nostrils as soon as Laura opened the door.

'Happy Thanksgiving,' she said, embracing them in turn.

'Happy Thanksgiving.' Romy handed her a large bouquet of tiger lilies and a bottle of wine.

'Oh my Lord, thank you, Romy – they're just beautiful. Come on through to the kitchen,' she said, leading them down the hall. 'We're all in there.'

Kit took off his coat and then started helping Romy off with hers, his American manners taking her by surprise. She had forgotten that Laura had raised her sons to stand when a woman entered the room, to pull out chairs and open car doors and never to walk on the street side of the pavement when they were with a girl. She had always found it rather charming, though a little disconcerting when you were used to more rough and ready Irish ways. It had always seemed especially incongruous coming from someone as wild and unconventional looking as Kit.

'Can I help you with anything?' she asked as they followed Laura into the kitchen.

'No thanks, dear, I think everything's under control. I have plenty of helpers.'

Ethan was standing over a large pot, aromatic steam rising

from it as he stirred, filling the air with the Christmassy smells of cinnamon, cloves and orange. On the far side of the room, Colm was setting the long oak table, the centre of which was already decorated with a brocade runner covered in fat pumpkin candles and pine cones.

'Hi,' Ethan looked up and smiled as they came in.

'Hello, Romy,' Colm called to her from across the kitchen, giving her a little wave. 'I've gone for blue today,' he said, indicating his shirt, which was the palest shade of duck-egg.

'Good choice,' Romy said, giving him a thumbs-up. 'Brings out the blue of your eyes.'

'My thoughts exactly,' he nodded happily, before returning to his table-setting.

'Hannah isn't here yet?' Kit asked.

'No, they should be here shortly,' Laura said. 'I'll just go and put these beautiful flowers Romy brought into water,' she added, bustling over to the sink.

'Have you warned Romy about Tank?' Ethan asked Kit.

'Warned me?' Romy asked.

'No. But he's not likely to go for her when he's only just met her, is he?' Kit answered his brother as if she hadn't spoken.

Ethan shrugged. 'Can't be too sure with Tank.'

'What do you mean "go for me"?' Romy asked exasperatedly.

Ethan abandoned his stirring, balancing his wooden spoon on the edge of the pot, and they both turned to her.

'He's just a bit … boisterous,' Kit said.

'He probably won't tackle you,' Ethan told her, 'since he's never met you before. But you never know. It's best to be prepared.'

'Hang on – *tackle* me?' Romy shrieked.

'Don't suppose you've ever played any rugby?' Kit asked her.

'Rugby? No!'

'What about self-defence?' Ethan asked. 'Have you ever done any martial arts or anything like that?'

'No. I've done a few kick-boxing exercise classes.' She was torn between alarm and amusement at the serious expressions on their faces as they discussed the possibility of their sister's fiancé grappling with her.

'Okay.' Ethan nodded thoughtfully. 'Well, maybe we could show you some basic blocking moves before he gets here.'

'Oh, come on! You're winding me up,' she said. Much as the idea of practising wrestling with Kit and Ethan appealed …

Ethan grinned. 'Well, maybe a little bit.'

'But not much,' Kit warned.

'Don't mind them,' Colm said, coming over. 'Tank's a good lad. He just doesn't know his own strength sometimes. That time he fractured Hannah's wrist was a freak accident.'

'Oh, now *you're* winding me up,' Romy said, laughing, slapping him playfully on the shoulder.

'No,' he said, his face the picture of innocence. 'That really happened.'

'Oh.'

'Don't look so worried,' Ethan said, giving her a consoling pat on the shoulder. 'It really was an accident. Hannah just dodged the wrong way and fell awkwardly.'

'It could have happened to anyone,' Colm said.

Surely not, Romy thought, but they didn't have time to explain further as the front door opened and two pairs of footsteps could be heard approaching.

'Hi, everyone,' Hannah called as she came into the kitchen, followed by a big blocky man with a tuft of dark hair standing up on his head. 'Happy Thanksgiving!' Hannah was tall like her brothers but without their reedy thinness, her body tending towards the curvy solidity of her mother's. She was strikingly like Laura, with a pretty, round face, huge clear blue eyes and thick strawberry blonde hair that fell to her shoulders. Romy was relieved that she didn't look too delicate and breakable, but alarmed that Tank had managed to injure her all the same.

While she hugged her brothers and father, Tank rushed over to Laura, who was standing at the sink arranging Romy's flowers, grabbing her from behind and wrestling her into a headlock.

'Oh hello, Tank,' Laura said, smiling up at him from under his arm, her voice vibrating as he ruffled her hair vigorously.

'Happy Thanksgiving, Laura,' he said, beaming as he released her and she tried to smooth her hair down and catch her breath, her cheeks flushed. He turned his attention to Kit and Ethan then, greeting them with a bout of shadow boxing while they feinted laughingly in reply. On the last punch, Kit didn't duck in time and Tank landed an actual blow to his stomach.

'Jaysus, sorry about that,' Tank said amiably, patting Kit on the back as he doubled over. 'And who have we here?' he asked, turning his attention to Romy, who leapt back instinctively.

Kit straightened up, and she was touched that both he and Ethan came to stand a little in front of her. 'This is Romy,' Kit said.

She braced herself, but got off lightly as Tank simply grabbed her hand, pumping it enthusiastically. 'Romy, pleased to meet you.'

'It's really nice to see you again, Romy,' Hannah said, smiling at her, but seeming somewhat bemused by her presence.

'Why don't you all go through to the living room while I finish up in here,' Laura said. 'I'll bring in drinks in a minute.'

They trooped through to the living room, and Romy sat on the sofa, Kit sitting unnecessarily close beside her, leaving a large gap between him and Ethan at the other end.

'Now that I've finally got you two here,' Hannah said to her brothers, 'I need to finalise plans for my wedding. Are you going to be bringing anyone, Kit? I take it Lauren won't be flying over for it?'

'No, definitely not. Lauren and I split up,' Kit said.

'Well, I can't honestly say I'm sorry to hear that,' Hannah said.

'God, no!' Tank agreed. 'She was a fierce pain in the hole altogether. Acted like she had something stuck up her arse the whole time.'

Maybe because she had, Romy thought.

'Gee, don't hold back,' Kit said.

'Well, you don't exactly seem gutted yourself,' Hannah said, looking at him closely.

'I'll live.'

'So are you planning to bring anyone to the wedding?' she asked.

'Yes, Romy's coming with me.'

'Oh, that's great!' she said, giving Romy a bright smile. 'I'd much rather have you there than stinky old Lauren. And you should come to my hen party. We're going to an adventure centre for the weekend, and we'll do archery and shooting and zip wires and all sorts of stuff.'

'That sounds unusual for a hen do.'

'Yeah, well, we're trying to save money, so I wanted to do something close to home. And it'll be loads more fun than going to some spa for facials and massages. It'll be great! What do you think? Will you come? It's the weekend after next.'

'Well, it sounds really fun, but I'd have to get a babysitter and I'm not sure about leaving Luke for a whole weekend—'

'Oh, you have a baby?'

'Yes.'

'I didn't know you had a baby!' Ethan said. 'How old is he?'

'Three months.'

'Couldn't his father babysit?' Hannah asked.

Romy knew she was probably fishing for information, but she didn't mind. She was used to people's curiosity about her circumstances. 'His father isn't around,' she said.

'Well, you should bring him. My friends all love babies. We could take turns babysitting so you'd get to do some of the activities.'

'If you're going to be doing shooting and zip wires at the hen party, I dread to think what's going to happen at Tank's stag,' Kit said.

'Well, you'd have to ask Wedgie about that,' Tank said. 'He's the one who's organising it.'

'I don't suppose there's any chance he's planning a Scottish theme,' Kit said sulkily. 'Spot of caber tossing, tug of war, that sort of thing?'

'I haven't a bog,' Tank said. 'He's planning a surprise for me, so it's all top secret.'

'Why would he have a Scottish theme anyway?' Hannah asked. 'There's no Scottish connection.'

'No reason. I was just hoping.'

'Really? I wouldn't have thought caber tossing would float your dinghy.'

'Kit was hoping to get a chance to wear a kilt,' Romy explained to Hannah.

'Ah!' She smirked. 'You're afraid of Wedgie, aren't you?'

'So would you be.'

'Drinks, everyone!' Laura called as she and Colm came in, carrying trays of mulled wine. 'Careful, it's hot,' she said as she held out a tray and Romy reached for a steaming glass, picking it up with one of the folded napkins Laura had piled alongside the drinks.

'What's this?' Tank said suspiciously, peering into his glass. 'Ribena?'

'It's mulled wine,' Hannah murmured to him.

'Mine's got a bit of twig or something in it,' he said, poking a finger into the glass to fish out the offending article.

'They're cloves,' Laura told him. 'They're supposed to be there. Ethan made it.'

'Oh, really? Great stuff, Ethan,' he said with a nod of his head in Ethan's direction. 'Fair play. Is that something you learned in the jungle?'

'Er … no,' Ethan said, his lips twitching.

'I knew a lad once who went into the army and got sent to the jungle. Fierce resourceful chap. Could make alcohol out of anything – bits of twigs, leaves, any sort of fruit you can think of – you name it, he could turn it into alcohol.'

'Well, Ethan hasn't been to the jungle,' Hannah said. 'He was in Haiti.'

'Ah, right,' Tank nodded, but from his baffled expression he clearly didn't see the distinction. 'Bark,' he continued dreamily, 'pine cones …

'Do you want to stay overnight at the hotel after the wedding, Romy?' Hannah asked. 'It's in Wicklow, so a lot of the guests are spending the night. I just need to know how many rooms we need.'

'Oh, yes, I'll stay the night. I've already arranged for Mum to take Luke.'

'Great! I'll book you a room, then.'

'She doesn't need a room,' Kit said. 'She'll be staying with me, in my room.'

To her surprise, Romy felt his hand on her leg in a seemingly casual gesture, and he squeezed even closer to her on the couch, so their thighs were touching.

'Oh!' Hannah seemed taken aback, her eyes narrowing as she watched Kit's hand. 'So you two are …'

'We're back together, yes.' Kit turned to smile at Romy,

putting an arm around her shoulders and pulling her into his side.

'Oh.' Hannah sounded disappointed, and Romy caught her and Ethan exchanging a glance. She wasn't sure what it meant, but neither of them looked pleased. Suddenly, she felt very disconcerted and uncomfortable – and hurt. She thought they liked her. They had both been friendly and seemed genuinely pleased to see her again. So why wouldn't they be happy that she and Kit were back together? At least Laura looked happy about it.

'Well, that was quick work,' she said, her face lighting up.

'When you know, you know,' Kit said, turning to look adoringly at Romy.

She felt a little frisson as their eyes met and enjoyed the feeling of being fancied, even if it was just pretend. Though it felt real enough.

'How about you, Ethan?' Hannah was asking now. 'Are you bringing anyone to the wedding?'

Romy was annoyed to realise she was on high alert for his answer.

'The bridesmaids are all attached – if that influences your decision,' Hannah continued.

'Shut up,' Ethan said, blushing and glancing at Romy. 'You make me sound like—'

'A total man-whore? That's what you are, my darling. But it doesn't make me love you any less.'

'Well, yeah, I guess I will bring someone.'

'Do we have a name? Who's the lucky winner?'

'Sinead. I'm meeting up with her tomorrow night. I'll ask her then.'

When Laura announced that dinner was ready, Kit indicated to Romy that he wanted her to hang back with him.

'Sorry about that,' he said when everyone else had left the room. 'I was kind of put on the spot. You don't mind, do you? Sharing a room?'

'No,' she said. 'It's fine.'

'I mean if you're supposed to be my girlfriend, it would seem weird if we didn't. But I can be a gentleman. I promise I'll keep my hands to myself. And you can break up with me right after the wedding if you like.'

'I'm not in any hurry to break up with you,' she said, smiling at him as they went to join everyone else in the kitchen.

'This all looks fantastic!' she said, as Kit pulled out a chair for her to sit down.

'It looks great, Mom,' Ethan said as they started passing bowls of soggy vegetables and lumpy mashed potato, and everyone else joined in, murmuring their appreciation. There was corn bread with chilli, bowls of stuffing and cranberry sauce, a green bean casserole and a couple of colourful salads. Whatever about the quality of her food, Laura couldn't be faulted on quantity.

'That turkey was a bugger to carve,' Colm said as he handed around plates of something resembling sawdust.

'Oh dear,' Laura fretted. 'Is it a little dry?'

'No, it's grand,' Colm said. 'It's that carving knife – wouldn't cut butter. We'll have to throw it out and get a new one for Christmas.'

'What's this?' Tank asked, poking his fork suspiciously at a dish of something orange with charred black stripes.

'They're glazed sweet potatoes,' Laura told him. 'My mom always made them just like that on Thanksgiving – except she didn't burn them.'

'They're not burned, they're *caramelised*,' Colm said. 'I've seen Jamie Oliver doing that.'

'Cremated, more like,' Tank said under his breath, nevertheless helping himself to a generous serving.

'This cauliflower cheese is gorgeous,' Romy said when she had tasted it, trying not to sound too surprised. Laura had obviously improved over the years, at least in some things. The mashed potatoes were still pretty awful, and the turkey was hard to swallow without choking, but at least there was something edible.

'Oh, Ethan made that,' Laura said, smiling at him. 'I don't know how he gets the sauce so smooth. I'm afraid I can't say the same for the gravy,' she said ruefully.

'Nonsense!' Colm huffed. 'We like a sauce with a bit of body, don't we?' he asked the table at large, and everyone nodded their agreement.

He should be happy with the gravy, then, Romy thought, as globules of it plopped onto her plate as she poured. It certainly had plenty of 'body'.

'Happy Thanksgiving everyone!' Laura said when they had loaded their plates, and they all clinked glasses. Then everyone started talking at once.

'So tell us about your boy, Romy ...'

'You won't have had a feed like this in a long time, Ethan. What do they eat in the jungle anyway?'

'Mom, I need you to come to the dress fitting with me next week.'

'Lumpy mashed potatoes are all the rage nowadays. *Crushed* potatoes, they call them. All the top chefs are doing them.'

As the sounds of chatter and laughter flowed around the table, Romy observed Laura at the head of it all and thought she looked ready to burst with happiness, her rosy cheeks warmed by the glow of candles, her joy palpable as she looked around at her family.

Later, when coffee had been served with a pecan pie so dry and hard that all conversation ceased as nothing could be heard over the crunching, Laura clinked her glass and everyone fell silent in what was clearly a Thanksgiving tradition.

'We have a lot to be thankful for this year,' she began. 'I'm so grateful to have the whole family together, and especially to have my two boys home. So I'm damned if I was going to miss the opportunity to have Thanksgiving with all of you. Ethan,' she said, looking at him, 'we're so proud of you, honey, but you do scare the bejaysus out of us sometimes.' Everyone laughed, while Ethan ducked his head, smiling shyly. 'It's good to have you home safe, sweetheart. And Tank,' she said, turning to him with a warm smile. 'You've made our Hannah so happy and we're all looking forward to you becoming a part of our family shortly. We couldn't have been blessed with a better son-in-law.' Romy was amazed to see Tank surreptitiously wipe away a tear. 'And we've forgiven you for that time you broke her wrist,' Laura added drily, causing more laughter to erupt. 'Romy,' she continued, 'it's wonderful that you and Kit have found each other again, and I hope we'll be seeing a lot more of you. You were always the nicest of his girlfriends,' she added with a cheeky grin at Kit.

'I won't argue with that,' Kit said, smiling at Romy.

'Neither will I,' Ethan mumbled.

'Or me,' Hannah chimed in.

'See,' Kit said to Romy, 'it's unanimous. All my family loves you.'

'As for me, I'm eternally grateful for this man,' Laura continued, touching Colm's hand, 'who loves me too much to see my flaws. And I'm delighted to hear that crushed potatoes are the latest thing, because I'm damned if I can make whipped ones.'

They all raised their glasses in a toast as Laura's little speech came to an end.

Looking around the table as the chatter resumed, Romy

marvelled at how much things had changed for her since she'd met Kit again. It had only been a little over a week, and already her life was opening up in all sorts of unexpected ways. She didn't really believe in fate, but she couldn't help wondering if they were meant to be together. Could it be that she'd found 'the one' all those years ago and they'd just lost each other for a while? As she watched Kit, she tried to assess her feelings for him, doing her best to take Luke out of the equation. She had loved him so much once – he was the only person she had ever been properly in love with. But that was a long time ago, and though they still had a connection, she felt in ways he was a stranger to her now. It was easy to fall back into loving him as a friend, but could she be *in love* with him again? Right now, she just knew that this felt good. Being with Kit and his family tonight she had a powerful sense of belonging. And try as she might, she couldn't take Luke out of the equation, because he was part of it. He was part of her and Kit, and he could be part of this family – and she wanted that for him. Maybe she couldn't love Kit again the way she once had. But she knew that she would like to try.

❈

By the time they were ready to leave, Romy felt cocooned in the soft cosy blanket that the warmth and conviviality of the evening had woven around her. While Kit called a taxi, she excused herself to go to the loo. She had just reached the top of the stairs when she heard Ethan and Hannah whispering on the landing.

'I thought now that he's home things would be different,' Hannah hissed. 'I thought he'd finally be forced to man up and get real.'

'I know,' Ethan whispered.

'I didn't think he'd go straight out and get himself another Lauren substitute.'

'Do you think she knows?'

Romy froze, the warm glow she had been bathed in moments before turning to ice. Suddenly, she just wanted to go home. She was about to turn around and go back downstairs, but it was too late – Hannah had seen her, and Ethan turned around to see what his sister was looking at. If Romy had been in any doubt that they'd been talking about her, their blushes and shifty looks erased it.

'Oh, hi,' she said awkwardly, stumbling on the top step. 'I was just …' she pointed towards the loo.

They both nodded at her before going back downstairs, leaving Romy dumbfounded on the landing, her heart pounding. Why were they so hostile to the idea of her and Kit being together? She couldn't understand it. Their friendliness earlier had seemed sincere. But they thought she was like Lauren – and they had made their feelings about Lauren abundantly clear.

On the way home in the taxi, she broached the subject tentatively with Kit. 'Am I like Lauren?'

He frowned, appearing surprised by the question. 'No. Not at all.'

'I don't mean looks-wise.'

'You're not like her in any way.'

Romy thought about what she had overheard. Maybe it wasn't that they thought she was like Lauren personally, but that they suspected she had the same sort of relationship with Kit. Perhaps they knew that Kit was involved in BDSM and disapproved of his lifestyle. If they thought she was taking Lauren's place as his submissive, that could explain their concern.

'Ethan and Hannah don't seem thrilled about the idea of us getting back together.'

'That's crazy. They all love you!'

'But that's just it. I don't think it's *me* they have a problem with. It's *us*.' She waved her hand between them.

'They just don't get us,' he said, putting an arm around her and pulling her into his side. 'No one ever did, remember? So sod 'em. It'll be you and me against the world, just like it used to be.'

She smiled, but she still felt uneasy, her sense of wellbeing evaporating. They weren't teenagers anymore. She didn't know if she liked the idea of them against the world. Tonight it had felt like the world was on their side, and it had been a good feeling.

Chapter Twelve

'So how's Kit working out?' Lesley asked Romy, as they settled in for another Saturday spinsters' night in.

'Great!' Romy said, handing her a glass of wine. 'Cheers!' They clinked glasses and Romy sat on the couch beside Lesley. 'Though he hasn't been around that much. He seems to have a pretty active social life already. He goes out a lot at night and doesn't come back until all hours – if at all.' Romy was disappointed that Kit wasn't around more. When he moved in, she'd imagined they would be like flatmates – sharing a bottle of wine in the evenings, having cosy chats and listening to music, getting together for coffee or supper – only with the added advantage of not actually having to share a flat. But it had been over a week now and she had seen very little of him.

'Lucky him,' Lesley said sulkily.

'*You* can't complain. You have a great social life. Though this is your second spinsters' Saturday night in a row. You'd want to watch yourself or you'll end up like me.'

'Well, I've decided to give the dating website a rest for a while. I had the most depressing date ever last night.'

'Oh God! That must have been bad. Worse than the guy who wanted you to wee on him?'

'Yep.'

'Worse than the one who dragged you all over Galway until he found a pub with a three euro lunch and then moaned about the standard of the food?'

'Worse than that. Worse than the guy who made me his wingman while he stalked his ex all night.'

'I still think he sounded right up your alley,' Romy said.

'Yeah,' Lesley grinned. 'I must admit that was kind of fun. And if he'd let me take the lead, she'd never have rumbled us and that whole thing with the cops could have been avoided. But would he listen?'

'Well, last night's guy must have been a real nightmare to top that lot. What was wrong with him?'

'Nothing. That's the depressing part.'

'Huh?'

'He was very nice.'

'But ...' Romy prompted.

'He's solvent, has a good job and a lovely apartment in Sandymount. He's nice looking – not gorgeous, but attractive, you know – and he dresses well. Good shoes.'

'Good shoes are important,' Romy said, nodding.

'He was good company, easy to talk to, has a good sense of humour. A proper sense of humour, not one of those I'm-alooper-and-all-my-friends-think-I'm-crazy idiots who'll laugh at any old shite, where you get a pain in your face pretending to find them as hilarious as they think they are.'

'He sounds great!'

'Yeah, he was really nice. We had a lovely time,' Lesley said, sounding really pissed off about it.

'So, what happened? Did he have his dead mother stuffed and sitting up in an armchair when you went back to his place?'

'Nope, there was nothing. He's just a nice, decent bloke.'

'What's your problem, then? He sounds ideal.'

'That's just it. There I was, out with this really nice, normal guy for once, having a perfectly nice time. But there was just … nothing.'

'No spark?'

'No. None. And it just made me think, what are the chances, you know? How likely am I to come across the love of my life on some dating website? It took me long enough just to find someone *normal*. It's so random and against the odds, and it was just … depressing.'

'Well, maybe you need to give it some time.'

'But I don't want to. I want to feel the spark! I don't want someone to grow on me like fecking fungus. I don't want to organise myself into falling in love. I want it to *happen*.'

'I know what you mean,' Romy sighed.

'I guess meeting Michael just brought it home to me. He's the guy I've been looking for the whole time – on paper anyway. All this time I've been so focused on just meeting someone nice and normal and reasonable looking – as if that's all it takes. And then I met him and I realise that isn't enough.'

'It doesn't help that you're working from home now,' Romy said, refilling their glasses. 'Maybe you need to widen your social circle.'

'But how? And don't say evening classes.'

'Well, don't look at me. I'm hardly the one to give advice. The last action I got was at David's Hallowe'en party.'

'No progress with you and Kit?'

'No. Like I say, I've hardly seen him since he moved in. I'm surprised he seems to have got a social life together here so quickly. I mean I don't think he kept in touch with anyone while he was in New York, so he'd be starting from zero.'

'Ah, well, he has certain advantages, doesn't he?' Lesley said, tapping her nose. 'He's probably hooked up with the local BDSM community.'

'You think he could have found them so soon?'

'Well, there can't be many of them around, can there?'

'I have no idea,' Romy said, taking a sip of her wine. 'Maybe there are loads of them. Or none. Do you think there even *is* a local BDSM community?'

'Oh, I'm sure there is,' Lesley said. 'Ireland isn't as backward as it used to be. And with the internet, it's so easy to find where your own kind hang out. Hey, why don't we Google it? Where's your laptop?'

'Danny will be here soon,' Romy said, glancing nervously towards her laptop in the corner of the room. 'We can't be looking at this stuff when he comes.'

'Well, get it quick then,' Lesley said, waving her hand at Romy impatiently.

Romy grabbed the laptop and brought it over to the sofa. She put it on the coffee table and moved the mouse around to bring it to life. 'What will I put in?' she asked.

'Try BDSM Dublin.'

Romy dutifully typed into the search engine, and, to her surprise, there were several results. As well as a site devoted to BDSM in Ireland, there was a blog and links for a couple of clubs as well as the inevitable sex shops, escort agencies and dominatrix services. There was even a website for a dungeon for hire.

'Well?' Lesley said, edging closer to look at the screen. 'Open that one,' she said, pointing to the main website for the BDSM community in Ireland.

For minutes, they sat in silence, reading the screen as Romy clicked through the pages. There were forums and discussion boards and information on meet-ups in Dublin.

'They call their meet-ups "munches",' Lesley commented. 'Sounds rude, doesn't it?'

'I can't believe there's so much of this going on in Dublin,' Romy said.

'Maybe you should become a member – find out more about it,' Lesley suggested. 'They seem like a friendly bunch.'

'Uh-uh. No thanks.' Romy added the site to her favourites so she could read it more thoroughly later. Then she clicked on the blog, which turned out to be by a Dublin couple, writing about their dominant/submissive relationship. Romy added that to her favourites too.

'Give us a look at that dungeon,' Lesley said.

Romy duly clicked on the link and they both gazed in silence at the screen as they read through the descriptions of the accommodation and looked at the photographs of the various equipment provided.

'Wow, I wish I'd known about this place when I was organising the Christmas party at my last job,' Lesley said. 'I'd have loved to have had a go at my boss on that rack.' She pointed to a particularly tortuous looking piece of apparatus.

'It looks medieval,' Romy said, shuddering. She shut the laptop down, replacing it on the table in the corner.

'So there you have it,' Lesley said. 'There's loads of this stuff going on in Dublin. Kit's probably out there shoving his butt plug up someone's arse as we speak.'

'Ugh!' Romy giggled, almost spitting her wine. 'But he wouldn't use that actual butt plug, would he?' she said, sobering up. 'I mean surely you wouldn't use the same butt plug on different girls? It's not very hygienic.'

'I don't know,' Lesley mused. 'But these are all questions we can ask May later. I was in with her today, and I told her you needed some advice. She said she'd call over tonight if she's not too ... busy.'

'Busy bonking Frank, you mean. Well, she'd better not come while Danny's here.'

'True. That's not a side of you he wants to see.'

'That's not a side of me, full stop.'

'But maybe it could be – with the right training. May was very excited when I told her you were interested in BDSM. She said she's got loads to show us.'

'Great!' Romy rolled her eyes.

Just then the doorbell rang. 'Here's Danny,' Romy said, getting up to answer it. 'Not a word of this while he's here, okay? And don't mention Paul – he's still pining.'

'He should come over to our side,' Lesley grinned. 'He's a terrible loss to womankind, and he's way too lovely for a man to appreciate.'

✳

'Hi, Lesley,' Danny said as he followed Romy back into the sitting room. 'Is my godson asleep?' he asked Romy as he handed her a bottle of red.

'Yes, he is, touch wood,' Romy said, tapping her forehead with her knuckles.

Lesley poured wine into the empty glass on the coffee table and handed it to him. 'Drink up!' she said, raising her own glass to him. 'You have some catching up to do.'

'So what are we talking about?' he asked as he took an armchair opposite them.

Lesley's eyes gleamed and she threw Romy a mischievous look. 'Men,' she said. 'What else?'

'We talk about lots of other things,' Romy said indignantly.

'So what have you been up to, Danny?' Lesley asked. 'Any new man in your life yet?'

'No,' he said. 'You?'

'No. All the good ones are taken – or gay.'

'I won't argue with that. Or taken *and* gay.'

'Lesley's taking a break from dating,' Romy told him. 'She was traumatised by a successful date.'

As they got mildly drunk together, they bemoaned their collective lack of anything resembling a love life.

'God, if we could even get one man between us,' Lesley wailed.

'We could do a time share,' Romy said, giggling.

'If you nab Kit, you'll have to share him,' Lesley said. 'One for all and all for one!' she exclaimed, sloshing wine from her glass as she jerked it up in salute.

'You're not – are you?' Danny asked. 'Nabbing Kit.'

'I don't know,' Romy said, a little needled that he seemed so shocked by the idea. 'Maybe.'

'Really?'

'Yeah … what's wrong with that?'

'Nothing. Just – you can do better.'

'Have you seen Kit?' Lesley said, looking askance at Danny. 'He's no slouch in the looks department.'

'I know he's very good-looking, but isn't he a bit … well, thick?' Danny said with an apologetic wince.

'No!' Romy frowned. 'That's mean.'

'He *was* a bit thick in school,' Lesley said.

'He just wasn't very academic,' Romy replied. 'He's clever

in other ways. He has street smarts. He was very successful at his job in New York. And it turns out he's good with his hands too. He put up some shelves for May during the week and she's been singing his praises to me ever since.'

'Who'd have thought? But you already knew he was good with his hands, didn't you?' Lesley said, wiggling her eyebrows suggestively.

'No, I never – we never … did anything back then.'

'What? You were glued to each other for two years.'

'But it was just snogging and … teenage stuff. We didn't—'

'You're saying you never shagged Kit?'

'No. Never.' *Except, of course, that time in the cupboard last Hallowe'en.* She caught Lesley's eye and she could tell she was thinking the same thing.

'Well, I can totally see the two of you getting back together,' Lesley said supportively. 'And if you don't, maybe I'll have a shot at him myself.'

'You can't do that. He's my ex, therefore he's officially off-limits.'

'That's the rule,' Danny nodded in agreement.

'But that was years ago,' Lesley said. 'There must be a statute of limitations on those embargos.'

'Nope. If I can't have him, no one can. In perpetuity. Now let's not talk about men anymore. That's not what spinsters' night is about.'

※

Several bottles of wine, a huge plate of nachos and a very giggly game of Pictionary later, Danny decided it was time to go before he passed out on the floor. Romy and Lesley poured him into a taxi and waved him off, and they were just starting to tidy up when there was a knock on the front door. Romy opened it to find May standing outside, clutching an armful of books and albums. She had forgotten all about May calling over.

'Hello, Romy. I hope I'm not too late,' she said, smiling. She looked bright-eyed and wide awake, her bird-like eyes dancing with excitement.

Romy stifled a yawn. 'Well, I was just clearing up before going to bed—'

'Only Lesley told me earlier that you'd like some advice, and I've been hunting out some things that might help,' she said, brandishing her books. She seemed so eager, Romy didn't have the heart to turn her away.

'Yes, well, come in,' she said, standing back to let her pass. 'Would you like a drink?' she asked as she led May into the sitting room.

'Yes, please. Brandy would be lovely.'

'Oh, hello, May,' Lesley said in surprise as she walked in from the kitchen.

'Hello, Lesley.' May turned to her. 'I brought those books and things I was telling you about.'

'Great!'

Romy handed May a glass of brandy and settled on the couch beside her. Lesley sat on May's other side.

'So, Lesley tells me you're interested in trying the BDSM lifestyle,' May said, turning to Romy.

'Oh, um … well, I'm not sure. I'm just interested in finding out more about it. There's someone I know who might be … into it.'

'So you're looking into it for a friend,' May said with a small smile, obviously convinced this 'friend' was actually Romy herself.

'It's this guy I know—' Romy began.

'Ah!' May exclaimed, her eyes lighting up. 'I understand.

You've met a chap you like who's into the scene, and so you're considering experimenting. There's nothing to be embarrassed about, dear,' she said, touching Romy's knee. 'I think it's wonderful that you're opening yourself up to new experiences, exploring the whole range of human sexuality.'

And she's off, Romy thought, smiling weakly at May.

'Now, are you interested in being a dominant or a submissive?' May asked.

'Oh, well, I'm not sure I'm interested in either. I'm just … curious about the whole thing. I mean I'm not even sure if this guy is into it. He's very secretive about his private life.'

'Yes,' May said, nodding. 'He would be. Discretion is very important in the community. BDSM is one of the last remaining taboos, and it's difficult for people to be open about it. If you were to enter into a relationship with this man, he may even want you to sign some sort of confidentiality agreement.'

'I bet!' Lesley piped up. 'I mean it's not exactly the sort of hobby you'd put on your CV, is it? "In my spare time I like to dress up in leather, whip my girlfriend and shove things up her bum."' She laughed, earning a stern look from May. 'Sorry, May,' she mumbled.

'If you're not going to take this seriously, Lesley—'

'No, I am, honest. I'll be quiet.'

'Well,' May said, turning back to Romy, 'I'll tell you all I can about the lifestyle. I lived as a submissive for several years, so I should be able to answer most of your questions. I've brought you some books,' she said, indicating the small pile of paperbacks she had deposited on the arm of the sofa. 'I've also brought all the albums and scrapbooks I kept of my time as a submissive,' she said, picking up another pile from the floor. 'There's a diary there too, which you're welcome to read.' As she spoke, she fished a pair of glasses out of her bag and put them on before flipping open a large scrapbook which she held on her knee. 'This is a record of my time with my master,' she said, flipping through the pages.

Lesley's eyes bugged out and she nestled closer to get a better look.

'What's this?' Romy asked, pointing to a long printed list in a plastic folder.

'They're the rules he gave me,' May said.

'You had rules?'

'Oh yes, there are always rules as part of a sub's training. The dom trains the sub to modify her behaviour in ways that are pleasing to him. It satisfies his desire for control, and at the same time helps her to develop in her role.'

Romy gasped as she ran her eyes down the list. It seemed to cover everything from diet and exercise to personal hygiene, right down to the waxing of pubes. She gulped. 'You had to wax … everything?'

'Oh, yes,' May said nonchalantly. 'That's quite usual. But you work out the rules between you. They're for your mutual benefit and pleasure. The same goes for the contract,' she said, pulling another printed document from a wallet in the scrapbook and handing it to Romy.

Romy flipped through it, feeling the colour drain from her face as she read the strange document, with lists of sexual activities that were agreed to, the toys that could be used and the punishments that would be administered if the rules were broken, all incongruously wrapped up in impersonal legalese. This had to be the strangest contract she had ever seen in her life.

'So these "soft limits" are …?' she asked, running her eyes down one of the appendices.

'Soft limits are activities that you're not sure about but are prepared to try. Hard limits are activities that are unacceptable to you and that you absolutely won't do.'

'Oh.' Romy didn't really need to know that her elderly tenant was open to the idea of caning, but she was glad to see May had drawn the line at anal fisting. '"Breath play" – what exactly does that mean?'

'Asphyxiation,' May explained calmly. 'As you see, that was a hard limit for me.'

'Christ! Doesn't that kind of go without saying?'

'Not at all. Some people find it very exciting. It's well known that it intensifies orgasm.'

'And this suspension …' Romy began.

'Why don't I show you some photos?' May said. 'They'll give you a clearer idea of what's involved. A picture speaks a thousand words, after all.' She picked up another album and opened it, flipping the pages. It was full of rather artistic black and white photographs of a couple playing out all sorts of scenarios. 'These are pictures of us in the playroom.'

'Is that …' Lesley hesitated, pointing to a photograph of a naked young woman suspended from the ceiling in a complicated looking piece of apparatus.

'That's me, yes,' May said, fingering the photograph fondly. 'I was so agile in those days. You need to be very fit to be a submissive,' she said to Romy. 'It's important to be strong and supple.'

'Yes, I can see that.'

'Those nipple clamps look painful,' Lesley commented, pointing to another picture.

'They're as painful as they are pleasurable,' May said with a serene smile.

Lesley and Romy looked on in stunned silence as May talked them through the photographs. 'This is a suede flogger … see the way my breasts are bound here … this was my collar that showed I belonged to my master … here I'm attached to a St Andrew's Cross …'

'Wow, it's a lot to take in,' Romy said when they got to the end of the album. She didn't know what to say.

'There is a lot to learn,' May said. 'But it's getting late and I can see you're tired. Why don't I leave all this with you, and I'll come back tomorrow and we can go over any questions you may have. And I can give you a little practical demonstration.'

'Demonstration?' Romy asked in dismay.

'Oh, don't worry, we'll just cover the very basics.'

'Really, May, that's not necessary. I'm sure the books will tell me all I need to know.'

'Nonsense, dear. It's no trouble,' she said. She finished her brandy and got up to go. So – does tomorrow suit you?'

'Er ... yes, that'd be great. Thanks, May.'

'Not at all. Happy to help. Will you be joining us, Lesley?'

'Absolutely. I wouldn't miss it for the world.'

'Excellent. I'll see you both tomorrow then.'

❋

'Golly,' Lesley said when she had left, 'she's like a sexual Jehovah's Witness.'

'Hmm,' Romy said absently, flicking through the album May had left with her.

'So,' Lesley said, edging closer to her. 'You've decided to give this a try.'

'No!' Romy said, horrified. How on earth had Lesley got that idea?

'But then why are you letting May come over to do her demonstration?'

'Because she was so keen to help and I didn't want to hurt her feelings. It's your bloody fault she thinks I'm interested in the first place. So I'll keep her books for a few days and pretend I'm reading them, and I'll let her do her demo if it makes her happy.'

'So you really don't have any interest in doing this stuff?'

'Er … no.'

'But what if Kit's into it? You said you wanted to try and make a go of things with him. And it might be your only chance of getting a boyfriend,' Lesley said cheerily.

'I'll take a vow of celibacy, then.'

'This one doesn't look too bad,' Lesley said, pointing to a picture of May trussed up like a turkey with a ball-gag in her mouth and blindfolded.

'I suppose it's not bad compared to, say, being kidnapped by fundamentalist terrorists.'

'May says this stuff made her feel very sexy and powerful.'

'I'd just feel like a right eejit. I mean how could you feel sexy, trussed up like a turkey ready for the roasting tray?'

'All she wants is stuffing.' Lesley giggled.

'I think she's about to get it.'

'What do you suppose yer man does when she's all tied up like that?'

'Whatever the hell he likes, I should imagine.'

Lesley sighed, flopping back against the sofa cushions. 'But, you know, this all looks like quite advanced stuff. I'm sure Kit would go easy on you to start with – work up to this stuff gradually. I'd say he'd be a kind master.'

'If I was an Alsatian I might find that comforting.'

'And I bet he'd get you your own butt plug if you asked him to.'

Romy snapped the album closed. 'Believe me, having a butt plug of my very own isn't my major concern in all this.'

'You never know, you might like it if you gave it a chance. That suede flogger didn't look too bad. May was a big fan.'

'May is a nutjob, hadn't you noticed?'

Lesley tutted. 'You're not supposed to say 'nutjob' nowadays. She's just a bit … challenged in the sanity department.'

'She's an OAP nympho.'

'You're so judgemental. I think she's great. She's ploughing a new frontier of sexuality. Fair play to her.'

'I have no problem with whatever May wants to get up to, honestly. It's just not for me.'

'What if you were the dominant one? You never know, Kit might want to be the one being tied up and ordered to wax his balls. Have you considered that?'

'You know, maybe he's not into this stuff at all. Have you considered *that*? You've just blown this up in your head and now you're talking like it's a known fact.'

'So what do you think this secret lifestyle is if it's not this?'

'I don't know.' Romy shrugged. 'Could be anything.'

'Could be drugs.'

'Yeah. I'm starting to hope it's drugs.'

Chapter Thirteen

Kit woke the next morning feeling disoriented, which wasn't unusual since he'd moved back to Ireland. It always took him a while to get his bearings, but there was no need to panic, he told himself as he looked around at the unfamiliar walls and shelves. He wasn't in his old room at his parents' house because he had moved into Romy's flat. He didn't remember seeing that Tiffany lamp before, and it was weird that he'd never noticed the Knuttel print on the wall opposite his bed until now. In fact, he was sure it hadn't been there. But maybe Romy had snuck in while he was out and put it up for him? That was nice of her, he thought dozily, rolling over – intrusive, but nice. He burrowed deeper into the pillow, reaching down to grab his morning wood, and froze when his hand brushed against warm skin that was not his own. He let his fingers explore a little, barely whispering over a warm mound of flesh. That was unmistakably an ass turned towards him.

Holy shit! He pulled his hand back and stilled, frozen to the spot. Then he gingerly raised himself on one elbow and leaned over to check out his sleeping partner. He was met with the composed features of a beautiful stranger. Bugger, bugger, bugger! Flattening himself down like a cartoon character who's been run over by a steamroller, he slid himself out of the bed. Then he gathered his clothes from the various corners of the room where they had been shed the night before and crept out into the living room to get dressed. He took in his surroundings as he dressed quickly, but nothing looked familiar. He had no recollection of coming here last night or of the sleeping stranger in the next room. He felt like he'd been gone over with a hammer. His eyes felt crunchy, like burned-out embers, and his head was pounding. His body was telling him that he'd had fun, but his brain couldn't remember a second of it. The last thing he could recall was walking down a winding metal staircase into a heaving, pumping club; the promise of excitement as he descended into the throbbing music and the press of bodies.

He looked around the room he was in, taking in the clues to last night – the empty champagne bottle, the dirty glasses, the overflowing ashtray – ugh, a smoker! He shuddered. He found his jacket strewn on a low red sofa, pulled it on and quietly let himself out of the apartment. Outside, he found himself on an unfamiliar street and he walked along aimlessly for a while trying to pick up clues about where he was. He passed several bus stops, but he had no idea what bus to get to Romy's house. He fished in his pockets to see if he had enough money for a taxi and found a crumpled five euro note and some change – that would hardly be enough to get him to Romy's unless he was really close. Maybe he could find a cash machine. Finally he came to a sign for the DART, the suburban train that runs along the Dublin coast. That would do. It didn't go anywhere near Rathgar, where Romy lived, but he could get it into the city centre and find his way home from there. Following the signs, he found his way to Blackrock station. It was a bright, clear morning, freezing cold, and he huddled into his jacket, trying to ignore the smell of smoke that clung to it, and breathed the sea air deep into his lungs as he waited for the train. He felt like he needed a detox – and not just for his hangover. He wanted to detox his whole life. He wanted to eat pure food and breathe fresh, clean air. He didn't want to spend his nights getting drunk in clubs, kissing smokers and sleeping with strangers, and his mornings feeling sick, seedy and remorseful. He needed to get some discipline back into his life.

❊

He arrived at Romy's place – his place now, he reminded himself – intending to have a bath and crawl into bed. However, he got to the house to find Romy up a ladder wrapped up in an enormous parka doing something to the guttering.

'Hello.' She turned to smile at him as he pushed open the gate, brushing muck off her gloved hand. 'Where have you been?'

'Hell,' he said, looking up at her. She looked so fresh and wholesome – vibrant and energetic, and completely in tune with the world, as if she was part of this crisp, clean morning. She looked how he wanted to feel.

'Well, you look like you could do with a cup of coffee,' she said, starting to climb down the ladder.

He was aware of how he must look and that she was being kind by putting it so mildly. He probably looked like he needed a shot of adrenaline and a blood transfusion. 'Thanks, I'd love a coffee. What are you doing?' he asked, nodding at the roof as she folded up the ladder and laid it against the wall.

'Just clearing leaves out of the gutter,' she said, removing her thick gardening gloves. 'They cause havoc if you let them build up.'

'Do you want a hand?'

'No, thanks. Luke will be due a feed soon, and I could do with a break myself. Anyway, I have something to show you. I've drawn up a plan for the house and done up some figures.'

She seemed really excited about it. He could tell from her tone and the light in her eyes that she wanted to do it, and his heart leapt. He was going to start turning his life around.

❋

In the kitchen, Romy took off her coat and put the coffee machine on. 'Wait here,' she said to Kit, 'I'll just go check on Luke and get the plans.'

When she left, Kit mooched around the kitchen aimlessly. He stood for a while looking out the window to the garden. Then he decided to make himself useful by getting out mugs for their coffee. As he searched through the cupboards, his eyes lit on a pile of books lying on the worktop. He picked up the top one idly – something called *The Loving Dominant* – and turned it over to read the blurb, surprised to discover it was a kind of manual for sadomasochistic couples – not what he would have expected Romy's reading material to be. Why would she be reading something like that anyway? She wasn't even with anyone. He turned over the next book and read the back cover. From what he could make out, it seemed to be some sort of guide to becoming a sex slave. Jesus!

His curiosity aroused, he picked up the well-thumbed paperback beneath it. It fell open at a section on genital bondage, complete with detailed instructions and – oh God – illustrations. He winced at the picture of a bound penis, dropping the book as if it had burned him. That wasn't an image he would forget in a hurry! His eyes ran over the rest of the titles – *SM101*, *The Compleat Slave*, *The Story of O* – even he had heard of that notorious erotic novel. There was a definite theme developing here. A photograph album lay at the bottom of the pile and he pulled it out and opened it. It was full of black and white photographs of a man and woman engaged in various sex games – the woman bound, gagged, blindfolded, bent over benches and suspended from the ceiling while the man brandished whips, canes and … a rather impressive boner.

Kit was shocked. Romy was the last person on earth he'd have figured for being interested in this sort of stuff. Obviously, she wasn't as wholesome as she appeared. And then another thought struck him. This was why she didn't know who Thingummyjig's father was! He remembered her telling him she had got pregnant at a party where everyone was wearing masks and she was blindfolded. Obviously little Whatsisface had been conceived at some kind of orgy and his father was just a nameless, faceless, gimp-masked stranger. He was flabbergasted. It was like discovering Snow White was on the game.

And then a thought occurred to him – was this why she wanted to talk about what happened at David's party? Was she looking for someone she could try these things with? Did she want him to do this stuff … with her? God, poor Romy!

He jumped guiltily, snapping the book shut as he heard Romy coming back towards the kitchen. He started opening cupboard doors randomly.

'Here we are!' She faltered in the doorway, her eyes darting to the books and she blushed bright red.

'I was just looking for some mugs,' Kit said, hoping she hadn't seen him looking at her books. She clearly hadn't intended to leave them lying around, and he didn't want to embarrass her.

'Oh, I'll get those. You sit down,' she said, waving him to the table.

He sat with his back to her and heard cupboard doors opening and closing.

'Here we go,' she said. He turned to see her approaching the table with two mugs and a pot of coffee. He noticed the books had disappeared from the counter.

'So here's my idea for the house,' she said, grabbing a folder from the counter and placing it on the table in front of Kit. He opened the folder while Romy poured them both coffee. He was impressed by how thorough and professional it was as he flicked through the pages. There were floor plans showing various proposed layouts with spreadsheets of the budget for each, as well as a detailed description of each proposal.

'Wow, this looks great!' he said as she sat down opposite him. 'You've put a lot of thought into it.'

'Well, it is what I do for a living. There's no point in going into something like this half-cocked and just hoping for the best.' She leaned over and flicked to one of the spreadsheets. 'This is the absolute minimum we could bring it in at, realistically,' she said, pointing to the total. 'And at that, we'd have to do as much as we can ourselves.'

Kit ran his eyes down the column. He had no idea what project managers normally earned, but the figure Romy had included for her own services seemed low to him. 'Is this what you usually charge?' he asked, pointing to the amount allocated for project management fees. 'I thought it would be more.'

She smiled. 'I've given you a discount. If you make way over the odds, you can give me a bonus if you like.'

'I will.'

'So what do you think? Could you manage that?'

'Yeah, I could just about cover it. But do you think it will work?'

'If we do a really high-end spec that would work as a country house hotel or something like that, yes. I've spoken to some estate agents and they think it has potential.'

She grabbed a thick envelope from the counter and pulled out a sheaf of glossy brochures. 'These are some similar properties,' she said, fanning the brochures out on the table in front of Kit. 'Just to give you an idea of what the end result could look like.'

The houses were amazing, grand and palatial with majestic staircases and sumptuous decor, the majestic gardens boasting well-manicured lawns and mature trees. He couldn't imagine his aunt's house ever looking like this. But what really caught Kit's eye was the price.

'Seriously?' he said, pointing to the figure. 'We could get *that* much for it?'

'Well, that's just the asking price,' Romy cautioned. 'It might not sell for that. It might not sell at all.'

'But it's possible?'

'Yes,' she said with a smile. 'It's possible.'

'Great! So when do we start?'

'We really need to spend some time down there first to make more detailed plans, and decide exactly what way we want to go.'

'Okay. When do you want to do that?'

'The sooner the better.'

'Well, I have Tank's stag do next weekend.'

'Oh yeah. Have you found out what it is yet?'

'Yes.' Kit sighed, looking morose. 'It's some kind of survival weekend bollocks. We get dropped out in the middle of nowhere, like we're survivors of a plane crash. Then we have to build our own shelters and do orienteering to find our way home again. Brilliant fun, according to Wedgie.'

'God, what happened to the simple days of just getting wasted?'

'I know. So anyway, next weekend is out. And the following weekend there's the wedding.'

'Well, why don't we wait until all that's out of the way and then maybe we could spend a few days there, camp out in the gate lodge and really get a feel for the place. In the meantime, we can get the electricity reconnected and I'll order a few skips and arrange for the chimney to be swept. That way we can get started right away on clearing the place out and getting the gate lodge into shape. It shouldn't take much to make that liveable, and then it'll be ready to move into as soon as work starts.'

'Wait – move into? You're planning to live down there? In the cottage?'

'Oh yeah.' Romy nodded. 'You really need to live on-site to keep control of a project like this. It will be easier than driving up and down from Dublin all the time anyway. It will speed things up a lot.'

'Okay,' he said uncertainly.

'You don't sound too sure.'

'No, it's fine. I just hadn't considered it, that's all.'

'It's not just a matter of managing the project. This budget is really tight and you can't afford to pay for anything you can possibly do yourself. We're going to have to get stuck in.'

'That's fine,' Kit said. He hadn't considered living in the property, but now that he thought about it, he decided a move to the country was just what he needed. He'd be out of harm's way in the middle of nowhere – no sleazy clubs and strangers' apartments. He would work hard, breathe clean air and go to bed early. He could see himself now, clear-eyed and ruddy-faced in some sort of healthy rustic wood-chopping scenario. 'Actually, it's great,' he said to Romy. 'I was just thinking this morning that I needed to get some discipline back in my life.'

'Discipline?' Romy seemed surprised by his use of the word – he couldn't blame her, considering the state he had turned up in this morning. He must look like he didn't know the meaning of the word. 'You had more … discipline in your life in New York?' she asked.

'Yeah, I did actually, believe it or not. I miss it.'

'So, we're on then?' she asked, grinning excitedly.

'We're on,' he said, holding out his hand. She grasped it and they shook.

✳

'This is the basic position the submissive usually adopts at the start of a session or whenever her master commands her to kneel,' May said later as she knelt on Romy's floor, while Lesley and Romy observed her from the sofa. To Romy's relief, May had arrived dressed as if she was going to a yoga class, in loose-fitting drawstring trousers and a tight white T-shirt. 'Sit back on your heels, legs wide apart, hands resting lightly on your legs, palms down,' she said, as if she was talking them through a yoga posture. 'The chin is slightly lowered and the eyes are down.'

Lesley took advantage of the fact that May's eyes were

lowered to smirk at Romy. Romy frowned back at her, anxious that May might catch Lesley and think they were making fun of her. Lesley wasn't taking this seriously at all. Neither was she, of course, but at least she was pretending to. She had only just managed to persuade Lesley that it wouldn't be appropriate to make popcorn for them to munch while they watched May do her demo.

'You must only raise your eyes to your master if he tells you to. If he commands you to look at him, you do so at once without hesitation,' she said, raising her eyes. 'That goes for all his commands, of course. You obey him immediately and without question. Failure to do so will result in punishment.'

Romy nodded. She wondered if perhaps she should take notes just so she would look like a diligent pupil. She felt she needed to look extra engaged to make up for Lesley.

'Only speak when you are spoken to directly or have been given permission to speak,' May continued. 'And you must always address your dom respectfully as "Sir" or "Master" unless he instructs you otherwise.'

'Would you be naked in that position?' Lesley asked, and Romy was surprised to see that she had managed to wipe all trace of humour from her face.

'Usually the submissive will be required to strip. It's a reminder of your status, apart from anything else. Or you might just be wearing your knickers, depending on what your master requires. But he'll give you clear instructions about what he wants.'

'What about the master?' Lesley asked. 'Would he be naked too?'

'Again, that's up to him. He might be fully dressed, or naked to the waist, depending on the scene and his personal preference.'

'Huh! It's all about what *he* wants, isn't it? And he gets to use all these toys on you, but you don't get to do anything to him? Seems like he has all the fun.'

'In many ways, the submissive's role is much easier than the dominant's,' May said. 'The submissive surrenders herself completely to the dom – she hands over control of her body and her will. Her role is simply to follow orders, to do her best to please her master and place her trust in him completely. All decisions and worries are taken out of her hands. The dom, on the other hand, has a lot of responsibility. He chooses what activities they will engage in. He's responsible for the welfare of the sub at all times. He must make sure that play is safe. He is responsible for taking care of all the sub's needs – material, physical and sexual. He can never really relax during a scene because he has to stay in control at all times. He must be ready to stop play at any moment if the sub uses her safe word.'

'Safe word?'

'Yes, the sub has a safe word that she uses if an activity goes beyond what she can endure. If the safe word is used, play ceases immediately.'

'And you don't get punished for that?' Lesley asked.

'Absolutely not. Safe words are taken very seriously in the community, and must always be honoured. It shouldn't be necessary to safe word, though. A good dom will be attuned to his sub's responses and won't push her beyond her limits.'

'And what about the, er, dom? Does he have any starting position?'

'Not really. It's more of an attitude, a bearing. Why don't you two girls try the submissive position and I'll show you what I mean,' May said, getting up from the floor.

Lesley and Romy looked at each other. Lesley shrugged and they both rose from the couch and knelt on the floor, adjusting themselves into the same position as May.

'Very nice, Romy,' May said, touching the top of Romy's

head. 'Legs a little wider apart, Lesley. Good. Excellent, you two.'

Lesley and Romy looked at each other from under their lashes and exchanged a smile.

'Observe my tone and manner,' May said, pacing in front of them. Her voice had changed, becoming deep and stern. 'Look up,' she said, and they both lifted their heads. 'My voice is firm and commanding. I have the demeanour of someone who expects to be obeyed. It's not aggressive, it's calm, assertive and controlled.' She did look like someone not to be crossed, Romy thought. May seemed to have grown a couple of inches before her eyes, her shoulders back, her chin firm and unyielding. 'When I give an order I expect it to be obeyed without question. If it isn't, I won't hesitate to administer the appropriate punishment.' She stopped pacing and came to stand beside Romy. 'I'm not cruel, but I am consistent and true to my word. Do you understand?' she asked Romy, adding, 'You may speak.'

'Yes, Mistress,' Romy answered, looking up at her.

'Very good,' May smiled. 'Likewise, if my sub has pleased me, I will let him know. I'll praise him, tell him he's a good boy, perhaps pet him a little.' She reached out and stroked Romy's hair from the top of her head to her shoulders.

'So it's a bit like owning a dog?' Lesley piped up, and Romy couldn't suppress a giggle.

May sighed. 'No, Lesley,' she said, rolling her eyes in exasperation. 'It's nothing like owning a dog.'

'Well, you give the sub collars and you train them, and they get treats for being obedient. And you give him a pat on the head and tell him he's a good boy. Sounds like a dog to me.'

'There's nothing undignified about being a sub,' May explained patiently. 'There is great satisfaction to be had in serving a master. Or mistress.'

'I'm sure Lassie felt the same,' Lesley said.

'If he has particularly pleased me,' May continued, ignoring Lesley's wisecracks, 'I might reward him by engaging in one of his favourite activities.'

'Like chasing a stick?' Lesley said, collapsing in giggles.

Romy threw May an apologetic glance, but May didn't seem unduly perturbed by Lesley's mockery. They were actually very fond of each other, and May knew Lesley well enough by now to recognise that it was just friendly banter and that Lesley didn't mean any harm by it.

'Yes,' May said, unable to suppress a smile and slipping out of her dom role, 'if he gets off on chasing a stick, then I might throw one for him. But I think you'll find most subs would prefer a blow job.'

'Hey, I won't be "finding" anything about what does or doesn't get them off. Romy's the one who's going to be doing that.'

As the practical part of the lesson was clearly over, Lesley and Romy got up off the floor and sat on the sofa again.

'Ah, yes. And you still don't know if this chap is a dom or a sub?' May asked Romy as she came to sit beside her.

'No. I don't even know if he's either.'

'Or he could be what we call a switch,' May said. 'Some people like to play both roles.'

'I'd say he's definitely a dom,' Lesley said. 'I can't see Kit letting anyone boss him around like that.'

'Kit!' May exclaimed, seemingly delighted. 'Is that who you're doing this for?'

'Well … like I say, I don't even know if—'

'I think Lesley's right,' May said. 'I doubt Kit has a submissive bone in his body.'

'I don't think *I* do either,' Romy said.

'Well, you might surprise yourself. And you'd be rewarded with the most intense pleasure you've ever experienced.'

'Well, thanks, May,' Romy said. 'That was really ... an eye-opener.'

'Any time, dear. Read those books I gave you, but don't worry too much about taking everything in. If you're with an experienced dom, he'll take care of your training and teach you all you need to know. If he knows you're new to this, a good dom will take it slowly.'

'And what if she wants to be the mistress?' Lesley asked. 'The sub wouldn't teach her, would he?'

'That would be a little more complicated,' May said. 'There are lots of books on the subject. But the ideal would be to train with another dom. Perhaps you could get involved in the local scene and find an experienced dom who could show you the, er, ropes,' she said with a little smile at the accidental pun. 'You might be able to find some meet-ups or even play parties where you could learn from more experienced people. Anyway, I don't think you need to worry about that,' she said kindly. 'I can definitely see Kit being a dom. He has a masterful way about him,' she said dreamily. 'There's something very firm about the set of his mouth ...'

'Great! Well, thanks again, May. You've certainly given me a lot to think about.'

'Happy to help, Romy. And if you have any more questions, don't hesitate to ask.'

✳

'Well, that has to be one of the weirdest afternoons I've ever spent,' Romy said when the old lady had gone.

'I thought it was very entertaining. And cheaper than the movies.'

Then Luke started to cry.

'Oh, thanks a lot, Luke,' Romy said as she went to get him,

'you couldn't have woken up a bit sooner and interrupted May's little lesson?' She lifted him out of his cot, holding him close and soothing him as she carried him back to the living room.

'Want to stay and get a pizza or something?' she asked Lesley.

'Yeah, love to. You should see if they do one with Pedigree Chum.'

'Shut up,' Romy said over her shoulder as she went to the kitchen to get Luke a bottle, Lesley following behind.

'Might as well get used to the taste,' Lesley said.

Chapter Fourteen

The following Thursday night Romy was pacing the floor with Luke, trying to lull him to sleep. He was fractious and moany, and every time she thought he was dropping off, he startled awake and began crying again.

'Maybe I shouldn't go out after all,' she said to Kit as he appeared in the doorway. 'I can phone Lesley and cancel.'

'She'll be on her way by now. Give him to me,' Kit said, holding out his arms for Luke. 'You go and get ready and I'll put him to bed.'

Romy looked at him uncertainly, but then handed Luke over. 'Okay.' She sighed. 'But we don't have to go out. We could stay here.'

'Wait and see what he's like when Lesley gets here,' Kit said as he settled Luke against his chest, rubbing his back soothingly.

'Some music might help,' Romy said. She wound up the little musical toy on the side of his cot and a plinky version of 'The Teddy Bears' Picnic' began to play.

Kit rolled his eyes. 'He doesn't like this muzak crap, does he?'

'It's what all the kids are listening to these days,' Romy said, smiling.

'Well, no wonder he's cranky. If I had to listen to that—'

'You can try singing to him instead, if you like,' Romy said as she left the room. 'He likes "Nellie the Elephant",' she called over her shoulder.

Kit rocked Luke gently in his arms to the rhythm of the music, feeling his juddering sobs as he squirmed against his chest, and his hot, damp breath as he nuzzled into his neck. He hoped he could get him to sleep by the time Romy got back down. He was glad she had taken him up on his offer to babysit. She was so capable and energetic, but still, it couldn't be easy being a single mum, and she didn't get to go out much and just have fun. She had always been so ready to help him, and he really wanted to do something for her for a change.

When the little wind-up toy ran down and the music stopped, Luke's cries had settled to little shaky sighs, and Kit could tell he was almost asleep. He didn't want to risk putting him in his cot just yet, so he kept up his rocking and started to hum, just to be on the safe side. He didn't know 'Nellie the Elephant', or any other children's songs – but Luke wouldn't know the difference.

He felt a strange sense of contentment wash over him as he paced the darkened room, feeling Luke go limp and heavy in his arms. There was something immensely comforting about the warm beanbag weight of him. Being here with Romy and Luke, he felt part of something – something real and solid. He felt connected and safe. He was beginning to think his mom was right and he had been lonely in New York. His friendships had been superficial, his relationships fleeting. He had always shied away from this kind of domestic life, but he was surprised how calm and grounded it made him feel. He was beginning to think maybe he could really do this. Maybe Romy had been lonely too. They could be good for each other. He could be a father to Luke, and they could be a family of sorts. He could learn 'Nellie the Elephant'.

❈

As Romy put the finishing touches to her make-up, she noticed Luke's crying had stopped. Maybe Kit had actually got him to sleep, she thought, smiling at herself in the mirror as she put on her lipstick. She didn't know what had got into Kit, but he was being a very good boyfriend lately – even when there was no one watching. Ever since that morning when he had come home looking like the wreck of the Hesperus, he'd changed. He had stopped going out all the time, and he had been spending lots of time with her. He was being really sweet too, cooking delicious dinners and offering to babysit tonight so she could go out for a drink with Lesley. Romy had hesitated at first, but he had been really helpful with Luke recently, and was applying himself to learning how to look after him with such determination that she didn't want to discourage him.

When she was ready, she left her bedroom and tiptoed softly to the door of Luke's room, which was slightly ajar. Kit had his back to her as she peered into the semi-darkness of the room, and she stood watching unobserved. What she saw made her heart melt. Luke was asleep, slumped over Kit's shoulder, while Kit swayed gently and sang so quietly that it took her a while to make out the words of 'At My Most Beautiful'. When he got to the bit about counting eyelashes, she felt like her heart would burst. She had to stop herself rushing in, throwing her arms around them both and telling Kit there and then that he was Luke's father.

Luckily, the doorbell rang. Kit emerged from the bedroom just as she was letting Lesley in.

'We don't have to go out, Kit,' Romy said to him. 'We can just have a drink here.'

'He's asleep now,' Kit said, shutting the door quietly behind him. 'We'll be fine.'

'Yeah, come on,' Lesley said. 'You haven't been out on the razz in ages.'

'Well, maybe we should just go to the local. I could be back here in five minutes if you need me.'

'But you're all dolled up now,' Lesley protested. 'And you look great. You don't want to waste that on the local.'

'Yeah, go on,' Kit urged her.

'Okay. Well … you have my mobile number. Call me if you have any problems – anything at all.'

'Jeez, anyone would think you didn't trust me.'

'It's not that, it's just—'

'I know. I'm kidding. Just go.'

Romy chewed her lip, while Lesley looked at her pleadingly. 'Okay,' she said finally. She dashed off to the hall and grabbed her coat. 'We won't be late,' she said to Kit as she pulled it on, slinging her bag across her shoulder. 'Thanks for this.'

'Yeah, thanks, Kit,' Lesley said. 'It's nice to have my old pulling partner back.'

'Oh!' Kit frowned. 'Are you on the pull?'

'No, of course not,' Romy said.

'Good. Okay. So, about what time do you think you'll be home?'

'You'll see her when you see her,' Lesley said. 'I mean it's not like she has a curfew. Is it?' she said, narrowing her eyes at Kit.

'No! Of course not. Stay out as long as you want.'

'Great! Well, wish us luck,' Lesley said, grabbing Romy's arm and heading for the door.

'Have fun!' Kit called after them.

When they were gone, he flopped onto the sofa. He was almost regretting offering to babysit now. He didn't like the idea of Romy out there meeting other men. When Lesley had put the idea in his head, he had felt a completely irrational stab of jealousy. Which was ridiculous. But it was there nonetheless and he had to remind himself that much as he loved this cosy domestic scene he was building with Romy, it wasn't real. She wasn't his girlfriend and Luke wasn't his son, and all the cosy dinners and babysitting in the world weren't going to change that.

※

'Well, did you see that?' Lesley said as they walked to the tram stop. There was an unmistakable note of triumph in her voice.

'What?'

'Kit. He didn't seem a bit pleased about you going out on the pull.'

'Well, you shouldn't wind him up like that. You know I'm not going on the pull. We're just having a girls' night out.'

'And he was just itching to give you a time to be home.'

'No he wasn't. He's just a bit nervous, that's all. It's his first time babysitting.'

'I think he wants to control you. Next thing you know he'll be giving you a set of rules and a curfew. Maybe you won't be allowed out at all.'

'It was him that suggested I go out, remember? He's been really sweet lately, actually,' she said, smiling. 'He's been coming over most nights, cooking amazing dinners and really making an effort to help out with Luke.'

'Really?' Lesley's eyes lit up. 'Almost like he wants to *serve* you?'

'You don't give up, do you?' Romy rolled her eyes.

'I'm just saying. Maybe he's used to pleasing a mistress.'

Romy couldn't help thinking of Kit's comment about having more 'discipline' in his life in New York, but she pushed the thought aside.

'Then again, maybe he's just into you,' Lesley said, 'and he's freaked out about you meeting someone else.'

'Maybe …' Romy had been wondering about things over the past few days. Kit didn't seem to want to do anything other than hang out with her and Luke. 'It would certainly be handy,' she said.

'Handy?' Lesley shrieked. 'Don't get carried away with the romance of it all, will you?'

Romy laughed uneasily. It was true that it would be convenient if Kit fell for her all over again and wanted to be with her, but she was starting to wonder how she felt. They got on well. She liked him a lot and she still loved him as a friend, but she didn't feel the spark she used to. Still, maybe that would come in time – or maybe it had been just a teen thing, made up of dizzy hormones and the heady novelty of first love. He was Luke's father, and they were good friends. Maybe that would be enough.

'Pity he didn't offer to babysit at the weekend,' Lesley said, breaking into her thoughts. 'Thursday isn't exactly party night, and I've got work to do in the morning. But maybe that's his plan. He wants you to enjoy yourself, but not *too* much.'

'Ah, he couldn't. He's got Tank's stag do at the weekend,' Romy said. 'Believe me, he'd much rather be babysitting while I shagged everyone in the town.'

✻

'Here we are, glass of wine for the condemned man,' Romy said, plonking two large glasses of red on the coffee table and joining Kit on the sofa.

'Thanks.'

'Have you packed the Swiss army knife I gave you?' Romy asked him.

'Yes,' Kit said morosely. He was all packed up and waiting for Ethan to collect him for Tank's stag weekend. He had spent a small fortune on outdoor gear and was all kitted out in brand-new hiking boots, a pair of trousers made out of some high-tech material designed to repel any weather, and an enormous down jacket that could house a small family. Romy had gone shopping with him, and fearing that his spending was eating into his budget for the house, had managed to talk him down from purchasing a very expensive rucksack and loaned him an old one of hers that she unearthed from the attic. Those trousers he was wearing alone would have paid a carpenter for a day, she thought ruefully. Despite all the money he had thrown at it, he still didn't look the part, more resembling a model from an outdoor clothing catalogue than someone who would actually engage in rugged activities himself. She could see him now, all designer stubble and carefully windswept hair, one shiny new boot resting on a rock while he gazed manfully into the distance.

'Want me to go through the attachments with you one more time?' she asked.

'No. I just need the knife so I can garrotte Wedgie if he comes near me, and I know where that is.'

He had been in a permanent sulk since he had found out Wedgie's plans for the stag, and his mood had got progressively worse the closer it came to the dreaded day. 'Never mind,' she said, 'you'll have Tank and Ethan. I'm sure they won't let Wedgie get you.'

Ethan was driving them in their mother's car, and Kit had decided that he should tell Ethan to pick him up from Romy's so it would appear as if he had spent the night with her. He had even arrived that morning with some of his belongings to strew around her apartment, leaving razors and shaving foam in the bathroom ('in case Ethan goes to the loo'), tossing a pair of his socks on her bedroom floor, halfway under the bed, and draping one of his sweatshirts over an armchair. She had drawn the line at letting him throw a pair of boxers on top of her linen basket.

'Kit, can I ask you something?' She took a gulp of her wine.

'What?'

'Why do you need a fake girlfriend?'

'Ah,' he said, turning to smile at her, 'I could tell you, but then I'd have to kill you.'

'Oh.' She frowned down at her glass, feeling frustrated.

'Well, not kill you,' he said. 'Maybe just get you to sign a confidentiality agreement.'

'Really?' Her ears pricked up. May had had a confidentiality agreement with her 'master'. 'Did you have a confidentiality agreement with Lauren?'

'Yes, I did, as a matter of fact. And with a couple of others before her.'

'Why would you need to have a confidentiality agreement with your girlfriends?'

'I had to tell them … certain things about myself that I want kept private.'

'I wouldn't tell anyone. If I signed a confidentiality agreement, would you tell me?'

'It's not that I don't trust you, Romy. It's different with you than it was with Lauren and the others.'

'How is it different?'

'My relationship with them was more … formal.'

'You make it sound like you exchanged contracts or something.' *Blimey, maybe they* had *exchanged contracts – contracts with lists of hard limits and soft limits and clauses about punishments and waxing of pubes.*

'Well, money did come into it – as I told you.'

Oh yes, the money. May's words echoed in her head. "A dom is responsible for all the sub's material needs." Maybe Kit wasn't able to have a sub now because he was broke and couldn't provide for one. 'Actually,' she said, 'I might have already guessed what your secret is.'

'Really?' Kit looked a little alarmed. 'Is it that obvious?'

'Oh, no.' She hastened to reassure him. 'It's not obvious at all. I'm sure most people would never guess.'

'I suppose you would be more alert to the signals than a lot of people,' he said.

What? Why on earth would he think that? Oh God, May's books! He hadn't seen them, had he? Romy thought she'd hidden them in time. Her panic attack was interrupted by the ringing of the bell.

'That'll be Ethan,' Kit said, his body slumping and his expression becoming even more hangdog, if that was possible.

'Your doom is upon you,' Romy said, smiling at him over her shoulder as she went to answer the door.

Wow, Romy thought as she let Ethan in, now he looked properly outdoorsy. His big stompy hiking boots had clearly seen plenty of action and his cargo pants looked lived in, their colour faded and their hems frayed. She could just picture him hacking his way through the Haitian wilderness to save cholera victims in a remote inaccessible village. It made this mock adventure weekend of Tank's seem very frivolous and silly.

'We're just having a glass of wine. Would you like a cup of coffee or something before you set off?' she asked him.

He glanced at his watch. 'Sure. Thanks.' He sat in an armchair opposite Kit. 'All set?' he asked him, nodding to his rucksack.

'Ready as I'll ever be,' Kit said sourly.

'You look very ... smart,' Ethan said, a smile playing about his lips as he took in Kit's outfit. 'Mr Manhattan goes camping.'

Kit glowered at him. 'Well, I didn't have any of the kind of clothes they said we should bring. Anyway, some of the stuff is old. Romy gave me the rucksack. And the sleeping bag.'

Romy had managed to intervene when Kit was allowing the sales assistant to persuade him that he should buy a spectacularly expensive sleeping bag.

'She says it'll take me all the way to Everest base camp,' he had told Romy.

'Really?' She had flipped the sleeping bag over, examining it. 'Does it have a plane built into it?'

'You know what I mean.'

'Yes, but you're not going to Everest base camp, Kit. You're going to Wicklow. I have plenty of sleeping bags at home. I'll lend you one.' It had taken some doing, but she had finally succeeding in convincing him that a normal four-seasons sleeping bag would be perfectly adequate for the Wicklow mountains.

'When do you get back?' she asked now as she handed Ethan a mug of coffee.

'I'll be back on Sunday, *if* I survive this weekend,' Kit replied.

'Don't worry, you'll be fine. You'll look after him, won't you?' she said to Ethan as she sat down beside Kit.

'Of course I will,' Ethan said.

'Hey, what makes you think Ethan will be more capable than me?' Kit asked indignantly.

'Well, obviously I'm a dab hand at all this survival stuff from my time in the jungle,' Ethan said, smiling crookedly.

'Oh yes, how could I forget about your time in the jungle?'

'And we'll have Tank with us too. He's bound to come in handy.'

'True. He could probably fell a tree with his bare hands.'

'And I'll make us all cocktails out of the bark,' Ethan said. 'It'll be fun.'

'If the worst comes to the worst and you don't manage to build a shelter,' Romy said, 'everyone can just move into your jacket for the night.'

'Very funny,' Kit said sulkily. 'The smile will be on the other side of your face tomorrow when you're zipping to your death on a wire.'

'Oh, are you going to Hannah's hen weekend then?' Ethan asked her.

'I'm just going down for the day. I'm not staying overnight. It's too awkward with Luke.'

To her surprise, Hannah had repeated her invitation for Romy to go to her hen do. After what she had heard Hannah and Ethan saying at Thanksgiving, she had assumed Hannah had only asked her out of politeness and wouldn't really want her there. But she had pressed, and seemed to genuinely want Romy to go. It was all very confusing.

'Come down for the day at least,' Hannah had begged.

'Then you can do some of the activities and have lunch with us, but you won't have to worry about staying over with Luke. And do bring him.'

It would have felt churlish to continue to refuse in the face of so much persuasion, so Romy had capitulated and agreed to go for the day. She was glad she wasn't staying overnight, though, not just because of Luke but because she wanted to be able to cut it short if she felt any hostility from Hannah. It was weird because she never did feel any antagonism from either her or Ethan – it seemed to be the idea of her as Kit's girlfriend that they didn't like.

'Well, I suppose we should be off,' Ethan said, draining his mug and putting it on the table.

'Okay. Bye, sweetie,' Kit said, turning to Romy and surprising her by giving her a lingering kiss on the mouth. 'Have fun tomorrow at Hannah's do.'

'I can't believe you guys are together again,' Ethan said, narrowing his eyes at them.

'Well, it's true!' Romy said brightly, snuggling into Kit as he put his arm around her, playing her part as one half of a loved-up couple perfectly.

Ethan frowned slightly, looking confused.

'I'll just go and say goodbye to … um … Luke!' Kit said, getting up from the sofa. Romy thought that was overdoing things a bit, but at least he had remembered Luke's name – though she was starting to warm to 'Whatsisface'.

'Be quiet,' she warned to his retreating back. 'Don't wake him up.'

'So, I hear you're employing Kit as some kind of handyman,' Ethan sniggered when Kit had left the room.

Oh – that snigger wasn't good. 'Not exactly "employing", but he's doing odd jobs around the place in lieu of part of the rent.'

'Right. Well, good luck with that.' Ethan smirked in a way that made Romy decidedly uneasy.

'Why do you say it like that?'

'Because ... have you seen his work?'

'No, but are you saying you don't think he's up to it?'

Ethan looked at her sceptically. 'Are you serious? You didn't even find out if he could actually do any DIY before you hired him? You always were too easy on him, you know.'

'Well, he told me he fixed things up in his apartments in New York all the time.'

'That's true,' Ethan nodded. Then he smiled to himself as if recalling something funny. 'Were you ever in any of his New York apartments?'

'Well, no, but he has his own tools! He wouldn't have his own tools if he wasn't into DIY, would he?'

'Yeah, he has his own tools all right.' Ethan chuckled. 'Have you seen his tools?'

'No.'

'You should get him to show you his tools some time,' Ethan said, seeming amused.

'It's very basic stuff,' she said, rattled by his attitude. 'Just fixing things for the tenants, putting up shelves, that kind of thing. I'm not going to be asking him to build an extension or rewire the house.'

'Thank God for that at least!'

'What? You really don't think he can do basic handyman jobs?'

Ethan sighed. 'Let me put it this way. Kit is a good handyman in the same way that Mom's a great cook.'

'No, I'm sure you're wrong about that. He put up some shelves for one of my tenants the other day and she's really pleased with them. She told me he did a great job.'

Ethan just looked at her, his eyebrows raised meaningfully, waiting for her to catch up.

'Oh,' she said when she realised what he was saying. Kit's mother was a terrible cook, but everyone pretended to love her food because they didn't want to hurt her feelings.

'Yeah.'

Oh, shit. She resolved to go and have a look at May's shelves as soon as possible.

'Okay, let's go,' Kit said, coming back into the room.

Romy saw them to the door. 'Have fun,' she said, 'and take care of each other.'

'See you Sunday,' Kit said, pulling her into his arms and giving her an enthusiastic kiss on the lips.

Mmm, he was still a really good kisser, Romy thought, winding her arms around his neck and kissing him back. By the time Kit released her, Ethan was already sitting in the car. But he was watching them, and he didn't look happy.

Romy waved them off, hugging herself as she stood on the doorstep. Damn Ethan! He had unsettled her, and it wasn't just the way he had been scowling at her and Kit just now. She thought of Laura's Thanksgiving dinner and felt queasy at the thought of what Kit might be doing to her beautiful house. Lesley would be coming over shortly, but as soon as she got the chance, she was going to check out May's shelves.

✳

'No Danny tonight?' Lesley asked later as they sat on Romy's sofa drinking wine and eating Romy's home-made pizza.

'No. He finally let some of his friends persuade him to go out on the razz with them.'

'Well, good. At least one of us is getting out there.'

'You know, I'm starting to think you might be right about Kit,' Romy said.

Lesley gasped. 'You mean – about the whole BDSM thing?'

'Yeah.' Romy nodded.

'Oh my God, did he come out to you about it?'

'No, but ... he's said a few things that make me wonder.'

'Okay, tell me everything,' Lesley said, leaning forward eagerly. 'From the top.'

'Well, it's not that much really. But the other day he was saying that he needs to get more discipline back in his life. He said he had discipline in his life in New York.'

'He actually used that word – "discipline"?'

'Yes.'

'Okay. It's definitely going into evidence, but it's not conclusive. Go on.'

'Well, today I asked him straight out what his secret was and why he needed a fake girlfriend. And he said he could tell me but I'd have to sign a confidentiality agreement first. He said he had them with his previous girlfriends.'

'Oh my God! May had a confidentiality agreement with her master.'

'I know. And then later, I said I had an idea about what his secret was, and he was a bit freaked and asked me was it obvious. When I said no, he said I'd probably read the signals easier than most people.'

Lesley frowned. 'Why would he think that?'

'I'm not sure, but he was in the kitchen the other day and those books May gave me were lying around. I shoved them in a cupboard as soon as I realised and I thought I got away with it. But he'd been on his own in there for a while. He might have seen them.'

'That must be it! He saw those books, so he thinks you're into it and can recognise one of your own kind.'

'Maybe. But if he thinks I'm part of that whole scene, why doesn't he just come out and tell me?'

'I don't know. Maybe there's some kind of secret handshake or something. So, anything else?'

'No.' There was also the blindfold, but she didn't want to bring that up. It would be case closed, as far as Lesley was concerned. Still, she couldn't help thinking how naturally it had occurred to him to use one. 'I just wish I knew one way or the other.'

'You need a way to smoke him out.'

'But how?'

'Hmm,' Lesley said, stroking her chin thoughtfully. 'I know! He's away at the moment, right?'

'Yeah, he's gone to Tank's stag weekend. He left earlier.'

'And you have a key to his flat?'

'Yes, but—'

'We should go down there and have a poke around.'

'And look for what?'

'Sex toys, leather gear … we might even be able to get into his computer,' Lesley said, her eyes lighting up.

'No! I can't go snooping around his flat.'

'Okay, then, I'll go,' Lesley said, jumping off the sofa. 'Give me the key,' she said, holding out her hand.

'Lesley, no!'

'He won't know I've been there, I promise. I'll do a really clean sweep. Do you have any plastic gloves?'

'What?'

'The ones you get with hair dye would do fine.'

'Seriously, Lesley, you can't! It's an invasion of privacy.'

'Okay,' Lesley sighed, her shoulders slumping. 'We'll have to think of something else.'

'Well, I'm going to Hannah's wedding with him next weekend and we'll be sharing a room. Maybe I could do something then.'

'That's perfect! We can set a honey-trap.'

'Huh?'

'Why don't you bring something with you – one of those floggers or something – and leave it lying around where he can see it. Then he'll think you're up for it and it's safe to tell you.'

'I don't have any of that stuff. And I don't want to buy it specially just to trap Kit.'

'I'm sure May would have something she could lend you.'

'Probably. But what if he's not into this kinky stuff? Then he'll think *I* am and it'll be weird.'

'Bring something really obscure, that most people wouldn't recognise. There was some pretty weird-looking equipment on those websites.'

'That's a good idea. I'll ask May.'

'Oh, but what if it turns out he is into it and he wants to hang you out of the ceiling?' Lesley gasped.

'I'll just say no. Besides, I doubt he'd bring all his equipment with him on the off-chance I'm going to let him hang me from the ceiling. Anyway, all the books say suspension is really tricky – and possibly dangerous. I don't think it's the kind of thing you'd set up in a hotel room.'

'True. But if he *is* kinky, it would be mean to lead him on and leave him hanging.'

'So what do you suggest I do?'

'Why don't you bring something you think you could handle if he wanted to use it on you? You can explain to him that you're just a beginner and you're not ready for the advanced stuff.'

'God, I don't know,' Romy fretted.

'Do you still want to have a relationship with him, if it turns out he's into this, or is it a total deal-breaker?'

'He's still Luke's father,' Romy said uncertainly. 'I suppose I'd still want to give it a go.'

'Well, you could let him spank you. That wouldn't be too weird, would it?'

'No … as long as I never had to see him again as long as I live.'

'How about bondage, then? You could let him tie you up and use a vibrator on you or something.'

'Yeah, that mightn't be too bad.' She thought about the blindfold – that had been sexy. She wouldn't mind doing that again.

'That's the spirit! Before you know it, you'll be letting him hoist you up to the ceiling in one of those harness contraptions.'

'Hmmm,' Romy said doubtfully.

'Well, keep an open mind. And maybe you'll be able to compromise – find something that's not too icky for you but would still keep him happy.'

Romy grimaced. 'I really don't think I could ever get into this stuff. Imagine having to call your boyfriend "Sir".'

'Or "Master".'

'Eew!' Romy squealed.

'And if someone gave me a pat on the head for being a good girl, I'd plant him! But what if it was the other way around – you calling the shots, him being the slave?'

Romy shook her head. 'I still don't think I could do it.'

'Well, maybe he could get cured,' Lesley said hopefully. 'He could try hypnotherapy!'

'I don't think it's really something you get cured of.'

'I don't see why not. I know lots of people who managed to quit smoking by being hypnotised. I don't see why it couldn't help fight the urge to truss up your girlfriend just as well. I mean I know it's not PC to say it, but let's face it – it's not normal, is it?'

'Even if it could work, he'd have to want to quit. If he does this stuff, it's because he likes it.'

'People like smoking. They still want to quit.'

'Hmm.' Romy wasn't convinced. 'Anyway, chances are he isn't into S&M at all,' she said briskly. 'But I wonder what his secret life is, if not this?'

'Well, there is another possibility,' Lesley said tentatively.

'Oh? What's that?'

'He could be gay.'

'He's not gay.'

'How can you be so sure?'

'Hello! He used to be my boyfriend, remember? I think I'd know if he was gay.'

'Look at the evidence. It would explain the butt plug. And he thinks you have good gaydar because of Danny. That's why he thought you were able to guess his secret. It all fits. And who needs a fake girlfriend more than a gay man who's not out? He wants you to be his beard. I don't know why we didn't think of it before.'

'Maybe because I spent two years joined to him at the mouth,' Romy said dryly.

'Ah, but not joined to him at your rude bits. That's the giveaway. Besides, that was a hundred years ago. He could have changed.'

'Are you forgetting that he's Luke's father?'

'Oh, yeah.' Lesley's face fell. 'But you said he was a bit freaked out about the whole thing. Maybe he doesn't normally shag women.'

Romy gasped as Kit's words came back to her. He'd had sex before, but '*not like that*'. 'Oh! I think you could be right.'

'Well, this is your perfect opportunity to find out for sure. We can make it a two-pronged honey trap. If he doesn't bite with the BDSM stuff, you could try seducing him – the plain old vanilla way. At least you don't need any special equipment for that – well, nothing you haven't already got.'

'I don't know ...'

'Come on, Romy. You're considering getting into a relationship with the guy. You need to know if he's gay. I mean if you think the kinky sex is a deal-breaker, how would you feel about no sex at all?'

'Oh!' Romy chewed her lip. She had to admit Lesley had a point. 'Right. I'll see if May has something I can borrow in the morning. There's something I need to see her about anyway.'

✳

The following morning, before setting off for Hannah's hen party, Romy called on May on the pretext of returning her books, but really because she wanted to inspect the shelves Kit had put up.

'Hello, Romy,' the old lady greeted her as she ushered her in.

'Hi, May. I just thought I'd return your books,' Romy said, sailing past her into the flat.

'Oh, thank you. But there was no need to return them so soon. Keep them for as long as you like. Would you like a cup of coffee?'

'That'd be lovely, thanks. Why don't I put these books on the shelf for you, and then we can discuss them over coffee? I have a few, um, questions.'

'Oh, excellent!' May's eyes lit up. 'You can just give them to me, dear.'

Romy handed the books over reluctantly, and May led her through to the kitchen. 'Oh, by the way, Kit left his tools here after he put up those shelves. Perhaps you'd take them for him? I've knocked a few times but I never seem to get him in.'

'Sure. He's away for the weekend. I'll give them to him when he gets back.'

'Here we are.' May rooted in a corner of the kitchen and then presented Romy with a tool box. It looked normal enough.

While May busied herself making coffee, Romy sat at the little table and opened the box. There was nothing unusual in the top tray, full of screws, nails and rawl plugs, but her heart sank when she lifted it out and saw what was inside – a hammer, scissors, screwdrivers, spirit level, even a little saw, all with pretty floral handles. They were the sort of tools you would buy in an upmarket department store rather than a DIY emporium or hardware shop – the sort of tools that were marketed as Christmas gift ideas for women. Still, she told herself as she pulled out the hammer and weighed it in her hand, a hammer was a hammer. It seemed heavy enough, and just because it had a decorative handle didn't make it any less functional. Her attempts to reassure herself were only marginally successful, however. She would still feel uneasy until she saw those shelves for herself.

'So you had some questions?' May said, placing a cafetière of coffee on the table along with two china cups and sitting opposite Romy.

'Oh, yes.' Romy racked her brain for something she could ask May. She already knew way more than she wanted to about her tenant's sexual exploits. 'Well, it's not so much a question,' she said finally, 'but I was wondering if you'd have something I could borrow. I was thinking of trying one of those, um … pinwheel things.' She and Lesley had explored the sex shop websites the previous night and decided that was a suitably obscure looking toy. Like a cross between a spoon and a mini pizza cutter, it also had the advantage of being small and easy to throw in a bag.

'Oh, yes,' May said, with a delighted smile. 'I'm sure I'd have one of those in my box of tricks. We can have a look later. Was that all?'

'Would that be quite recognisable to anyone who was involved in BDSM?' she asked. 'I mean would it be something quite commonly used?'

'Oh, yes, anyone in the lifestyle should know what that was – and what to do with it.'

'Good.'

'You can have a lot of fun with that,' May said with a twinkle in her eye. 'If there's anything else you'd like to try, just let me know.'

'Thanks.' Romy sipped her coffee. 'You obviously enjoyed this … lifestyle,' she said.

'I loved it. It answered a very deep need in me at the time. I found it very liberating.'

'Liberating? Really?' Romy thought of the images of May bound and restrained. It looked anything but liberating.

'The irony isn't lost on me,' May said, with a smile.

'So why did you give it up?'

'My dom died,' she said sadly.

'Oh, I'm sorry.'

'Thank you, dear,' she said. 'I could have found another, of course. But we had a real relationship and I found I didn't want to submit to anyone else after him. Many dom/sub partnerships don't have any romantic or emotional side to them at all – they're more like business relationships. But we loved each other, and when he died, well, I didn't want to replace him.'

'How old were you when he died?'

'I was about thirty-five.'

'So you never went back to being a sub?'

'No. I felt I'd already explored that aspect of sexuality to the full anyway. I would have found it too limiting to continue. Not that it was restricting while I was with Marcus, because we had more. But to go back and start again with someone else …' She shook her head.

'So what did you do then?'

She smiled wryly. 'I ran away and joined the circus – literally.'

'Really?' Romy breathed.

'Yes. I joined a circus in Barcelona and travelled all over Spain with them for a year.'

'As a trapeze artist?' Romy asked, thinking of the photos of May suspended from the ceiling on ropes. Her time as a sub must have qualified her for some pretty complicated acrobatics.

'Oh no, dear! Nothing so exciting. As a wardrobe mistress. I sewed the costumes. Very dull, I'm afraid.'

It sounded anything but dull. And at least her job description still included the word 'mistress', Romy thought.

'It was an exciting time, though,' May said, smiling fondly as she reminisced. And I met the most marvellous people. There was a Jamaican acrobat …' She trailed off, draining her coffee. 'Well,' she said briskly, 'shall we go and look for that pinwheel?'

'I just want to have a look at those shelves Kit put up for you too,' Romy said as she followed May through to the sitting room.

'Oh, yes, I'm very happy with them,' May said over her shoulder. 'Didn't I tell you? There they are,' she said as they entered the room, pointing to the shelves running along an alcove – at a distinct angle.

'Oh, May, I'm sorry. I didn't realise.'

'Aren't they great?' May beamed at her, to Romy's astonishment.

'Well, they're …'

'They're the perfect height for me to reach, and he even painted them the exact colour I wanted.'

'They're fine, I suppose, as long as you don't want to use

them as actual shelves. But if you were thinking of putting anything on them—'

'Oh!' May frowned. 'Don't you think they look strong?'

Romy stepped closer, examining the brackets underneath the shelves, which barely adhered to the wall. She jiggled a shelf a little and it wobbled precariously. 'No. To be honest, I think they'll collapse if you put so much as a card on them.'

'Really?' May squinted at the shelves through narrowed eyes.

'But there's no danger of that,' Romy reassured her, 'because anything you put on them would slide right off. They're at an angle.'

'Are they?' May peered at the shelves. 'I can't say I'd noticed. But my eyesight's not what it used to be.'

'Anyway, don't worry about it. I'll fix them.'

'I'm very happy with them,' May said, folding her arms and giving Romy a challenging look, as if daring her to criticise Kit's work further. 'I think he's done a fine job.'

'But I can't leave them like this, May.'

'Well, maybe you could tell him what's wrong and he could fix them himself. He's coming back next week anyway, to put up our swing.'

Romy gulped. 'There's no way I can let him put up the swing, May. You'll get killed.' Wonky shelving was one thing, but there was no way she was going to trust Kit to install a sex swing that would have to bear the weight of two cavorting old folks. She certainly didn't want to be the one to have to rescue them when it came crashing to the ground.

'Oh.' May paled.

'I'll put up the swing myself.'

'Well, perhaps that would be best. But could you put it to Kit in a way that won't hurt his feelings? And please don't mention the shelves to him. He's such a lovely young man, and I'm sure he did his best. Maybe we could just leave them as they are?'

'But what if you want to put something on them? They're not much use like that!'

'Well, there are more important things in life than my knick-knacks. And it's not good for a man's ego to have a woman second-guessing him all the time – especially when it comes to things like DIY. They like to feel useful and … handy.'

'Yes, but Kit's clearly *not* handy, is he?'

May gave her a stern look. 'You know, Romy, if you're going to be Kit's sub, you're going to have to lose this attitude. You'll have to get used to not questioning his judgement.'

'Even if his judgement is clearly abysmal?'

'That won't be for you to decide.'

'But as the dom, wouldn't he be in charge of the equipment? Some of that stuff could be dangerous if it's not set up properly.'

'Well, often it can be one of the sub's duties to take care of the equipment. You would sort out the ground rules between you before you begin. But, after that, you have to let him make the decisions and trust that he's doing the right thing for both of you. You must submit to his will completely – at least while you're playing.'

'While you're playing?' Romy pounced. 'So you do get time off from all the submission and obedience?'

'Oh, yes. There are some couples who do it twenty-four/ seven – it's called total power exchange – but it's rare. It's too intense for most people to keep up constantly.'

'And the rules don't apply when you're not playing? You don't have to call him "Sir" or "Master" and do whatever he says?'

'Well, no. You still have to be respectful—'

'So it would be okay, then, to point out that he's done a bloody crap job in your downtime?'

May sighed sadly. 'Romy,' she said, patting Romy's shoulder consolingly, 'you know I'm very fond of you, and I think you're a great girl, so please don't take this the wrong way, but I'm not at all sure you have what it takes to be a submissive.'

No, Romy thought, me neither.

'Are you still interested in borrowing that pinwheel?' May asked.

'Oh, er, yes, please. No harm in trying, eh?'

'Okay, you wait here. I have all my toys in a box in the bedroom.'

As she waited for May to come back, Romy looked around the room. There was a stack of framed photographs in an armchair under the alcove, no doubt waiting to go on the shelves, and Romy picked them up and looked through them. Some of them she had seen before – a young and very beautiful May playing Ophelia in the Abbey Theatre; slightly older as Lady Macbeth with the RSC. She had already known that May had led an adventurous and rather eccentric life – cut off by her father after some scandal with a boy and leaving her very wealthy aristocratic family to become an impoverished actress in Dublin and subsequently London. That would have been enough excitement for most people in a lifetime, but she had discovered in the last two days that it was just the tip of the iceberg for May. Romy sighed. She felt like she hadn't lived – and never would, by May's standards. She set the bar very high – dark sexual adventures, Jamaican acrobats, circuses … Romy felt that no matter what she did, she would never catch up.

'Here we are,' May came back, bearing a large box. 'Everything's in here,' she said, placing it on the coffee table and opening the lid. 'You're welcome to take anything you like.'

'Wow!' Romy gasped as she delved into the box. It was an Aladdin's cave of sex toys, many of which she wouldn't have recognised only a few days ago. She quickly located the little pinwheel. 'Can I take this too?' she asked, lifting out a spreader bar. Despite May's assurances, she still wasn't convinced the pinwheel would be instantly recognisable as a sex toy. It was so innocuous looking. She decided she should take a spreader bar too, to be on the safe side.

'Yes, of course, dear. Take as much as you like.' May began rooting through the box. 'If you're taking the spreader bar, perhaps you should take some handcuffs as well,' she said, handing a pair to Romy. 'And a ball gag. And you really should try these nipple clamps. They're fun.' She handed item after item to Romy until her arms were full of floggers, whips, blindfolds and restraints of every kind.

'Gosh, thanks, May. This lot should keep me going for a while.'

'Not at all, Romy. Let me know how you get on.'

'I will.' She had no intention of trying any of this stuff, but she didn't like to refuse May's kindness. She would bring the pinwheel and spreader bar to the wedding with her to test Kit. The rest she would stash in her wardrobe for a suitable period before returning them to May unused.

'I'm still not sure you have what it takes to be a submissive,' May said.

'No, me neither,' Romy said, smiling. 'Still, only one way to find out!'

Chapter Fifteen

That evening, Romy was relaxing with a glass of wine while Danny bathed Luke and put him to bed for her. It had been a tiring day. After leaving May's flat with her booty, she had driven through a violent rainstorm to the adventure centre where Hannah's hen weekend was being held. Fortunately, the rain stopped and the sky cleared just before the activities were due to start, and she had spent the day shooting arrows and guns, leaping from towering platforms and swinging across wires suspended between tall trees. It had been good fun, but exhausting.

She hadn't been sure of the wisdom of bringing a baby to a hen party, especially one held in an adventure centre, but Luke had been a huge hit with Hannah's friends, and had been in constant demand all day. Romy had hardly seen him from the moment they arrived, when Laura had whipped him out of her arms and fell instantly in love. After that, he had been passed from one person to another while they took turns for archery or shooting. As the day progressed and the activities had become more extreme, the hens had even started to fight over him.

'Oh, I'll have to sit out the zip wire,' Denise, Hannah's bridesmaid had said casually. 'It's my turn to mind Luke, and his nappy needs changing.'

'You had Luke for the climbing wall,' another bridesmaid had said. 'You go ahead, I'll change his nappy.'

'I don't expect any of you to deal with that,' Romy had said, breaking into their argument. 'If his nappy needs changing, I'll do it.'

'Oh no, it's no bother,' both girls had chorused, and several others joined in, claiming they had changed lots of nappies for nieces and nephews or that it would be good practice for when they had babies of their own, and generously offering to sit out the zip wire or the climbing wall so that Romy could have a go.

'We've got tomorrow as well,' they'd said to her. 'You're only down for the day. We don't want you to miss out.'

Clearly, Luke's dirty nappy held no fears when compared with zip-wiring.

Feeling duty bound to be a good sport for Hannah's sake, especially when some of her friends were being so negative, Romy had taken part in everything and had thoroughly enjoyed herself. The only time she had got to sit down with Luke was at lunch, and even then Laura had insisted on giving him his bottle while Romy ate. Laura was excusing herself from the more hair-raising activities and had offered to take

Luke for the rest of the day so everyone else could enjoy themselves. But once lunch was over, a small, thin girl had raced up to Romy with a rather desperate look on her face.

'*Please* can I have Luke next?' she begged. 'We're doing high ropes, for fuck's sake! What possessed Hannah to think this was a good idea for a hen party? I thought we'd go to a spa and have a few facials and manicures, not go to a feckin' boot camp and swing out of the trees.'

Laura had taken pity on the girl and reluctantly handed Luke over to her for a short stint, while Romy put on her helmet again and strapped herself into another harness. By the time they were leaving, Luke had had a bevy of devoted fans waving him off, and she'd known that when everyone told her they were sorry she wasn't staying for the next day, they'd meant it.

She smiled as she thought of the forlorn faces of the girls as she had driven off with their hero. She was probably lucky they hadn't kidnapped him.

'He's asleep,' Danny said softly, padding back into the room.

'Great. Thank you. The food's on its way.' Too exhausted to cook, Romy had ordered an Indian takeaway and was looking forward to a quiet night in with Danny in front of the TV.

Danny sat beside her on the sofa and she poured him a glass of wine.

'So how was last night?' she asked.

He shrugged. 'It was okay. We ended up at a party of some guy Neil met in The George. It got a bit messy, so I went home fairly early.'

Romy gave him a sympathetic smile. Danny had always been quiet and rather shy, and she knew wild parties and nights out clubbing weren't his scene. But where else did gay guys go to meet someone? Evening classes?

'Maybe you should try a dating website, like Lesley.'

'Hmm, maybe. But you've seen Gaydar. Fucking terrifying!'

Romy had to agree. She had seen the gay dating website and it scared the living daylights out of her. The guys who posed in only their underpants were mild. Some just had pictures of a penis as their avatar (allegedly their own penis, but who knew?). And they made no bones about what they were looking for either – there was none of the coy guff about long walks on the beach or trips to the movies that you get on most dating websites. Instead, they went straight in with lists of their preferred sexual activities. Lesley may find internet dating difficult, but at least she wasn't required to include details of her genitalia in her profile, or whether or not she would take it up the bum. Romy couldn't help thinking it would be nice to at least get to know someone a little first before finding out they had a huge dick or that they were interested in having a threesome. It seemed to her that a little bit of mystery was no bad thing.

'Well, maybe you'll meet someone through work,' she said. That seemed to be her answer to everyone these days. 'In the meantime, pick a movie to watch,' she said, getting up as there was a ring at the door and she went to collect the takeaway. 'Anything as long as it's *Moulin Rouge*.'

They were just settling down with the Indian and starting to watch *Moulin Rouge* when there was a knock on the inner door. 'Must be one of the tenants,' Romy said, pausing the DVD and getting up to answer it.

To her astonishment, she opened the door to find Kit standing on the threshold, panting and looking rather manic, his eyes wild. He bound in past her, waves of cold damp air rolling off him.

'Kit!' She followed him into the living room. 'What are you doing here? Shouldn't you be building a shelter on some mountainside right now?'

'I escaped!' he said breathlessly, spreading his arms like the Messiah. He flopped into the nearest armchair and started taking off his jacket. 'Hi, Danny.'

'How did you get here?' Romy asked.

'Oh shit! I forgot, there's a cab outside and I'm all out of cash. Could you get it? I'll pay you back tomorrow.'

Romy sighed. 'Okay.' She saw Danny scowl out of the corner of her eye as she grabbed her purse and went out, running down the steps to the waiting taxi. She paid the driver quickly and dashed back into the house.

'So, what happened?' she asked Kit as she returned to the room, dropping her purse on the coffee table.

'Well, turns out I'm more resourceful than I thought I was – than anyone thought I was, actually,' Kit said. 'Oh, is that Indian?'

'I'll get you a plate,' Romy said resignedly, since he was practically drooling at the sight of the takeaway. She went to the kitchen and heated a plate in the microwave, and collected cutlery and a glass.

'Here you go, she said, depositing the lot on the coffee table and pouring a glass of wine. 'Oh my God, you're frozen,' she said as she handed Kit the wine and her hand brushed against his.

'I know. You should be wrapping me in aluminium foil and making me hot cocoa. I've survived a horrific ordeal.'

'Well, wine and curry will have to do. But I can get you a duvet if you want?'

'No, thanks. I'm fine. I'll warm up in a minute.' He took a gulp of wine.

'You're lucky you had that jacket,' Romy said, nodding to the armchair where Kit had left it.

'I credit it with my survival,' Kit said, getting up and crossing to the coffee table. 'It was worth every penny.' He sat cross-legged in front of the low table, helping himself to rice and curry, and tearing off a large chunk of naan bread. 'Oh my God, this is amazing, Romy. You're a life-saver.'

Romy couldn't help smiling as he attacked the food and wine like a starving man. 'So tell us what happened. How did you get away?'

'Like I said, I was resourceful – which was pretty much the point of the exercise, so I win!'

'I don't think that was quite the idea,' Romy said.

'We were supposed to pretend we'd been in a plane crash and had to survive and make it back to civilisation using only our wits and whatever we had with us. Well – here I am,' he said, making an expansive gesture with his arms. 'In civilisation.'

Romy laughed. 'You were supposed to see if you could survive in the wilderness.'

'Bollocks to that! I'm the one sitting here having takeaway and wine. I'm the true survivor. Where are the rest of them? Still stuck out on that godforsaken mountainside eating berries and dodgy looking mushrooms. Much use *they'd* be in a plane crash.'

'Yes, but it's supposed to be fun. You're not meant to "escape" from a stag party.'

'I don't know,' Danny said. 'I've been to a few stag parties that I wouldn't have minded escaping from.'

'So how did you find your way home? Did the others even know you were going?'

'I told Ethan I was going to make a break for it whenever I got the chance. But I haven't been able to contact him since. They don't have any mobiles – because they wouldn't survive a crash, you see.'

'They'll probably be worried about you.'

Kit shrugged nonchalantly. 'That'll teach them to leave me to fend for myself out in the middle of nowhere.'

'So, did you orienteer your way back?'

'Like hell I did! They gave us a lesson about navigating by the sun or some shit, but I had no idea what they were talking about. I just figured there's nowhere in Ireland that's *that* far from civilisation. So I took off and I just kept walking until I found a road. Then I hitched a lift to the nearest town – well, it wasn't so much a town as a pub. From there, it was just another hitched lift, a bus, a train, a tram and a cab home,' he finished, looking very pleased with himself.

'Christ! How long have you been travelling?' Danny asked, wide-eyed.

'Since around dawn this morning when I left the actually quite impressive little shelter that Tank and Ethan had built.'

'You must be exhausted!' Romy said.

'You'd think. But actually I feel quite buzzed. I think I must be having an adrenaline rush. I've heard people who survive disasters often react this way. It's the sheer joy of being alive!'

'But you didn't survive a disaster,' Romy pointed out. 'You survived one night of a stag weekend. It's quite common.'

'You're just in denial because you don't want to face up to the very real danger I was in.' Kit divided the remainder of the wine between their three glasses. 'Another one?' he asked, waving the bottle.

'In the rack in the kitchen,' Romy told him.

Kit went to the kitchen and came back with another bottle. 'You survived Hannah's hen in one piece I see,' he said to Romy as he opened it.

'Yes, it was fun. Well, *I* thought it was. Some of the girls there would have liked to escape too.'

'That pair are a match made in heaven,' Kit said, shaking his head.

'Luke was a big hit with the girls.'

'That's my boy.' Kit grinned. 'So what did you do – zip-wiring, water-boarding?'

'Well, not water-boarding,' Romy said, laughing.

'No?'

'Er, no.'

'Water-boarding isn't an adventure activity,' Danny said. 'It's a form of torture.'

'Same thing, isn't it?' Kit said, shrugging.

Romy was glad she'd over-ordered as Kit wolfed down everything in sight and continued eating long after she and Danny had finished, forking up every last grain of rice and crumb of naan. 'You must have been starving,' she commented.

'I was. We had to *forage* for food,' he said disgustedly. 'Not very realistic, if you ask me. I mean if a plane really crashed there'd be bound to be some airplane meals lying around, wouldn't there? They could have left us some tubes of Pringles at the very least.' He pushed his plate away with a sigh of satisfaction.

'We were going to watch a DVD before you came,' Romy said. 'Do you want to watch it with us?'

'I feel like going out and celebrating,' Kit said. 'I'm alive! Let's go out and get plastered.'

'I can't,' Romy said, glancing towards the bedroom.

'Oh yeah, little Whatsisface. Well, we could bring him with us!'

Romy fixed him with a glare.

'Only joking!' Kit added hastily when he saw her stony expression.

'Anyway, I'm wiped out,' she said, yawning and sinking back against the sofa.

'How about you?' Kit asked Danny. 'Will you come and drink to my survival with me?'

'Well ...' Danny looked at Romy.

'Go if you want to,' she said. 'Really, I'm ready for bed. All that water-boarding takes it out of a girl.'

'Okay, then,' Danny said to Kit.

'Have fun you two,' Romy said as they got up to go. 'And Kit, send Ethan or Tank a text to let them know where you are. I know they don't have their phones, but at least they'll see it as soon as they get them back.'

'Will do.'

※

'So, Romy tells me you're gay,' Kit said conversationally to Danny as they walked down the steps.

Danny gave a small smile. 'Well, I haven't got the bumper stickers printed up yet, but, yep, it's true.'

'God, sorry! Bloody stupid thing to say.'

Danny laughed. 'It's fine.'

'So where are we going?' Kit said when they got to the gate. Is there a decent pub around here? I know I'm high on life, but I don't think I'm up to going into town.'

'There's a good pub in the village. It's not far.'

'Great! Unless you want to go into town? I mean I don't mind if you want to go to one of … your places.'

'We are allowed mix with the heteros, you know,' Danny said, laughing.

'I know, God, I didn't mean—'

'Hey, relax,' Danny said. 'I'm just messing with you. Thanks for the offer, but I really fancy a quiet drink. Had a bit of a wild night last night.'

'Great! Lead the way. I just hope it has dim lighting. I still have bits of countryside stuck to me. I probably smell too – just to warn you.'

'You're definitely in no state to go to a gay pub, then,' Danny said. 'We have much higher standards.'

'True. There's no way I could go to a gay bar wearing this

stupid jacket.' Though Kit had to admit that right now he was damn glad of the stupid jacket. It was bloody freezing! The icy air bit into his face and made his eyes water, and he began to regret leaving the cosy warmth of Romy's flat. He'd had enough of the outdoors in the past twenty-four hours to last him a lifetime.

'So, I hear you've just broken up with someone,' he said as they walked.

'Er, yeah.' Danny glanced across at him warily. 'Are all your conversations like this?'

Kit sighed. 'Sorry, I'm an idiot. Honestly – Romy will tell you. Just tell me to mind my own business.'

'No, it's okay. But I think maybe we should walk a bit faster. If this is your idea of small talk, I'm going to need a drink quick.'

※

The pub was warm and sufficiently dark to satisfy Kit, and they found a free sofa in a cosy corner by an open fire. Kit had been surprised that Danny had agreed to come out with him. He'd got the impression he didn't like him very much, and Danny's behaviour now as they sat over a couple of beers was doing nothing to make him think he was wrong. He was so quiet, and it was all Kit could do to drag a few words out of him. Why the hell had he come if he was just going to sit there being so cool and detached, observing Kit from behind his inscrutable façade like he was some kind of science project? The adrenaline high that had got Kit here in the first place had gone, and he felt fed up. God, they should have stayed at Romy's! He was starting to sweat, and it was nothing to do with the roaring fire. He was doing all the talking, either talking about himself or trying to draw Danny out with questions to which he got monosyllabic answers. He still knew next to nothing about Danny, other than that he was a landscape gardener and loved his job.

'So, you're an uncle now!' he said heartily, trying another tack.

'Yeah,' Danny said with a fond smile. 'And a godfather.'

'Oh, you're Whatsisface's godfather? That's great!'

'Luke.'

'Luke, exactly.' Brilliant! He could probably expect to find a horse's head in his bed any day now, just because he couldn't remember the kid's name. He cast around desperately for another topic of conversation. 'I was sorry to hear about your father,' he said.

Danny just nodded in acknowledgement. 'It hit Romy really hard. I mean it did us all, but she was …' he didn't finish the thought. 'Having Luke seemed to help her get over it.'

More than two sentences – that was progress! 'She seems to be a great mother.'

Danny drained his glass and stood, and Kit knocked his back too, grateful that this awkward evening was coming to an end. It had been a stupid idea and he just wanted to go home.

'Same again?' Danny asked, and Kit looked up at him in astonishment. *Dear God! Surely he doesn't think we're having a good time?*

'Well, it's getting late … we should probably go.' Then it occurred to him that Danny felt he should buy a drink because Kit had got the first lot. 'You can get me one another time,' he said.

'Just one more,' Danny persisted, with such an appealing look that Kit couldn't say no, even as his heart sank at the prospect of prolonging this agony. Though why Danny would want to sit here any longer with someone he didn't like and couldn't be bothered to talk to was beyond him.

He watched Danny up at the bar, smiling shyly as the barmaid flirted with him. Poor thing, he thought, she didn't realise she was wasting her time.

Danny returned with the drinks and they both sipped their beers in silence. 'You must find it a big change moving back here after living in New York,' Danny said eventually.

'You can say that again,' Kit said with a wry smile. 'Not what I would have chosen. Still, it's not all bad. I was lucky to bump into Romy again.'

'Yeah. She's a good person to know.'

Was that a dig? Kit wondered. He wasn't sure. He decided to confront it anyway. 'Look, I know you think I'm taking advantage of her, but I'm really not. At least I don't mean to.'

'I'm sure you're not.' Danny smiled. 'Romy kind of invites it – she can't help herself. Anyway, it makes her happy. She likes to help people out, fix things … it's just the way she is.'

As he spoke about his sister, warming to his theme, it struck Kit that Danny wasn't aloof or unfriendly, he was just shy. He looked so like Romy, he thought as he watched him, his face warmed by the alcohol and the flickering firelight. The same thick dark hair, the same big brown eyes framed by long sooty lashes, the same sallow skin. No wonder the barmaid had been trying to chat him up. He was very cute. 'Have you ever been to New York?' he asked.

'Yeah, I went there last year for the first time with Paul – my ex.' A shadow passed across Danny's face momentarily, but he quickly replaced it with a smile. 'It's a fantastic city! I'd love to go back.'

'Pity I didn't know you then. I could have shown you around. So how long were you with Paul?'

'A couple of years. I met him at the Chelsea Flower Show. I had a show garden there. It won silver.'

'Well done,' Kit interjected.

'Thanks. Anyway, I met him there and he was from Dublin, so we got talking, and we went out for dinner together. Then when we got home, he hired me to do his garden.'

'But he didn't just want you to mow his lawn,' Kit drawled.

'Something like that.'

Danny loosened up with the second drink, and the conversation began to flow. His whole face lit up when he told Kit about the garden he had designed and made for Paul, his enthusiasm for his work evident. 'Sorry, this must be really boring for you,' he said finally. 'You're probably not a garden person.'

'No, it's interesting – though I haven't a clue about gardens myself. Couldn't tell a tulip from a turnip. So what happened with Paul?'

Danny shrugged, a hurt look clouding his face. 'He said there wasn't anyone else, but I'm pretty sure there was.'

'Just a general feeling, or do you suspect someone in particular?'

'Someone in particular. What really kills me is they'd never have met if it hadn't been for me. I'd dragged Paul to this gig—'

'What was the gig?' Kit interrupted. He knew that wasn't the right question, but he couldn't help being interested.

'The Rocket Monkeys.'

'Oh my God! I can't believe you even know who they are! You must be one of a handful of people in the world who know them.'

'Well, it's thanks to you that I do,' Danny admitted, blushing. 'I used to listen to those mixed tapes you were always making for Romy.'

'Well, I'm glad *someone* appreciated them. So anyway, you were at this gig …'

'Yeah. Paul wasn't into them at all and only came under protest.'

'Philistine!'

'I know. Anyway, we met this guy there – James. I knew him slightly. He was a friend of a friend of a friend. But Paul had never met him before. I just knew there was something as soon as they met. Paul started acting weird, making out like he was a major Rocket Monkeys fan, like he was trying to impress this guy. And he kept disappearing to the loo and coming back looking all flustered and smelling of booze. Anyway after that night he started acting shifty – working late, cancelling plans at the last minute ... the usual.'

'Well, you're better off without him,' Kit said airily. 'Anyone who doesn't like The Rocket Monkeys ... so what did you think of their latest album?'

'Best thing they've ever done.'

'Is the right answer!' Kit slapped the table enthusiastically. 'Wasn't it fantastic?'

'Yep. Though nothing can beat their gigs. I suppose you've seen them live lots of times?'

'A few, yeah. I caught them in New York last year on the American leg of this tour. So who else do you like?'

'Well, I don't know if you remember a band called Dirt Bikes for the Elderly?'

'That's funny, Romy and I were just talking about them the other day.'

'Really? Well, they've re-formed and they're coming here in January. I have a spare ticket, if you're interested. I was going to bring Paul, but—'

'I'd love to see them!'

'Do you want another drink?' Danny asked, jumping up abruptly.

'Oh, I think it's my turn, isn't it?'

'Well, it's just if you want one, we'd better get it now. It's last orders.'

'Is it?' Kit looked around the pub, which was almost empty, and glanced at his watch. It was almost eleven thirty. 'How on earth did that happen?'

Later, after he had waved Danny off in a taxi and was winding his way homewards somewhat unsteadily, Kit felt a warm glow that wasn't entirely alcohol induced. He was so glad he'd had the initiative to escape from Tank's stag weekend. Otherwise, he would have missed the best night he'd had since moving back to Dublin and he wouldn't have missed tonight for the world, let alone for another night on a godforsaken mountainside with Wedgie offering to start a campfire by lighting his farts.

❋

The next day Ethan dropped by Romy's flat to return Kit's rucksack.

'He's not in downstairs,' he said to Romy, 'so I thought he might be here.'

Ethan had two days' worth of stubble on his face and big bags under his eyes. He looked weary and utterly delicious.

'No, but you can leave it with me. I'll give it to him. The rucksack's mine anyway, and I doubt he'll ever have use for this stuff again.' She took the bag from him and dropped it inside the door. 'I can't believe he took off like that without telling anyone. You must have been going crazy.'

'Nah, I wasn't really worried,' Ethan said, leaning against the door jamb. 'I knew he'd be okay. Kit always lands on his feet.'

Kit was lucky his brother was so laid back, Romy thought. If he'd pulled a stunt like that on her, she'd have been frantic.

'Do you want to come in?'

He hesitated for a moment, then shook his head. 'Better not. I still have to drop one of the other guys off. And Mom will be worrying. She wasn't happy about this adventure weekend at all. She won't relax until we're all home.'

'God, yeah, I can imagine! I know how I'd feel if it was Luke out there fending for himself on some mountain.' She shuddered. It didn't bear thinking about!

'Well, you don't have to worry about that for a few years yet,' Ethan said, smiling.

'No, thank goodness. So was it fun?'

He shrugged. 'Well, Kit ran off, another guy went into anaphylactic shock after eating a berry, Wedgie ended up in hospital and another guy is suffering from hypothermia. But apart from that – yeah, it was great!' he said, widening his eyes enthusiastically.

Romy laughed. 'What happened to Wedgie? Did he break something? Was it Tank?'

'No, nothing like that. He had to go to the burns unit after he tried to start a campfire in an, er, unusual way.'

'Oh! Well, I hope he's okay for the wedding.'

'I'm sure he'll be fine. Though he might not be able to sit down. Don't ask.'

'I don't think I want to know.'

'Well, I'll see you next Saturday, if not before.'

'Okay, see you Saturday.'

Chapter Sixteen

'I hope you don't mind sharing a room,' Kit said for the umpteenth time as they drove down the long tree-lined avenue to the hotel where Hannah's wedding was being held.

'No, not at all,' Romy said with a reassuring smile.

If only he knew! She had no problem with that whatsoever. In fact, it was crucial for her to put her and Lesley's plan into action. The pinwheel was nestling in her suitcase along with the spreader bar, but she was increasingly confident that Kit wouldn't have a clue what they were. Once that test was out of the way, she would move on to phase two of the honey-trap – the vanilla seduction. She had packed her best underwear specially. And who knew where that would lead? *No, I have absolutely no problem with sharing a room.* She looked across at Kit, resisting the urge to do an evil laugh.

'It's a gorgeous setting for a wedding,' she said as she stepped out onto the gravel in front of the hotel and surveyed her surroundings. There were acres of sweeping grounds, dotted with mature trees and benches. The lawn sloped gently downwards from the hotel to a small stream, a little wooden bridge across the water leading to the tiny chapel where Hannah and Tank would be married later that day. The wedding wasn't for another four hours, but they had driven down early to give themselves plenty of time to check in and get changed.

There was a queue at reception, mostly of guests for the wedding, and there were so many burly rugby types that Romy felt like she was in the middle of a scrum. Kit introduced her to the man behind them while they waited, a stocky ruddy-faced man called Peter.

'It's a terrible pity you ran off like that,' Peter said to Kit in an almost impenetrable Limerick accent, his bellowing voice echoing around the entrance hall. 'You missed the best stag do ever. 'Twas mental altogether! You should have stuck around – things really kicked off after you left.'

'I'd already had enough excitement to last me a lifetime.'

'But you missed all the fun. Poor Jack nearly died of anorexic shock from a poison berry, and Ethan had to give him an adrenaline shot. He could have literally died!' From his thrilled tone, this was clearly the highlight of the weekend for him. 'Thank God we had Ethan with us. He's a handy fella, isn't he? I believe he's been away in the jungle.'

'Yeah,' Kit said. 'He's basically Tarzan with a stethoscope.'

'And then Wedgie set his arse on fire. It was brilliant!' Peter's face got even redder as he laughed at the memory of Wedgie's pyrotechnic display. 'Fair play to Wedgie for organising it all.'

'I don't know why he doesn't go into party planning full time,' Kit mumbled to Romy, who suppressed a giggle. 'At least you made it out alive,' he said to Peter.

'Aye, we all did, thank God. Though we had a good few casualties, in fairness.'

'Is Wedgie okay now?' Romy asked him. 'Was he able to come today?'

'Oh yes. He's not the Mae West, but he's here all right.' He craned his neck, looking out to the gardens. 'That's him there,' he said, pointing to a man walking slowly across the grass with a pained expression and a gait like an arthritic John Wayne.

'Ha, so it is!' Kit said, chuckling.

'Hey, that's not nice,' Romy said to him under her breath. 'You shouldn't laugh at his misfortune.'

'It's not misfortune, it's his own bloody stupid fault. Maybe that'll teach him a lesson.'

'Poor Wedgie,' Peter said. 'I think he feels bad about Mick. He's still above in the hospital, the craythur.'

'What happened to *him*?' Romy asked.

'Unfortunately, Wedgie burned down his shelter with one of his farts. Sorry, now,' he said, raising an apologetic hand to Romy, 'but that's the way 'twas. And sure, it was fierce cold out there at night and he'd a lot of drink taken. Anyway, in the heel of the hunt he suffered from exposure and they had to take him to hospital to warm him up.'

'Oh, poor him!' Romy said. Mick must be the hypothermia victim Ethan had mentioned. 'Will he be all right?'

'Arra, he'll be grand. 'Tis an awful pity he had to miss today, but, sure, what can you do?' he said, shaking his head philosophically.

'Not much in the face of Wedgie,' Kit murmured to Romy.

''Twasn't entirely Wedgie's fault. Ethan had warned us

that it wouldn't be a good idea to drink too much, but he went ahead and got locked anyway. Oh, it's your turn,' he said, pointing to the reception desk which was now free. 'I'll see ye later,' he said as they stepped forward to take their turn to check in.

'Wow, good call escaping from that stag,' Romy said as they took their seats in front of the desk.

※

When they had checked in, Kit carried their bags up to the room, dropping them just inside the door. 'I'm just going to check out where everyone else is.' He pulled his mobile from his pocket. 'I'll be back in a sec,' he said, dialling as he went out the door.

Romy did a little internal happy dance as she surveyed the room. She wandered around, exploring the bathroom and checking out the TV, room service menu and mini-bar, then threw herself on the big double bed, spreading her limbs out in a starfish shape and grinning to herself. She loved hotel rooms, and this one was lovely. And much as she missed Luke, she was going to make the most of having some time to herself – and some time alone with Kit. Maybe she would even get to have sex tonight in this bed. After all, as Lesley had pointed out, it would be mean to get him all worked up and then not follow through. She hugged herself, her stomach tingling with a mixture of nervousness and excitement at the thought. It had been way too long.

She got up and moved to the deep window seat overlooking the lawn. People who she assumed were wedding guests, judging by their attire, were already starting to mill around outside. A winter wedding was always difficult to dress for, but most of them seemed to have pulled it off admirably, achieving the difficult combination of warmth and glamour. There were just a handful of girls who had refused to make any concession to the weather and sported pale, goose-pimpled limbs, visibly shivering in their thin dresses as they huddled into inadequate wraps and tried to look comfortable.

'Right,' Kit said, coming back into the room and pulling her from her people-watching, 'I've got everyone's room numbers. Ethan and Sinead are just next door, and everyone else is somewhere along this corridor. Apart from Hannah and Tank, of course. They're in the bridal suite.'

'Makes sense,' she said, turning from the window.

'Hey, why is it called the bridal suite?' Kit asked, frowning. 'Why not the groomal suite? Or just the wedding suite?'

'The bride always gets top billing at a wedding.'

'That's not fair! It's discrimination,' he mumbled as he picked up Romy's case and put it on the luggage stand. He placed his own flat on the floor and zipped it open. 'Right, we'd better get this show on the road,' he said, hanging his suit carrier in the wardrobe. 'They've already started drinking without us. We'll never catch up if we don't get a move on.'

'Okay.' Romy hopped off the window seat. 'Do you want to go first?' she asked, waving towards the bathroom.

'I don't mind. Whichever you prefer.'

'Yeah, you go first. Then I can take my time.'

She opened her suitcase and pretended to be engrossed in unpacking while Kit stripped down to his boxers before heading into the bathroom, though she did allow herself a surreptitious peek as she hung her dress in the wardrobe. He was certainly fit, she thought, checking out his taut stomach, long muscled legs and broad chest that still bore the traces of a golden tan. Once he was in the bathroom, she took out the pinwheel and spreader bar from the depths of her case and laid them carefully on top, leaving the case open so that Kit would see them. Now all she had to do was wait.

✳

And wait, she thought later as she lay on the bed and watched Kit move around the room as he dressed. He had emerged from the bathroom after about half an hour in a cloud of citrusy-smelling steam and she had been waiting patiently for him to notice the sex toys ever since. He had to pass right by her case every time he went to the wardrobe or dresser, but he was lacing his shoes now and he still hadn't noticed them. Unless he had, and wasn't saying anything because he didn't know what they were. Or because he did … She was just going to have to draw his attention to them deliberately.

'Could you help me with these?' he asked, coming over to her and holding out a pair of cufflinks in his strong, tanned hands.

She sat up and fastened the cufflinks in the stiff cuffs of his snowy white shirt, breathing in the delicious male scent of his aftershave. He looked so gorgeous. She really hoped he wasn't a fan of the kinky stuff – or gay. She thought about that night in the cupboard. Gay my arse! she snorted to herself. Darth Vader was no stranger to shagging women. But this was her chance to find out what made him tick – she had to make the most of the opportunity. She needed to get the kink out of the way so she could move on to phase two of the plan.

Kit went to the mirror to knot his tie and she noticed that his hair was already dry. 'Why don't I go downstairs so you can have the room to yourself, and then you can join me whenever you're ready?' he said as he finished with his tie and took his jacket from the wardrobe.

It was now or never. 'Okay,' she said, hopping off the bed

and going over to her case. She had to act fast. She began unpacking make-up and jewellery and piling them onto the dressing table. 'God, how on earth did *that* get into my case?' she said, slinging the little pinwheel onto the pile.

To her relief, Kit took the bait. 'What is it anyway?' he asked, picking it up and looking at it curiously.

'Oh, it's just … a massager,' she said, taking it from him and rolling it along her arm to demonstrate.

'Really? Looks painful.'

'Yes,' she said, smiling to herself. 'Doesn't it just?' One test down, and Kit had passed with flying colours. But she wanted to make sure.

'I don't know what I was thinking when I packed,' she mumbled, lifting the spreader bar from her case. 'I must have been half asleep. I certainly didn't mean to bring this!' She held it up to Kit, laughing at her own absent-mindedness.

'What the hell is it?' he asked, taking it from her hands, screwing his face up in confusion as he pulled at the straps.

'Oh, it's just … er … an exercise thing,' she said, making an effort to sound casual. 'It's for toning your abdominals.'

'Well, you won't be needing that this weekend, will you?'

'No, I certainly won't,' she said, taking it from him and throwing it back into the case. Or ever, she thought to herself.

'Well, I'll see you down in the bar.' He bent to the mirror to give his hair a final flick. 'Call me if you need anything,' he said, straightening up.

Romy waited until she was sure he was safely down the hall before doing a little victory dance.

'Yes!' she shouted, punching the air with her fist. She was relieved she wouldn't have to consider BDSM if she wanted to be with Kit. Now she just had to rule out the gay thing. She raced around the room excitedly, stripping off and laying out her prettiest underwear on the bed. 'I did the right thing bringing you,' she said, smiling down at it smugly. 'Let phase two of the honey-trap commence!'

Before heading for the bathroom, she grabbed her mobile and sent Lesley a text: 'Vanilla seduction is go.'

✳

'Wow, you look amazing,' Kit said when she found him in the bar, his eyes raking over her appreciatively.

She had gone all out and she knew she looked good. Her purple crushed velvet dress and soft suede boots were sexy without sacrificing warmth and comfort, and her long dark hair fell in soft snaky curls around her shoulders.

'Thanks,' she said.

'Let me get you a drink. Champagne?'

'Yes, please.'

Kit was standing with his father and brother, and a pretty redhead who stood beside Ethan – presumably his date. All the Masterson men were sporting snowy white shirts for once. Tuxedos really did something for men. They all looked really well, Romy thought, as she looked around the circle, her eyes lingering on Ethan, but he was … breathtaking.

'I went for white today, Romy,' Colm said, pointing to his shirt. 'Father of the bride – had to be done.'

'Sometimes you have to go with tradition,' she said, smiling at him. 'Where's Laura?'

'She's up helping Hannah get ready.'

'Romy, this is Sinead,' Ethan said, introducing the girl at his side.

'Hi, nice to meet you,' Sinead said, smiling as they shook hands. She had merry eyes and dimpled cheeks in a pale freckled face, and she looked like fun and trouble.

'Here you go,' Kit said, returning and handing her a glass

of champagne. His arm snaked around her waist and he pulled her into his side.

'Thanks.' She put her free arm around his back, blushing as she caught Ethan watching the movement closely. But that was ridiculous – why should she feel guilty for putting her arm around her boyfriend? She felt as if Ethan had caught her out in a lie – which technically, she supposed, he had, since Kit wasn't really her boyfriend. Not yet. But that could be about to change.

✳

Twenty minutes before the ceremony was due to start, the guests were invited to take their places in the chapel, and they tottered across the lawn in varying degrees of inebriation, some still carrying champagne glasses with them. One woman got stuck in the grass and just stayed put, laughing maniacally until her partner came to haul her out. Spindly heels, soft earth and too much champagne were not a good combination.

'Sinead seems nice,' Romy commented to Kit as they walked arm in arm towards the chapel. Romy had discovered that Sinead was a journalist who had met Ethan when she was doing a feature on volunteer workers. She had kept them entertained with wildly indiscreet stories about various celebrities and politicians that had never made it into the press.

'Yeah, she's great,' Kit said. 'But don't get too attached.'

'Why? Do you not think Ethan's that keen on her?'

'I'm sure he likes her as well as the next girl, but he doesn't usually stay with one person for long. Wouldn't be fair on the next girl.'

'Huh!' She looked ahead at Ethan, who was crossing the

little wooden bridge now, his arm around Sinead. He seemed far too nice to be such a man-whore.

'He's very nice to all his girlfriends,' Kit said, as if he had read her thoughts. 'He just likes to spread himself around. It's fairer that way. Everyone gets a turn.'

'Very nice of him, I'm sure,' Romy said archly.

'Anyway, Sinead's well able to take care of herself.'

Romy could believe that. She certainly didn't seem the needy type.

'She doesn't take it seriously any more than he does. I think they're fuck buddies more than anything – friends with benefits. It's the way they do things nowadays, apparently.'

Romy sighed. 'Kids these days,' she said, shaking her head. 'I don't get the whole friends with benefits thing. Do you?'

'Well, it's not for old fogeys like us,' he said, giving her a squeeze. 'Ethan's young, he likes girls. There's nothing wrong with that. It's normal at his age to put yourself about a bit.'

'I suppose.'

'Ethan doesn't sweat the small stuff,' Kit said as they crossed the bridge, which was decorated with flowers and ribbons wound around its wooden posts. 'Maybe it's something to do with the work he's been doing, the places he's been. I guess it makes you realise what's important. All this worrying about who's shagging who, or "where's this relationship going" must seem like so much toss when you've seen people struggling just to survive.'

Romy looked at him, surprised at this defence of his brother. Usually, he was more than happy for an opportunity to slag him off. 'So, women are "the small stuff"?' she said indignantly.

'No, that's not what I meant. But sex … people make too much of a big deal out of it. It doesn't have to be that complicated. You eat, you sleep, you shag – it's simple.'

Romy rolled her eyes. 'You're such a romantic!' she said as they stepped into the chapel.

✳

It was working, Romy thought that evening as Kit took her hand and led her to the dance floor.

Stage one of the vanilla seduction was going brilliantly – no doubt aided by the hearts and flowers theme of the day. After all, if you couldn't get off with someone at a wedding, when could you?

It had been a perfect day. The ceremony was lovely, the pews of the little chapel adorned with ribbons and flowers. Hannah was a stunning bride, and Colm beamed with pride as he walked her down the aisle. Tank was surprisingly emotional, his voice hoarse with tears as he took his vows, while Laura beamed and cried at the same time, glowing with happiness.

After a champagne reception in a lovely old galleried hall, they sat down to dinner in the sumptuous banqueting room. Romy and Kit were seated with Ethan and Sinead, and Peter, who they had met in reception, and his mousy wife Mary. The food was delicious, the champagne and wine flowed, and the company was fun. Even Kit had to admit that Wedgie made a very funny speech – with anecdotes from the stag do providing plenty of material – but he still smirked as Wedgie finished and lowered himself gingerly back into his chair with a pained wince as he passed the mic.

Romy felt lit from within. Kit had hardly been able to keep his hands off her all through dinner, constantly touching her leg, stroking her hair, or dropping little kisses on her cheek. Now he was pulling her into his arms and they began swaying softly to the music. She melted against him, breathing in the male smell of him as he laid his cheek against hers, and sighed contentedly. Kit had passed the gay test with flying colours, and she felt sure that this lovely day was going to end with delicious, vanilla-flavoured sex.

As the band began playing a recent hit with a salsa beat, Kit began to dance properly, spinning her away from him and pulling her back to wrap his arms around her, twirling her around, his legs moving between hers, their limbs entangling and their hips bumping as they moved in perfect harmony. She had forgotten how nice it was to dance with someone who knew what they were doing. She felt graceful, elegant and sexy as she glided and spun. And she definitely felt turned on as Kit's strong, hard body crashed against hers.

The party was winding down and many of the guests were starting to drift towards their rooms. Peter and Mary had already left when Kit and Romy returned to their table. Ethan had pulled Sinead onto his lap and they were wrapped around each other, kissing and talking, smiling into each other's eyes. Ethan couldn't seem to stop touching her, running the back of his hand down her bare arm, or stroking the hair back from her face while he gazed at her like she was the most fascinating woman in the world. They both seemed oblivious to the presence of anyone else. Was that really just sex? Romy wondered. She felt Kit's hand on her shoulder and jolted. She turned towards him, and then he was pulling her into his arms, his lips descending to hers.

He was still one of the best kissers of all time, she thought, as their mouths moved together. Kit's tongue ran along her bottom lip and she opened her mouth to his, their tongues tangling as the kiss deepened. It was soft and wet, and luscious as chocolate, and Romy couldn't get enough. She wanted more and more, her fingers clutching needily in the short hair at the nape of Kit's neck.

Finally, Kit pulled away gently, but only just enough so that he could speak. He was still so close she could feel his breath on her face when he murmured, 'Do you want to go upstairs?'

'Oh yes!' Romy nodded eagerly, not caring if she looked desperate. She was!

'Are you sure?' He glanced across at Ethan and Sinead before bending to whisper in her ear 'You don't have to come up now if you don't want to. If you're not ready to leave the party—'

'No, I am!' she assured him, afraid he would change his mind.

'You sure?'

'Absolutely.' She grinned and bent to kiss him again.

'Okay, then,' Kit said, standing and pulling her up. 'We're going to call it a night,' he said to Ethan.

Romy had forgotten Ethan and Sinead were still there. She looked across at them now and found Ethan looking at her with a strange expression on his face that she couldn't make out, but that appeared oddly like a mixture of bafflement and concern. She couldn't understand why he would be staring at her like that, but it left her feeling off-kilter. Still, it only niggled at her consciousness for a fleeting moment as they said their goodnights. She was far too anxious to get upstairs with Kit to worry about it.

They took their leave of Hannah and Tank, Tank now obviously feeling that he knew Romy well enough to grab her in a half nelson and rub her head so vigorously that she felt her neck might snap.

'It's just his way of showing affection,' Hannah said to her when Tank had released her and turned his attention to sparring goodbye to Kit. 'It means he likes you.'

'It was such a lovely day,' Romy said. 'Congratulations again.'

Hannah pulled her into a heartfelt hug, but as she let her go, something passed across her face that reminded Romy of the look Ethan had just given her.

She brushed it aside as Kit took her hand, his fingers interlacing with hers as they made their way out of the room. She wanted to scream every time they were stopped by someone wanting to talk to them on their way to the door. Kit's little touches were the only thing just about keeping her grounded, his thumb stroking over the back of her hand or his arm wrapping around her, squeezing her to his side as they made small talk. Still, she was in a frenzy of desire by the time they made it out to the lobby and were finally heading for the lifts, the throb of music fading behind them.

This was it, Romy thought as Kit pressed the button for the lift, his other arm going around her and pulling her closer as they waited. She knew something was going to happen, excitement curling deep in her stomach as they stepped into the lift. Kit pushed the button for their floor and she turned to him, expecting him to kiss her as soon as the doors closed. Instead, he released her hand as the doors swished shut and leaned back against the wall of the lift, putting a little more distance between their bodies.

Romy tried to quell the crushing disappointment she felt. He probably didn't want to start shagging her in the lift like some movie cliché. He was right, she told herself, it was better to wait until they got to the room. Once they were safely behind closed doors, they could really let it rip. She was an adult. She could wait a few minutes to be ravished, though she was practically hopping from foot to foot as she counted off the numbers of the floors. Thank goodness it was a low building!

Kit walked ahead of her down the corridor and slipped the keycard into the door, and she followed behind, fully expecting him to grab her as soon as they got inside. Kit closed the door and slid the keycard into the slot for the lights, then threw himself on the bed with a loud exhale.

'Well, that went well, I thought,' he said, leaning against the headboard with his hands behind his head, his legs stretched out in front of him. 'Did you enjoy yourself?'

'Yeah, it was great,' Romy mumbled, thrown off by Kit's sudden change of demeanour. Downstairs, he had seemed ready to devour her. It was like he couldn't wait to get her up here alone and start ripping their clothes off. Now he was lying there on the bed and she was standing stupidly by the door not knowing what to do with herself, all worked up with nowhere to go. How did that happen?

'Do you want to go to bed right away?' he asked, sitting up to remove his jacket and slinging it on the end of the bed.

Romy hesitated, not sure how to answer that. There was nothing seductive in the way he asked and, somehow, she got the feeling that he wasn't suggesting sex. She just wanted to get back to where they'd been before they came upstairs. 'I'm not that tired,' she said. 'I just need to get out of these boots and into something more comfortable.' Yes, that was it! She would 'slip into something more comfortable' – the oldest, corniest seduction trick in the book.

'Great! Fancy something from the mini bar?' Kit asked, getting off the bed and opening the little fridge.

'Mmm, I'll have a bottle of white wine if there's one in there,' she said, taking off her boots and sighing with relief as her feet sank into the soft, thick carpet. 'Could you help me with the zip on this?' she asked, going to where he was hunkered down by the mini bar and turning her back to him, sweeping her hair out of the way over one shoulder.

'Sure.' She felt him stand behind her, and then his fingers barely touching her as he slid the zip down, stopping at the small of her back, though it went right down to the top of her bum.

'Thanks.' She stood still for a moment, hoping to feel his hands on her bare skin as he turned her around and pulled her into his arms.

'Pinot Grigio or Sauvignon Blanc?'

She turned to find him hunkered down again, peering into the fridge.

'Um … Pinot Grigio, please,' she mumbled. And a bucket of cold water, she added in her head. Maybe there would be some ice in there that she could throw over herself. 'Well, I'll just … get changed,' she said, heading for the bathroom.

Once inside, she leaned on the sink surround, her head in her hands, and wondered where it had all gone wrong. Had she misread the signals? There was no doubt that Kit had been blatantly flirting with her all night, but maybe that was just how he was. Or was he simply doing it to keep up the pretence that they were a couple? Yet it had felt so real … she couldn't believe she had imagined the desire in his eyes and the passion of his kisses. Then, suddenly, she remembered his promise that he would be a gentleman and keep his hands off her while they shared a room. Could that be what was holding him back? If so, she just needed to show him that she was up for it. There was only one thing for it.

She wasn't going to let this hotel room or her sexy underwear go to waste without a fight. She had to give this vanilla seduction one last try. She stripped off her dress and looked at herself in the mirror, piling her hair up on top of her head and trying out a sexy pout. Damn it, she looked hot. And Kit was a man. He was hardly going to refuse sex if she offered herself to him on a plate, was he?

Taking a deep breath, she opened the door and walked back into the bedroom. Kit was lying on the bed, flicking through the channels on the TV. He had removed his shoes and tie, and his shirt was open halfway down.

'I've poured your wine,' he said, patting the bed beside him without taking his eyes off the TV.

Romy crawled onto the bed. 'Thanks,' she said, reaching for the glass on the nightstand. The wine was lovely and cold and she gulped a mouthful gratefully. Then she put the glass down and very slowly and deliberately leaned down and kissed Kit on the lips.

'Oh.' He pecked her lips in return and finally dragged his eyes from the TV and turned to look at her, his eyes widening as he took in her underwear. 'Didn't you bring anything to sleep in?'

'Well, I …'

'Why don't you get in?' he said, pulling back the duvet and patting the space beside him. 'You'll get cold.'

Romy got into the bed uncertainly and Kit piled up pillows behind her, smiling at her as he tucked the duvet around her until she was mummified up to her neck. 'There, that's better, isn't it?'

He turned his attention back to the TV, oblivious to Romy's dismay at suddenly finding herself bundled up like a toddler. 'Oh look, *Friends*,' he said. 'Want to watch that?'

'Sure.'

As the familiar theme tune filled the room, he put his arm around her and pulled her close, snuggling her against him as he relaxed back against the pillows with a satisfied sigh. 'This is just like old times, isn't it?' he said.

'Yeah,' Romy said weakly, returning his smile. But it wasn't. It was nothing like old times.

Chapter Seventeen

Romy woke early the next morning, feeling restless and edgy. After Kit had joined her in bed last night, she had lain awake for what felt like hours, twitching with frustration. She had slept fitfully, the events of the evening on a constant loop in her brain. Her mind raced as she went over what had happened again and again, and tried to figure out what it meant.

Kit was still sleeping peacefully beside her, snoring gently. She picked up her phone from the nightstand and checked the time. It was only seven-thirty, and it would probably be hours yet before anyone else surfaced, but there was no chance of getting back to sleep. She was too fidgety to stay in bed any longer so she decided to get up and go for a walk. She needed exercise to calm her thoughts and to work off some of her pent-up energy and frustration. A shower could wait until later, she thought, pulling back the duvet and sliding out of bed – she didn't want to risk waking Kit by rattling around in the bathroom. She dressed quickly in the dark, relieved to be back in the comfort of jeans and a sweatshirt after glamming it up yesterday. Then she let herself out of the room quietly and walked down the hushed corridor.

Outside, it was a beautiful crisp winter's morning, the grass dusted with a light coating of sparkling frost that shone in the darkness. She set off at a fast pace across the lawn away from the hotel, feeling better already as she breathed in lungfuls of the fresh morning air. There was no one around and she relished the feeling of having the world to herself for a while. Her mind wandered as she walked, her thoughts soon drifting back to the previous night and Kit.

How could she have got it so wrong? Chuckling to herself, she thought of her efforts to seduce him with her sexy underwear, only to have him smother her in bedclothes and cosy up with her to watch TV, completely immune to her semi-naked charms. When Kit had asked her to be his fake girlfriend, he had meant it. He just wanted her as camouflage. Last night he had been playing a part, and he had assumed she was too. He just happened to be very convincing, and somewhere along the way she had forgotten they were faking it and had let her libido run away with her.

Now in the calm of the morning, she was able to get some perspective. She could even see the funny side – though she still cringed a little at her ridiculous attempts to get off with him. God, what had she been thinking? At least she'd ruled out the BDSM thing. But the vanilla seduction had been a total bust. Did that mean Kit was gay? She knew Lesley would think so, but Lesley hadn't spent a night with him in a wardrobe. Maybe he was bisexual …

Anyway, it didn't matter, she thought, as she started heading back towards the hotel. Though one thing was for sure – whatever Kit was into, he wasn't interested in doing it with her. So that was that. At least she knew where she stood, and she found she didn't mind. Some sex would have been nice, but other than that … she realised she just didn't feel that way about Kit anymore.

It was light by the time she retraced her steps, the sun bright in a clear blue sky. Following the stream, she came to the little wooden bridge leading to the chapel. A few ribbons still clung to its posts, fluttering in the light morning breeze. As she turned in the direction of the hotel, she realised she wasn't the only person up and about. A lone figure was sitting on one of the benches across from the bridge. He was bent over, his arms resting on his knees, but as she drew closer, she saw that it was Ethan. He looked up as she approached.

'Good morning.' He smiled up at her, shielding his eyes from the low sun.

'Morning.' She slid onto the bench beside him.

'You're up early,' he commented.

'Yeah, I didn't sleep very well.'

'Are you okay?' he asked, studying her face intently.

'Yes, I'm fine,' she said, brushing off his concern. 'I guess it's just sleeping in a strange bed, and missing Luke.' She couldn't very well tell him the real reason – sexual frustration, head spinning after your brother rejected my advances. 'So what's your excuse?'

He shrugged. 'I woke up early and couldn't get back to sleep, so I went for a run.'

'Wow, that was very energetic of you. Kit's still sleeping like the dead – at least, he was when I got up.'

'Yeah, Sinead's the same.'

Literally shagged out probably, Romy thought, after a

thorough seeing-to last night. Lucky thing! 'So, it was a good night last night, wasn't it?' she said, drawing her feet up onto the bench and wrapping her arms around her knees.

'It was. Though I have one major regret.'

'Oh? What's that?'

'That I didn't get to dance with you.'

'Oh! Yeah, that was a startling omission.'

'It really was. My younger self would be disgusted with me for letting the opportunity go by.' He shook his head ruefully.

'That's very sweet of him. But maybe it's just as well. Your girlfriend mightn't have been too happy about it.'

'Sinead? She's not the jealous type. Anyway, she's not my girlfriend. She's just ... someone I hang out with.'

'And you hang out with her in bed?'

His answer was a sheepish grin. 'Sometimes.'

She grinned back, rolling her eyes. 'Anyway, I hope your younger self isn't too upset with you.'

'Oh, he is. He's outraged. You were in my top three, you know.'

She smiled. 'Wow, I'm flattered.'

'Yep, you were up there with Jennifer Aniston and Lara Croft.'

'In what order?'

'First you, then Jennifer, then Lara.'

'You don't have to say I was number one just because I'm here. I can handle losing out to those two.'

'No, it's true. That was the order.'

'I can't believe Lara Croft came last! I'm impressed. That seems very mature of you.'

'Well, I think it went in order of realness. Lara was really fit, obviously—'

'Obviously.'

'Very hot. But she was just a graphic image. Jennifer Aniston is a real person—'

'But you only ever saw her on TV.'

'Exactly. Whereas *you*,' he said, eyeballing her, 'you were a real live girl, walking around our house in 3D. I could speak to you and you'd answer me! It was very exciting.' He shook his head, smiling.

Romy laughed. 'Well, I can see why your younger self would be mad at you.'

'He may never forgive me.'

'I wish there was some way we could make it up to him.'

'Maybe there is,' he said, getting up off the bench. He stood in front of her and held out his hand.

'What? You want to dance? Here?' She looked around. There was still no one else outside.

'Why not?' He grinned.

She wasn't exactly dressed for dancing – but then neither was he.

'Come on, this is a big deal for me,' he said when she hesitated. 'Imagine if you got to be with someone from your laminated list.'

'Well, when you put it like that …' She took his hand and stood up slowly. 'We don't have any music.'

'Ah!' he said, raising a finger in the air. He dug into his pocket with his other hand and pulled out an iPod.

'Very smooth,' Romy said while he turned it on and began scrolling through songs. 'Young Ethan would be proud. You might redeem yourself in his eyes yet. Or maybe not,' she added, giggling as he took ages to choose a track.

'Don't rush me, woman,' he growled. 'This is a big moment for me. It has to be right.'

Romy dug her hands into her pockets and waited.

'Okay, here we go.' He stretched out the earphones, and placed one of the buds in his ear and the other in hers. Then he took one of her hands, placing his other hand on her waist, and raised his eyebrows questioningly.

Romy nodded, wrapping her free arm around his back as the opening bars of REM's 'I've Been High' filled her head. 'I love this song,' she said.

'I'm not a very good dancer, by the way,' he whispered quickly as they began to move slowly together.

'That's okay.'

They looked at each other in silence as they shuffled around on the grass, occasionally exchanging little smiles. As the music swelled, Ethan let go of her hand, wrapping his arms around her and pulling her close. Romy laid her head against the solid wall of his chest with a contented sigh. As she relaxed against his body, she forgot their surroundings, losing herself in the music and just enjoying the feel of Ethan's arms around her. She didn't want it to end.

When the music stopped, they stood in each other's arms for a moment, still connected by the thin wire of the headphones, neither of them moving to pull away. Romy lifted her head with difficulty. She felt like she was just waking up from a lovely sleep.

'Damn,' Ethan breathed, 'I should have picked a longer song.' He shot her a look that made her breath hitch.

God, he was an accomplished flirt, Romy thought. No wonder he'd got so many girls lining up to sleep with him. 'Well, that was … nice,' she said softly, pulling away. 'Do you think your younger self is appeased?'

'Yes, I think he's pretty chuffed with me right now.' He smiled smugly, gently removing the earphones before releasing her. 'Thank you.' He dropped a kiss on her forehead.

'You're welcome.' She shoved her hands in her pockets, suddenly feeling awkward. 'Well, I suppose I should go and have a shower.'

'Yeah, me too,' he said, but made no move to go.

Finally she turned to leave, but he stopped her with a hand on her elbow. 'Romy, can I ask you something?'

'Sure.'

He swallowed hard, appearing nervous. 'You and Kit …' he began hesitantly, and Romy's heart plummeted. 'You're not really together, are you?'

'What?' She looked at him sharply. 'What makes you say that?'

'That's not an answer.'

'I said you could ask me a question. I didn't say I'd answer it.'

'Hmm. I think maybe you just did,' he said with a gentle smile.

'No! I didn't—' she started to protest, but she was interrupted by his phone chiming with a text alert. He pulled it out of his pocket to read the message.

Damn! Why hadn't she just automatically said that of course she and Kit were together? She could have said that they'd slept together last night and it wouldn't even have been a lie. Instead, she'd increased his suspicions. But he'd caught her off guard. It was one thing pretending to be Kit's girlfriend, but she hadn't been prepared to be called out on it. She had no idea that Ethan wasn't buying it – or Hannah, she guessed. That would explain the strange looks they'd been giving her, and their whispered words on Thanksgiving. They knew she was a fake girlfriend, just like Lauren and the others before her.

'Sinead,' he said, waving the phone at her before shoving it back in his pocket. 'Everyone's meeting for breakfast in about half an hour. We'd better go and get ready.'

They walked back to the hotel in silence, Romy frantically scrabbling around in her brain for something she could say to allay his suspicions. If she was too defensive, it would just have the opposite effect, but she needed to say something. She felt she had let Kit down.

'Ethan,' she began as they got to their floor and were about to part ways. 'What you said—'

'Forget it,' he said, shaking his head. 'I'm sorry, I shouldn't have said anything. I'll see you at breakfast.'

'Yeah, see you.' She felt deflated that she wasn't going to get to say her piece – though she still wasn't sure exactly what she would have said.

'And thank you for the dance,' he said before turning and striding down the corridor to his own room.

✳

Kit was up and dressed when Romy got back to the room. She felt she should tell him what Ethan had asked her, but she couldn't bring herself to do it. He was so happy that they were fooling everyone, and she didn't want to upset him by telling him otherwise – not yet anyway. They went down to breakfast together after she had showered and dressed, joining Ethan and Sinead, who were already seated at a large table. Other members of the wedding party gradually filtered in to join them.

Kit was as attentive to her as he had been the previous night, back in the role of solicitous boyfriend now that they were in public again, but Romy felt horribly self-conscious, aware of Ethan and Hannah watching them and not buying it. She was glad now that she hadn't told Kit. She would hate him to feel as embarrassed and uncomfortable as she did. It wasn't just knowing that Ethan and Hannah suspected their relationship was bogus; she felt awful about deceiving Laura and Colm, and it gave her no satisfaction that they were taken in by her and Kit's act. It was different when she thought they might get together for real. Now that she knew that wasn't going to happen, she felt very awkward playing his girlfriend in front of them, and much as she loved them, she was anxious to get away.

There was also the fact that her behaviour around Ethan was becoming worryingly crush-like. She found her eyes constantly straying in his direction throughout breakfast, and she didn't even want to name the emotion she felt as he fussed over Sinead. Their dance on the lawn hadn't helped, bringing a warm, fuzzy feeling every time she thought of it. Sinead looked rested and well taken care of, Romy thought with a pang of resentment. And she seemed to have worked up a gargantuan appetite, putting away vast quantities of food, Ethan smiling indulgently at her as he passed her yet more soda bread.

All things considered, she was itching to get away, so when Laura invited her to dinner at their house later on, she didn't hesitate to decline.

'Thanks,' she said, 'but I really need to get home and collect Luke from Danny's.' She was looking forward to having a quiet night in with her son. It was amazing how much she'd missed him, even though she had only been away for one night.

'Oh, is Danny babysitting him?' Kit asked. 'I thought it was your mum.'

'No, mum's away on holiday at the moment – in Egypt.'

'Oh, right.'

'She'll be back next week, though, so she'll take him when we go down to the house.' Romy had decided they should fix up the gate lodge first so it was fit for her and Luke to move into before starting work on the main house. It wouldn't take much to make it liveable, and it was all work they could do themselves, which would save money for the rest of the renovations. She had suggested organising a working party for the following weekend, roping in as many people as they could to help so that they could get the work done quickly.

'Fancy a weekend in the country?' Kit asked Sinead now. 'Unlimited fresh air in exchange for a lot of hard work.'

'You're not selling it properly,' Romy said to him. 'You didn't even mention the beer. There'll be beer,' she said to Sinead. 'And wine. It'll be fun.'

'Next weekend? It sounds great, but I'll be in Paris.'

'Oh, shame. That makes Ethan my only recruit,' he said to Romy.

'You're coming?' Romy asked Ethan.

'Yeah, definitely.'

'He's not starting his new job until January, so he's going to help us with the house,' Kit told her.

'Oh?' Romy said to Ethan. 'Have you got skills?'

'I'm a pretty decent carpenter,' he said. 'And I'm good at the general grunt work.'

'Oh God,' Kit groaned, 'don't get him started on his time building houses in South Africa.'

'You did?' Sinead looked at him in surprise. 'I never knew that.'

'It was just a volunteer thing I did in my gap year.'

'It's a pity Tank will be away on honeymoon,' Kit said. 'He'd be good at the demolition side of things.'

'I thought I'd ask Danny to come,' Romy said to Kit. 'He could take a look at the grounds, maybe make a plan for the gardens.'

'That'd be brilliant! We can ask him when we go to collect Thingummy.'

'*We*? Aren't you going to dinner at your parents'?' Laura had a big family get-together planned with some of the relations who had come to the wedding and she had assumed Kit would be going.

'Well, since *you're* not, I thought I should spend the night with you and—'

'Luke.'

'Yeah. I mean, I'm sort of his dad now, amn't I?'

'What do you mean?' Romy looked at him aghast, her heart hammering. How could he have found out?

'Well, you know, because we're … going out together. That sort of makes me his father, doesn't it?'

'Er … no. It really doesn't.'

'Okay, stepdad.'

'Still no.'

'Isn't the mother's boyfriend usually called a stepdad?'

'Maybe if they're living together. Certainly not when they've only been going out for about a week.'

'Oh. Still, I'm sort of the father figure in his life now, amn't I? He's a boy – he needs a male role model.'

Romy smiled, glad that Kit was so willing to be part of Luke's life. Even if they weren't going to be together, she felt he would be a good father to Luke. 'Well, there's plenty of time for that. He's only four months old. You should go for dinner with your family tonight. You can show him how to be a man another time.'

'Oh. Okay.'

'And see who else you can rope in for next weekend,' Romy said. 'Call in all your favours.'

'I don't really have any to call in.'

'Don't worry,' she said, smiling. 'I have loads.'

❋

'It'll be fun,' she said to Lesley the next day when she dropped in for coffee. 'Road trip, a weekend in the country, lots of wine. We'll bring sleeping bags and camp out indoors.'

'Does it count as a road trip if you're only going to Wicklow?'

'We'll be driving there. On the road.'

'Fair enough. Will I be able to smash stuff up?' Lesley asked.

'You can smash stuff up and tear stuff down to your heart's content.'

A little smile curled at the edges of Lesley's mouth. 'Can I have a lump hammer?'

'Of course you can have a lump hammer. I'll reserve one just for you.'

'Right, I'm in.' She shook her head ruefully at Romy. 'You know all my weaknesses.'

'I do. Resistance is futile.'

'So anyway, tell me all about the weekend. How did the vanilla seduction go?'

'It was a total bust.'

'What?' Lesley shrieked. 'When I didn't hear from you, I assumed … what happened?'

'Nothing,' Romy said flatly. 'Absolutely bugger all.'

'Wait,' Lesley said, grabbing Romy's arm and pulling her up.

'Where are we going?'

'To the incident nook,' Lesley said, dragging Romy into the study and over to the whiteboard in the corner.

Romy glanced at the board. It had changed since the last time she saw it. Now the Darth Vader in the centre had Kit's face stuck on. On one side was written 'BDSM' with a picture of a butt plug taped beneath it, on the other 'Vanilla' with a picture of an ice-cream cone, and at the bottom was the word 'Gay' with a picture of Elton John.

'Okay,' Lesley said, folding her arms, 'tell me everything. He didn't recognise the sex toys?' She pointed to the butt plug.

'No. He obviously had no idea what they were. He's definitely not into BDSM.'

'So you proceeded to phase two – the vanilla seduction.' She waved at the ice-cream cone.

'Yes, and it seemed to be going really well. He was all over me at the reception, and I got quite, you know, wound up. But then when we went back to the room, it was like he threw a switch and just turned it off.'

'Did you show him your underwear?'

'Yes! At first, I thought maybe he was trying to be a gentleman and didn't think I'd be up for it.'

'But you put him straight on that?'

'Definitely.'

'And there's no way he could have misread your signals? You know, there's such a thing as too subtle. Sometimes, you can err on the side of Doris Day.'

'I crawled on top of him wearing practically nothing and started kissing him.'

'Nice move – very proactive.'

'Thank you.'

'And what did he do?'

'He – he *tucked me in*!'

'He did *what*?'

'He said I'd get cold and I should get into bed. And then he tucked me in, and we watched TV.'

'You're joking!'

'No.'

Lesley looked at Romy in silence, chewing her lip. 'That's it, then – he's gay,' she said finally.

'But he's not! I used to go out with him, remember?'

'That doesn't mean anything. Lots of gay men start out with girlfriends. Elton, if you remember,' she said, rapping her knuckles on his picture, 'even had a wife at one point.'

'I suppose.' Romy frowned, struggling to get her head around the idea.

'Look at the facts.' Lesley turned to the whiteboard. 'He's not kinky,' she said, pulling off the picture of the butt plug. 'He's not vanilla.' She removed the ice-cream cone. 'What does that leave?'

Romy looked at the board. 'Elton John,' she said. 'He's Elton John.'

'You jumped him in your underwear and he tucked you into bed, for feck's sake! What more proof do you need?'

'It was really nice underwear too,' Romy mused.

'I'm sure it was.'

'But that doesn't necessarily mean he's gay. Maybe he just doesn't fancy me.'

'I've seen you in your underwear. It's not you, it's him.'

The more Romy thought about it, the more obvious it seemed. Except ... 'He wasn't gay that night at David's party.'

'Well ... maybe that was a once-off for him. Or he could swing both ways. Look, why don't I put a tail on him so we'll know for sure?' Lesley said.

'No, don't do that. What does it matter? Anyway, he's entitled to his secrets.' If he *were* gay, Kit clearly didn't want anyone to know – including her.

'So, what happens now?' Lesley asked.

'Now I have to tell him about Luke.'

✳

Romy had been agonising over a way to bring up the subject of David's fateful Hallowe'en party. She didn't want to freak Kit out, but now that she knew where they stood, she had to tell him that he was Luke's father – she just couldn't think how to start. But a couple of nights later, she was reading through the TV listings in the paper when something caught her eye.

'Oh,' she said to Kit, 'The first two *Star Wars* movies are on tonight. Let's have a marathon.'

'Really?' Kit frowned. 'What is it with you and *Star Wars*? I don't remember you being such a fan.'

'Well, I've developed a bit of a thing for Darth Vader,' she said with a playful smile. 'I think it's the mask, and the air of mystery.'

'Oh!' Kit's eyebrows shot up.

Shit! He looked totally freaked out. So much for introducing the subject in a light, casual way.

'I have very fond memories of a night I spent with a masked man.' She gave him a significant look.

'Oh, right.' Kit tugged at his collar. He appeared to be breaking out in a sweat. 'Um … cup of tea?' he asked, shooting off the sofa and practically running to the kitchen before she could even open her mouth to answer.

'Yes, please,' she said to his retreating back.

Well – that went well, she thought, smiling wryly to herself.

❋

In the kitchen, Kit put the kettle on and stood waiting for it to boil while he took deep breaths and tried to calm himself down. Jesus, why did Romy suddenly feel the need to regale him with the details of her penchant for masked sadists? He really didn't want to hear about it. And now she insisted on bringing up that awful night at David's party. He drew out the process of making the tea, stalling for time while he tried to think of a way to change the subject when he went back to the living room. If only he knew how to do a Chinese tea ceremony …

He didn't want to think about that night ever again. He should never have got so drunk. If he hadn't been completely arseholed there was no way he'd ever have let that fat fuck David talk him into a threesome. The mere thought of his big stupid head sticking out of that Shrek costume made him want to puke. And by some horrible, ludicrous twist of fate, it turned out Romy was the woman he'd roped in as the token third party – token because it quickly became clear that the threesome was just a pretext for David to satisfy his bi-curiosity by shagging another man. It hadn't taken long for Red Riding Hood to figure out that she was surplus to requirements. After some cursory fumbling with her breasts, David had completely ignored her while he concentrated on fucking Kit's mouth with his tongue and groping his crotch. Eventually, she'd got pissed off and left in a huff.

He hated knowing that that was Romy, and he couldn't understand why she would want to talk about it. Even if that was the sort of thing she was into, she must have been annoyed that she hadn't been included more. He just never wanted to think about that night again as long as he lived.

Finally, he had no option but to return to the living room with the tea. 'So I got a text from Hannah,' he said as he entered the room, determined to cut Romy off before she could go back to the topic of David's party. 'They seem to be having a brilliant time,' he said as he handed Romy her mug. 'The weather is fantastic. They went on a boat yesterday. Tank got a bit sunburned and—'

'Kit,' Romy interrupted, almost shouting. 'About that night at David's party—'

'Please, let's just never mention it again.'

'We need to talk about it,' she said firmly.

'But why?' Kit wailed desperately.

'Because—'

Oh Christ, she's not going to suggest we have another go, is she? 'Look, I'm sorry about what happened – and I'm sure you are too. But can't we just forget about it?'

'No, because—'

'I don't usually do that sort of thing—'

'Well, me neither, but—'

'And I didn't even go through with it that time, so—'

'But—' Romy began, but then she suddenly went very still. 'Wait – what do you mean you didn't go through with it?'

'I mean, I didn't, you know … have sex with …' Kit trailed off, blushing.

'But you did.'

'No. I don't know what he told you, but—'

'No one told me anything.' Romy was flailing around now, looking very confused. 'I was *there*, Kit.'

'No.' He shook his head. 'You left, remember?' Finally, she'd gone quiet and he could say his piece.

'What are you talking about?' she asked now in a faint voice.

He sighed heavily. 'At David's party. When the three of us—'

'What three of us?'

'You, me and David.'

'*David*?' She frowned. 'David wasn't there. It was just us …' Then she gasped suddenly, and her eyes flew to his. 'Kit, what costume where you wearing?'

'Vampire.' He frowned. Didn't she already know that?

'Oh my God!' she gasped, pressing a hand to her forehead. 'I don't believe it! You weren't Darth Vader?'

'Darth Vader? No,' he said, frowning. 'I thought … you mean that wasn't you – in the Red Riding Hood costume?'

'No.' She shook her head weakly. 'There was … someone else at the party dressed as Red Riding Hood. It must have been her.' She gave a weak mirthless laugh. She was so stunned, it took her a while to realise that she was also disappointed, and sad that it wasn't Kit. She had got to really like the idea that he was Luke's father, and even if there was no hope of a real relationship between the two of them, he was shaping up to be a good dad.

'So what happened with you and this Darth Vader, then?'

'It's just … I sort of have something of his …' She shook her head. 'It doesn't matter,' she said, blinking rapidly.

'Are you okay?'

'Yeah, fine.'

Oh, God, Kit thought, was she going to cry? He swallowed hard. 'Look, sorry I cut you off there. If you want to talk about that night, we can.'

'No, it's okay. What happened at David's party stays at David's party. Okay?'

'Okay,' Kit said, breathing a sigh of relief. 'So, will I make popcorn?'

'What?'

'For this *Star Wars* marathon. If you still want to do that?'

'Oh, yeah. I do.' It was probably the only way she would ever see Darth Vader again.

Chapter Eighteen

'You're sure your mother really doesn't mind babysitting for the weekend?' Romy asked Kit the following Friday morning as they loaded Luke's paraphernalia into her van. The trip to the house in Wicklow had almost been cancelled when Romy's mother had returned from Egypt with a severe case of food poisoning. But then Laura had stepped in and offered to take Luke for the weekend instead.

'No, she's thrilled,' Kit said, stuffing a giant bag of nappies into the van. 'Anyway, it's sort of her job. She's practically his granny now, isn't she?'

'What with you being his dad and all?' Romy said, laughing as she handed him another holdall.

'Exactly,' Kit said, tucking the bag in among the others. 'God, does he really need all this stuff?'

'I'm afraid so,' Romy said, shutting the doors. 'Your son is very high maintenance.'

'Huh! Well, he doesn't get that from his mother,' Kit said, smiling at her.

'No, no one's ever accused *me* of being high maintenance. It must come from your side of the family.' Though they were joking around, Romy felt a little pang as she went back into the house to get Luke. It made her sad that she would probably never know in what ways Luke took after his father, and his story would always remain incomplete. She pushed the thought aside as she locked the door behind her and carried Luke down the steps.

'Now,' she told him as she strapped him into his car seat, 'we're going to leave you with your Granny Masterson for the weekend, and we're going to pick up your Uncle Ethan.' She kissed him on the head, giggling as he grasped at her hair so she had to prise it gently out of his hands when she pulled back.

Kit was already in the passenger seat and she jumped in beside him. 'Do you think maybe it's too early to call over?' she asked, glancing at the clock on the dashboard. It was only eight o'clock. 'Maybe we should wait until a bit later.'

'No, it'll be fine. I told them we'd be dropping Luke off first thing. We still have all the gear to pack up, and we want to get down to the house as early as possible.'

'True.'

'It'll be okay. Mom and Dad are early risers anyway.'

'What about Ethan?'

'Well ... apparently he was going out on the piss with a bunch of his old college friends last night, so who knows what shape he'll be in – or whose bed, for that matter.'

'Oh. Maybe he won't even want to come. I mean he is supposed to be having some R&R, isn't he?'

'No, he's really keen to come and help with the house. Don't worry – whatever state he's in, we'll scrape him up and throw him in the van. He can thank us later.'

'Okay, then,' Romy said, starting up the engine. 'Let's get this show on the road.'

✻

'Boy, am I glad to see you two,' Laura said when she opened the door, a beleaguered expression on her face as she waved them in. She smiled down at Luke, who had fallen asleep in the car. 'Do you want to leave him somewhere quiet?' she asked.

Romy nodded.

'You can put him in here,' Laura said, showing her into the sitting room, while Kit started unloading Luke's stuff from the van.

'I know it looks like a lot,' he said, when he had put everything in the sitting room, 'but that's just because it is.'

'Well, come on through to the kitchen,' Laura said. 'We're all in there.'

'Is Ethan up?' Kit asked.

'He is,' Laura said softly, 'but he has … guests. We have a bit of a situation on our hands.' She pursed her lips. 'It's a Mexican standoff.'

Romy wondered what she meant as they followed her down the hall. In the kitchen, they found Ethan serving breakfast to a pouty girl with long dark hair who was sitting at the table. She was wearing a pink-tinged T-shirt that was far too big for her and clearly belonged to Ethan, and nothing else, her legs and feet bare under the table. Ethan stood beside her, shaking cereal into a bowl and placing it in front of her, while a pretty blonde in a similarly outsized T-shirt and a pair of Ugg boots paced around the kitchen talking into a mobile and darting anxious glances at them both.

Ethan looked up and smiled as they came in. He was dressed in jeans and a thick wheat-coloured jumper, and he looked fresh-faced and totally edible, his hair sticking out in every direction. 'Hi, this is Sarah,' he said to Romy, indicating the dark-haired girl, who looked up unsmilingly and acknowledged them with an infinitesimal raising of her eyebrows. Kit evidently already knew her, nodding hello. 'Sarah, Romy. And that's Fiona,' he said, indicating the other girl. She gave them a little wave, mouthing, 'Hi'.

'I'll just go and put Luke's things away upstairs,' Laura said. 'I'll leave you to it.' She bustled off, seeming anxious to get out of the kitchen.

'Say when,' Ethan said to Sarah as he began pouring milk onto her cereal.

'I don't have time for breakfast,' she said, shoving the bowl away from her. 'I'll be late for work as it is.'

'It's the most important meal of the day,' Ethan said, sliding the bowl back in front of her. 'You should eat something.'

'I'm going to call a cab,' she said, pushing away from the table and hitting a button on her mobile, holding it to her ear as she strode into the hallway.

Kit rolled his eyes at Ethan when she was gone.

'What?' Ethan said defensively.

'What's eating Godzilla?' Kit said, glancing over at Fiona to make sure she wasn't listening, but she was too engrossed in her phone call.

Ethan just shrugged, crossed to the fridge, and having taken out a bowl, sat down at the table. Grabbing the spoon he had put out for Sarah, he began to eat. Kit and Romy sat opposite him.

'Where's Luke?' Ethan asked.

'He's asleep,' Romy said. 'We put him in the living room so as not to wake him.'

'Oh,' Ethan said, looking disappointed. 'I was hoping to finally meet him. Oh, well, maybe he'll wake up before we go.'

'Ethan loves babies,' Kit told Romy. 'He's a bit weird like that.'

'That's not weird!' Romy protested.

'It's a bit weird for a bloke, though, isn't it? I mean, it's different if it's your own baby, of course,' he added hastily. And obviously I love … Whatsisface.'

'Luke,' Romy and Ethan said simultaneously.

'But liking complete randomer babies – you have to admit that's a bit weird for a guy.'

They were interrupted by Fiona coming over to the table. 'Okay, crisis averted,' she said, snapping her phone shut.

Ethan introduced Romy and Kit. 'What do you want for breakfast?' he asked her. 'Cereal? Toast?'

At least he was a good host, Romy thought – even if he was a total slag.

'What's that you're eating?' Fiona asked with a flirtatious smile, sliding into the seat beside him.

'It's chocolate pudding. Mom made it for my homecoming.'

'You can't eat chocolate pudding for breakfast!' she said, laughing.

'Why not? It's fantastic.'

She tutted. 'You're such a baby.'

'Do you want some?'

'Oh, I want some all right,' she murmured with a cheeky grin. 'But I'm not going to get any, am I?'

Just then Sarah came back into the room, dressed now in a very short skirt, thigh high, spiky-heeled suede boots and a sparkly sequinned top. She marched up to the table and everyone froze, the tension palpable as she glowered at Fiona and Ethan. 'I've called a cab,' she said to Fiona, her eyes flinty. 'It'll be here in about ten minutes. Do you want to share it?'

Fiona looked back at her, conflicting emotions crossing her face. For a moment, they faced each other in silence, seeming to size each other up.

'Are you going home first, or—'

'Well, obviously I'm going home first,' Sarah said, rolling her eyes. 'I can't go to work dressed like this.'

'Why not? You look great,' Ethan said.

'Ethan, just … shut up,' Sarah said crossly. 'So, are you coming or not?' she asked Fiona.

'Yeah, all right,' Fiona said finally, with an air of defeat. 'I'd better go get dressed,' she said to Ethan, getting up.

Sarah sat down in her vacated chair, picking up the bowl of cereal Ethan had poured her earlier. No one spoke as she began to eat in a way that somehow managed to convey the impression that she was doing it under protest.

Fiona came back into the kitchen all dressed up for a night out. 'I've decided I'm just going to walk-of-shame it into work,' she said to Sarah. 'I can't be bothered going home to change.'

Just then, the doorbell rang.

'That'll be the taxi,' Sarah said, getting up.

Ethan stood and grabbed Sarah's coat from the back of a chair, holding it open for her like a waiter in a restaurant.

'Jesus, Ethan,' she said, snatching it from him, 'just because I have a vagina doesn't mean I'm completely helpless. I'm quite capable of putting my coat on all by myself.'

'Sorry,' Ethan said, stuffing his hands into his pockets. 'I'll just see you out.' He followed the two girls out to the front door, and they could be heard saying their goodbyes.

Romy raised her eyes questioningly at Kit. 'What the hell?'

'They're both exes of Ethan's,' he said.

'Oh, right.'

'Yeah.'

'Do you think he …?' It was obvious both girls had spent the night, but surely Ethan hadn't, not in his parents' house.

'Shagged them both? Wouldn't put it past him.'

Before they could say any more, the front door closed and Ethan came back into the kitchen.

'Now that you've got rid of your harem, are you ready to go?' Kit asked him.

'Sure.'

'We don't have to leave right away,' Romy said. 'You can finish your … breakfast.' She glanced at the bowl of chocolate sponge.

'Great!' He grinned, sitting back down at the table. 'Would you like some of my welcome-home pudding?' he asked, holding out a piece to her on a spoon. 'This is the last of it.'

'No, thanks.' God, he was incorrigible. Those girls were barely out the door and he was flirting with her.

'And it's not pudding, it's cake,' Kit told him.

'Whatever, it's amazing!' Ethan spooned the last bite into his mouth.

'You've spent too long in the jungle,' Kit said dryly.

Ethan yawned widely and laid his head on his arms on the table.

'Tired?' Kit asked.

'Mmm. I didn't get much sleep last night.'

'I bet you didn't,' Kit said.

'No rest for the wicked,' Romy said tartly.

'What?' Ethan said, lifting his head. 'Why are you both looking at me like that?'

'We just can't believe you had both those girls spend the night.'

'They didn't give me much choice. I couldn't get them to leave.'

'Oh, right – so you were just doing them a favour.' Romy cringed at how bitter she sounded when she had no cause to be.

'Look, what you get up to is your own business,' Kit said, 'but while you're living here, you should be more respectful. Whatever about having one girl sleeping over, two is really pushing it. It's not fair on Mom.'

'Mom doesn't mind,' Ethan said, shrugging. 'And I cleared up after us and made them breakfast, so—'

'Christ, I don't believe you!' Kit fumed. 'It's not about who made their breakfast – it's about what you were doing last night.'

'We were just hanging out,' Ethan said, shrugging innocently. 'What's the big deal?'

Hanging out, Romy thought, like he 'hung out' with Sinead? Kit seemed to have been rendered speechless, so she answered for him. 'He just can't believe you think it's okay to … to *hang out* with two girls right under your parents' noses,' she sputtered.

Ethan looked at her, frowning in confusion. Then his eyes widened. 'Oh my God! You think – you think I *slept* with both of them?' He seemed torn between amusement and outrage.

'You mean you didn't?'

'No! Jesus!'

'Sorry, I thought—'

'God, I can't believe you think I would do that.' Ethan looked genuinely hurt, and Romy felt bad for having misjudged him.

'Well, you had two half-naked girls vying for your attention, who'd obviously spent the night,' Kit said. 'And we know what you're like. What were we supposed to think?'

'You could have given me the benefit of the doubt.'

'We could,' Kit said, 'but where's the fun in that? So which one *did* you—'

'Which one did I what?'

'Which one did you sleep with?'

'Neither!' Ethan huffed, rolling his eyes. 'Christ! They only stayed over because I couldn't get them to leave. A few of us came back here after the pub, and eventually it was just the two of them, and they just wouldn't go. In the end, I said they could crash here because it was the only way I was going to get to bed. Sarah slept on the couch and Fiona slept in your room. Okay?'

Kit laughed. 'They were cock-blocking you,' he said.

'What?'

'Obviously they were both afraid that if they left first, you'd take the other one to bed as soon as they were out the door.'

'Hmm. Possibly,' Ethan mumbled reluctantly.

'And were they wrong?'

A sheepish smile twitched at the corners of Ethan's mouth. 'Possibly not.'

Romy rolled her eyes. 'You're disgusting!'

'Hey, you're the one thinking about threesomes. According to you two, I didn't even have to wait for one of them to leave.' He shook his head. 'I can't believe you thought that. I mean, apart from anything else, can you honestly see those two sharing ... like that?'

'I can't even believe they got in a cab together,' Romy said. She felt light-hearted, almost giddy with relief that Ethan hadn't slept with either of those girls – even if it was only because he didn't get the opportunity.

'I thought maybe they were having an attack of morning-after remorse and that's why they were being so stroppy,' Kit said.

'Actually, they're usually not like that.'

'Sarah is. Sarah's *always* like that.'

'She's feisty,' Ethan said, shrugging. 'I like that in a woman.'

'She's not feisty, she's mean.'

'That's a mean thing to say,' Ethan said.

'That's a true thing to say. Jeez, you were just being polite helping her on with her coat, and she savaged you.'

'She just has this idea that people are always treating her differently because of her vagina,' Ethan said, smiling. 'It's a sore point with her.'

'Who has a sore vagina?'

Their heads all spun to the back door, to see Colm sticking his head in. 'Are they gone?' he asked, his eyes darting around the room.

'Yes, the coast is clear,' Kit told him.

He came into the kitchen and closed the door behind him. 'So who has the sore vagina?' he asked.

'No one,' Ethan said, at the same time as Kit answered, 'Sarah.'

'Ah, poor girl,' he said, nodding understandingly. 'That would explain it.'

'Explain what?' Ethan asked.

'Why she was in such a temper this morning. I mean that can't be much fun, can it?' He winced.

Ethan rolled his eyes. 'She doesn't have a—'

'I'll stop you there, son,' Colm interrupted, holding up one hand in a halting gesture. 'I don't want to know how she got it or what it has to do with you. That's on a need to know basis, and I do not need to know.'

'But there's nothing to—' Ethan began.

'God, it was like *High Noon* in here this morning, Romy,' Colm interrupted, rubbing his hands together and seeming hugely amused by the situation. 'You should have seen the pair of them squaring off against each other. I wouldn't like to bet on who'd come out on top in that fight.'

'My money would be on Sarah,' Kit said.

'She's a scary woman, isn't she?' Colm said admiringly. 'Though, in fairness, the other one's not to be underestimated either.'

'I saw a cab pulling away,' Laura said as she came into the kitchen. 'Are those girls gone?'

'Yeah,' Ethan answered.

'Did they share a cab?' Colm asked. 'Is that wise?'

'They'll be fine,' Ethan said, shrugging. 'They're friends.'

'Friends!' Kit exclaimed. 'They looked ready to tear each other to pieces.'

'They were like something out of a David Attenborough programme,' Colm said. 'Two lionesses circling each other around a carcass on the Serengeti.'

'And what am I in this scenario?' Ethan asked, laughing.

'You're the piece of meat they're fighting over,' Kit said.

'Well, they usually get on fine. I don't know what got into them.'

'Not you,' Kit murmured under his breath. 'That's why they were so pissed off.'

'Have you guys got time for coffee before you go?' Laura asked as she switched on the machine.

Before anyone could answer, they were interrupted by the sound of Luke's crying from the other room.

'We might as well stay for coffee,' Romy said to Kit as she jumped up. 'I'll change Luke and feed him before we go.'

As she changed Luke in the living room, Romy took advantage of the time out to give herself a talking to. She had been shocked by how jealous she had felt of those girls. She hated thinking that Ethan had slept with both of them – or even one of them – and it had made her stupidly happy to discover he hadn't. It was ridiculous because who Ethan did or didn't sleep with was nothing to do with her – and never would be. She fancied him – who wouldn't? He was gorgeous. But she mustn't let it get out of hand. He was too young for her, he was out of her league, and besides, as far as he was concerned, she was his brother's girlfriend. She had to stop thinking about him in that way.

When she had dressed Luke again, she carried him back to the kitchen, clutching him in one arm while she took one of his pre-prepared bottles out of the fridge.

'So this is Luke – finally,' Ethan said, jumping up and coming over to her. 'Can I hold him while you're doing that?' he asked, holding out his arms.

'Um … sure,' Romy said, surprised by his eagerness.

'You can trust me, I'm a doctor,' Ethan said, when she hesitated to hand Luke over. 'I know how to hold a baby.'

'Oh, okay,' she said, passing Luke to him carefully.

Ethan's face lit up as he grinned down at Luke, cooing at him as he chucked his cheeks and played with his fingers, while Luke gurgled happily. He walked back to the table and sat down with Luke on his lap, and soon they were making each other laugh.

'He's great!' Ethan called across the kitchen to her.

'He is, isn't he?' she said, smiling as she placed his bottle in the microwave.

'And that's an expert opinion,' Kit said. 'Ethan's doing paediatrics, so he knows his babies.'

Romy turned towards them while she waited for Luke's bottle to heat up, and she felt her heart melting as she watched Ethan playing with Luke, clearly delighted by him. Damn him! How was she ever going to avoid a full-blown crush with him behaving like this? These days, the surest way to her heart was through her son, and Ethan seemed to have found the path with the unerring instinct of a Sherpa.

By the time Luke's bottle was ready, Laura had placed a tray of coffee and mugs on the table.

'Why don't I feed him while you have your coffee?' Ethan asked, holding out a hand for the bottle.

'Oh, no – it's fine,' Romy said, sitting down.

'Come on, please? I'd really like to. And I don't want more coffee.'

Looking at his eager face, Romy softened. He seemed to genuinely want to feed Luke – and she still felt bad about accusing him of having a threesome. 'Okay, thanks,' she said, handing him the bottle.

'Cool!' Ethan grinned as he settled Luke in his lap, laying him back against one arm and pressing the bottle to his lips. He laughed softly as Luke began to drink enthusiastically, with loud sucking noises. 'Aw, he's so cute. I wish he was coming away with us for the weekend.'

'I told you he was weird,' Kit said to Romy.

❊

Later, Danny and Lesley met them at Romy's house, and when Romy had introduced everyone, they all helped load the van and Danny's Land Rover. It was a bright, frosty day, the cold snapping at their faces as they moved between the house and the cars with tools, camping equipment, and boxes of food and booze.

'So that's the brother,' Lesley mumbled to Romy while they retraced their steps to the house to collect another load of supplies. 'I can't say I blame you for going all goo-goo over him. He's gorgeous.'

'I haven't gone goo-goo over him,' Romy hissed. But she knew that wasn't true. It was useless trying to kid herself any longer. She had a full-on heart-pounding, knee-wobbling, massive great crush on Ethan. She just hoped it wasn't as obvious to everyone else as it was to Lesley – especially when they were all going to be spending the whole weekend together. That would be mortifying – not to mention the fact that she was supposed to be with Kit. It would be awful if everyone could see she was lusting after his brother.

'I'm going to leave my car here,' Lesley said as she pushed another camp bed into the back of the van. 'Unless you need me to bring more stuff?'

'No, that's everything,' Romy said, slamming the doors closed. 'You can come in the van with me and Kit.'

'Why don't I go with Danny?' Kit called across to her as he loaded the last box into the Land Rover.

'I don't mind,' Danny said, shrugging. 'Whatever.'

'Cool.' Kit grinned. 'I've brought my iPod. This way we can have one car with good music.'

Huh, Romy thought, so much for Kit playing the devoted boyfriend. She thought he'd be all over her this weekend, grabbing the opportunity to convince Ethan that they were really a couple. But then, of course, he didn't know that Ethan needed convincing because he didn't know that he and Hannah suspected anything. Maybe she should warn him.

Lesley climbed into the middle passenger seat of the van, and Ethan got in beside her.

'So you're the doctor?' she said, turning to him as they set off. 'I've heard a lot about you.'

'You have?' Ethan glanced across at Romy. He seemed a little subdued and she hoped he wasn't still upset with her over the threesome thing. 'Not all scandalous, I hope.'

Shit! He *was* still brooding about it. 'Look, Ethan,' she said, 'I'm really sorry about … what I said.'

'What did you say?' Lesley asked Romy.

Ethan shrugged, pouting sulkily – which only made his mouth more gorgeous than ever. 'Romy thinks I'm a total sleazeball.'

'I don't!' she protested. 'That's not true. I just … wasn't thinking. Forgive me?'

'It's fine,' he said, a smile spreading across his face. 'I'm just winding you up.'

'What happened?' Lesley asked, looking back and forth between them.

'She thought I'd had a threesome in my parents' house.'

'Fair play to you!' Lesley said.

'But I didn't.'

'Good man yourself. I'm glad to hear it.'

Ethan grinned at her.

'So, Ethan, you're a man, right?' she asked.

'Um … yes. Last time I checked.'

'Right, because I'd like to get your opinion on this date I went on last week – from a male perspective. And in fact, from a doctor's point of view as well, so you're ideal for the job.'

'Oh? Sounds … intriguing.'

'Yes, well, I don't know if "intriguing" is the word, but there was a rash involved that was certainly the wrong side of mysterious. So, anyway …'

Romy relaxed as Lesley kept up a steady stream of chatter the whole way to Wicklow.

Chapter Nineteen

When they had unpacked the cars and carried everything into the gate lodge, they wandered around the little cottage together, inspecting the rooms, while Romy made mental notes about what needed to be done. There were two bedrooms, a small bathroom and a cosy combined kitchen/living area. The plan was to make it habitable as quickly as possible so that she could stay on-site to oversee work on the renovation. It really wouldn't take much. The cottage was dingy and grubby, but it had been lived in much more recently than the main house and had no major problems. With a bit of work, it would be perfectly adequate as a temporary home for the duration of the project. It would need more extensive redecoration and updating before it could be sold as an adjunct to the main house, but that could wait until the major work had been completed.

'I hope you're not planning on moving in anytime soon,' Lesley said, wrinkling her nose as she peered into a built-in wardrobe and the smell of mildew wafted out. 'There's no way we're going to get this place in shape in a weekend.'

'Oh, we're just the advance party,' Romy said. 'There are reinforcements coming down for the day tomorrow.'

'I didn't know that,' Kit said. 'Are we paying them?'

'Just in beer and grub,' Romy told him.

'Really? I know times are hard, but can you really get people to work for food?'

'*I* can. I told you I'd be calling in some favours.'

'Wow, you're a handy girlfriend to have,' Kit said, putting an arm around her and grinning at her. 'It's like I'm going out with Don Corleone. Though you're much better looking, obviously,' he added hastily. 'And slimmer … and less mumbly. And you don't have that jowl thing going on.'

'So, hardly like Don Corleone at all, then,' she said, smiling.

'Just in having troops of people at your command, ready to do your bidding.'

'Right,' Romy said, pulling away, 'before we do anything else, I'm going to see if I can get the boiler going. Then I think we should start on the kitchen.'

In an airing cupboard beside the bathroom she had found an immersion heater which seemed to be working, so at least they would have hot water.

They all trooped into the small, grungy kitchen, falling silent as they surveyed it despondently.

'It's not as bad as it looks,' Romy said. 'What it mainly needs for now is a really good scrub. But first, let's have some lunch while we're waiting for the water to heat up. I brought a picnic.'

'Yay, lunch!' Lesley said, visibly brightening. 'I'm starving.'

'Me too,' Kit said, 'but isn't it a bit cold for a picnic?'

'I meant indoors. Having a picnic means we don't have to bother about cleaning anything first. There are a couple of blankets in that box,' she said, pointing.

'Okay, we'll sort that out while you go and look at the boiler,' Lesley said, shooing her out the door.

The boiler remained dishearteningly cold and lifeless, despite Romy's best efforts at resuscitation – though her knowledge of plumbing was severely limited, so she didn't have high hopes. After extensive fiddling with the switch to no avail, she gave up and went to explore a large shed to the side of the house. Among the inevitable rusting bicycles, clapped-out lawnmowers and bags of mouldy compost, there was a large chest freezer. That would be handy if it still worked. And the shed would be useful for storage if she got rid of all the junk. She had had some skips delivered during the week so she put clearing out the shed on her mental to-do list. As she headed back to the lodge, she was pleased to see a small pile of logs and peat stacked neatly against the side wall. It wasn't covered, but thankfully it hadn't rained much in the last couple of weeks, and touching it with her fingers, she found that it was reasonably dry.

When she stepped back into the kitchen, a picnic blanket was laid out on the floor along with a couple of cool boxes, two large catering flasks of tea and coffee, and a pile of paper cups.

'Lunch is served,' Lesley said, gesturing to the blanket with a flourish.

'Mmm, this looks great,' Romy said as they all settled on the floor and Danny unloaded the cool boxes, laying open foil-wrapped sandwiches and slabs of cake, while Lesley dispensed tea and coffee and passed it around. 'What's this?' she pointed to a large circular aluminium parcel.

'Mom made that for us,' Ethan said, peeling back the foil. 'It's a giant biscuit.'

'It's not a biscuit, it's a cake,' Kit said.

'Really?' Romy scrutinised the flat chocolate-coloured disc.

'It looks like a biscuit,' Ethan said.

'Well, it's a cake – a chocolate cake.'

'Are you sure?' Lesley asked. 'It could be a chocolate biscuit.'

'It's flat like a biscuit,' Danny said.

'It's got layers like a cake – look.' Kit pointed out its double layer construction with some kind of chocolate coloured creamy stuff in the middle.

'That doesn't prove anything,' Lesley said. 'Lots of biscuits have layers like that. Custard creams, Oreos, Jammy Dodgers …'

'Bourbon creams,' Romy supplied.

'Well, I know for a fact that it's a cake, okay? I hope you didn't call it a biscuit in front of Mom,' Kit said to Ethan.

'I don't think so,' Ethan said, frowning. 'Anyway, whatever it is, I'm sure it'll taste great.'

'God, it's freezing in here,' Lesley said, huddling over her tea so the steam warmed her face, her hands wrapped around the cup.

Romy looked around the circle. They were all still wearing their coats, except Danny and Ethan.

'We might as well have had the picnic outside,' Kit said from the depths of his massive down jacket.

'The boiler's dead, so I'm not going to be able to get the heating going today,' Romy said apologetically, 'but I brought down a couple of heaters. And we can have a fire in here,' she added, nodding to the open hearth in the living area. 'The chimney was swept last week and I found some logs and turf by the side of the house.'

'I shouldn't have let you talk me out of buying that arctic sleeping bag,' Kit said to her. 'It would have come in handy tonight.'

'Never mind,' she said, 'I've brought a load of hot water bottles.'

'Anyway, you'll get warm once you start scrubbing,' Danny told him, smiling mischievously.

'Great!' Kit said dryly. 'It's like that bloody survival weekend all over again.'

'Don't you even think about escaping from this one,' Romy said. 'I'll hunt you down.'

'I wouldn't dare,' he said, reaching for a piece of lemon drizzle cake. He groaned as he bit into it. 'Oh my God, did you make this?' he asked Romy.

'Yeah, I did.'

'Well, that's it, then – I won't be going anywhere. In fact, I think I'm going to have to marry you,' he said, throwing an arm around her. 'What do you say?'

'Okay,' she said, shrugging. 'Why not?' She smiled at him, leaning into his squashy jacket. But then she became aware of Ethan watching them and felt uncomfortable. She pulled away.

'Anyone for a bit of this, er, thing Mom made?' Ethan asked, picking it up.

'I'm game!' Lesley said.

He broke off a piece and handed it to her.

'It snaps like a biscuit,' Lesley observed as he broke off another piece for himself.

Ethan nodded in agreement and they both watched each other as they chewed thoughtfully.

'It's crunchy like a biscuit,' Ethan said when he had swallowed.

'For God's sake!' Kit roared. 'It's a *cake*!'

❋

When they had finished eating and cleared away the picnic things, Romy handed Lesley a lump hammer.

'You can smash up all that mouldy built-in furniture in the bedrooms for starters,' she said. 'And save the wood – we can use it for the fire.' Then she doled out cleaning supplies, rubber gloves, goggles and face masks to everyone else.

'Hey, why does she get a lump hammer and I just get a pair of Marigolds?' Kit asked peevishly.

'Because she bagsied the lump hammer.'

'Oh, fair enough,' he said, snapping on his rubber gloves.

'This isn't my first rodeo,' Lesley said, grinning smugly as she gave a few practice swings with the hammer.

'I can see that.'

While Lesley skipped off to start demolishing wardrobes, and Ethan, Kit and Danny got stuck into cleaning the kitchen, Romy went to work on the bathroom. Time passed quickly, and the more she did, the more there seemed to be still to do, but finally she was finished.

'You've done a great job in here,' she said, joining the others in the kitchen, looking around admiringly at the sparkling countertops and see-through windows. She moved around, absently opening cupboard doors and peering into the fridge and oven. 'Well,' she said, straightening up and leaning against the counter, 'the good news is that the shower is working. The bad news is you have to take your clothes off to get into it. And the bathroom is *freezing*.'

She had got warm as she worked, but as soon as she stopped, she felt the cold start to creep through her again straight away.

'I don't have the energy to take my clothes off,' Lesley said, crossing into the living room and flopping onto the sofa, 'even if I could bear the cold.'

Everyone else murmured their agreement.

'Pizza time, then? There's a takeaway in the village. Why don't I go and get us all pizza, and you guys try and get a fire going?'

※

When she returned laden down with boxes of pizza and garlic bread, Romy found everyone tucked up in their sleeping bags sitting in front of a roaring fire. It looked like a convention of giant snails. A couple of bottles of red were open and warming on the hearth.

'This looks cosy,' she said.

'Your sleeping bag is here, warming up for you,' Ethan said, patting her bag in front of the fire.

'Oh, thank you,' she said, slipping off her shoes and jacket. She doled out the pizzas and burrowed into her sleeping bag. It was toasty warm and felt like heaven.

Kit poured wine and handed it around, and the air was filled with fragrant pizza steam as they all opened the boxes and began to eat. The fire hissed and sizzled as Ethan pushed another log into the flames, sending a rush of red sparks flying up the chimney.

Biting into her pizza, Romy closed her eyes in ecstasy as the hot dough and melting cheese suffused her with warmth and comfort. The wine was the perfect temperature and she felt all her muscles relax as heat seeped through her. She didn't know when she'd felt so profoundly snug.

'We've decided we should all sleep in here,' Danny told her, 'to be near the fire.'

'Good idea. It's only fair.'

'And since none of us are taking squat off, we don't have to worry about flashing our inappropriate bits,' Kit said.

'Should we have a sing-song or something?' Lesley said. 'Since we're sort of sitting around a campfire.'

'Please, God, no,' Kit said.

'I can do better than that,' Romy said. 'I brought some games.'

'Oh God, not board games,' Kit groaned. 'Let's have a sing-song!'

Romy laughed. Kit had always mocked her love of board games, which he found excruciatingly boring. 'Don't worry, it's not a board game.' She wriggled out of her sleeping bag and came back bearing a box. 'Hedbanz,' she announced.

'Oh, I love that game!' Lesley said.

'It looks like a board game to me,' Kit said, eyeing the box suspiciously.

'Well, it's not. You wear a headband with the name of someone famous on it, so everyone can see it but you. Then you have to ask questions to find out who you are. It's very straightforward.'

'It's fun,' Lesley assured him. 'I'll start.'

Lesley was Audrey Hepburn, which by some fluke she guessed very quickly. Then, Ethan was Abraham Lincoln, which took somewhat longer. Next, Kit wore a headband bearing the legend 'Jesus Christ'. They had finished the pizza and were onto the second bottle of wine, and he still hadn't got it. He knew he wasn't an actor or singer, that he was male, vaguely political and possibly a revolutionary of some kind, but that he wasn't Che Guevara. When he asked if he had magical powers, there was a great deal of consultation and discussion, but no one could quite decide how to answer.

'Some people think so,' Romy finally said.

'Santa Claus!'

'No.'

'Give me a hint.'

'Some people believe you've performed miracles,' Lesley said.

'Harry Potter!'

'You're not fictional, remember?' Romy reminded him. That had been one of his first questions.

'I'm not fictional and I've performed miracles.' He thought. 'Saint ... Somebody,' he said, clearly racking his brain to come up with the name of a saint. 'Oh, I know – the pope!'

'Um … no. I don't think he's done any miracles, has he?' Lesley said.

'Saint Jude!'

'No.'

'Saint Joseph!'

'No.'

'Saint ... Peter!'

'No, but you're getting warmer,' Danny said.

'Give me another hint.'

'Okay,' Danny said, scanning the ceiling as he thought. 'You were at the Last Supper.'

'Moses!'

Everyone laughed.

'Moses wasn't at the Last Supper,' Ethan said, chuckling.

'He wasn't?' Kit frowned. 'Why not?'

Ethan shrugged. 'Who knows? Maybe he was washing his hair that night.'

'He did have a lot of hair,' Lesley said. 'And it was in rag order if those paintings of him are anything to go by. Frizz city.'

'Well, in fairness, it can't have been easy keeping your hair in good condition when you lived in the desert all the time,' Romy said to her.

'True. And in Olden Times too. They didn't have any of the advanced technology shampoos and conditioners that we take for granted.'

'Or any shampoo at all – not even Sunsilk.'

'God, yeah – total nightmare! I suppose unmanageable hair would have been a given.'

'Okay, so I was at the Last Supper, but I'm not Moses,' Kit recapped, bringing them back to the game. 'Abraham!'

Romy collapsed back on the floor in a fit of giggles. 'Abraham wasn't at the Last Supper either.'

'Well, how am I supposed to know who was there? I wasn't the bloody sommelier.'

'Yeah,' Danny said, laughing. 'Obviously we only know who was there because we were involved in the catering.'

'There were only thirteen people at the Last Supper,' Lesley told Kit gently. 'Jesus and the apostles.'

'I know that! I'm not a complete ignoramus.'

'Well … why did you say Moses, then?' she asked tentatively.

'You mean … Moses wasn't in the apostles?' Kit asked, frowning.

'You make it sound like a band.' Romy laughed. 'And now, The Apostles with their number one hit single!'

'Yeah,' Lesley giggled, 'maybe he was in the original line-up but got kicked out.'

'Because no one liked his hair,' Romy said, giggling with her. She felt woozy and giddy, on a natural high from the pizza and wine and the relief of being warm.

'Not with the hair again!' Kit huffed. 'Jesus Christ, can you—'

'Yes!' Lesley pounced.

'Huh?'

'Yes – Jesus Christ! That's the answer.'

＊

The following morning, Romy woke to the delicious smell of bacon frying. Still in her sleeping bag, she shuffled into the kitchen to find Ethan and Kit presiding over a couple of frying pans, making an enormous breakfast. Lesley and Danny were sitting at the table expectantly, also still cocooned in their sleeping bags.

'Ah, just in time,' Kit said, smiling at her. 'How do you like your eggs?'

'Sunny side up.'

'Same for everyone, then,' he said. 'That's easy.'

'There's tea and toast,' Ethan said, waving her to the table. 'This'll be ready in a minute.'

She pulled out the chair beside Lesley and sat down. 'I can't believe how well I slept,' she said, rubbing her eyes.

'Well, I'd say you had a lot to catch up on,' Lesley said, pouring her a mug of tea. 'And that cleaning was knackering. I ache all over.'

'Me too!' everyone chorused, comparing notes about sore muscles and stiff backs.

'Dig in,' Ethan said as he put a plate piled high with rashers, sausages, eggs, tomatoes and potato cakes in the middle of the table, and he and Kit sat down.

'So what's the plan for today?' Kit asked as they all helped themselves.

'Well, we've done the groundwork,' Romy said, 'so there won't be much for us to do once the workmen get here, other than stay out of their way and keep them fed and happy. I want to go up and spend some time in the house – take measurements and stuff, so I can make some proper plans.'

'And I'll take a look around outside,' Danny said, 'and start thinking about a design for the grounds.'

'And we can start clearing stuff out into the skips.'

'Well, I'll take care of the cooking, if you like,' Kit offered.

'Really?'

'Sure. I'm a very good cook, you know.'

'I know. You both are,' she said, looking between him and Ethan.

'Learning to cook was kind of a priority when you grew up in our family,' Ethan said with a crooked smile. 'When all our classmates were doing football camps in the summer holidays, Kit and I would beg to go to cooking ones.'

'And I'm used to catering for the masses,' Kit said. 'I told you I was a short order cook for a while in New York, didn't I?'

'Yes, you did.'

'That was probably my favourite job. The pay was shit, of course, but I had a blast.'

'Well, if this breakfast is anything to go by, I'd say you have a calling,' Lesley said. 'It's amazing.'

'Fantastic!' Danny agreed.

'Okay, then – you're hired,' Romy said. 'I just need you to come up to the house so I can go over my ideas with you, and then you can channel Jamie Oliver to your heart's content.'

✳

Shortly after they finished breakfast, a vanload of burly Poles descended on the house led by Stefan, Romy's tenant, who was the biggest and burliest of them all.

'Wow, this is impressive,' Kit said as they poured out of the van and swarmed into the house. 'It's like one of those barn-raisings you see in films.'

Once Romy had briefed them on what needed to be done, they infiltrated every corner of the house like a colony of ants, and soon the cottage was being transformed with impossible speed as they moved through it with methodical diligence. Leaving them to it, Romy and the others trooped up to the big house. On the doorstep, Romy handed out hard hats to everyone.

'Hats don't suit me,' Lesley said, trying to hand hers back.

'Humour me,' Romy said firmly, not taking the hat from her.

'But they make my hair go all funny.'

'Well, if a piece of ceiling fell on you, it could make your head go all funny.'

Lesley sighed, reluctantly putting the hat on. 'See?' she said. 'I look like an eejit, don't I?'

'Well, at least you'll be a safe eejit,' Romy said, smiling as she put on her own hat.

'It's all right for you,' Lesley said sulkily. 'You look good in yours.'

'Hardly.'

'You do,' Ethan nodded. 'It's very sexy.'

Romy met his eyes, and the way he was looking at her made her feel hot and prickly. She turned away to hide her blush.

'And the guys all look great in them,' Lesley continued. 'It's just me – they do nothing for me.'

'Well, it might save you from getting clocked on the head by falling debris, so that would be more than any other hat has ever done for you. Come on,' Romy said, leading the way into the house.

'Wow, this is amazing!' Ethan said, looking around as they stood in the vast hall. 'I haven't been here in so long.'

'Takes you back, doesn't it?' Kit said to him.

'We used to have epic games of hide and seek up here,' Ethan said. 'It would take hours to find everyone.'

As they walked through the large, echoingly empty rooms, Romy outlined her ideas for the renovation, all of which Kit enthusiastically approved.

'It's a fantastic house,' Danny said, looking out the window of one of the upstairs rooms. 'I'm going to go and take a walk around the grounds.'

'I'll go with you,' Kit said.

'See if the tree swing is still there,' Ethan called after him.

'Oh yeah, I'd forgotten about that. I'll have a look. And when we're done,' he said to Danny, 'maybe we could go into the village and get some supplies for dinner.'

When they were gone, Romy got out her tape measure and a notepad, and prepared to get down to the nitty-gritty of measuring the rooms and making lists of what work needed to be done.

'You two don't have to stay,' she said to Ethan and Lesley, who were perched together on a window seat, watching her.

'We can help,' Lesley said eagerly.

'These rooms are big,' Ethan said. 'You'll need someone to hold the other end of your tape measure.'

'And I'll write everything down,' Lesley said, picking up Romy's notepad and pen.

'Okay then. Let's get started.'

❋

It was after dark when they got back to the house, and the workers were just knocking off, loading debris into the skips and tidying away tools. Kit had been busy in the kitchen, and they all sat down together to steaming bowls of chilli with pasta, and garlic bread.

'Is it just the heat from the oven or is it warmer in here?' Romy asked.

'No, it's warmer,' Kit said, smiling. 'Stefan got the heat working.'

'Oh, thank you!' Romy beamed at him. 'You're a godsend. And thank you all for your hard work,' she said, raising her glass to the table at large. 'The place looks amazing. I'll be giving you all a call when work starts.'

All the men raised their glasses to her in a silent toast.

'Is no problem,' Stefan said. 'You are good pirson to work for, Romy. You hev been good to all of us, so vee be good to you,' he said with an expansive shrug.

'Oh shit!' Kit gasped. 'That reminds me, I told May I'd go back and put up that … thing for her. I completely forgot. I'll do it as soon as I get back.'

'No need,' Stefan said. 'I put trapeze on ceilink for her.'

'You did?' Romy said. 'Thanks. I hope it's not too noisy,' she added apologetically.

'No, is better for me. Now she swink out of ceilink, is much quieter. I get good sleep.'

'Oh, that's good. I'm glad it's worked out well for everyone.'

'You have a tenant who does trapeze?' Ethan asked, wide-eyed.

'Not exactly,' Romy said. 'It's hard to explain.'

'She hev sex on trapeze,' Stefan explained unabashedly. 'Before it was beng, beng, beng all the time. And the screamink!' He raised his eyes to heaven. 'Oy – so much noise! Now is just the screamink – is not so bad.'

'May is quite eccentric,' Romy explained to Ethan.

'I think she's lovely,' Kit said.

'Yeah, she's a big fan of yours too,' Romy told him. 'And your work. She showed me those shelves you put up for her.'

'Good, weren't they?'

'She was very happy with them,' Romy said obliquely, catching Ethan's eye. He was smiling at her smugly, knowing damn well he'd been right.

'Oh, I fix those shelves too,' Stefan said. 'They were crep. You are crep hendymen,' he said bluntly to Kit.

'Gee, thanks!'

'Crep hendymen, but good cook!' Stefan said heartily, pointing to his empty bowl.

Romy and Ethan buried their faces, giggling into their chilli.

Well, Romy thought, at least she was being spared having to break it to Kit that his work wasn't up to scratch. There was a lot to be said for Stefan's bluntness.

'But May was delighted with those shelves,' Kit protested. 'You said so yourself.'

'May was just being nice. She didn't want to hurt your feelings.'

'Unlike some,' Kit said, glowering darkly at Stefan.

'Hey, you can't be good at everything,' Danny said consolingly. 'And you really are an amazing cook.'

'Yes, great cook! But crep hendymen,' Stefan reiterated.

✻

'Well, I guess our work here is done,' Danny said as they looked around the cottage after the Poles had piled into their van and driven off.

The transformation in the cottage was amazing, and it was hard to believe it had been achieved in such a short time. Only yesterday it had been dingy and miserable, and now it was bright and cosy. Once she brought down some furniture, Romy decided, it would be quite homely. She had plenty of pieces in storage that she could use to furnish the place.

'So, anyone fancy going to the pub?' Kit asked.

'I think I'll stay here and play with the hot water,' Romy said. She was longing to get clean and into her pyjamas.

'Me too,' Lesley said. 'I'm dying for a shower.'

Ethan and Danny were both for the pub.

'Perfect!' Lesley said. 'You can all have a boys' night out, and we'll have a girls' night in.'

✻

Later, when they were both showered and in their pyjamas, Romy and Lesley sat in front of the fire in their sleeping bags and shared a bottle of wine. At first their conversation consisted entirely of extolling the virtues of the shower, and groaning with delight over the hot water.

'You have to dump your fake boyfriend,' Lesley said, when they had finally exhausted the topic of how amazing it felt to be clean.

'What? Why?'

'Because you have to get with the brother. He's so into you.'

'He's just flirty. He's like that with everyone.'

'He's not like that with me.'

'Well, that's just because he's polite and it would be rude if he was flirting with both of us at the same time. If I wasn't around, I bet he'd be just the same way with you. It's a reflex with him.'

'I don't think so. Have you not seen the way he looks at you? It's obvious he has the hots for you.'

'He's a total man-whore. He fancies anyone with a fanny and a pulse.'

'Well, all the more reason. You've got a fanny and a pulse, so he's a sure thing. You need to get back in the game. This is your chance.'

'But I don't want to be just another notch on his bedpost. You know I'm not good at casual sex and one-night stands.'

'I don't think he just wants a one-stand with you. Honestly, Romy, you're there in your Bob the Builder outfit, not a curve in sight or a screed of make-up on, and he's looking at you like you're Playmate of the Month. He's got it bad.'

'Don't be daft,' Romy said, though she couldn't help smiling at the thought of Ethan wanting her like that. She caught the desire in his eyes sometimes when he looked at her, but she tried not to read too much into it. It was just his way, she told herself.

'I'm telling you, he couldn't look more enthralled if you were spread-eagled with your chuff in the air, your tits falling out of a bustier and a staple through your stomach.'

'What a charming image!'

'I bet Ethan would think so. Seriously, he looks like he wants to eat you – in the good way.'

Romy thought longingly of having a man touch her – having Ethan touch her. 'A fling would be nice,' she said wistfully.

'There you go.'

'A lovely, uncomplicated fling with a nice, straightforward guy.' God, it would be wonderful, she thought. It was way too long since she'd had sex – and sometimes, lately, she was overwhelmed with panic that she might never have it again. Ethan was certainly uncomplicated.

'You really like him, don't you?' Lesley said.

'Yeah,' she admitted, 'I do. But nothing can happen,' she said firmly, not sure if she was trying to talk herself or Lesley out of it. 'I mean, even if I did break up with Kit, what would his family think if I ditched him and took up with his brother straight away? I'd look like a right ho. They probably wouldn't be too pleased with Ethan either.'

She sipped her wine, gazing into the fire. If only she'd never agreed to be Kit's fake girlfriend. Still, maybe it was just as well. She really did like Ethan – a lot – and she was rubbish at casual sex. A fling would be nice while it lasted, but she would just end up wanting more.

'No,' she said finally, 'I'm just going to have to be faithful to my fake boyfriend – for better or worse.'

Chapter Twenty

The following morning, they all slept late and after another big breakfast, packed up to go home. As they had hardly left the house in two days, they decided to spend some time checking out the surrounding area and then go to one of the local pubs for lunch before heading back to Dublin. The village was tiny, but quaint, with brightly painted cottages and a pretty stone bridge over a small, rushing river. Despite its size, it boasted three pubs, a couple of cafés and a Chinese restaurant as well as the pizza takeaway they had already made use of. After exploring the village, they went for a walk in the woods that were at one end of it. It was a bright, cold day, bringing the surrounding landscape into the vivid Technicolor of an old movie – the browns, greens and russets of the rolling hills contrasted sharply by the clear blue sky. Their breath hung in clouds before them as they crunched through the crisp leaves underfoot.

'It's very scenic around here,' Romy said as they made their way back through the village. 'And there's a championship golf course nearby too. It'd be a good location for a country house hotel.'

'Ooh, this is lovely,' Lesley said, looking around as they entered the pub. It was large but broken up into lots of cosy little nooks and crannies. The decor was comfortingly old-fashioned, with exposed ceiling beams and whitewashed stone walls adorned with a plethora of horsey paraphernalia.

'This is nicer than the one we went to last night,' Kit said as they settled into a pair of squashy sofas in front of an open fire.

'Well, this situation just calls out for lunch-time drinking,' Lesley said. 'I think I'll have a hot whiskey – or an Irish coffee.' She chewed her lip thoughtfully. 'I know – both!'

'That sounds like heaven,' Romy said. 'I wish I could join you.'

'Why don't you?' Kit asked.

'Can't – driving.'

'Oh, yeah.'

'What kind of insurance do you have on the van?' Ethan asked.

'Not the kind that covers drink driving.'

He gave her a patient look. 'I mean, can anyone drive it?'

'Oh, yeah – it's open insurance.'

'Well, why don't I drive back and you can drink whatever you want.'

'Oh, no – it's fine. But thanks.'

'Go on. I'm not bothered. And I don't imagine you get many opportunities to be decadent now you have Luke.'

'Go on,' Lesley nudged her. 'I hate drinking alone.'

'I'm sure you won't be alone,' Romy said, nodding at the others.

'Ah, they're boys. It's not the same.'

'All right, then. Thanks,' she said to Ethan, really touched by his thoughtfulness.

'Great!' Lesley said. 'Why don't we start with a pair of hot whiskies, and then have Irish coffee for dessert?'

'Good plan,' Romy smiled, sinking back into the plush sofa with a contented sigh.

'So what'll we have to eat?' Lesley said, picking up a menu. 'God, I love a roast lunch in a pub, but I'm still too full after breakfast.'

'Me too,' Romy said. 'I'll have the smoked salmon.'

Ethan ordered roast turkey with all the trimmings, but everyone else declared themselves too full to manage more than soup and sandwiches. As he laid into a huge roast dinner, which he pronounced amazing, Romy couldn't help wondering where Ethan put it all. How did he manage to eat so much food without racking up a single ounce of extra flab?

After two hot whiskies, piles of silky soft smoked salmon on thick slices of home-made brown soda bread and Irish coffee for dessert, Romy felt mellow and contented as a cat, every instinct urging her to curl up on the sofa and fall asleep in the glow of the fire.

'C'mon, sleepyhead,' Danny said, pulling her off the sofa as they all got up to leave, and she realised she had nodded off. He kept a steadying arm around her as they walked back to the cars and she staggered along beside him, her legs protesting wildly about being made to move and refusing to co-operate.

'I thought I might drop into the garden centre on the way home,' Danny said to Kit when they reached the cars. 'So maybe you should go back with Romy in the van.'

'Oh, no – I'll go to the garden centre with you, if that's okay.'

'Sure, it's fine by me. I could show you some of the stuff I'd be thinking of for your grounds.'

'There's plenty of room in the van, now that we've got rid of all the stuff,' Ethan said to Kit.

'I know, but I'd like to go to the garden centre.'

'Really?' Ethan could hardly have looked more surprised if Kit had said he quite fancied going to a Justin Bieber concert.

'Yes, really,' Kit said a little defensively.

'Okay, if you're sure.' Ethan looked at him doubtfully.

'I am. I'll see you all back at the ranch,' Kit called as he climbed into the Land Rover beside Danny.

'Well, that was weird,' Ethan said as they watched them drive away.

❄

Kit wasn't surprised Ethan had looked askew at him when he was so keen to go to the garden centre with Danny. Trips to the garden centre with their parents had been the bane of their childhood lives. He, Ethan and Hannah hadn't agreed on much, but they were unanimous that a visit to a garden centre was the worst weekend outing ever. But he was enjoying Danny's company, and he wanted to enjoy it a bit longer, even if it meant traipsing around endless aisles of muck and greenery that all looked the same to him. He figured he could get through it, and then maybe he could persuade Danny to go out for a drink or something to eat when they got home.

He was shocked to discover that he was actually having a good time. Danny was so knowledgeable, and his enthusiasm was infectious. Kit didn't have a clue what he was talking about half the time, but he liked listening to him as he showed him plants that he thought would work for his house and explained how they would look in full bloom and how certain flowers and shrubs would complement others. He got quite animated as he outlined various ideas for the garden, and he painted such a vivid picture that Kit actually found himself becoming excited about weird things like topiary trees and rhododendrons.

All the staff seemed to know Danny – and adore him – and he was constantly stopping to chat to people as they walked around. Despite his shyness, he had that gift for talking to strangers that Kit had always admired in others, not possessing it himself, and he often fell into conversation with other Sunday shoppers, swapping notes and giving advice, or just enthusing over a plant they both loved. Right now he was engaged in telling a young couple how to revive a dying rose bush, and Kit hung back, listening happily as they spouted gobbledygook at each other.

'Thank you so much,' the woman said with a wide smile.

'No problem. Good luck with it,' Danny said as they turned to go. 'I hope it works.'

Danny reminded Kit so much of Romy sometimes. It wasn't just the way he helped other people out – he had the same quiet assurance that she had, at ease with who he was and with a complete lack of pretence.

'Sorry,' Danny said, turning to him. 'This must be really boring for you.'

'No, not at all,' Kit assured him. 'I'm glad I came.'

'Well, I'm almost done. I just want to pick up some things in the hardware, and then we can go and have afternoon tea if you like. They have a brilliant café here. It's all home-made stuff – mostly organic.'

'Yeah, that'd be great.'

When Danny had been around the hardware section, they

went to the checkout. Kit watched as Danny chatted with the checkout girl, who was clearly a fan, judging by the way she was smiling adoringly at him, fluttering her eyelashes and sticking her chest out.

You can stick your tits out until they poke him in the eye, sweetheart, Kit thought, *but he's never going to be interested.*

Danny remained his charming, affable self as they bantered back and forth.

'What?' Danny turned to him, laughing as he shoved his wallet back into his pocket, and Kit realised that he'd been standing there goggling at him admiringly like a total fan-boy.

'Nothing,' he said, feeling flustered and caught out. 'Let's go get that tea.'

The checkout girl handed Danny a ticket. 'Give Declan there a shout when you're ready to go,' she said, nodding to a brawny shaven-headed youth with little silver hoops in his ears, 'and he'll bring that out to the car for you.'

'Thanks.' Danny put the ticket in his pocket and wheeled the trolley towards the exit. 'I'll just get this lot in the car first,' he said to Kit.

'I was just thinking that poor girl doesn't realise she doesn't stand a chance with you,' he said as they walked to the car park.

'Leah? She knows I'm gay. I used to come here with Paul a lot.'

'Really? She seemed to be giving it her all.'

Danny shrugged. 'She enjoys flirting – it's just a bit of fun. And I don't have any objections,' he said, grinning. 'I mean it's nice to feel fancied, isn't it – even by someone you don't fancy back?'

'I guess.'

Kit helped him put the stuff in the back of the Land Rover. 'Right, that's it,' Danny said, slamming the boot door shut.

'Wait, there's something missing,' Kit said. 'Where's your mud?'

'My *mud*?' Danny frowned, his lips twitching.

'Mud … earth … whatever it's called. You bought bags and bags of it, remember?'

'Oh, the compost! That's what Declan's going to bring out when we're ready to leave.'

'Oh. Okay.'

Danny led the way to the café and they sat on benches at a big rustic wooden table.

'Everything here is good,' he said, 'but the apple tart is *amazing*.'

'I'll take your word for it,' Kit said, smiling as he put the menu back on the table. 'Apple tart it is.'

A young girl came to take their order. 'Ah, my favourite customer,' she said, smiling at Danny as she pulled a notepad from her pocket. 'Don't tell me,' she said, pen hovering over the paper, 'hot apple tart with cream and a large pot of tea.'

'You know me so well.' Danny smiled back at her.

She turned to Kit.

'I'll have what he's having.'

'Good choice. And I don't just mean the apple tart,' she said with a wink, nodding to Danny. She skipped off, smiling to herself.

'Sorry,' Danny said, blushing. 'She seems to think you're my new boyfriend.'

'I don't mind,' Kit said, shrugging.

'You don't?'

'Actually, I'm kind of flattered. You seem to be considered quite the catch around here.'

The waitress came back with a tray and placed a huge slice of apple tart with cream in front of each of them.

'You'll never guess who we had in here earlier today,' she

said to Danny as she unloaded a teapot, milk and sugar onto the table. 'I couldn't believe he had the nerve to show his face.'

Danny looked alarmed. 'Paul?' he asked.

The girl nodded. 'I didn't let him have any apple tart. I told him we'd sold out. You should have seen his face.' She laughed. 'He could see it, right there on the counter in front of him. "What's that?" he says, pointing to it. But I just said we had to keep enough for our *loyal* customers. I let him have a scone. Unfortunately, we didn't have any of yesterday's left, so I had to give him a fresh one.' She sighed.

'What time was this? Is he still here?' Danny looked panicked, his eyes darting around the café.

'No, it was a while ago,' the girl said with a wave of her hand. 'I'm sure he's long gone. Anyway, you've done much better for yourself,' she said with a little smile at Kit. 'And he's traded down big-time, so all's well that ends well.'

'He … he was with someone?'

'Yeah, creepy-looking fella,' she said, wrinkling her nose. 'Good enough for him, if you ask me. Well, enjoy your tart. If you need anything else, just shout,' she said cheerily and bustled off.

Danny was a bit subdued after that. Poor guy, Kit thought – he was obviously freaked at the thought of running into his ex.

'You were right,' Kit said, 'this tart is incredible.' The pastry was thick, almost like shortbread, and the apples tasted fragrant and sweet as spring air, like they had just been picked from the tree that morning – which they probably had.

Danny smiled weakly in return. Kit tried to engage him in conversation, but he was edgy and distracted, and he was anxious to leave as soon as they finished their tea.

'I just have to go and pee,' Kit said as they stood up to go.

'Okay. I'll give Declan a shout, and I'll wait for you at the front door.'

When Kit came out of the toilets, he saw Danny standing by the exit fidgeting. As he walked over to him, Danny was approached by two men. *Shit!* Kit could guess who they were by Danny's body language even before he got close enough to see that they were holding hands. Danny looked awkward and uncomfortable, his hands shoved into his pockets and his shoulders up around his ears. The smile on his face did nothing to disguise the stricken look in his eyes. Kit was in no doubt that this was Paul and his new man. The waitress was right – he did look creepy. All that hair! He was like a walking carpet. Unless, of course, that was Paul. But either way, she was right – the baldy one looked creepy too. If only they could have shared the hair out between them, they'd both be better off.

Kit felt guilty. If he hadn't gone to the loo, they'd have got away in time and Danny could have avoided having to face Paul and his new boyfriend. Still, he thought, maybe there was a way he could make it better. He ran his fingers through his hair, took a deep breath and strode up to Danny.

'Sorry to keep you waiting,' he said, slinging an arm casually around Danny's shoulders. He felt him start. 'Aren't you going to introduce me?' he said, nodding to the couple. Fuzzy-Wuzzy's eyebrows had shot up into his hairline – which wasn't much of a distance, in fairness.

'Oh, um … yeah.' Danny recovered quickly and Kit felt his shoulders relax. 'This is Paul,' he said, indicating Fuzzy-Wuzzy. 'Paul, Kit.'

Paul eyed Kit up speculatively as they shook hands, and Kit was pleased that he looked put out. *Yeah, in your face, sucker! Danny's done much better for himself. And that baldy weasel is much more in your league.* He didn't think he was being arrogant. It was just realistic. By any objective standard, Kit knew he was way hotter than Paul.

'And this is his … um, this is James.' James was short and stocky. He looked older than any of them, but was refusing to make any concession to the fact that he was middle-aged. His close-shaven head was clearly meant to look like a fashion choice, but only drew attention to the fact that he was balding. His too-tight jumper was designed to show off his muscles, but unfortunately also clung to every roll of flab and didn't quite cover his jutting beer belly. God, what ugly children the pair of them would have, Kit thought, feeling triumphant on Danny's behalf.

When they were done shaking hands, Kit slipped an arm around Danny's waist, pulling him into his side. 'So, you've been shopping, I see,' he said, nodding to the full trolley beside Paul and James.

'Yes. We've just moved into a new place, so we're starting from scratch,' Paul said, with a wary glance at Danny.

'Oh! Didn't you take any of the stuff from your old place?' Danny asked.

'No, James didn't think there was anything worth taking,' Paul said.

Kit felt Danny flinch.

'It's not worth the hassle, is it?' James said. 'Digging things up and replanting them.'

'Besides, James has a vision of how he wants the garden, don't you?' Paul said. 'The old stuff wouldn't really work.'

'Well, it was a bit old-fashioned, wasn't it?' James said. 'A bit chintzy. I mean, it was very nice in its own way, don't get me wrong. But I want to do something a bit more contemporary – a bit funky.'

'So, what do you do, James?' Kit asked, more to change the subject than because he wanted to know.

'I'm in the music business.'

'Ah. Right.' That explained the desperate clinging onto youth.

'How about you?'

'I'm sort of between jobs at the moment, taking some time out.' He didn't want to say he was unemployed for Danny's sake. 'But I'm developing an old property I inherited and Danny's helping me with the grounds. I'm completely clueless about gardening, I'm afraid.'

'Well, you couldn't have a better person to guide you than Danny,' Paul said, earning a scowl from James.

'I know. Coming here with him has been a complete revelation. It's like a whole new world. And the café is amazing! Have you been?'

'Er, yes, we went there earlier.'

'Isn't it fantastic? Such friendly staff! What was that girl's name?' he asked Danny.

'Susie.'

'Yes, such a pet! And the food! Did you have the apple tart?' he asked James. 'It is literally to die for.'

'So I hear,' James said, glowering.

'I've been raving about it to James, but they didn't have any ready when we were there,' Paul said.

'Oh, shame. Well – next time maybe. Come on,' he said to Danny, 'we'd better get going. Where's that hunky boy who was going to take the stuff out to the car for us?'

'If you mean Declan,' Paul said, 'apparently he's not available today. They're a bit short-staffed. We had to do all the heavy lifting ourselves.'

Danny looked around. 'Oh no, there he is,' he said, waving at the boy who was striding towards them.

'Yo, Danny,' he said as he reached them. 'And you must be Danny's new fella.' He turned to Kit. 'Pleased to meet you.' He held out his hand and they shook. 'I've heard a lot about you.'

'You have?'

'Word travels fast in this place,' he said with a grin. 'So, you're ready to go now, Danny?'

'Yeah.'

'I have your stuff out front, so lead the way.'

'Well, it was good to see you, Danny,' Paul said. 'Nice to meet you, Kit.'

'Yeah, you too,' Danny said.

When they had all said goodbye with studied politeness, Declan followed Kit and Danny outside where he picked up several bags of compost, and they loaded it into the car. When Declan had taken his leave and was walking back into the store, Danny burst out laughing. 'Oh my God, that was brilliant! Did you see Paul's face?'

'Yeah. He looked like he'd just eaten roadkill and it didn't agree with him.'

'Thanks,' Danny said shyly, slapping Kit on the back.

'No problem,' Kit said, relieved that Danny hadn't taken offence at his interference. He had acted on the spur of the moment, and it was only afterwards that it occurred to him that Danny may not appreciate his little stunt. He was glad he had managed to cheer him up.

But once they were in the car, Danny's buoyant mood seemed to evaporate, and he sat gazing out the windscreen, seemingly lost in thought. 'I don't know how James could say there was nothing worth taking from Paul's place,' he said sadly. 'I'd put a lot of work into that garden, and we'd spent a fortune on it. It was really beautiful.' He turned to Kit with big mournful eyes.

'I'm sure it was.'

'I mean, maybe it wasn't cool or "funky", but Paul isn't a cool, funky kind of guy, you know?'

'I can tell.' Kit sighed. 'Look, clearly Paul doesn't know a good thing when he has it. If he could throw you away, what would it cost him to get rid of a few trees and plants? You deserve better than him,' he said, touching Danny's cheek with the back of a finger.

Danny recoiled instantly. 'Hey, what are you doing?' His eyes were filled with confusion.

'Sorry, I just—' Kit's eyes flicked to the window behind Danny. 'It's just that Paul's there, looking right at us.'

'He is?'

Kit nodded, glancing towards the window again. 'Why don't we really give him something to look at?' he said before bending his head and pressing his lips to Danny's in a soft, innocent kiss. He felt Danny stiffen in surprise, his lips remaining rigid, and he pulled back slightly. 'Only if you want to,' he said, searching Danny's eyes, watching the conflicting emotions that passed across his face as he hesitated. Finally, he gave a barely perceptible nod, and Kit kissed him again, stroking the short hair at the nape of his neck until he felt him relax, his eyes fluttering closed. This time Danny's lips were soft and yielding and they started to move tentatively under his as he started to kiss Kit back. His eyes were still closed when Kit finally pulled away. Then they fluttered open, a small smile lifting the corners of his mouth as he blinked at Kit.

'Wow, that was …' He shook his head. He looked confused, scared and happy all at once, which was pretty much exactly how Kit was feeling himself. He really shouldn't have done that. And yet he couldn't quite bring himself to regret it.

'It was nice. You're a good kisser,' he said to Danny.

'Um … thanks. So are you. I mean, I know it's not what you're into – kissing blokes, but …'

Kit shrugged. 'A kiss is a kiss. It's like flirting. It's nice whoever you do it with.'

Danny smiled, seeming a little reassured. Then he turned to look out his window. 'I don't see Paul,' he said.

Kit followed his gaze. 'Oh, he's gone now. They just drove away. But believe me, he saw every second of that. He couldn't take his eyes off us.'

'Really?' Danny grinned.

'Absolutely,' Kit smiled back, as Danny started up the car. 'And if you thought he looked sick before …'

Chapter Twenty-One

Had developing always been this knackering or had she just forgotten, Romy wondered, several days later as she leaned wearily against the worktop of the gate lodge kitchen and gazed out the window into the darkness of the morning. She flicked on the radio while she waited for the coffee to brew, and 'Fairytale of New York' was playing, an unwelcome reminder that Christmas was fast approaching. She was usually prepared weeks in advance for Christmas, but this year she had nothing organised and the thought of it just made her feel even more overwhelmed.

The work had always been tiring, but in a satisfying

way that left her feeling content and guaranteed a restful, refreshing sleep. She had missed the physicality of it, the satisfaction of doing something practical and seeing real, concrete results for your efforts. But they were only three days into the project and she was so exhausted she felt physically sick – and work had barely begun. Perhaps she had been away from developing for too long and had gone soft. She couldn't seem to summon her old energy, and she couldn't remember feeling this bone-aching weariness before. But then, she hadn't had a small baby to look after in those days. Maybe she had been naive to think she could just go back to her old routine and expect everything to be the same now that she had Luke.

It was probably just lack of sleep, she told herself, yawning and rubbing her eyes. Luke had been peevish the previous night and had woken up several times. She had only just got him back to sleep about half an hour ago. However, despite her exhaustion, she had been unable to fall back asleep herself. These dark winter days didn't help either; it was almost eight o'clock and there was only the merest hint of light creeping across the sky. It was hard to feel energetic when it was so gloomy all the time.

At the start of the week, she had moved down to the gate lodge with Kit and Ethan, and together they began to do what work they could on the house while waiting for planning permission. At the moment, it mainly consisted of gutting the place of all its junk and old furniture, stripping walls and laying bare foundations, while Romy lined up contractors and sourced materials. The roofers were due to start tomorrow, so at least they should be able to get something major accomplished before Christmas.

Having Ethan staying with them meant that Romy and Kit had to keep up the pretence that they were together, and share the double bed she had installed in one of the bedrooms along with a cot for Luke. But it didn't feel awkward now that sex had been taken out of the equation and she knew they would never be more than platonic friends – and she enjoyed the giggly, whispered conversations they had in the dark. Besides, she was glad to have Ethan there. As well as being hard-working and energetic, he was great with Luke. Kit always showed willing and tried his best to do the dad thing, but Ethan was a natural. It was good having him around as long as she didn't let herself dwell on how much she'd rather be sharing a bed with him than Kit.

She was just pouring herself a mug of coffee when the door opened and Ethan came in, bringing a blast of cold air with him. She looked up in surprise. 'I didn't think anyone else was up.'

'Yeah, I went out for a run,' he said, still panting slightly. He was dressed in light grey sweats and he looked energised and vital, his cheeks flushed and his eyes bright. She could practically feel the energy rolling off him and she felt a little stab of envy.

'Coffee?' she offered.

'Yes please.' He rubbed his hands together.

'It must be freezing out,' she said, handing him a mug.

'Yeah, but it feels good when you get going.' He cupped his hands around the mug, warming them.

She knew just how that felt – lungs bursting with cold, crisp air, heart pumping, the sheer animal energy of it. 'God, I miss that,' she said as they sat at the table together.

'Miss what?'

'Running.'

'You run?'

'Well, I used to. I stopped when I was pregnant, and since Luke was born, it's all I can do to have a shower.'

'I'll watch him, if you want to go out.'

'You would?'

'Sure.'

Despite how tired she felt, the thought of running was appealing. She knew how invigorating it could be. Maybe if she started running, she could get back to the right kind of tired. 'Thanks. I might take you up on it tomorrow.'

'You look tired,' he said, his eyes raking over her.

'I'm knackered,' she said, rubbing her hair. 'Luke didn't sleep much last night.'

'Yeah, I heard him.'

'Sorry. I hope he didn't wake you.'

'Not so that I couldn't get back to sleep. Did Kit get up with him at all?'

'Oh, yes. He takes his fatherly duties very seriously,' she said with a wry smile.

'He does.' Ethan laughed softly.

'Sometimes I think he's almost convinced himself that he's really Luke's father – which he's not, by the way,' she added.

'I know he's not.'

'I don't know why he feels he has to act like he is. It's almost like he thinks it's expected of him or something.'

'I think Mom's largely to blame for that,' Ethan said. 'I've heard her lecturing him on the responsibility that comes with going out with a single mother. He's had dire warnings about being good to Luke and not messing you around.'

'Oh.'

'You can put him in with me tonight, if you like – since his dad won't be around.'

Kit had been contacted out of the blue by one of the companies he'd sent his CV to when he first returned to Ireland and was going back to Dublin later that day to get ready for an interview early tomorrow morning. Romy was already feeling jittery at the thought of being left alone with Ethan for the night. She couldn't deny the attraction she felt for him, and what really killed her was that it seemed to be mutual. She hadn't admitted it to Lesley, but, like everyone else, she knew when someone fancied her, and she was fairly certain that if Kit wasn't in the way, something would happen with Ethan. Just her luck that when she finally felt that spark again, it was with someone she couldn't have.

'That's really sweet of you, but I'm hoping last night was a once-off. He's usually a really good sleeper.'

'You're not talking about this guy, I take it?' Kit said, striding into the kitchen carrying a wide-awake Luke and handing him to Romy.

'What are you doing up again, Mister?' Romy chided.

Luke stared back at her with the face of a Zen master, inscrutable and all-knowing.

'I think he needs changing. I'd do it, but I'm heading off.'

'Already? You're not even going to have any breakfast?'

'No, I'm meeting Mark, a guy I know who works at this company. He's going to give me some coaching for the interview,' he said, shrugging on his jacket. 'Then I have to sort out a suit, and try to find a shirt Mom hasn't put through the wash.'

'At least you'll get a decent night's sleep tonight. Well, good luck.'

'Thanks.' He bent and kissed her, and then planted a soft kiss on Luke's forehead. 'I'll see you tomorrow.'

'Knock 'em dead,' Ethan called after him.

And then there were two, Romy thought, suddenly very aware of being alone in the house with Ethan.

'So, alone at last,' Ethan said with a cheeky grin, echoing her thoughts. She tried not to let it rattle her. After all, it was only for one night. Kit was coming straight back down tomorrow as soon as the interview was over. Nothing could happen in one night …

＊

That evening as she and Ethan ate dinner, Romy felt quite pleased with herself. She had worked companionably with Ethan all day and she had managed to play it cool and not act like an infatuated idiot. Luke was back to his smiley, happy self and she was grateful for the focus he provided as they ate. In a couple of hours, they could go to bed – separately – and tomorrow Kit would be back, and everything would return to normal. She was almost there. Then something caught her eye through the window and her heart sank.

'Oh, no – that's all we need,' she groaned, jumping up and going to the window. Snow was falling thickly, fat swirling flakes dancing in the light from the kitchen.

'Maybe it won't stick,' Ethan said, coming to join her at the window.

But Romy knew there wasn't much chance of that. It had been freezing hard for the past week, it hadn't rained in ages, and the snow was falling so heavily. Even as they watched, it settled on the grass in a dense layer. 'It's already sticking,' she said.

＊

When Romy woke the next morning, she sprang out of bed and opened the curtains, hoping that by some miracle the snow might have melted in the night. Her hopes were dashed as she looked out at the Christmas card scene before her. Everywhere was covered in a thick white icing, the boughs of the trees bending under the weight of it, the deep forest green of small shrubs peeking through the frosting like the decorations on top of a Christmas cake. That special snowy silence had descended, like someone had pressed the mute button. Bright sunlight glinted on snow-laden branches and fat heavy flakes were still falling from the leaden sky. It was very beautiful – and an absolute bugger.

'Shit, shit, shit!' she cursed. There was no way the roofers could work today, even if they were able to get here, which was highly unlikely. The snow would bring everything to a grinding halt – for who knew how long? Not only that, but she was now stuck here alone with Ethan. How could she ignore him if she had no work to occupy her all day? She would just have to find something she could do to keep herself busy. She checked on Luke, but he was still sleeping soundly. She pulled on a big thick cardigan and a pair of Uggs and made her way downstairs. The smell of frying bacon told her Ethan was already up before she got to the kitchen. He was standing by the cooker watching over bacon and sausages that hissed and spat in a pan.

'Morning!' He turned and grinned at her. He looked rugged and utterly delicious, dressed in a thick wool jumper, faded jeans and chunky hiking boots. 'You're just in time,' he said, indicating the pan. 'Fried egg?'

'Yes, please,' she said, flicking the switch on the kettle as she went to stand beside him. 'Well, this is a bit of a disaster,' she said, nodding out the window.

'I know. And according to the weather forecast, it's set to last all week.'

'Oh God!' Romy groaned in anguish, leaning on the worktop as she waited for the kettle to boil. 'We're not going to be able to get on with anything. Maybe we should just go back to Dublin.'

'No chance of that,' he said, shaking his head. 'I've been

out. The roads are completely impassable. Even if we could make it, it'd take about two days to get there.'

'So Kit won't be able to get back down either.'

'No. According to the radio, it's bad everywhere. The whole country seems to have ground to a halt.'

Christ, she was stuck here on her own with Ethan for God knows how long – no way out and no way in for anyone else who could act as a buffer. And no work she could focus her energies on. This was a nightmare. She made the tea, and Ethan finished cooking the breakfast in silence, placing two plates on the table.

'So, you've been out?' she asked him as they sat down to eat.

'Yeah. It's a beautiful day. I chopped some more logs for the fire.'

'Oh. Good. Thanks.' *Gah!* The thought of Ethan chopping logs was making her go all funny. It was ridiculous – could he get any more hunter/gatherer? She tried not to picture him cutting wood, looking all manly and outdoorsy in his thick jumper and stompy boots, the muscles shifting in his arms as he swung the axe— 'Well, there must be something we can do today,' she said.

'We could make a snowman.'

'Yeah, great suggestion,' she smiled. 'Thanks.'

'It could add a lot of value to the house. We could make it a feature.'

'I was thinking I might get on with choosing the bathrooms and doing some ordering.'

'Or we could have a snowball fight.'

Oh God, a snowball fight – was he trying to kill her? She imagined them wrestling on the ground, wriggling around in the snow, his icy hand on her skin as he tried to stuff a snowball down her top … Her nipples hardened just thinking about it.

'Um … yeah, I think I'll get on with choosing the bathrooms. This is great, by the way,' she said, indicating her plate. 'Thanks.'

'No problem.' He smiled at her. 'Well,' he sighed, 'if you're not up for a snowball fight, I suppose I could get on with stripping out the old kitchen.'

'Yeah, that's a good idea,' she said, pushing her plate away. 'Right, I'm going to hop in the shower and get going. See you later.'

'Okay. See you.'

✳

The steps up to Romy's house were treacherous, and Kit clung to the rail as he climbed, his body rigid with the effort of staying upright. His good shoes had no grip, but he didn't feel he could turn up for an interview in Wellingtons. When he finally made it into the house, he bounded up the stairs and knocked on May's door.

'Oh, hello, Kit!' She smiled at him as she opened the door. 'You look very smart!'

'I'm going to an interview this morning.' He had been relieved when they had phoned to tell him it would still go ahead, though a little later than originally planned because of the traffic difficulties. 'Anyway, I was just wondering if you wanted me to get you anything while I'm out.'

'Oh, that's very thoughtful of you. Yes, I could do with a few things and we haven't been able to get out. Come in for a moment – unless you're in a hurry?'

'No, I have plenty of time.' He had booked a cab so far in advance that even if the taxi driver crawled there on his hands and knees with Kit on his back, they would still make it with time to spare.

She brought him in and sat him down at the kitchen table while she made a list.

'We could do with more milk,' she said, thinking aloud as she wrote, 'and might as well get more bread. We can always freeze it, and who knows how long this weather will last. Better get some fresh fruit too – don't want us getting rickets, do we?' She paused in her writing and looked up at him. 'Is there any chance you'd be passing a chemist?'

'Sure,' Kit said with a shrug. 'I can go to a chemist if you like.'

'I think Frank's out of his ointment. Let me go and check.' She stood and left the room, coming back shortly afterwards with a tube of cream. 'I'll just write down the name,' she said, adding it to the list. 'And if you could get us a few boxes of condoms too?'

Kit gulped and nodded.

'If you could get an assortment, it'd be great. Some ribbed ones, and a few boxes of flavoured ones as well,' she said, writing again. 'I'm doing a Tantric sex workshop next week, and I like to have plenty of condoms to hand out. I do try to promote safe sex, and if you can make it fun, that's half the battle isn't it?' she said. 'So, if you see any novelty ones – glow in the dark or whatever – you could pick those up too.'

She handed the list over and Kit frowned down at it. 'Um … any particular flavour?' he asked.

'Just get as wide a variety as you can.'

'Okay, well, I'd better be off,' Kit said, standing.

'Just let me get my purse,' she said, leading him into the sitting room. 'It's really very good of you to think of the old people in this weather,' she said as she handed him a couple of fifty euro notes. 'I'm terrified of slipping on the pavement, and those steps are a death trap. You have to be very careful at our age.'

Kit's eyes drifted to the swing on the ceiling. 'Yes, I'm sure,' he murmured. 'Well, I'll see you later.'

'Bye,' she said as she saw him to the door. 'And best of luck with the interview!'

✳

Romy spent the rest of the morning holed up in her bedroom with her catalogues and spreadsheets, deciding on fittings and furniture for the bathrooms and placing orders online, in between feeding and playing with Luke. When she got hungry around midday, she went to the kitchen and made herself a sandwich, relieved that Ethan wasn't around. She knew she should ask him if he wanted anything, but she was too much of a coward. She made a mug of tea, devoured her sandwich quickly and went back to work, feeling sneaky, but glad she had managed to avoid him.

In the afternoon, when she was starting to suffer from cabin fever, she wrapped Luke up in all the warmest things she could find, put on her Wellingtons and took him out to show him the snow.

'Look, Luke, isn't it pretty?' she said, her breath clouding in front of her. Luke chattered away to her as she carried him around the grounds, taking off his mittens to let him touch the snow, his nose wrinkling at the cold. She shook branches and watched his eyes dance in wonder as the snow cascaded from them like a sprinkling of talc. Glancing up at the house, she saw Ethan standing at an upstairs window watching them. He waved, and she waved back, smiling up at him, and she made Luke wave too, shaking his arm for him. Then she felt guilty because Ethan looked like a little boy with his nose pressed against the window, longing to go out and have fun in the snow, so she beckoned to him to join them. He disappeared from the window, and moments later the front door opened and he came out, pulling on a thick jacket as he walked down the steps and strode over to them.

'Changed your mind about the snowman?' he asked, and Romy had to grin at the boyish enthusiasm that lit up his face.

'Um … I've kind of got my hands full,' she said, indicating Luke. 'But feel free.'

'Maybe later. It's no fun on your own. Here, let me take him for a while,' he said, holding out his arms.

Romy passed Luke to him, grateful to be relieved of his weight for a while. They walked around the field in front of the house, chatting about their morning's work, and playing with Luke. Luke shrieked with laughter when Ethan ran very fast with him and Romy chased them, her feet sinking into the deep snow as she lumbered after them. Ethan would slow down to let her catch up, making Luke squeal with delight when he swerved away again just as she reached them.

He was really good with babies, Romy thought as they walked back to the house. God, was there anything he wasn't good at?

'Well, time for this one's nap,' she said when they got to the lodge. They stamped snow off their boots at the door and she took Luke from Ethan.

Probably tired after all the fresh air, Luke went to sleep really quickly. When she came back into the kitchen, Ethan was still standing there in his jacket. 'Cup of tea?' she asked, moving to put the kettle on.

He shook his head. 'Later,' he said, grabbing her hand. 'Come outside again.'

'What?'

'I want to make that snowman.'

'You're serious?'

'Absolutely. Come on,' he pleaded. 'It never snowed like this when I was a kid. I never got to make a proper snowman. I had a deprived childhood.'

Romy looked at him helplessly. How could she resist that face? 'I still have things to do ...' she said, making a token protest, but already knowing she was going to cave in.

'You can do them tomorrow. Come on, we can skive off – no one will know. Besides, everyone else is having a snow day. We should get one too.'

'Okay,' she smiled, and was rewarded by his face lighting up. She grabbed her coat from the hook and pulled it back on, along with her gloves, hat and scarf, and they went outside again.

✳

Snowman-building turned out to be hard work, especially as Ethan was insistent that it had to be a substantial one, in keeping with the grandeur of the house. The garden now boasted a very impressive model, constructed of two huge boulders of snow, and even sporting a classic carrot nose. It took Romy a while to cool down after their exertions and it was only when she was starting to cook dinner that she noticed how cold it had got in the house and went to check the radiator. Finding it stone cold, she turned the knob the other way, even though she knew it was already turned on and she was switching it off. Shit! She went to check the radiator in Luke's room and found that cold too. There was obviously something wrong with the heating. It was snowing again already and the weather forecast was for more snow tomorrow. They'd freeze to death. She went out to check the boiler and found it dead, but she didn't have a clue what was wrong. When she had tried switching it off and on again a few times to no avail, she decided to check the oil tank. She found a dipstick, got a ladder from the shed and confirmed her worst fears. They were out of oil. Damn! What a time for this to happen! There was no way of getting an oil company to deliver anytime soon. She had listened to the news on the radio, and it seemed the whole country had come to a standstill. When she got back to the house, Ethan was in the kitchen, stirring the sauce on the hob.

'The heating's clapped out,' she told him. 'There's no oil.'

'Oh shit! I thought it had got very cold.'

'And there's no hope of getting a delivery until the snow clears.'

'Well, at least we've got the fire – and we still have those heaters you brought down.'

Romy nodded. 'They won't be enough on their own in the bedrooms, though. We should camp out in here. I guess one of us could sleep on the sofa, and we can use one of the camp beds.'

Ethan shook his head. 'After dinner I'll bring your mattress in here and you can have a proper bed in front of the fire. I'll take the sofa.'

Chapter Twenty-Two

When he returned that afternoon, Kit was surprised to see that the path had been cleared, the snow shovelled to one side. As he headed for the steps, Danny emerged from the door to the garden with a shovel. Out of the corner of his eye, Kit saw his Land Rover parked outside the gate, surprised he hadn't noticed it as he came in.

'Hi, Danny.' He stopped at the bottom of the steps.

'Kit! What are you doing here?' Danny asked, coming to a halt in front of him.

'I came back for an interview this morning.'

'Oh. So I guess you're stuck here now.'

'Yeah, for the time being.'

'Big weekend planned?' Danny asked, nodding to the

groceries Kit held in his arms. Following his gaze, Kit saw a jumbo box of ribbed condoms peeking out of a Boots bag.

'Oh! No – I was just doing some shopping for May.'

'Oh, right.' Danny smirked. 'Well, I told Romy I'd come over and do the steps for her since she's snowed in down there. I'd better crack on.'

'Okay. I should go and give May her groceries. See you later, maybe,' Kit said as he gripped the railing and started up the steps.

✳

As he let himself into his apartment, Kit felt strangely hollow and he couldn't figure out why. The interview had gone really well. He could do the job in his sleep, and finding himself back on his own turf, with people who spoke the same language, he had felt competent and in control. He had been in no doubt of their approval. They were obviously impressed by his experience and abilities, and saw him as a highly desirable employee. One of the guys who had interviewed him was an old acquaintance – a former colleague from New York who Kit knew could be relied on to put in a good word. He had even invited Kit to join them for Christmas drinks and told him to bring his partner.

Sitting in the harsh light of that smart, shiny office, he had felt the threads of his old life start to knit together again and wrap themselves around him. That familiar world of suits, back-slapping machismo and high stakes deal-making could be his again – and he wouldn't even have to go to New York. Romy could come to the Christmas drinks with him. He could take her to business dinners and functions and show her off to his colleagues and clients. He would have his old life back. It was practically a done deal.

So why did he feel so edgy? He should be buzzing. Instead he felt empty, nervous and … hemmed in. He flopped onto the sofa, pulled off his tie and threw it on the coffee table. It was probably just that he'd been out of that world for a while so it was a bit daunting going back to it – like returning to school after the summer holidays. After the first week he'd be fine, and it would be as if he'd never been away. He went to the kitchen, took a bottle of Chablis from the fridge and poured himself a huge glass, wishing Romy was there to have a drink with him.

Taking his wine back into the living room, he sat on the sofa, put his feet up on the coffee table and turned on the hi-fi. Three tracks later, he retraced his steps to the kitchen to top up his glass. He glanced at the clock on the kitchen wall. It was only three o'clock, but what the hell? Soon he would have a job again and he wouldn't be able to drink in the middle of the day. Might as well make the most of it while he had the chance. Maybe he would even go out later, let his hair down … hook up, even. It had been a long time since he'd had a good night out.

Back in the living room, he called Romy. He felt even worse about her being stuck down in the country when she told him the heating had broken down, but she seemed remarkably cheerful despite everything, and genuinely didn't seem to mind being marooned there with Ethan.

'You okay?' she asked, after he had told her all about the interview. 'You sound a bit … flat.'

'Yeah, I'm fine. I guess it's just a bit of an anti-climax when there's no one here to celebrate with.'

'Is Danny there? He said he'd go over to clear the snow.'

'Yeah, I saw him.' He was still out there. Kit could hear the scraping of his shovel on the steps.

'Well, he's staying over at my place tonight. I'm not sure – I think he might be going out later. But you could try him.'

*

A couple of hours later, Kit was opening a second bottle when he realised the scraping outside had stopped. He heard the front door open and close. That must be Danny knocking off work. Maybe Danny would have a drink with him, help him celebrate. Maybe they could go out to a club together, perhaps even … He sloshed a mouthful of wine into his glass and knocked it back. Then he picked up the bottle, grabbed his keys and went out. He bounded up the steps, which were now cleared, the snow piled up on either side. He went inside and knocked on Romy's door.

'Hi,' he said when Danny opened the door. 'Drink?' he offered, raising the bottle.

'I was just about to get ready to go out,' Danny said.

'Oh, okay,' Kit said despondently.

Danny's face softened. 'Well, just a quick one, then,' he said, standing back to let Kit in.

'Great!' Kit strode into Romy's living room and planted himself on the sofa.

Danny got a couple of glasses and put them on the coffee table, and Kit poured the wine.

'Here's to me,' he said, handing a glass to Danny and raising his own in salute. 'I think my interview today went really well.'

'Oh, good for you!' Danny said, clinking his glass against Kit's as he sat down beside him. 'Does this mean you're planning to stay in Dublin, then?'

'Yeah, I think so – for now anyway.'

'So how's work going on the house?'

'It was going okay, but of course it's all come to a standstill now with this snow.'

'And now Romy's snowed in down there with your brother,' Danny said thoughtfully.

'Yeah. I feel really bad about that. I spoke to her earlier, though, and she seems very upbeat about the whole thing. She takes things in her stride, doesn't she?'

'She does,' Danny said, smiling.

'So, where are you off to?' Kit asked, refilling his glass. Danny still wasn't even halfway through his. 'Hot date?'

'No. Just a party.'

'Oh, a party? Sounds like fun.' Kit gulped down more wine while he waited for Danny to invite him along.

'I'd ask you to come, but I'm sort of going on someone else's invite, so …'

'Oh, no – that's fine. Will your wanker ex be there?'

'Paul? No,' Danny said, narrowing his eyes at Kit.

'Good. Glad to hear it,' Kit slurred. 'So who are you going with? New bloke in your life?'

'Just some friends,' Danny said curtly. He glanced at his watch. 'Well, I'd better go and get ready.'

Kit looked at him unhappily. 'Do you have to go? Why don't you stay here and we'll get drunk together? It's going to be hell trying to get anywhere tonight anyway with this weather.'

Danny hesitated, looking tempted for a moment. 'Sorry, but they'll be expecting me.' He drained his glass, put it back on the coffee table and got up. 'You can stay and finish your drink if you like.'

'Oh, come on,' Kit wheedled. 'You don't want to go out in that cold, do you? Or are you hoping to hook up at this party?'

'None of your business.'

'Because if you're not, you might as well stay here and get shitfaced with me. Or we could go to the local pub.'

Danny sighed. 'Look, I'm not Romy, okay? I'm not going to throw everything in and prop you up just because you're feeling a bit sorry for yourself.'

Kit was taken aback. He'd never seen this assertive, almost

aggressive side of Danny before. He rather liked it. 'I'm not feeling sorry for myself. I'm celebrating.'

'Doesn't look like it to me. Anyway, I've no time to stand here arguing with you. I'm going to get ready. Stay as long as you want.' With that, he turned on his heel and stalked off to the bathroom.

When he was gone, Kit poured the remains of the bottle into his glass and continued to drink. He was starting to feel quite mellow. He took off his jacket and stretched out full-length on the sofa. He was still lying there when Danny reappeared, wearing black jeans and a black polo neck jumper, his thick dark hair still damp from the shower. *Holy shit!* He scrubbed up well, Kit thought, sitting up. He watched as Danny moved around the room, picking up keys and wallet and stuffing them into his pockets. The black clothes accentuated his dark colouring, and he looked sleek and elegant as a panther – maybe even a little bit dangerous.

'Is that what you're wearing?' Kit asked, waving his wine glass in Danny's general direction.

'Well … yeah. What does it look like?'

It looked mighty fine, Kit thought. But he said, 'You'll never pull in that.'

'What?' Danny looked at him, aghast. 'What's wrong with it?'

'Nothing if you're playing a cat burglar in a Hollywood B movie. But if you want to hook up with a hot gay man …'

'And what the fuck would you know about that?' Danny said scathingly.

'Quite a lot, actually,' Kit said, getting up and walking over to him, backing Danny into the wall until they were standing toe to toe eyeballing each other. 'For instance,' he said, taking Danny's face in his hands and kissing him forcefully, pushing him back into the wall.

For a moment, Danny was too stunned to respond. He stood there lifelessly, his lips remaining rigid while Kit kissed him. Then he suddenly came to with a jolt and pushed him away. 'Kit, stop!' he gasped. 'We can't do this.'

'Sorry,' Kit said, stepping back. 'You don't want to?'

Danny looked away. 'I can't do this to Romy.'

'Romy!' Kit said, laughing in relief. He had noticed Danny's evasive answer to his question. 'That's not real,' he said. 'Romy and me – we're not really together.'

'You're not?'

Kit shook his head. 'No.'

'You've never been with her?'

'I've never slept with her, no.'

'With any woman?'

'Not since I was eighteen.'

'So you're … gay?'

'As I was saying,' Kit said, bending his head to Danny's again. This time he kissed him softly, gently, and Danny relaxed, winding his arms around Kit's back and opening his mouth to his coaxing tongue, and then the kiss became more passionate, their tongues tangling and wrestling with each other.

'Right,' Danny said breathlessly as Kit sucked on his neck. 'I see your point.'

'There's more,' Kit whispered, his hands roaming under Danny's jumper. 'You want to hear it?'

'I'm all ears.'

Kit grabbed the hem of Danny's top and pulled it off and then he was kissing his chest, licking and sucking his nipples.

'Shit!' Danny gasped. 'You really know what you're talking about, don't you?'

'And you're such a great listener.' Kit smiled against Danny's skin as he kissed his way down his stomach until he was kneeling before him, unbuckling his belt.

'I'm going to be late,' Danny breathed, groaning deep in his throat as Kit unzipped his jeans and his hand moved over the bulge in his boxers.

'Shut up,' Kit murmured. 'You've pulled.'

❋

After dinner, Romy lifted Luke into his Moses basket and carried it gently into the living room, careful not to wake him. Then she pulled back the couch while Ethan dragged her mattress in, dropping it in front of the fire. They had set up the two electric heaters at the far corners of the room, so that between them and the fire, it was now quite cosy and warm. While Romy washed up, Ethan piled up her bed with pillows, duvets and blankets. There was something incredibly sexy about a man making a bed for you – even if his intention was simply to prevent Romy dying of hypothermia, and not to spread her out on it and have his wicked way with her. He threw a couple of pillows and a duvet onto the sofa for himself.

'There – looks cosy,' he said, standing back to survey his handiwork.

The bed did look cosy – but Romy couldn't help thinking it would be even cosier if he was in it with her.

'So, uh … are you ready to go to bed now?' he asked her.

'Um … yeah. I'm pretty beat.' Suddenly, everything felt very stilted and awkward between them.

'Yeah, me too. Well, I'll just go and get ready then.'

While he went to his bedroom to get changed, Romy raced to the bathroom to brush her teeth, then went to her bedroom and flung off her clothes, scrambling into her pyjamas so that she could get into bed before he came back. She heard him in the bathroom as she sprinted across the hall and she dove under the duvet just in time before he came into the room wearing a T-shirt and boxers. He looked surprised to see her already in bed.

'I'll just put a few more logs on,' he said, bending down close to her to stoke up the fire. The fresh logs crackled and sparked as he pushed them into the flames. 'That should keep it going until morning.' Then he got up and went over to the light switch. 'Will I turn the light off?'

Romy looked over at him and nodded. 'Night,' she said, closing her eyes and turning away towards the fire.

'Night.' She heard him walk back to the couch, and waited for the squeak of the springs as he lay down on it, but it didn't come.

'Um, Romy?' His voice was close and she turned around to find him standing beside her makeshift bed, looking down at her.

'Yes?' she whispered, her heart hammering in her ribs.

'Um … would it be okay if I slept here too?' he said, indicating her mattress.

'Oh. Uh … yes. Of course.' She pulled back the covers on the side nearest him and edged further towards the fire, turning away from him. *Oh God, shoot me now.*

How was she going to survive a night lying beside him in bed, not touching him, him not touching her? But she could hardly refuse. The couch wouldn't be very comfortable, especially for someone as tall as Ethan, and she had a double bed. Was it too late to opt for hypothermia? She felt the mattress give as he lay down beside her, felt the warmth of his body at her back. 'Good night,' she whispered again, scrunching her eyes tight and praying that sleep would overtake her soon. This was just unbearable.

'Good night,' he whispered. She was surprised to feel him lean over her, and then she felt the wet warmth of his lips on her cheek. Little flames of desire curled and leapt in her stomach as his lips lingered on her face, trailing down to her chin. And then they were gone and she felt bereft, her fingers digging into the mattress as she forced herself not to turn around and grab him.

She felt him move closer behind her, and then his fingers were moving lightly through her hair – so lightly she thought she might be imagining it until his other hand moved to her side, edging up underneath her pyjama top and stroking her skin softly.

'Romy?' His voice was husky. 'You're not really with Kit, are you?'

She realised she'd been holding her breath. 'No,' she managed to whisper. God, she'd tell him anything if it meant he'd keep touching her like this. He could get a job with MI5 getting spies to tell him all their secrets.

'Thank Christ for that!'

His warm hand continued to caress her hip, and as he pulled her gently back into his body, she felt a burst of triumph to discover that he was rock hard. Her inner slut did a happy dance, thrilled that he wanted her too. Or wanted sex, and she happened to be handy – whatever. She didn't really care. Her libido was already having its very own ticker tape parade in celebration of the victory, and it didn't much care how it had been achieved.

Then he was leaning over her again, his lips finding hers in the darkness, kissing her softly, sensuously, his tongue tracing along her bottom lip. He pulled back slightly, but she could still feel the warmth of his breath on her cheek. 'Is this okay?' he whispered and she nodded, turning to him to grant better access to his roving hands, to show him just how okay it was. He looked more beautiful than ever, his face flushed with desire and warmed by the golden glow of the firelight.

'Are you warm enough? Can we take this off?' he asked huskily, grabbing the hem of her pyjama top. 'I want to see you.'

She nodded and he pushed back the blankets before pulling off her top and then her bottoms and she was naked. For a while, he just looked at her in the light of the flickering fire, watching his hand as he touched every inch of skin he'd exposed, gently caressing her breasts, stroking the gentle swell of her belly and the curve of her hip, while he told her how gorgeous she was and how much he wanted her, until she thought she would go mad if he didn't put his mouth on her again.

Finally, he kissed her as his hand moved between her legs and he groaned into her mouth when he felt how wet she was. Then he was kissing her everywhere, nibbling and licking and sucking her belly, her breasts, the soft flesh of her inner thighs, until at last he was at the place where she wanted him most, and the waves of pleasure built and built until they reached the zenith and her body rose off the bed, suspended on an invisible thread like an achingly sweet note held on a string, before the vibrations passed and she crashed back down to earth, still trembling as after-shocks rippled through her.

'Oh my God, you're so beautiful,' he panted, pulling her to him.

'That was amazing,' she breathed, almost teary with gratitude. She knew it had been a long time for her, but she was pretty sure that would have been a mind-blowing experience under any circumstances.

With his body pressed against hers, she realised that he still had a raging hard-on and she pulled off his boxers so his erection sprang free. She stroked the silky skin, longing to feel him thrusting inside her. But they didn't have any protection. She was about to slither down the bed to reciprocate when he suddenly sat up.

'Just give me a minute,' he said, kissing her swiftly before hopping out of bed. He returned moments later with a string of foil packets.

'You have condoms?' she gasped, practically whooping with joy.

'Always prepared,' he said, grinning as he opened one of the packets and rolled on a condom before jumping back into bed.

'You're a regular boy scout,' she said as he settled between her legs. And then he was plunging into her and the pleasure started building all over again.

✳

'Seriously, that was it? You were going out with *one* condom? You obviously didn't have high hopes for that party.'

'I was going to get more when I was out, if I needed to,' Danny said defensively. 'How come you don't have any?'

'I've been … going through a dry patch, I suppose,' Kit admitted reluctantly, running a hand through his hair. 'But you were going to a *party*, for fuck's sake! With *one* condom!'

Danny sighed. 'We're a disgrace to the gay community.'

'We'll be drummed out if anyone finds out.'

They had gone downstairs and were in Kit's bed ready for round two, when they discovered they had exhausted their resources when they used Danny's lone condom. Now they were sitting up side by side in the bed, bewailing their fate.

'Shit!' Danny kicked the sheet in frustration. 'Maybe you should look again. Have you checked all your pockets?'

'I've looked everywhere. I don't have any.' Kit put his head in his hands and sighed. 'Oh!' he exclaimed, suddenly sitting up straight. 'But I know a woman who does,' he said, turning to Danny with a grin, his eyes lighting up.

Danny looked at him questioningly, and then realisation dawned. 'No way! You're going to ask May for a condom?'

'Why not? That's what neighbours do, isn't it – borrow stuff from each other?'

'Yeah, eggs and cups of sugar … maybe a bog roll at a pinch.'

'Well, why should a condom be any different? But you'll have to ask her,' Kit said, giving Danny a little kick to shunt him out of bed.

'What? Why me?'

'Because she'll think I'm cheating on Romy – she thinks we're together and she knows Romy's not here.'

'But – she's *your* neighbour. I don't really know her.'

'All the more reason. I'll have to face her every day. You never have to see her again.'

'Oh, all right,' Danny sighed, throwing back the duvet and getting out of bed. 'What will I say?' he asked as he pulled on his clothes.

'You could say you're going to a party and you only have one condom. She knows you're gay, right? I'm sure she'll understand.'

'Very funny.' Danny grinned at Kit as he shuffled into his shoes.

'Get plenty – we can pay her back tomorrow. Oh, and get some of the flavoured ones – chocolate, if there are any!' Kit called after Danny as he went out the door.

❋

Romy woke early the next morning. Ethan was still sleeping deeply, his limbs knotted around hers, warm and heavy. She turned and looked at the fire. It was mostly ash now, but there was still the odd glow of red. She carefully disentangled herself from Ethan and crept out of bed, pulling on her pyjamas. She blushed as she remembered Ethan pulling them off her, kissing her bare skin, nibbling her nipples, her clit, putting his tongue inside her, and his fingers, and finally his big, beautiful cock. He had teased and tormented her for hours and given her the most explosive orgasms of her life. She shivered, fighting the urge to wake him up and start all over again.

Despite the fact that she had been awake for most of the night, she felt amazing. Sex was better than sleep any day of the week! She pulled on a cardigan and crept over to Luke's basket. He was still sleeping too, so she went into the kitchen and put on some coffee, relishing the time to herself to relive the details of the previous night, smiling to herself as she recalled the little sounds Ethan had made as he thrust inside her, his groans of pleasure and satisfaction, his whimpers of need.

But as she started to come down from her sex-induced high, a million questions flooded her brain. Had Ethan been thinking about her that way all along? When had he decided he would try to have sex with her last night? When he was making the bed? Before that? Would he have made a move on her if they hadn't ended up in this situation? Was it just a case of any port in a storm – he wanted to have sex and she was the only woman in the vicinity? And the most burning question of all – would he want to do it again or was last night just a one-time-only special?

She suddenly felt very insecure and desperate to know where she stood with him. Kit had told her that Ethan didn't go in for serious relationships, and casual sex was the order of the day for him. But how casual? Would he think she was being clingy if she wanted to do it again? What if she wanted to do it again lots of times? Did he have a limit to the number of times he'd sleep with the same girl? And what about tonight? Would he expect them to sleep together again? So many questions! Her head was spinning.

Well, she couldn't carry on like this – she would drive herself mad. As she stood at the counter, sipping her coffee, she looked out the window. The snow was still thick on the ground and another light sprinkling was starting to fall. They would be stuck here for another day at least. She couldn't spend the whole day on tenterhooks, wondering what was going to happen that night. She would be a nervous wreck, not knowing how to act, what to say, or if she should just say nothing and pretend it hadn't happened.

She would have it out with him when he got up, she decided. She would make it clear that she wasn't expecting anything from him, but she needed to know where she stood one way or the other. She would be straightforward and honest and grown-up about it. If he just wanted a one-night stand, that was fine. Well, not fine – the thought that he might not want to do it again made her feel like crying – but she would deal with it. It was the uncertainty she couldn't bear.

Then she looked up and he was standing there in the doorway, bare-chested, and all she could think was how beautiful he was.

'Good morning,' he said, giving her a lazy smile.

God, she just wanted to lick him. She felt her insides melt, and all her resolve sliding away. *Stop it*, she told herself firmly, *you need to sort this out now*.

'Morning,' she said, standing up and taking her cup over to the sink. She stood there with her back to him for a second while she rinsed it out, regaining her composure. Then, taking a deep breath, she turned to him. 'So are we having sex now?' she asked.

He gave a startled laugh. 'Oh! Um ...' he scratched his head and smiled at her sleepily. 'Sure,' he said finally. 'But ... um,' he hesitated. 'Do you mind if I just have some Coco Pops first?' He pointed to the cupboards behind her. 'Keep my strength up ...'

'Oh no!' she gasped, feeling herself blushing. 'I wasn't asking you to – I didn't mean right this minute! I meant now as in the present continuous.'

She was babbling and he just stood there, smiling at her. Why didn't he say something?

She ploughed on. 'I just need to know. Was last night just a one-off or ... I mean it's fine either way—'

He frowned slightly, stepping closer to her. 'You really don't mind either way? That's not very flattering.'

'Oh, no, I didn't mean it like that. I just meant – no pressure, you know. If it was just a one-night stand ...'

'You do realise that isn't just up to me, right?'

'Yes, I know that. I just wanted to know, um ... what do you think?'

'Well, for my part, I vote yes.'

'Yes to ...?

'Yes, we're having sex now – in the present continuous.'

She smiled and felt her body melting with relief. She hadn't realised how tense she'd been.

'What about you?' he asked.

'I vote yes too.'

'Yes to?'

'To us having sex now, in the present continuous.'

He grinned. 'That's unanimous then,' he said, putting a hand on the side of her face and bending to kiss her while his other hand slid up inside her pyjama top, cupping a breast.

'What about your Coco Pops?' she breathed as he nuzzled her neck.

'Coco Pops can wait.'

'Don't you need to keep your strength up?'

'I'll be fine,' he murmured between kisses.

'Well, something's up anyway,' she said, as she felt his erection pressed against her. 'You really want to do this again now? Before breakfast or anything?'

'No time like the present continuous.'

✳

'How did you get so good at this?' she asked later as they were once more snuggled up on the mattress in front of the fire. 'You're twelve. You're not supposed to know about this stuff.'

'I aced anatomy.' He grinned, tracing a lazy pattern on her thigh.

'Yeah, I can tell.' She sat up, stretching contentedly. 'Well, I don't know about you, but I've worked up a hell of an appetite. I need my breakfast.'

'Me too. I'm starving.'

She turned her head, looking down at him. 'You don't really eat Coco Pops do you?'

'Of course. It's the breakfast of champions.'

She rolled her eyes. 'No, it's the breakfast of five-year-olds. Makes me feel like more of a cradle-snatcher than ever.'

✳

'Well, that was a turn-up for the books,' Danny said the following morning, as he and Kit lay wrapped around each other in bed.

'You didn't know I was gay?' Kit asked, stroking Danny's hair. 'Didn't even suspect?'

'No, not at all. So Romy knows?'

'I haven't exactly told her, but I think she guessed. I suppose she's got good gaydar because of you.'

'She never said anything.'

'Well, she wouldn't. She knows I'm not out.'

Danny stirred, pulling back a little. 'Why aren't you?' He frowned.

Kit sighed. 'It just sort of … happened that way. I was already in New York when I realised I was gay, so there was no need to tell my family. They didn't have to know about the life I lived over there.'

'Do you not think they'd have been cool about it?'

'No, that's the funny thing – I'm sure they would have been. But at first there seemed no need, and then the more time passed without telling them, the harder it became. I felt they'd be hurt that I hadn't told them before – like it meant I didn't trust them. I suppose I kind of painted myself into a corner.'

'So, Romy is like your … *beard*?' Danny said the word like it was something completely preposterous that he'd only ever come across in movies – which somehow struck Kit as quite likely.

'Basically, yeah.'

'And you had girlfriends like that in New York? Fake ones?'

'Yeah, all the time.' Kit sighed. 'I was working on Wall Street, it's a very macho environment. It's tough enough without giving yourself added complications. It's just a lot easier doing business if you can be one of the guys, you know?'

'Not really,' Danny said, smiling wryly.

'No, I don't suppose you would.' Kit leaned over and placed a soft kiss on Danny's forehead. 'That's one of the things I like about you.'

'That I'm not one of the guys?'

'That you don't pretend to be something you're not.'

'That's ironic, coming from you.'

'Believe me, I know.'

They were interrupted by the buzzing of the text alert on Danny's phone. He scrabbled around on the floor for his jeans and pulled his mobile out of the pocket.

Kit threw back the duvet and got out of bed while Danny read his text. 'I'm going to make coffee,' he said as he pulled on jeans and a sweater.

'Okay, I'll be out in a sec,' Danny said, smiling as he began typing a reply.

❋

'What do you want for breakfast?' Kit asked when Danny joined him in the kitchen. 'Eggs? Croissants?'

'Actually, I thought we might go out for brunch,' Danny said.

'Okay.' Kit shrugged. It was a bright, sunny morning, and it had finally stopped snowing, though the ground was still covered. It would be nice to get out. 'Where do you want to go?'

'Well, some of the friends I was meant to be going to the party with last night are meeting up at Odessa.'

'Oh. That was them texting you just now?'

'Yeah. So – what do you say? They do fantastic huevos rancheros.'

'Were they mad at you for not turning up at the party?' Kit asked, smiling crookedly.

'No. Not when I told them why.' Danny grinned.

Kit's smile faded instantly. 'You didn't tell them about me?'

'Well … yeah. I mean, I told them I got lucky.'

'But you didn't say who with?'

'No. They wouldn't even know you.'

'And you won't … tell anyone, will you?'

'What?' Danny said scathingly.

'You won't tell anyone about this?' Kit said uncertainly, surprised by Danny's sudden coldness.

'No, don't worry,' Danny said, his lip curled contemptuously. 'Your secret's safe with me.'

Kit looked after him in confusion as he stormed off towards the bathroom. A moment later, he heard the shower running. What the hell had got into him all of a sudden? He thought they had had a nice time – a *very* nice time. And now suddenly he was getting the cold shoulder.

When Danny returned, he was fully dressed and pulling on his jacket. Kit jumped in front of him, barring his way as he headed for the door.

'Hey, where are you going?'

'I'm going to meet my friends in Odessa,' Danny said implacably. 'I take it you're not coming?'

'I can't. You know that.'

'Why can't you?'

'Because – they'll know it was me you were with last night. Why don't you stay here with me?' Kit said, putting a hand on Danny's shoulder. 'I'll make us huevos rancheros.'

'What's the point?' Danny said huffily, shrugging off his hand.

'Is this because I asked you not to tell anyone?'

'Yeah, it is. I'm not interested in being anyone's dirty little secret, okay?'

'But I'm not out. I *told* you. What did you expect?' *Damn it, why was he being so obtuse?*

'And why aren't you out?'

'Jesus! Were you not listening to a word I said in there?' Kit raged, waving to the bedroom.

'Yes, but – you're not on Wall Street anymore, Kit. Why do you still need all the pretence, the fake girlfriends?'

'It just makes life easier,' he said, shrugging.

'Whose life?'

'Look, Danny, I really like you. This wasn't just a casual shag for me. I want to be with you.'

'Just not in public.'

Kit sighed. 'No,' he admitted finally.

Danny flinched. 'Well, sorry, but that doesn't work for me.'

With that, he stomped off and slammed out the door. Kit went to the window and watched as everything he most liked about Danny – his honesty, his integrity, his refusal to compromise – took him farther and farther away.

Chapter Twenty-Three

Having wished the snow away when it first came, Romy now wanted it to last forever. First thing every morning, she raced anxiously to the window to check that it was still there, hoping for the thaw to hold off just a little longer. She loved living with Ethan and Luke in their little bubble, cocooned from the outside world. She and Ethan did what work they could on the house during the day, and spent the rest of the time making love, playing with Luke and having fun in the snow. They cooked and ate, they talked endlessly, and because the hot water still wasn't working, they boiled pots of water and took baths together. It was like a lovely holiday, and Romy was afraid that it would all melt away with the snow, and she would be dumped back into reality with a thud. She knew Ethan didn't want a serious relationship, and that was fine. But she was having so much fun, she just wanted it to last a bit longer. She was having a fling with a gorgeous, uncomplicated man who seemed to want her as much as she wanted him. She couldn't remember when she'd felt so happy, and she hadn't had this much sex in … well, ever!

Still, she couldn't help feeling a twinge of guilt when she thought of Kit.

'Don't tell Kit I told you, okay?' she said to Ethan one night when they were in bed together. 'That I'm not really his girlfriend.'

'Okay,' Ethan said, his brow furrowed. 'Not that I really needed you to tell me.'

'Yeah, how did you know?'

Etha smiled. 'Let's just say, I don't think you're his type.'

'Huh! That's not very nice.'

'I'm very glad you're not,' he said, tucking a strand of hair over her ear. 'Believe me, his type does nothing for me.'

'Is he … is he gay?'

Ethan raised his eyebrows. 'I thought you could tell me. I mean, what other reason could he give you for wanting you to be his fake girlfriend?'

'Well, he didn't tell me in so many words – he just said he didn't want people prying into his private life and stuff.'

'But it must have been obvious why?'

'Well, yeah,' she said, feeling silly that it hadn't been. 'Pretty much. But I couldn't be absolutely sure.'

'What other explanation could there be?'

'None, really.' She didn't want to get into Lesley's BDSM theory. 'So he's never actually come out to anyone?'

'No. But Hannah and I have always suspected, and then one time she decided to surprise him in New York. He didn't know she was there and she turned up at his apartment unexpectedly. There was this guy there … Kit tried to explain him away, but Hannah wasn't convinced. And there was other stuff too – she said he'd obviously spent a lot of time clearing away any evidence from the apartment if he knew we were coming.'

'Wow.'

'Plus his girlfriends weren't very plausible.'

'Gee, thanks. Now I'm implausible.'

'I don't mean you,' Ethan said, smiling at her. 'Well, not when you really were his girlfriend – I doubt he even knew he was gay himself back then.'

'Poor Kit. It must be exhausting keeping up that pretence all the time.'

'I know.' Ethan sighed. 'Hannah and I were hoping that when he came back to Ireland, he'd come out. We just think he'd be so much happier if he could be open about it and be himself.'

'So that's why you were angry with me?'

'We weren't angry with you – well, maybe Hannah was a little bit. But mainly she was just pissed off with Kit.'

'Well, you can't tell her about this,' she said, waving her hand between the two of them.

'You mean about all the sexing we've been doing?' he grinned wolfishly, leaning over her and planting a kiss on her chest.

'We can't tell anyone – especially Kit. It has to be a secret.'

'I know. But it's going to be difficult when we're back in Dublin. I mean, Kit lives in your house.' He started nuzzling her neck.

'You mean – you want to keep, um … doing this when we're back in Dublin?'

'Hell, yeah,' he said, his breath hot on her skin as he

pressed little butterfly kisses down her neck. Then he stopped suddenly, pulling back to look at her. 'Don't you?' he asked, his expression anxious.

'Yes!' she squealed, putting an arm around his neck and tugging him back to her. 'We'll just have to be careful.'

'Don't worry. We'll figure it out.'

✻

Romy had adapted the old adage 'when your baby sleeps, you sleep' to 'when your baby sleeps, you have sex', and she had never been more grateful that Luke was such a good sleeper.

'Has Luke gone for his nap?' Ethan asked as he appeared at the door of her bedroom, his eyes glittering with intent.

'Yeah. We've got about an hour, hopefully,' Romy said, grinning.

'Cool.' He wasted no time, removing his jacket as he strode into the room. He pulled her into his arms and kissed her. Then he blew on his hands to warm them before sliding them up under her top, tickling her sides, and cupping her breasts. She grabbed the hem of his jumper and he broke the kiss to lift his arms so she could yank it off over his head. Then they were kissing again, Romy's hands moving to the waistband of his jeans.

'Mmm,' he groaned, pulling away. 'I'll just be a sec.' He darted off to the bathroom, leaving Romy practically hopping from foot to foot as she waited for his return.

When he came back he stood in the doorway with the box of condoms in his hand, looking worried. *Damn!* What's wrong? she thought. Why wasn't he lunging for her and throwing her on the bed? They didn't have any time to waste.

'Um … problem,' he said, running his hand through his hair. 'We're running out of supplies.'

'Oh, no, I'm sure not. There was plenty of milk in the fridge this morning. And don't forget we've got all that stuff in the freezer too. Don't worry about it,' she said, beckoning him to her, impatient to get on with the ravishing.

But Ethan was shaking his head. 'No, I don't mean food. We're running out of condoms,' he said, waving the box. 'Look.' He crossed the room to her.

'Oh!' They both gazed down forlornly into the box. There was one foil packet at the bottom. 'Is that it?' she asked in a tiny voice.' *That can't be it!*

'Yeah.' He sighed. 'I didn't realise.'

'Noooo!' Romy couldn't suppress her cry of anguish. How could this have happened? Why had they been so profligate? They had been going at it like rabbits on ecstasy, with no thought of tomorrow, and now suddenly they only had one shag left. One shag!

'I know.' He gave her a pained look. 'I'm sorry.'

'It's not your fault. It's just – aaargh!'

'So, do you want to – I mean, maybe we should save it for tonight or—'

'But what if the snow doesn't clear tomorrow?' Romy asked with rising panic. She knew she wasn't behaving in a very dignified manner, and if she wasn't so damn horny, she might actually feel quite ashamed of herself. But the lust was all-consuming. Her libido had staged a mutiny and taken over her brain, and was already hatching plans for her to hike through the snow to the nearest pharmacy.

'I could pull out,' Ethan suggested.

Her mouth twisted. 'It's a bit risky.'

'I always use protection. And I've been tested regularly for work, so I know I'm clean. But if you're not comfortable—'

'It's not that. But I'm not on the pill.'

'Oh! Okay. Too risky, then.'

'Yeah.' She chewed her lip.

'Well, there's lots of other stuff we can do,' Ethan said.

'True.' She smiled, relaxing a little. 'But what about tomorrow? And the day after? If the snow lasts—'

'Ssh,' he said, bending to kiss her before pulling her sweater off in one fluid movement. 'We'll worry about tomorrow when it comes. We're wasting time here.'

✱

'You okay?' he said later as they lay in each other's arms, their skin sticky with sweat and saliva.

'More than okay,' she grinned at him. 'Fabulous. You?'

'Fantastic.'

'Other stuff is fun.' She wrapped her arms around him and laid her head on his chest. 'Was it really okay for you?'

'Uh, *yeah*,' he said. 'Couldn't you tell?'

'I thought maybe you were just being nice.'

She felt his chest rise and fall as he laughed. 'You're funny,' he said, his fingers moving through her hair. 'It's not easy to fake that, you know.'

'Sorry. It's just – I haven't done this in a long time – a *very* long time. Not since Luke's father. And that hardly even counts.'

'Who was he?' he asked, immediately adding 'You don't have to tell me.'

She propped her chin on his chest and looked up at him. 'No, I don't mind. But there's not much to tell. It was just a one-night stand with a stranger. I don't even know his name.'

Ethan stroked her cheek. 'Do you mind – not knowing?'

She sighed. 'Not so much for myself. But I wish I had something better to tell Luke when he grows up.'

'What will you tell him?'

'The truth. And I'll tell him what little I do know about his father.'

'And what's that?'

'That he was a good man,' she said, reciting the words she often said to Luke as she lulled him to sleep. 'A compassionate man. And he was kind to me once when I was very sad.'

She already told Luke about his father, repeating it like a bedtime story, as though he could absorb it into his psyche, though he was too young to understand. Since discovering she was pregnant, she had dissected every detail of that night, scrutinised every word spoken for what it could tell her about the father of her child. Then she wove it into a fable that she told Luke as she soothed him to sleep, imbuing her narrative with all the classical elements of a fairytale – a mysterious knight, a healing kiss, the gift of a baby. 'Your father is a good man, Luke,' she would say, as she stroked his soft cheeks. 'Young, but wise, with a good heart. He understood human suffering. Even though I told him my worst secret, he still kissed me.'

'It's not much,' she said now to Ethan, as he stroked her hair.

'It seems like a lot to me – for a one-night stand.'

'Yeah,' she said, smiling as she laid her head on his chest. 'We didn't bother with small talk – thank goodness. I know so little about him – I don't even know his name or what he does for a living. But at least I feel I know what kind of person he was.'

❋

The following morning, Romy placed the condom box on the windowsill in the kitchen, like a monument to their resourcefulness and frugality. She felt like a wartime housewife, storing up their meagre rations for when they would need them most.

They wouldn't have to hold out much longer, she thought, looking out the window. There had been no fresh snow in the past couple of days, and when she flicked on the radio, the weather reporter said that there was a thaw on the way. It seemed to have already started, fat dollops of snow dropping off the branches of the trees, the whole landscape shimmering and glistening in the dazzling sunlight. At least their snowman was still intact. She felt sad at the thought of him melting away and wished there was some way they could preserve him.

She and Ethan had agreed that they should return to Dublin as soon as the roads were driveable. It was less than a week to Christmas, and the long-term forecast was for more snow. If they didn't leave when they got the chance, they could end up stuck here for Christmas. When the oil company rang to say they would deliver the following day, she knew it was time.

'We'll use it tonight,' she told Ethan, nodding to the condom.

But Luke had other ideas. He was fractious all day and kept them awake most of the night, crying incessantly. It was impossible to pacify him, and Romy began to worry that there was something seriously wrong with him. But Ethan checked him out and assured her he was fine.

'I think he's probably teething,' he told her – which made sense considering the way Luke was frenziedly gumming every available object.

Though they took turns pacing the floor with him, neither of them got much sleep, and when Ethan got up with him the following morning, it felt like only minutes had passed since Luke had finally settled down and fallen asleep.

'You stay here, get some rest,' Ethan said, kissing Romy on

the forehead as he slid out of bed. She was about to protest, but her eyes were already closing.

She woke hours later to a deep rumbling sound outside. Getting up and going to the window, she was greeted with the welcome sight of the oil truck chugging down the drive. Ethan was standing outside with Luke, both of them bundled up in coats and gloves while they waited for the truck.

She hopped back into bed, listening to the pumping of oil and then the truck rumbling away again into the distance. When all was silent again, Ethan came in, stamping his feet on the mat before coming over to sit on the couch with Luke on his lap.

'What time is it?' she asked, raising herself up on one elbow.

He glanced at his watch. 'Two thirty.'

'Oh my God! I must have slept for hours.'

'Well, you needed it.'

'So, what did I miss?'

'Loads.' He grinned. 'We have oil. Luke said his first word.'

'He did? What was it?'

'Ethan.'

'Huh!'

'Aw, don't be jealous. I'm sure it would have been 'mama' but you weren't around, so ...' He shrugged. 'Babies live in the moment.'

'Oh, well – at least I got my lie-in. That's the main thing.'

'What else?' He thought. 'I took him for a go on the tree swing. He liked that. And he took his first step.'

'Damn! I miss everything.'

'I recorded it all on my mobile.'

'Oh, that's okay, then,' she said snuggling back into the pillow. 'But wake me up for his first day at school.'

'So, what do you think of today's outfit?' he asked, removing Luke's jacket.

Romy held out her arms and he handed Luke to her. 'Very nice,' she said. 'I wouldn't have put those colours together, but they really work.' She put Luke down on the bed and lay down next to him. Luke promptly grabbed his feet, babbling tunefully to himself.

Ethan removed his jacket, kicked off his shoes and slid in beside them. He placed a soft kiss on Luke's forehead, then Romy's, and lay back against the pillows with a contented sigh. 'Let's stay here all day,' he murmured, putting his arm across them both as his eyes closed.

❉

Romy was tidying up the kitchen the following morning, when there was a loud banging on the door. She opened it to find Lesley, Danny and Kit standing outside.

'Surprise!' Lesley said, jumping up and down in glee – or maybe just to keep warm. 'We've come to rescue you.'

She barged past Romy, Kit and Danny following her. She stopped abruptly in the living room, her gaze fixed on the mattress in front of the fire. 'Oh!' Her eyes drifted to Kit and Danny, but they had headed straight for the kitchen. 'Maybe you don't want rescuing,' she whispered to Romy, nodding at the mattress.

'Don't be daft! The heating broke down and we had to sleep in here with the fire, that's all. I slept here and Ethan slept on the couch, and it was all very civilised.'

'Oh, pity,' Lesley shrugged, seeming to accept her explanation. 'Well, I'm going to get the sausages on. I'm starving. We brought bags of food!' She headed to the kitchen.

When she was gone, Romy scanned the room quickly for any incriminating evidence, but there was none. They had spent all day yesterday in bed, dozing on and off, only getting up to eat and to feed and change Luke. Even so, they had still been too tired last night for anything more than some chaste kissing before falling asleep in each other's arms. So the condom lived to fight another day. *Shit, the condom!*

She followed Lesley into the kitchen. Kit and Danny were standing in opposite corners of the room, glowering at each other, creating a decidedly frosty atmosphere, while Lesley unloaded what looked like the contents of an entire butcher's counter into a couple of pans. Romy's eyes darted to the windowsill, where the condom box still sat. She waited until she was sure no one was looking and grabbed it, shoving it into the cupboard under the sink. They had been planning to use it today, their last hurrah before heading back to Dublin. So much for that, she thought sadly.

She heard Ethan's quick step on the stairs.

'Your bath's ready, babe,' he called as he came into the room, and Romy spun towards him, raising her eyebrows in warning. 'Oh, hi!' He stopped in the doorway, looking around at everyone, then walked over to Luke's cot and lifted him out. 'Come on, babe,' he said. 'Bathtime.'

Phew, good save, Romy thought.

'Why don't I give him his bath?' Danny said, holding out his arms to take Luke. 'I haven't seen him in ages.'

'Oh, I'm not sure that's … I mean, I think it would be better if I—'

'What?' Danny gave an incredulous laugh. 'Who do you think you are – his dad or something?'

'No, but—'

'Just give him to me.'

'Um … okay,' Ethan said, handing Luke over with obvious reluctance.

Danny stalked off with Luke, but reappeared moments later. 'Christ, are you trying to drown him or something? You should see the bath he was planning to put Luke in,' he said to Romy. 'It's full to the top – and it's got bubble bath!'

'Oh … um, I guess I got a bit carried away in the excitement of having hot water again – forgot who it was for,' Ethan mumbled.

'It's scalding hot too,' Danny frowned at him.

'Sorry. Seems a shame to waste all that water, though. Why don't you use it, Romy?' Ethan said.

'Oh, good idea. Thanks.' She threw him a sympathetic smile.

'I guess I'll just go and get started on packing up the car,' he said, and walked out, his shoulders hunched miserably.

Danny rolled his eyes. 'He's a bigger eejit than his brother, if that's possible,' he muttered, apparently not caring that Kit was within earshot.

'I'll go and help Ethan,' Kit said, shooting Danny a sulky look and stomping out of the kitchen.

Luke started crying, and Danny wandered off to the living room with him. 'What's got into them?' Romy whispered to Lesley once they were alone.

'God knows,' Lesley said, rolling her eyes, 'but they've been like that all day.'

It wasn't like Danny to be so bad-tempered and belligerent. What on earth could have happened between him and Kit? Then she almost gasped aloud as a thought struck her. Surely not … But she dismissed the idea almost immediately. It couldn't be that. As far as Danny was concerned, Kit was her boyfriend – and Kit wouldn't do anything to make him believe otherwise.

'Thank God you'll be coming back with us,' Lesley was saying. 'I couldn't stand being stuck in a car with glum and glummer for another three hours.'

'Three hours!'

'The roads still aren't great around here.'

'What possessed you all to come down anyway?'

'It was my idea. I suppose I was feeling a bit stir crazy after being cooped up for so long because of the snow. I just felt like a jaunt. I thought it would be fun – three crazy dudes hitting the open road. Seemed like a good idea at the time,' she said sourly.

Romy smiled sympathetically.

'You seem very cosy with Ethan,' Lesley said after a pause. 'Are you sure you don't mind us being here?'

'No, don't be daft!'

'Well, you'd better go and have that bath before it gets cold. Breakfast will be ready in about half an hour.'

'Okay, thanks.'

On the stairs, Romy met Ethan coming down, carrying a box in his arms. He made desperate eyes at her, and she silently signalled to him to follow her back up. There was no one upstairs, but just in case, she waited until they were in the bathroom with the door closed before she spoke.

'Sorry,' she whispered, 'I had no idea they were coming.'

He just looked at her, his expression full of sadness and longing. 'Shit!'

'I know.'

He bent and kissed her, his fingers pulling her jumper up slightly, lightly playing with the bare skin of her back and stomach, barely touching her, but already driving her crazy. Damn, why had they wasted so much time? Why hadn't they spent every waking moment they had doing this? Every time Ethan pulled back, it was only milliseconds before he leaned in and kissed her again. Finally, he wrenched himself away with a groan.

'You'd better have your bath before it gets cold,' he said. 'I wish …' he looked longingly at the bubble-filled water.

'I know, me too.'

Still he didn't budge, instead grabbing her jumper by the hem and pulling it over her head, followed by the long-sleeved T-shirt underneath. Then he started to unhook her bra.

'Ethan!' Kit called from the stairs.

'Shit, better go.' With one last lingering kiss, he hurried out of the room and Romy locked the door behind him.

How are we going to keep our hands off each other for the next few days? She sank into the warm water. She was looking forward to going home in a way, but she wasn't prepared for her time with Ethan to be cut short so abruptly. She had thought they would have today at least. She realised how, even in the short time they'd had, she'd become addicted to having sex with him, and even though he said he still wanted them to be together in Dublin, she was scared that it wouldn't happen. They would have to sneak around, and maybe he would decide that it was too complicated and not worth the bother – especially when he had so many other opportunities. There were plenty of girls who wanted to be with him – girls he wouldn't have to see in secret. Would he forget about her once they were out of their little bubble? She scooped up the largest bubble from the top of the bath and blew it into the air, watching as it floated above the water until it burst and disappeared.

❋

'I was talking to Mom,' Ethan said later as they all sat around the kitchen table eating Lesley's enormous fry-up. 'She wants you guys to come for drinks at our house on Christmas morning,' he said to Romy.

'You mean all of us?'

'Yeah. You and Luke, your mom, Danny.'

'Oh, great! That's really nice of her.'

'Brilliant!' Danny said, rolling his eyes.

'Bloody great!' Kit said, sounding far from happy.

Romy, Ethan and Lesley exchanged puzzled looks. What the hell was going on with those two? Romy wondered. Whatever it was, it was going to be a very long drive back to Dublin.

'I get the impression she's got a few presents for Luke,' Ethan said, smiling at Romy. 'And she figured you'd want to spend some time with him on Christmas Day,' he said to Kit.

'Of course I want to spend time with Luke – and Romy,' Kit said pointedly.

'Well, I think it's great. I'm looking forward to it already,' Ethan said. Kit merely scowled at him in response.

❋

Romy tried to engineer it so that Ethan went in the van with her, and the other three drove back together, but Lesley was having none of it.

'No way!' she said. 'I'm not going to be stuck in a car with those two for another bloody three-hour journey. At least now we can separate them, so no one has to put up with the pair of them.'

Romy conceded that it wouldn't be fair to inflict that on Lesley again, so Danny and Kit were separated like a pair of squabbling children. Lesley drove Kit and Ethan, while Romy took Danny.

'Try and find out what's going on with them,' Lesley whispered to her before they got into their cars. 'I'll do the same. That way we'll get both sides of the story.'

But Danny wasn't very forthcoming when Romy tried to press him for details. All she could get out of him was that Kit had called round a bit pissed and outstayed his welcome, drinking wine on the sofa while Danny was trying to get ready to go out. She didn't feel she was getting the full story by a long shot.

'Well, I just hope you can both behave yourselves on Christmas Day,' she said.

'Yeah, and I think that's a crap idea, by the way. I don't want to spend any of Christmas Day with that wanker!'

Romy gave up and dropped the subject. She could only hope that the two of them had got over their strop by Christmas.

When they stopped at a petrol station for coffee, she took Lesley aside to see if she had discovered anything more from Kit.

'No, I couldn't get anything out of him – Ethan tried too. He just kept saying Danny was a sanctimonious jumped-up prick.'

Romy sighed. She loved Christmas, but she had a feeling that this year it would not be without its difficulties.

Chapter Twenty-Four

The Mastersons were assembled in the hall to greet Romy and her family on Christmas morning. Romy was hyper-aware of Ethan from the second she walked through the door. He looked so beautiful in a thick cream cable-knit sweater and black jeans and her heart was pounding as she made her way to him, greeting first his mother and father, then Hannah and Tank, until finally she came to him.

'Happy Christmas,' he said, kissing her on the cheek. She wished she could have more than a brotherly peck, but there was no way that was going to happen today. Kit, on the other hand, pulled her into his arms and made a show of giving her a lingering kiss on the lips. She felt her cheeks redden, conscious that everyone else was watching. She would have to break up with him after Christmas. She just wasn't cut out for this beard business.

Marian had got away with a handshake from Tank, probably in deference to the fact that he hadn't met her before. But Danny, being male, apparently warranted no such concession and was treated to a brief sparring match before being wrestled into a headlock. Kit and Danny were civil, but just about, nodding coolly at each other.

They were ushered into the living room where there was a roaring fire and Laura served champagne with smoked salmon canapés, while Luke was passed around and fussed over by everyone. No matter who Romy was talking to, she always knew where Ethan was in the room, her senses on high alert whenever he came close to her. At least, she had a good excuse for watching him when he took Luke, and she didn't have to hide her enchantment as he played with her son. But the urge to dart across the room and throw herself into his arms was almost overwhelming. They hadn't seen each other since coming back from Wicklow, and it was driving her crazy not being able to touch him the way she wanted to. Being so close to him only increased the agony.

She was pleased to see that her mother seemed to be really enjoying getting to know her old neighbours again, and she and Laura were chatting away like old friends while Colm bounced Luke on his knee and showed him the big fluffy polar bear they'd bought him. Danny and Kit were clearly avoiding each other, always on opposite sides of the room, neither of them looking happy.

'Come up to my room for a minute,' Kit murmured in her ear as he sidled up to her.

'Why?'

'I just thought we should disappear for a while – you

know, so everyone will think we can't keep our hands off each other.'

'Oh. Okay,' she said, putting down her glass. He took her hand and she followed him from the room, feeling Ethan's eyes on them as they left.

'We'll just stay up here for a few minutes,' Kit said as they sat on his bed. 'You don't mind, do you?'

'No, it's fine.' It was on the tip of her tongue to tell him that she wanted them to stage a break-up, but he seemed a bit down, and she didn't want to upset him at Christmas. It could wait until the holidays were over.

'So, we're having our New Year's Eve party this year – Ethan, Hannah and I. I presume you'll come?' Kit asked her.

'You still do that?' Kit's parents always spent New Year's Eve with Colm's family in Cork, and as teens, the three siblings traditionally took advantage of being left alone in a parent-free house, and threw a party.

'Well, we haven't for ages, but we decided we'd re-instigate it this year since we're all home.'

'Sounds great! I'll definitely be there if I can get a babysitter.' Maybe she could even get some time alone with Ethan. 'Do you think we've been up here long enough?' she asked, anxious to get back downstairs. She may not be able to touch Ethan, but at least she could talk to him.

'Sure. Why don't I go down first and you follow in a few minutes – that way it'll seem like we're trying to be discreet. And muss yourself up a bit before you come down.'

'Okay.' She sighed as he left the room.

She came out of Kit's bedroom a few moments later. As she made her way along the landing, another door opened and Ethan appeared. Grasping her arm, he pulled her into the room, then shut the door and backed her up against it.

'Happy Christmas.' He grinned, gazing into her eyes before

swooping in for a kiss. All Romy's pent-up longing whooshed over her like a wave at the feel of his lips on hers, leaving her gasping for breath. She grabbed him, kissing him back feverishly, running her fingers through his hair and over his chest like she could never get enough of him.

When they finally broke apart they were both flushed and breathless.

'God, I needed that,' Ethan said, leaning his forehead on hers. 'I've missed you so much. I'm going crazy not being able to touch you. And kiss you.' He leaned in and kissed her again.

'Me too,' Romy breathed as his lips moved to her neck. 'But we should probably go back down. We'll be missed.'

She felt him nod, the softness of his hair tickling her chin, but he made no move to let her go as he nuzzled the sensitive skin of her throat.

Finally, he lifted his head with a sigh. 'I wish we could …' His eyes drifted regretfully to the large bed that dominated the room, and Romy suddenly realised that they were in his bedroom. The thought gave her goose bumps. If only there was time, she thought, looking longingly at the bed – even for a quickie. Maybe on New Year's Eve – perhaps in the commotion of the party they could slip away unnoticed.

'We should probably go down separately,' Ethan was saying, 'so no one gets suspicious.'

Romy nodded. 'I'll go first.' She knew the drill by now.

This had gone beyond ridiculous, she thought, torn between annoyance and amusement as she peeked out the door first to make sure no one was looking, then crept along the corridor. Her life had turned into a French farce.

'Good job!' Kit said when she rejoined him in the living room.

'What?' She frowned at him in confusion.

'The mussing up,' he said. 'You look like your feathers have been well and truly ruffled.'

Romy smiled weakly at him and took a big slug of champagne. She had to force herself not to turn around when she heard Ethan return to the room moments later, but it wasn't long after that that her mother declared that it was time to go because she needed to get the turkey in the oven. They collected their coats in the hall and took their leave with more hugs and kisses and wishes of 'Merry Christmas'. When they were on the doorstep, Danny pulled a rolled up sheet of paper from the inside pocket of his coat and turned back, marching up to Kit.

'That's for you,' he said gruffly, handing it to him.

Kit looked down warily at the scroll in his hand. 'What is it?'

'It's the design I did for your garden.'

'Oh, thanks. I didn't think—'

Danny bristled, and turned to go.

'Thanks!' Kit called after him.

❄

As the days passed, Romy started to feel very antsy about not seeing Ethan. She had felt sure he would call over on Stephen's Day on the pretext of visiting Kit, and they would at least be able to see each other, but he didn't. She missed him desperately, and the more time passed without seeing him, the more on edge and insecure she felt, fretting about who he was with and worried that he was forgetting her. Out of sight is out of mind, and Ethan wasn't renowned for having much of an attention span when it came to women. Perhaps her time was up.

She tried to reassure herself that she was being silly and

had nothing to worry about. After all, he had told her how much he missed her on Christmas Day – more than that, he had shown her. She repeated his words over and over again in her head, and relived his passionate kisses. He had seemed as desperate to have some time alone together as she was. She had to have a little faith. But as the days after Christmas passed with no sign of Ethan, it became harder and harder to believe.

When she arranged to meet Kit for a drink the day before New Year's Eve, she was fully expecting Ethan to take the opportunity to come along. So she was disappointed when Kit turned up alone.

'I thought Ethan might come with you,' she said when they were seated at a table with a couple of drinks. She tried desperately to keep her voice light and sound casual.

'No. He was going to when I originally mentioned it to him, but that was before Anna turned up. I don't think we'll be seeing much of Ethan for the rest of the holidays.'

Oh fuck! Icy tentacles crept through Romy's veins, chilling her blood, as all her worst fears were realised in those two syllables: Anna. Feeling her throat constrict with tears, she told herself to hold it together. 'Who's that, then?' she asked, trying to sound offhand.

'She's one of Ethan's bevy of fuck buddies.'

'Oh!' She took a big gulp of her drink. Don't cry, don't cry, don't cry, she chanted in her head.

Damn it, why was she so upset anyway? She knew Ethan slept around – a lot. She knew they were just having a fling and weren't serious about each other. But the thought of Ethan with someone else made her want to throw up and scream and cry all at the same time.

'Yeah, she turned up on Stephen's Day. She's been travelling and she was trying to get back to France for Christmas, but her flight was cancelled. The snow over there is even worse apparently. So she got stranded here.'

'Is she … staying there – at your parents' house?'

'Yes. "Sleeping in the spare room",' Kit said, doing quotation marks in the air.

'But you don't think she is really?'

'I doubt it. Unless Ethan's sleeping in there with her. It wouldn't be like him not to offer a bed to a hot French girl in need. He's very charitable that way.'

Romy forced a smile.

'He's seemed a bit lost the past few days,' Kit mused. 'Hasn't been himself.'

'In what way?'

Kit shrugged. 'He just seems really restless and on edge – like a hen that can't lay, as Dad puts it.'

'Really?' Romy felt a tiny stirring of hope.

'More like a cock that can't *get* laid,' Kit said with a laugh. 'He didn't seem to have anyone lined up, and it's not like him to go without for so long. But I'm sure Anna will sort him out.'

Of course, she thought, her heart plummeting. What an idiot she was. It wasn't *her* Ethan had been missing, it was sex. And now because she was unavailable, he was having it with someone else. She should have known and she berated herself for her stupidity. She knew what he was like – Kit had told her often enough. What did she expect? He had only slept with her in the first place because they were snowed in together and she happened to be convenient. Probably anyone else would have done just as well.

She had known all along that it was just sex and it wasn't going to last. So why did she feel so damn *hurt*? Of course, she knew bloody well why, and it wasn't just that she wanted their fling to last a little longer. She hadn't meant to fall for

Ethan, but that hadn't stopped it happening, and she had fallen hard. She was crazy about him. And he was out there somewhere fucking Anna.

She knew she had no reason to be angry with him. He had never said anything to make her believe she was any different to the countless other girls he had slept with. It wasn't his fault that she felt more than he did and that their time together had meant so much more to her. But how could he go around being so damn sweet and adorable, and making her happier than she'd ever been if he was just going to take it all away again? It was too cruel. And it was torture to think of him being that way with someone else. She couldn't bear it.

'Romy? Are you okay?' Kit asked, frowning concernedly at her.

'Oh, yeah, I just – I just have to go to the loo. Sorry.'

She darted to the loo, where she gave vent to the tears that she couldn't hold in any longer and allowed herself a quick cry. The rest would have to wait until she got home. Then she splashed her face with cold water until she was confident the redness around her eyes was gone, and rejoined Kit.

'So, have you any news?' he asked her when she got back to her seat. 'How's Luke and … everyone?'

'Luke's great!' She smiled. 'He's started teething, so he's gumming everything in sight.'

'And how's Danny?'

She made a face. 'He's okay, I guess. He's been a bit down in the dumps lately.'

'He should have come out tonight – might have cheered him up.'

'He couldn't. He was meeting Paul,' she said, raising her eyebrows. 'That's his ex.'

'I know. I met him.' Kit took a big swig from his drink.

'You did?'

'That time we went to the garden centre.'

'Oh. Danny never said.'

'Why is Danny meeting him?'

'Paul's been ringing him lately.' She looked down at the table, tracing a pattern on the wood with her finger. 'I think maybe he wants to get back together.'

'Oh. Do you think Danny would take him back?'

'I don't know. I hope not – so does Mum. I mean, we used to like Paul, but he was really shitty to Danny in the end.'

Kit sighed. 'So, you're still coming to our party tomorrow night?'

'Oh! Yes, I guess so. Mum said she'd babysit.' Oh Christ, would Ethan be there with his latest fuck-buddy? Would she be forced to act cool while watching them snogging at midnight, pretending she didn't care about him any more than he cared about her? *Shit!* But it would be weird now if she didn't go. She would just have to tough it out.

'Bring Lesley. And Danny.'

'Danny? Really? I thought the two of you didn't want to be on the same planet these days, much less in the same room.'

'Well, it'll be a big party,' Kit drawled. 'I'm sure we'll be able to stay out of each other's way.' He sounded flip, but she couldn't help noticing that he looked sad.

'Yeah, I'll bring him. I'll bring them both.'

❉

Romy felt queasy the following night as she rolled up at the Mastersons' house. She was not looking forward to this party in the least and she really didn't know how she was going to get through it.

'Hi Romy, Danny,' Ethan smiled as he opened the door. 'Hi, Lesley – nice to see you again.'

'Hi,' Romy answered quietly, thrusting a bottle of wine at him as they stepped into the hall and were greeted by the sounds of a party in full swing.

When they had removed their coats, Ethan led them through to the packed living room.

'What do you want to drink?'

'Um … I'll have red wine please,' Romy said.

Lesley and Danny both asked for white and Ethan disappeared to get the drinks.

Romy had expected Kit to make a beeline for her and monopolise her all night as his 'girlfriend', and for once she would have been happy to act the part. It would provide a useful shield against Ethan. But Kit was on the other side of the room and made no move towards her when she came in – perhaps because she was with Danny.

'There are nibbles over there,' Ethan said as he returned with their drinks, waving to a table where chips and dips were laid out. 'But we'll be having proper food later.'

Romy was relieved that as soon as he had distributed their drinks he was called away by Hannah as more of his friends turned up. She recognised Fiona and Sarah among the new arrivals.

Somehow, she managed to avoid Ethan, strategically moving around the room so that she was always on the opposite side to him. As co-host, he was busy and in demand, so it wasn't too difficult to keep out of his way, but it wasn't the most relaxing way to spend a party. Now he was across the room, chatting to a group of girls and drinking beer from a bottle. She scanned the group, wondering if one of them was Anna.

'This party sucks,' Danny said beside her.

'Yeah.' She sighed. 'Maybe we should blow it and go to the local for midnight.'

At least Lesley seemed to be enjoying herself. She was getting chatted up by a tall rugby-playing friend of Tank's.

'Having a good time?' Kit asked, striding up to them.

'Yes, great!' Romy said, plastering on a cheery smile. 'Oh, excuse me, I'm just going to say hi to Hannah,' she said, leaving Kit and Danny alone as she saw Ethan heading their way.

'I really loved your garden design,' Kit said to Danny. 'Thanks.'

Danny just shrugged in response.

'It's really nice to see you, Danny. I'm glad you came.'

'Actually, I was just thinking of leaving.'

'Oh? Got somewhere better to go?' Kit asked, but was greeted with a churlish silence. 'Romy told me you were meeting Paul the other night,' he pressed on.

'So? What's it to you?'

'I thought you might bring him tonight.'

'We're not back together.'

'Good.'

'Not that it's any of your business.'

Kit sighed. 'Well, anyway, I'm glad you're here. There's something I wanted to tell you.'

'Yeah? What's that? You're getting engaged to my sister?'

'I've made a New Year's resolution,' Kit said. 'And I'm going to start it right now.'

'Oh yeah?' Danny said disinterestedly.

'Well, aren't you going to ask me what it is?'

'Uh, no – I wasn't planning to.' Danny lifted his drink jerkily to his lips and took a gulp, twitching with bad temper.

'Why not?'

Danny looked at him askance. 'Because I don't give a fuck. Do what you like.'

'Oh, I plan to,' Kit said. Then he very deliberately set down his drink, took Danny's face in his hands, and kissed him softly on the lips.

Danny grunted in surprise, too stunned to move. But as Kit's mouth moved against his, coaxing and teasing, gently prising his lips apart, Danny relaxed into it. He put his arms around Kit and kissed him back, and the rest of the world zoned out as they stood there in the middle of the party kissing and kissing, completely oblivious to the open-mouthed stares of everyone around them.

'Is that—' Lesley stuttered. 'Oh, my God!'

'What the hell?' Ethan echoed her sentiments.

'Am I really seeing this?' Romy said, dazed.

It felt like the whole room had gone still and quiet as everyone watched Kit and Danny snogging like a pair of loved-up teenagers.

Finally, they broke apart. 'Was that public enough for you?' Kit asked Danny, a slightly smug smile on his face.

Danny just grinned back at him in answer. Then they seemed to simultaneously become aware that they had an audience, and Kit raised their joined hands in the air before taking a theatrical bow.

'Thank you, ladies and gentlemen. We'll be here all week.'

Everyone clapped, and Danny and Kit took more bows.

'About bloody time,' Hannah said.

'So Kit's definitely—' Ethan began. Somehow in all the excitement Romy had dropped her guard and he had ended up beside her.

'Gay,' Romy finished. 'I'd say that's pretty conclusive proof, wouldn't you?' she said, turning to Ethan, forgetting in her shock that she wasn't speaking to him.

She looked at Danny and Kit, both beaming at the crowd and each other. Well, at least someone was happy, she thought. They looked ecstatic. Clearly, she wasn't going to be required for role-playing duty tonight.

'I haven't seen you all night,' Ethan was saying, turning the full force of that heartbreaking smile on her. 'I'm beginning to think you're avoiding me.'

'Ethan!' Sarah rushed up and grabbed him before Romy could reply. 'You're needed in the kitchen. We're running out of margarita mix. Sorry, I just need him for a minute,' she said to Romy, an unmistakable gleam of triumph in her eyes as she pulled him away.

'I'll be back in a sec,' Ethan said, as he let Sarah drag him off.

Romy looked around the room, her eyes raking over all the pretty glossy-haired girls and wondering once again which one Anna was. What did it matter anyway? she thought. If it wasn't Anna it would be someone else. She saw Fiona watching beadily as Sarah dragged Ethan out of the room. Was tonight going to turn into another who'll-get-to-sleep-with-Ethan contest? Well, she wouldn't be throwing her hat in the ring. At least she had more self-respect than that.

She found Lesley still chatting to her rugby player and pulled her aside.

'Do you mind if I go?' she asked. 'I'm not feeling great.' It wasn't really a lie. The thought of Ethan with any of these girls made her feel nauseous.

'Aw, that's a shame. But no, go on. I'm grand.'

Romy was pushing her way to the door when she felt a hand on her arm, stopping her.

'Where are you going?'

'I'm going home,' she said, trying not to look as pathetic and heartbroken as she felt.

'What? You can't go home yet,' Ethan said, beaming at her. 'I haven't even had a chance to talk to you. And you have to be here at midnight.' He leaned close to her ear and whispered, 'We'll finally have an excuse to kiss in public. Though, now that Kit has very publicly dumped you for your brother—'

'Ethan!'

Just then a slight dark-haired girl with a pixie haircut to match her equally pixyish face came rushing up and clutched onto Ethan's arm. 'I want to dance,' she said in a French accent, and Romy immediately knew that this was Anna. She was stunning. 'Come and dance with me.'

'Well, don't let me keep you,' Romy said, turning on her heel and rushing from the room. She scrabbled for her coat in the hall, desperate to get out of there before she started crying and made a complete fool of herself.

'Romy!' Ethan emerged in the hall looking rather bedraggled – mauled by his hordes of adoring fans, no doubt, she thought bitterly. 'Don't go, please.' He looked at her with a pained expression. 'Look, I'm sorry I haven't been able to see you the past few days. Anna just turned up out of the blue and—'

'It's fine, Ethan. You don't have to explain anything to me.'

'But I want to. I feel like you're angry with me for some reason.'

'I'm not angry,' she said flatly, and in that moment she meant it. She wasn't angry. She just felt dead inside – tired and numb and fed up. 'I'm just – disappointed,' she said honestly. 'And I know I've no right to be,' she interrupted as he opened his mouth to speak. 'I know we were just … hanging out or whatever, and it didn't mean anything.'

'Hanging out?'

'And now I'm not convenient anymore and you have another fuck-buddy to keep you company—'

'A what?' he asked, screwing his face up in what looked like genuine confusion and horror. 'What are you talking about?'

'Kit told me about Anna—'

'Kit! Well, I don't know what he told you, but Anna is not my … my fuck buddy!'

'Isn't she?'

'Romy, I am not fucking Anna or anybody else, and if you came upstairs with me right now I could show you a hard-on with your name on it that's been nearly two weeks in the making.'

She was stunned into laughing despite herself. 'Oh my God, that is so romantic!'

'I know,' he said with a sheepish smile. 'Smooth, huh?'

'You do know you can, um … handle that yourself?'

'Oh God,' he groaned, 'is that what you've been doing?' His eyes darkened.

'Be mindful of your thoughts, young Skywalker,' she said.

Ethan smiled, relaxing a little. 'I don't want to handle it myself. I want you to handle it for me.'

She sighed. 'Why haven't you called me, Ethan? Why haven't I seen you for days?'

'Why haven't *you* called *me*?'

'Uh-uh, don't throw this back at me. As soon as Anna showed up, you disappeared. You really expect me to believe you didn't sleep with her – as you have every right to,' she continued when he began to protest. 'You're young, free and single, and we never said we were exclusive or anything.' To her horror, she felt her lip tremble, all the strain and anxiety of the past few days overwhelming her, and tears spilled from her eyes before she could stop them.

'Oh, Jesus, don't do that, please,' Ethan begged, taking her hand and pulling her into the relative privacy of the corner under the stairs.

Romy swiped at her tears impatiently with the back of her hand.

'I should have called you, and I'm sorry.' He sighed. 'I guess I was afraid. Anna's someone I used to sleep with, okay? That's all in the past. It was over ages ago. But she just turned up out of the blue, and I said she could stay here, and I didn't want you to find out and get the wrong idea. That's all.'

'The wrong idea being?'

'That I was sleeping with her.'

'And you're not?'

'No!' He raked a hand through his hair impatiently. 'If you don't believe me, you can ask her yourself,' he said, grabbing her hand and pulling her back into the party. He weaved through the crowd until he found Anna chatting to a group of Tank's rugby friends and tapped her on the shoulder. 'Anna,' he said firmly, as she turned to face him, 'can you tell Romy here – have we slept together while you've been staying?'

Anna looked startled, but she recovered quickly. She raised an eyebrow, her eyes flicking over Romy coolly. 'No,' she said finally with a wry smile that wasn't entirely unfriendly. 'I guess now I know why.'

'Oh,' Romy said in a small voice as Anna turned away.

'See?' Ethan said to her.

'Well, that wasn't embarrassing at all.'

'So – you'll stay? Please?'

'Yes.'

'Do you want another drink? Red wine?'

She shook her head. 'I think you said you had something with my name on it. I'd like to see that.'

Chapter Twenty-Five

'So – you and Ethan!'

'You and Kit!'

Romy and Danny faced each other across the table the following morning, while Ethan, Hannah and Kit bustled about the kitchen making breakfast. Despite the slight awkwardness of the situation, they couldn't stop grinning at each other like a pair of loved-up idiots. Kit placed a plate of bacon and sausages in the middle of the table and sat down beside Danny, while Ethan sat next to Romy.

'Help yourselves,' Hannah said, plonking a pile of toast and a pot of tea in the centre of the table. Then she went to the door of the kitchen and yelled to Tank that breakfast was ready.

He shuffled into the kitchen, yawning and bleary-eyed. 'Good party last night,' he said as he and Hannah took their places at either end of the table.

'Where's Anna?' Kit asked. 'Isn't she staying here?'

'She, um … decided to move to a hotel,' Ethan said.

'It was like musical beds here last night,' Hannah said.

Romy smiled, thankful that when the music stopped, she had ended up with Ethan.

'You two are going to be in so much trouble with Mom,' Hannah said, grinning evilly at her brothers.

'Hey, it was your party too,' Kit said. 'Anyway, the place isn't that bad, is it?'

'And we still have plenty of time to clear up before they get back,' Ethan added.

'I'm not talking about the mess. That's the least of your problems.'

'Why will we be in trouble, then?' Kit asked.

'You,' she said, pointing her fork at Ethan, 'for messing around with someone who has a baby.'

'I'm not messing around with her,' Ethan said, taking Romy's hand under the table and entwining his fingers with hers.

'Yeah, right. Let's see how long that lasts,' Hannah said with a cynical laugh. 'Sorry, Romy,' she added. 'No offence.'

'That's okay,' Romy said shakily. Under the table, Ethan pulled her hand onto his thigh and gave it a reassuring squeeze.

'And as for you,' she said, turning her attention to Kit. 'I don't even know where to begin. Subjecting us all to Lauren for starters, when it was completely unnecessary – not to mention treating Mom and Dad like a pair of throwbacks. I mean, what did you think they'd do – disown you or something?'

'Come on, Hannah,' Ethan said. 'Give him a break.'

She smiled, softening. 'It *is* nice to see you happy,' she said to Kit.

'God, we're going to have an awful lot of explaining to do, aren't we?' Kit said with a sigh.

'You most of all,' Ethan said chirpily.

'At least I'm not screwing around with a mom.'

'I am *not* screwing around with her.' Ethan rolled his eyes. 'Don't listen to them,' he said to Romy.

'Ugh, I'm suddenly not hungry anymore,' Kit said, pushing his plate away. 'I mean, how the hell are we going to explain all this to Mom and Dad? Where do we even start?'

'Well, don't look at me,' Tank said as he piled bacon between two slices of toast. 'I haven't a clue what's going on.'

'I'll explain it to you in the car on the way home, sweetie.'

'We'll have to tell Mum too,' Romy said to Danny.

Hannah stirred her tea thoughtfully. 'Mom and Dad will be back this evening. What do you say we make them dinner and just tell them everything? We could invite your mother too, Romy – kill a whole flock of birds with one stone.'

'I'm on for that,' Romy said. 'Mum was going to keep Luke as long as I wanted today anyway, and we were going to go out for dinner. She could just come here instead.'

'Are you sure that's a good idea?' Kit asked. 'It's an awful lot to hit them with all at once.'

'I think the sooner everything's out in the open, the better,' Romy said. It would be such a relief – she couldn't wait. She had had enough intrigue to last her a lifetime.

'I agree,' Danny said, smiling shyly at Kit. 'I mean, what's the point of having a hot boyfriend if you can't show him off?'

'You're so shallow,' Kit said, looking hugely pleased.

'So, what are we going to have for this dinner?' Hannah mused. 'We'd better make it a good one.'

'With lots of wine,' Kit said. 'Lots and lots of wine.'

❉

They spent the rest of the day planning and preparing the dinner. They all worked companionably together, cleaning and cooking, chatting as they chopped and stirred, polished and tidied. Romy felt deliriously happy being close to Ethan and not having to hide how she felt about him. Even doing simple domestic things like chopping vegetables together was bliss. They made beef in Guinness with creamy mashed potato and roast root vegetables, and Hannah made a dense, luscious chocolate cake for dessert.

'Anyone would think we were trying to butter them up,' she joked as she and Romy put the finishing touches to it.

By the time Colm and Laura got home, the house was sparkling, the table was set and the candles lit, and several bottles of wine were open and breathing.

'This is a lovely surprise,' Laura said, smiling delightedly as she surveyed the scene. 'And something smells wonderful.'

'We're almost ready to eat,' Hannah told her. 'We're just waiting for Romy's mum.'

'Oh, Marian is coming? That's nice.'

'We have something we want to tell you,' Kit said, 'but we'll wait until we're all together.'

'Oh, I think we can guess what that is,' Laura said, her eyes twinkling as she smiled knowingly at Romy.

'Um … I really doubt it,' Ethan said.

'Do you think she *does* know?' Kit whispered to Romy when they were alone in the kitchen.

'No, of course not. She thinks we're getting engaged.'

'Does she?' he groaned. 'Oh, fuck!'

'Never mind,' she said, patting him on the shoulder. 'It'll all be over soon.'

Just then the doorbell rang. 'That'll be Mum.' Romy went to answer the door.

'Let's get this over with,' Kit said, following her.

✻

Luke was awake when Marian arrived, so everyone started on drinks while Romy fed him and put him to bed in Kit's room. All eyes were on her when she returned to the dining room, and she could feel the excitement in the air, the eager anticipation in the expressions of Laura and Colm – and even her mum. She tried to ignore it as she busied herself with helping Hannah to serve the food while everyone took their seats.

'This all looks terrific,' Colm said.

'Right, are you all sitting comfortably?' Hannah said when they were all seated. While everyone nodded and began serving themselves, she added, 'Don't get used to it,' under her breath with a sly smile.

'Well, you had something to tell us?' Laura prompted, her eyes darting between Kit and Romy.

'We're not getting engaged,' Kit blurted out.

'Oh.' Laura's face fell.

'You've called us all here to announce that you're not getting engaged?' Colm asked. 'Not that I'm complaining, mind. You can tell us you're not getting engaged any time if we get a feed like this.' His eyes had glazed over as he ate, his face flushed with pleasure.

Romy looked around the table, but no one seemed inclined to begin. Hannah and Ethan were both looking expectantly at Kit, who was clearly struggling to think what to say. He opened his mouth several times, only to shut it again. She didn't blame him. She wanted to do this, but it really was hard to know where to start.

'I'm not Kit's girlfriend,' she said to get the ball rolling.

'Oh! You've broken up?' Laura asked.

'Er, no – not exactly.'

'She's sleeping with Ethan,' Kit piped up.

'Ethan!' Laura gasped, turning to him. 'How could you do that to your own brother?'

'She told you – she's not his girlfriend,' Ethan said.

'Well, not now that *you've* slept with her,' Colm said. 'For feck's sake, son!'

'But *he* wasn't sleeping with her,' Ethan said defensively.

'Oh, so you thought you might as well!'

'No! Anyway, he slept with Romy's brother.'

'With her *brother*?' Laura gasped, and all eyes shot to Danny. 'Why would he do that?'

'I'm gay,' Kit said.

'No, you're not, son. Just because you've had one …' Colm cleared his throat, 'you know … experience … it doesn't mean you're gay.'

'But he *is* gay,' Hannah said.

'Since when?'

Kit shrugged. 'Always, I suppose.'

'And you knew?' Laura turned to Hannah accusingly. 'And you never told us!'

'*I* never told you! What about Kit? He should have been the one to tell you. Anyway, Ethan knew too.'

'God, this is better than *EastEnders*,' Colm said, grinning.

'We didn't *know*,' Ethan said. 'We just suspected. Kit never told us.'

'Well, good on you for coming out anyway, son! That can't have been easy.'

'Dad, he's thirty-one,' Hannah said, rolling her eyes.

'Still … But what about your girlfriends?' Colm asked Kit.

'They were beards,' Ethan said. 'Including Romy.'

'His girlfriends wore beards?' Tank whispered to Hannah.

'I'll explain later,' she said, patting his hand.

Kit turned to his mother. 'A beard is what they call a—'

'Good Lord, I know what a beard is, Kit,' Laura said indignantly. 'I do watch television, you know.'

'So Romy wasn't really with Kit at all,' Ethan said. 'We weren't doing anything wrong.'

'No,' Laura said gently, 'but honey, when there's a child involved—'

'I'm not going to mess her around, Mom. I swear.'

'He's not,' Romy said, feeling the need to stick up for Ethan when everyone was having a go. She wanted him to know that she trusted him.

'Thank you,' he said, taking her hand and smiling at her. 'It's nice to know *someone* has some faith in me.'

'So, everyone's happy, in the heel of the hunt?' Colm summed up, looking in turn at Kit and Ethan, Romy and Danny, who all beamed and nodded in response. 'Well, that's the main thing, isn't it?'

'You're right,' Laura said, a fond smile softening her features as she looked at all the happy faces around the table.

'Well, I think it's great,' Marian said. 'I always liked Kit.' She smiled approvingly at him.

'She did,' Danny said to Kit. 'She never trusted Paul – thought he was sly.'

'Ah, for feck's sake!' Tank swore. 'I was just getting the hang of this. Who's Paul?'

'I don't know, actually,' Hannah said.

'He's Danny's ex,' Kit told her.

'Ah, okay. All clear now?' Hannah asked Tank.

'Yeah,' he said uncertainly. 'But I still don't get where your man comes into it all.'

'Who? Paul?'

'No, the little fella who was here on Christmas Day – the baby.'

'Oh, Luke! He's Romy's son.'

'And are we not going to find out who his father is?'

'Er ... no, I don't think so.'

'Oh. I thought we would.'

'I suppose *you'll* be like a father to him now,' Kit said to Ethan, looking downhearted. 'I kind of liked having a son.'

'Well, you can be like an uncle to him,' Romy said, and he brightened.

'Same as you,' he said, smiling at Danny. 'He can be my sort-of nephew.'

'So, I take it this means you won't be moving back to New York?' Laura asked Kit.

'No, definitely not.'

'Well, that's great news,' she said, beaming at him. 'It's good to see you so happy, honey.'

'This is better than an engagement any day,' Colm said. 'I think we should have some champagne.'

❈

'Well, that was certainly an interesting evening,' Marian said to Romy as they got into a taxi later, replete with chocolate cake and champagne.

Colm had insisted that they drink toasts to Kit and Danny, and Romy and Ethan, and to Kit coming out of the closet. And then, so that they wouldn't feel left out, they had toasted Hannah and Tank as well. The party broke up shortly after dinner as everyone was flagging after the celebrations the night before.

Romy and her mother were the first to leave. Romy wanted to get Luke home and settled – and she was longing for bed herself. Though she and Ethan had left the party early last night and were in bed before midnight, they had got very little sleep, and she had struggled to keep her eyes open throughout dinner. As fantastic as last night had been, right now she was looking forward to conking out in her own bed. Besides, she didn't feel comfortable about sleeping with Ethan in his parents' house when they were home. In the next couple of weeks, he would be starting work and moving out, but in the meantime they would have to stay at her place if they wanted to sleep together.

'Not too weird for you, I hope?' she asked her mother.

'No, it was lovely.'

'It was, wasn't it? She smiled. 'Danny and Kit seem really happy.'

'They do. Is it strange for you, seeing them together?'

She considered. 'No,' she said. 'Is it strange that it's not?' She laughed.

Her mother cocked her head to one side, regarding her thoughtfully. 'You're back to your old self,' she said. 'It's good to see.'

'I feel more like my old self. Only different – better.' She felt so light-hearted and free now that everything was out in the open. She couldn't remember ever feeling so happy. Suddenly a thought occurred to her. 'Dad would have loved tonight, wouldn't he?'

Her mother threw back her head and laughed. 'He would. He always liked Colm.'

'He was never a big fan of Kit's, though.'

'If only he'd known he was gay,' Marian said, laughing.

'Yes, he'd have felt duty-bound to approve of him then.'

'I think he'd be very impressed with how he turned out,' Marian said seriously. 'And he'd have loved Ethan.'

'Do you think so?'

'Of course.' Her mother's eyes sparkled as they flickered over her. 'He'd have loved anyone who made you this happy, Romy.'

❋

After he had seen Danny off in a taxi, Kit walked down the hall and into the kitchen, where Ethan was sitting at the table with a cup of coffee. Kit poured himself a cup and sat down opposite him. Hannah and Tank had already left, and their parents were in bed. It was just the two of them.

'Strange night, huh?' Ethan said, blinking tiredly.

'But in a good way.'

Ethan smiled. 'Yeah, it all went really well. And somehow you managed to get treated like the conquering hero – jammy bastard!'

Kit grinned.

'So – out and proud,' Ethan said, doing jazz hands. 'How does it feel?'

'Like I should have done it years ago.'

'Well … better late than never. And if you'd done it earlier, you probably wouldn't have ended up with Danny. He's great.'

'Yeah,' Kit smiled fondly. 'And so is his sister.' He took a deep breath, bracing himself. 'Look, there's something I wanted to talk to you about,' Kit said. 'I think it's great about you and Romy, but—'

'Oh God, not again! For the umpteenth time, I am not going to mess her around, okay?'

'That's not what I was going to say.'

'Oh. What is it, then?'

'It's just that – there are things you don't know about Romy. She's not as … straightforward as she seems.'

'Hey, I know you used to go out with her, but that was a long time ago. I think I probably know her better than you do now.'

'I don't think you know everything. I just feel I should warn you, so you know exactly what you're getting into.'

Ethan's face changed, his smile disappearing. 'What do you mean?'

'Romy's … into certain things that, well, I'm pretty sure you're not.'

'Oh, is that all?' Ethan laughed, his relief obvious. 'Don't worry, I know about that.'

'You do? And it doesn't bother you?'

Ethan shrugged. 'No. Why should it? If it makes her happy.'

'But it's not just about what makes *her* happy, is it? She'll expect you to, you know, join in.'

'You think so?' Ethan still looked unconcerned. Kit felt he wasn't grasping the seriousness of the situation.

'Of course. You're her boyfriend – naturally she's going to want to do that stuff with you.'

'I suppose … maybe. But so what if she does? I mean, it's not my cup of tea, but I'm sure I could put up with it if it's what she wants.'

'How could you – if you're not into it?' Kit could hardly string a sentence together. He couldn't believe Ethan was so cool about all this.

'It's not a lot to do for someone you, you know …'

'Love?'

'Yeah,' Ethan said, smiling shyly. 'Anyway, she probably has friends she could do that stuff with – people who'd be more into it.'

Kit gulped. 'And you wouldn't mind? Her doing that with other people?'

'Of course not.' Ethan laughed at the shocked expression on Kit's face. 'Jesus, we don't have to be joined at the hip.'

'No, but—' Kit spluttered.

'I'm sure she'd rather do it with people who like the same stuff. It'd be more fun for her.'

'I don't believe you can be so—'

'Anyway, if she really wanted me to, I'm sure I could sit through it if need be—'

'*Sit through it?*' Kit shrieked, aware that probably only dogs could hear him now. '*Sit* through it?'

Ethan rolled his eyes. 'It's not a big deal. You always put way too much importance on that kind of stuff, you know.'

'What kind of stuff?'

'You know, what bands it's cool to like and all that.'

'*Bands?*' Another one for the dogs. 'Seriously, you think I'm talking about bands?'

'Look, I know Romy likes Take That, okay? And I'm not saying it's been easy, but I've come to terms with it,' Ethan said solemnly.

The little shit was being sarcastic, Kit thought. He was trying to help him, and he was taking the piss. He should be angry – but instead he just felt sorry for him.

'And if she wants me to go to a concert with her next time they're on tour,' Ethan was saying, 'I'm sure I can cope. I'll be there for her.'

Kit gave him a pitying look. 'Ethan, I'm not talking about Take Bloody That.'

'You're not?'

'No.'

'Well … whoever. I don't care. Even if she likes Chris de Burgh. I don't care, okay?'

'You don't mind if she likes Chris de Burgh?'

'No,' Ethan said, but he looked upset at the thought. 'Well … I wouldn't be happy about it, you know? Obviously. But it's fine,' he said, shrugging. 'It wouldn't change the way I feel about her.'

'Wow!' Kit breathed. 'You've really got it bad, haven't you?'

'I know.' Ethan ducked his head, smiling sheepishly.

Bloody hell, Kit thought. If Ethan could get over Chris de

Burgh, maybe Romy's sexual proclivities wouldn't be such a big obstacle after all.

'She doesn't, does she?' Ethan was looking at him anxiously.

'Sorry? Doesn't what?'

'Like Chris de Burgh.'

'No, not as far as I know.' Kit thought. 'No, I'm sure not.'

'Phew! That's good. I mean I've nothing against Chris de Burgh fans per se, but—'

'You don't want them moving in next door and marrying your children.'

'Exactly. Bringing down the neighbourhood.'

'You could test her, just to make sure.'

'How?'

'You could put on 'The Lady in Red' and see if she squeals and demands that you dance with her to it.'

'I'd have to download it first.'

'That would be a bit awkward. It would be on your iPod. Your iTunes would think you liked that sort of thing.'

'I'd get recommendations based on it.'

'It would follow you for the rest of your days.'

'I think I'll just give her the benefit of the doubt.'

'Good thinking.'

'So this thing you were going to tell me ...' Ethan began nervously. 'Is it better or worse than Chris de Burgh?'

Kit thought. 'Worse. No, better! Hang on ... I'm not sure. You'll have to decide for yourself after I tell you.'

'Okay. So?'

Kit was almost sorry he'd started now. Romy and Ethan had been so happy tonight. They obviously loved each other and he didn't want to spoil things for them. But wasn't it better that Ethan knew up front what he was getting into?

He thought for a moment, not sure where to start. 'Has Romy ever told you about Luke's father?' he said finally.

'She doesn't know who he is,' Ethan said, relief passing over his face. 'She's told me that.'

'But do you know why?'

Ethan shrugged. 'It was a one-night stand—'

'It's because it was at some kind of kinky orgy where everyone was wearing masks and blindfolds.'

'I don't believe you!' Ethan reddened, but he looked more scared than angry.

'It's true,' Kit said with an apologetic grimace. 'Romy told me so herself.'

'But—' Ethan spluttered.

'That's the sort of thing Romy's into,' Kit said gently. 'S&M. She wants to be tied up to stuff and whipped. She wants a boyfriend who'll boss her around and make her call him "Sir".'

'But that's – that's not true. I mean we've …' Ethan shifted uncomfortably. 'We've … done stuff. And she's never—'

'Well, I suppose it's not the easiest thing to come out with when you're with someone new. Maybe she's afraid you'd laugh at her – or run for the hills.'

'I'm sure you're wrong,' Ethan said. 'You must have got the wrong end of the stick.'

'Sorry, Ethan. I know it's hard to believe. She seems so … *normal*. But it's true. You should see some of the books she has in her flat,' Kit said, widening his eyes.

'Well, just because she's reading books about it doesn't mean she wants to do it.'

'It's not just that. Have you ever met her tenant May?'

Ethan shook his head.

'She's some kind of sex expert on the internet. Anyway, she knew I was supposed to be Romy's boyfriend and she told me that Romy was getting lessons from her about how to be a submissive. She thought Romy was doing it for me, so I had to pretend to be thrilled that she was making the effort.'

Ethan just blinked at him uncomprehendingly. Then he looked down, his brows beetled together, his eyes darting back and forth as if he was searching his brain for something and coming up blank.

'Still, could be worse,' Kit said cheerily, trying to lighten the mood.

Ethan lifted his head and looked at him hopefully.

'She could like Chris de Burgh.' He threw in a wink for good measure, but Ethan still looked gloomy.

'God, I wish she just wanted me to dance with her to "The Lady in Red".'

'Come on, cheer up. It's not the end of the world. You know, maybe you should try some of that stuff. It might be fun.'

'I doubt it.'

'You never know until you try. Maybe you'd like it.'

'I just – I really don't think I could do it.'

'Hey, you were willing to go to a Take That concert a minute ago,' Kit reminded him. 'It's amazing what people will do for someone they love. Look at Dad – hasn't had a decent bit of grub in over thirty years.'

Ethan laughed a little at that. 'And he's the happiest man in Ireland.'

'Exactly. Maybe you should try and find some easy things you could do that would keep Romy happy without having to go the whole hog.'

'Like what?'

'I don't know – do some light bondage, work a few slaps into your routine or something.' He tried to remember some of the images from the books he had flicked through in Romy's kitchen. 'You could make her give you a blow job while she's hanging upside down off a table. That doesn't sound too bad, does it?'

'Ugh! It sounds awful. Why would I want to do that?'

'Don't ask me. I'm just trying to help you out here. Why don't you look it up on the internet – maybe you could come up with some ideas?'

Ethan shrugged miserably.

'You could spank her—'

'Look, I know you're only trying to help, but I don't think we should even be talking about this.' Ethan bowed his head, raking a hand through his hair.

'You're right. Why don't I take you to see May?'

Chapter Twenty-Six

The first weeks of January brought more snow, making a return to Wicklow impractical, and Romy was secretly glad that work on the house was on hold once again. Ethan started work and began looking for a place of his own as soon as the holidays were over, and she was glad of the excuse to stay in Dublin with him and spend as much time together as possible while they could. He had been practically living with her since New Year's Day, sleeping at her place every night and taking her apartment-hunting with him, seeking her approval before making a decision. She was touched that he was clearly taking her and Luke into account – he didn't say it in so many words, but she knew it was no coincidence that he only looked at two-bedroom apartments or that the place he finally chose was only a couple of streets away, within walking distance of her house.

But even though they spent almost every moment together, and despite the fact that he was very much behaving like they were a couple, Romy couldn't help feeling that he was drifting away from her. He had seemed preoccupied lately, and more guarded – even a little distant at times – and she worried that maybe he was having second thoughts. It probably wasn't much fun for a guy his age to suddenly find himself sitting home with a baby every night. Perhaps living at her place had brought the reality of it home to him and he had got cold feet.

She had thought he might suggest they move in together on a more permanent basis, but when he didn't, she wasn't going to push it as everything Kit had told her about Ethan came back to haunt her – how he liked his freedom and didn't tie himself to one person. If he was already having doubts about commitment and monogamy, she didn't want to do anything that might make him feel trapped.

By the third Friday in January, she was starting to wonder if it was over. She hadn't seen him all week. She had helped him move into his new place the previous weekend, and he had started work on Monday. She knew he was working long hours at the hospital and he was busy getting settled in his new place, but she missed him and apart from a few brief calls and texts, she hadn't heard from him. They hadn't even christened his new bed yet.

She wished she knew what he was thinking, but at the same time she dreaded finding out that he wanted to end it. She was just about to cave in and call him that evening when the phone rang and the caller ID showed his number. She let it ring a few times, almost afraid to pick up.

'Hi, Ethan.'

'Hi. How are you?'

'Good. You?'

'Yeah, good. Tired. Sorry I haven't seen you all week. I had a lot of stuff to sort out here.'

'That's okay,' she said, picking nervously at a cushion as she waited for the axe to fall. He was going to tell her he'd changed his mind, she thought, her body rigid with tension.

'So, do you want to come over tomorrow night?'

'To your place? Yeah, sure – that'd be good.' Relief coursed through her body.

'Can you get a babysitter? I thought just the two of us—'

'Yes, I'm sure Mum will do it. We can finally christen your new bed.'

'Um … yeah.'

Oh God, he sounded so awkward and shifty. That clearly wasn't what he had in mind at all. Maybe he just wanted to break up with her in person?

She couldn't bear any more waiting. She had to know. 'Ethan, you – you haven't changed your mind, have you? About us?'

'No! No, of course not.'

Thank God, he sounded genuinely shocked by the idea.

There was silence. Then he said, 'I really want to be with you, Romy. But—'

Oh, God – that 'but' filled her with dread. He was supposed to reassure her that she was worrying about nothing. He wasn't meant to get all serious and admit that there was a 'but'. She swallowed hard and forced herself to ask.

'But?'

He sighed heavily. 'I'm just not sure I can be what you want me to be – that I can give you what you need.'

'But you are – you do!'

'I just … I don't know if I can have the kind of relationship you want.'

And so began the age-old commitment speech, she thought.

Despite all the warnings, and the efforts she had made to prepare herself for it, it came as a blow. Ethan was always so open, so ready to take life as it came – it was one of the things she loved most about him. She couldn't believe he was being so rigid about this. Didn't he realise how happy they were together?

'But I want to try,' he continued, and her body sagged with relief. 'Just don't expect too much, okay? I don't want to disappoint you.'

'You won't,' she said. 'You could never disappoint me.'

'Well, I'll see you tomorrow night, then. Eight o'clock?'

'Tomorrow night.'

❉

The following evening, she arrived at Ethan's apartment at eight on the button. She had decided to go all out, and she was feeling sexy and pretty in a purple jersey dress that clung to her curves, the scooped neckline showing plenty of cleavage. Underneath it she was wearing her sexiest underwear, confident that it wouldn't be wasted on Ethan as it had been on his brother.

'Hi.' She smiled when he opened the door, feeling suddenly shy. It seemed like a long time since she had seen him. He looked casually sexy in black jeans and a tight black T-shirt.

'Hi.' He didn't smile, but led her in and helped her off with her coat. He seemed nervous, his fingers trembling as they brushed against her skin. 'Wow, you look amazing!' he said as he hung her coat on a hook by the door, his eyes devouring her. Then he seemed to pull himself up and his expression was blank once more.

He led the way into the living room. Candles flickered on

the mantelpiece, and a stapled sheaf of A4 paper lay on the coffee table beside a tumbler of dark amber liquid.

'The place looks good,' she said, looking around.

Ethan stood in front of her, his hands on his hips. She could smell the whiskey on his breath. She waited for him to pull her into his arms, but he just stood there. She was about to close the distance between them when he spoke.

'Go into the bedroom,' he said. 'Take all your clothes off and wait for me.'

'Wh— what?'

He just continued to regard her impassively.

'Oh, er, okay.'

She felt a bit unnerved by the way he was acting. He was so cool and aloof. But he obviously had something planned and she decided to go along with it, heading for the bedroom.

Feeling a bit silly, she took all her clothes off and folded them neatly, putting them on a chair by the bed with her boots lined up underneath it. So much for her sexy underwear, she thought sadly as she placed it on top of the pile. She wasn't sure what to do with herself while she was waiting. Should she lie on the bed in a provocative pose? She felt a bit stupid just standing here naked in the middle of the room. In the end, she opted for sitting on the edge of the bed with her legs crossed, feeling slightly less exposed and ludicrous that way.

Then she waited and waited. She looked around the room as the time passed. It was still full of boxes that Ethan hadn't unpacked yet. She tutted as she thought of their jumbled contents. She had tried to impose some kind of order, but Ethan's method of packing had consisted of sweeping the contents of drawers, cupboards and wardrobe higgledy-piggledy into boxes, claiming he would sort them out at the other end. It seemed likely that might never happen.

She wondered if Ethan would be naked when he came

in. If he came in, she thought, looking at her watch. Then she realised her watch looked silly when she wasn't wearing anything else, so she took that off too and placed it on top of her clothes. She hoped this wasn't some awful practical joke. Maybe she was being secretly filmed. This didn't seem Ethan's style at all. He hadn't even offered her a drink.

Finally, the door opened and she jumped off the bed as Ethan strode into the room. He was still dressed, making her feel more naked than ever. His eyes widened, as if he was surprised to see her there, and he looked a little freaked out for a moment, but then he seemed to compose himself again.

'I bought you a present,' he said, handing her a long, thin box from behind his back.

'Oh, thanks.' She smiled, taking it from him. 'Will I open it now?'

He nodded, and she opened the lid to find ... *What the hell?*

'Oh! Um, it's ...' She lifted it out of the box, expecting it to turn out to be something else altogether. But no, it was a riding crop. 'Um ... thanks?' she said, looking at him in confusion.

'Do you like it?' he asked with a strange smile.

'I'm sure it's very nice, but ... I don't ride.' She felt like there was some joke that she wasn't getting.

'Well, I wasn't—' Ethan gulped. 'I wasn't planning to whip a horse with it.'

'Oh!'

'Maybe we can use it later,' he said, taking it from her hands and tossing it on the bed.

Crikey, what the hell had got into him this evening? Why was he acting so weird?

'Now, get on your knees,' he said, pointing to the floor in front of him, 'and, um ...' He put a hand to his mouth and the rest of what he said was muffled, but Romy could have sworn it sounded like 'suck my cock'.

'Sorry? What did you say?'

'You heard me. I said get on your knees.'

Romy sank obediently to her knees in front of him. This was the most bizarre evening ever! He'd better get to the punchline soon. 'But after that?'

'Oh God,' Ethan groaned. 'Don't make me say it again.' He put a hand to his forehead and took a deep breath. 'I said ... suck my cock,' he said, with an apologetic wince. His face was bright red and he was breathing heavily, and Romy was worried that he was going to pass out.

She popped open the button of his jeans and pulled down the zipper, her fingers brushing against the front of his boxers. Hmm, he didn't seem very excited about this blow job he was demanding. She sank back on her heels. 'Ethan, are you sure you want to do this right now? You don't look very well. Maybe you should lie down.'

'Don't argue. If you don't do what you're told, I'll – I'll be very cross with you,' he said, shaking a finger at her like an angry parent. 'I'll ... um ...' He swallowed hard. 'I'll put you across my knee and ... spank you.' He closed his eyes as he said the last words, seemingly in an agony of mortification.

'Like hell you will,' Romy said with a laugh.

'Oh God,' he groaned. 'This is terrible, isn't it?'

Laughter bubbled up inside her at the absurdity of the situation, but Ethan looked so embarrassed and miserable that she tried to swallow it down.

'It's pretty awful, yes.'

'Sorry,' he said, hanging his head. 'Oh, I forgot, I've got handcuffs.' He pulled a pair of handcuffs from his pocket and dangled them in front of her. 'Will I put these on you?'

'I don't think so.'

'Blindfold?' he said, pulling one from another pocket.

'No thanks,' she said distractedly. Jesus, what else did he have in there? He was like some kind of weird kinky magician.

'I could tie you up,' he said hopefully.

'You could take a hike.'

'Oh, I shouldn't ask you, should I? I should just—' He rushed at her suddenly, grabbing her wrists.

'Hey!' She yanked away from him. 'What are you doing?'

'I'm handcuffing you.'

'Well don't.' She pulled away as he grasped for her hands again.

'Stop struggling.' He frowned as she twisted out of his hold. 'I don't want to hurt you.'

'Stop trying to frigging handcuff me then.'

'Hey, are you supposed to answer me back like that?'

'Answer you back!' she shrieked. 'Who do you think you are – my dad?'

'Come on, settle down,' he said, running a hand down her hair. 'Just … be a good girl and let me put these on you, okay? I don't want to have to … um … p– punish you.'

'*Punish* me? Are you kidding me?' She sprang up from the floor and backed up to the bed.

Ethan looked startled. 'Do you not want me to handcuff you?'

'No.'

'Oh.' He frowned. 'Wait – do you really not want me to or is this part of the—'

'What part of "no" do you not understand?'

'Oh shit!' he said, slapping a hand to his forehead. 'I forgot to give you safe words. I'm such an idiot.'

'What do I need safe words for?'

'You know, so you can tell me if you want me to stop – like, red means stop, green means go.'

'Haven't you ever heard the expression, "No means no"?'

'But it doesn't always, does it? I don't know if you mean it or if it's part of the scene. That's why we need the safe words.'

'Believe me, when I say no, I mean no.'

'You really don't want me to … force you?'

'No.'

'And you're not just saying that because you want me to whip you or something?'

'Jesus! No. Or red. Whatever will make this stop, okay? I'm naked here, Ethan!' She was starting to feel upset. This was not how she had seen tonight panning out at all.

'I know,' he said, looking at her longingly, 'and you look so gorgeous. I wish we could just—' He sighed, putting his hands on his hips. 'This isn't working, is it?'

'What exactly is it you're trying to do?'

'I'm trying to, you know, turn you on.'

'Oh!' She resisted the urge to burst out laughing. 'Well, in that case, no, it's definitely not working.'

He hung his head despondently. 'I told you I couldn't be what you want me to be.'

'You think I want you to be some … weirdo with a spanking fetish?'

'Well, yeah. Basically.'

'Oh!'

'Not that I'm saying it's weird. I mean, whatever you're into, it's fine. It's just … not my thing.'

'Well, it's not my thing either,' she said indignantly.

'Romy, I know you're into this kinky stuff – and I don't mean that in a judgemental way. But I just can't do it. I mean, I couldn't even get through this bit, and I'm sorry, but I *really* don't want to hit you.'

'Good. That makes two of us.'

'Really?' He frowned. 'Oh!' he said, his eyes widening. 'Do you want to be the one in charge? You could hit me!' he said, like it was a really bright idea.

'You want me to hit you?' she asked, biting her cheek to stop herself laughing. 'With a riding crop?'

'Well … no, not really,' he admitted. 'But I'd prefer it to hitting you.'

'These are the options?'

He raked a hand through his hair agitatedly. 'I don't know – maybe there's a class I can take or something.'

'Really? You'd do that for me?'

He hesitated. 'I wouldn't have to … wear one of those leather masks, would I? You know, with a zip on the mouth? Only I'm a bit claustrophobic.'

'Okay, no gimp masks then. How do you feel about being with another man?'

'Wh— what?' He gulped. 'Um, I don't really think …' He rubbed the back of his neck fretfully, looking pained.

'Oh my God, you're adorable,' Romy said, rushing over to him and throwing her arms around him. She suddenly felt very aware that she was naked while he was fully dressed. 'Do you mind if I put my clothes back on? I feel at a bit of a disadvantage here.'

'No, of course not,' he said, still looking utterly miserable. Then he turned and stood with his back to her. Everything felt weird and awkward. He was treating her with the polite deference of a virtual stranger, turning away to give her privacy while she dressed, as if they hadn't seen each other naked countless times.

'Okay, I'm decent,' she said when she had pulled on her clothes. He turned around as she was pulling her hair out of the collar of her dress, shaking it loose. He looked heartbroken.

'Would you like me to call you a cab?'

'No!' she gasped, horrified. 'You want me to leave?'

'No. But I didn't think you'd want to stay. Not after ...' He trailed off, unable to meet her eyes.

She put a hand to his face, forcing him to look at her. 'I think we need to talk.'

He nodded and she led him back to the bed, sitting down on the side of it and pulling him down beside her.

'Were you drinking before I got here?' she asked, smelling the whiskey fumes on his breath.

'Yeah. I thought it might help.'

'Well, you could have got *me* one. I was stone cold sober through all that.'

'I'm sorry I was such a disaster,' he said.

'Ethan, I'm not into any of this ... S&M stuff. Honestly.'

'You're not?'

'No, not at all.'

'Oh, God. Sorry.' He buried his head in his hands. 'You must think I'm an awful pervert, saying those things to you – and trying to make you—' he broke off with a whimper.

'I don't,' she said, prising his hands away. 'I think you're incredibly sweet for trying to do that for me because you thought it was what I wanted – even though you obviously hated it.'

She was finally rewarded with a crooked smile. 'You could tell I wasn't enjoying myself?'

She grinned. 'You looked like you were going to have a seizure. You have to be the worst dominant in the world ever!'

'Well, I think I can live with that.'

'But what made you think *I* was into it?'

'Kit told me.'

'Kit, really?'

She eyed the riding crop on the bed. She wasn't normally a violent person, but if Kit was here right now ...

'He said you got pregnant with Luke after some orgy where everyone was wearing masks and blindfolds.'

'Oh!' She laughed. 'That's not true. Well, it's true that everyone was wearing masks – but that's because it was a Hallowe'en party.'

'And he said you had all these books in your apartment, and May told him you were taking lessons from her about how to do this stuff.'

'They got the wrong end of the stick about something, that's all.'

'It wasn't just them, though,' he said, looking at her anxiously. 'You know I used to use your computer sometimes when I was staying at your place, and I saw all that stuff you had on it.'

'What stuff?'

'All the websites and blogs about BDSM that you had in your favourites.'

'Oh, I'd forgotten about those.'

'And I found your box of toys in the wardrobe. I wasn't snooping. You'd asked me to get your slippers, and they were just there.'

'Oh, God!'

May's toys – she'd forgotten they were there. She finally couldn't hold it in any longer and she fell back onto the bed, collapsing in giggles, her whole body shaking, tears streaming down her cheeks.

'Romy?'

'Sorry!' she said, wiping her eyes and pulling him down beside her.

'It's not funny. That was horrible. It was one of the worst experiences of my life.'

'Aw, come here.' Romy pulled him into her arms, stroking his hair soothingly. 'It's okay now. You'll never have to do that again.'

'It was worse than the time I had to be in the school play,' he said piteously.

'What was the play?' She thought if they talked about other things it might help take his mind off his recent trauma.

'The Nativity.'

'Did you have a big part? Even then?' she asked, giggling at her own joke.

'Not really. I was just a wise man.'

'Oh, I bet you were cute. Did you wear dressing gowns?'

'Yeah. And white tea-towels on our heads. Except mine was pink, of course.'

'Obviously. So what did you have to do – point to the star?'

'No. That was one of the other wise guys.'

'Or say, "Please accept this gift of frankincense"?'

He shook his head. 'I brought myrrh. What is myrrh anyway?'

'I have no idea.'

'Anyway, I didn't have to speak. I just had to hand over my present, and then kneel down and look awestruck.'

'Well, that doesn't sound too bad.'

'God, I hated it. I kept trying to hide behind one of the other kids.'

'That must have been hard. Or did you not get tall until later?'

'No, I was one of the tallest in the class. I crouched.'

Romy giggled.

'Mom and Dad came to see me in it,' he said, smiling, 'and they tried to get their money back.'

'They did not!'

'Romy,' he said after a silence, 'if you're not into all this, why were you taking lessons from May?'

'I was just being polite.'

He raised his eyebrows.

'It's a long story – I'll explain it all to you later.'

'And why did you ask me if I could be with another man?'

She smiled guiltily. 'I was just winding you up.'

'That was mean.'

'I know. I'm sorry.' She took a deep breath. 'Ethan, when you said you didn't know if you could have the kind of relationship I wanted, is this what you meant?'

'Yeah. I thought you needed the S&M stuff. I mean, you always seemed happy with … what we did. But I thought it wasn't going to be enough for you in the end. May said if it's in your nature you'd never be satisfied with—'

'You've been talking to May?'

'Where do you think I got the ideas for tonight?'

'Oh my God, May gave you notes, didn't she?' Romy said, jumping off the bed and racing to the living room. Ethan chased her, but she got there before him, snatching the sheaf of A4 from the coffee table and dodging him as he tried to grab it from her. She ran back to the bedroom and threw herself on the bed, flicking through the pages, and Ethan lay back down beside her.

'You changed the script. You were supposed to say, "You may have the honour of my cock".'

'Yeah, well, I put it in my own words.'

'You took it and made it your own. That's nice.'

She turned the page. 'Wow! I'm glad you didn't start with this one,' she said, pointing to another of May's suggested scenes. 'I thought the whole "suck my cock" scenario was bad, but you were letting me off lightly.'

'Yeah,' Ethan said, grinning. 'I don't think I'd ever have got up the nerve for that one.'

'And I don't even know what's going on here,' she said, frowning at an illustration.

'You're holding it the wrong way up.'

She turned the page around. 'Oh!'

He snatched the bundle of paper from her hand and tossed it on the floor. 'Romy?'

'Yeah?'

'What did you think I meant?'

'I thought you were afraid of commitment – that you didn't want to be tied down with me.'

He gasped, reaching out to stroke the side of her face. 'Romy, I love you. You know that, right?'

She nodded. She did know that. She could feel it. But it was still nice to hear.

'I think you're spectacular.'

'Wow! I don't think I've ever been called spectacular before.' She grinned.

'I'd love nothing more than to be tied down with you. I just don't want to get tied *up* with you.'

'I love you so much,' she whispered as he leaned over to kiss her, pressing her into the bed. She felt something hard digging into her back and she groped around behind her, pulling out her present.

'What am I going to do with this?' she said, looking at him teasingly.

'You could take up riding.'

'Or I could whip you if you've been a naughty boy.' She giggled, but Ethan looked pained.

'Sorry,' he said. 'I can't joke about it.'

'Too soon?'

He nodded. 'Maybe never.' He took it from her. 'I'll take it back and get you something else.'

'No!' she said, grabbing it out of his hand. 'It was a present. You can't take it back.'

'You don't really want it, do you? What will you do with a riding crop?'

'It has sentimental value. Maybe I'll have it framed. It'll be a reminder of how far you were willing to go to please me.'

'I want to make it my life's mission to please you,' he said, pulling her to him.

'Well, lucky for you, I'm very easily pleased.'

Chapter Twenty-Seven

'Well, this is lovely,' Marian said the following Sunday evening as Romy showed her around Ethan's apartment.

'Ignore the mess,' she said, as she opened the door to the bedroom, where packing boxes still littered the floor. Ethan still hadn't got around to sorting through them – but that was largely because he had spent most of his spare time in bed with her, so she wasn't about to complain.

She opened the door to the second bedroom softly and they both tiptoed to the side of the cot where Luke was sleeping. They spent a few minutes in silent adoration, watching him breathe, before creeping out again.

Back in the kitchen, Ethan was stirring sauce on the hob.

'Almost ready,' he said. He took a spoonful of sauce, blew on it and held it out to Romy to taste.

'Pinch more salt?' she suggested.

'That's what I thought.'

Romy poured wine for them all, and they stood around the kitchen drinking and chatting while they waited for Danny and Kit.

'Sorry we're late,' Danny said when they arrived shortly afterwards in roaring high spirits, their cheeks flushed and their eyes bright from the cold. 'I couldn't drag Kit away from the garden centre.'

Ethan shook his head. 'Next thing you know you'll be listening to Phil Collins and staying in on Friday night to watch *The Late Late Show*,' he said, grinning at his brother.

'Where's our nephew?' Kit asked, ignoring him as they unwound scarves and removed their jackets. 'Have we missed him?'

'Afraid so,' Romy said. 'He's asleep.'

'Oh, shame. Anyway, I've got loads to tell you,' he said. 'And I have an announcement to make. But I'll wait until we're sitting down.'

'Is it that you're not getting engaged?' Romy said.

'Very funny.'

'Well, you can go on through and sit down,' Ethan said, bending to take a roast leg of lamb out of the oven. 'Dinner's just about ready.'

When they were all sitting around the table, Romy looked expectantly at Kit. 'So? What's the big announcement?'

'I heard back from that interview,' Kit said. 'I got the job.'

'Oh, congratulations!' Romy beamed, raising her glass to his.

'Thanks.' He clinked glasses with her. 'I'm not taking it,' he said as everyone else started to raise their glasses to him.

'Oh.' Marian and Ethan put their glasses back down.

'Wow, not getting a new job – that's almost as exciting as not getting engaged,' Romy said.

'Why aren't you taking it?' Ethan asked.

'Because I've changed my mind about the house. That's what I want to discuss with you,' he said to Romy.

'Oh. You don't want to carry on with it?'

'No, I do. But I want to do the hotel. So I need you to make different plans.'

'Okay – that's no problem. But you don't need to be there, Kit. I can manage the project on my own – that's what you're paying me for, after all. You should take the job.'

'But I don't want to. I don't mean I want to convert the house into a hotel and sell it. I want to run it as a hotel myself.'

'Oh! Are you sure?'

'Positive. The thing was, I knew I could do that job in my sleep, and the money was great. But every time I thought about starting it, I just felt miserable. Getting offered that job was the best thing that could have happened to me – it made me realise how much I didn't want it.'

'We're going to move into the gate lodge for the moment,' Danny said. 'So we'll be on-site and you won't have to be down there.'

'I'll still need you to project manage,' Kit said, 'but you'll be able to do it from here mostly once we're there to oversee things, won't you?'

'And I can run my business from there just as easily as from Dublin,' Danny said.

'That's good, isn't it?' Ethan said to her.

She smiled at him. 'Very good.' She had made a commitment to Kit and she fully intended to see it through, but she hadn't been looking forward to having to spend days apart from Ethan while she stayed on the site in Wicklow.

'Have you told Mom and Dad?' Ethan asked.

'Yeah, and they're all for it. Mom's really glad that the house will stay in the family.'

'Well, that's great news,' Marian said, raising her glass again.

As Romy clinked glasses with Kit, she thought how glad she was that he had come back into her life and how much both their lives had changed for the better because of it. If Kit hadn't crashed out of that tree on Hallowe'en, they wouldn't all be here now. She would never have met Ethan. The thought made her shudder. Kit and Danny wouldn't have each other, and Kit would most likely still be living a lie, keeping his family at arm's length and sleepwalking through a life that he didn't even realise made him unhappy. Thank God they had found each other again.

Everyone was so much happier now that everything was out in the open – no more secrets. Well … except one. And suddenly she knew she didn't want to have any secrets from these people anymore.

'There's something I want to tell you,' she said, catching her mother's eye. From the way her smile faded, she could tell her mother knew it was something serious.

'Is this about Luke's father?' she asked.

Romy felt Ethan stiffen beside her. 'No,' she said. 'I don't think I'm ever going to find out who he is.' If she was honest, she didn't really want to find out. Ethan loved Luke, and she couldn't imagine a better father for her child. She hated the thought of someone turning up to take Ethan's place in their little impromptu family, and she knew he dreaded it too.

'It's about Dad,' she said, and she felt Ethan relax again. 'I was there the day he died.'

'Yes, I know. You found him.'

'No. I was there when he died. He was alive when I arrived at the house that day.'

Suddenly everyone at the table was very still. Her mouth was dry, but she forced herself to continue.

'I knew he was on his own in the house, so I called in to check on him. You had a meeting with your editor, remember?' she said to her mother.

She had gone upstairs and found him in his bedroom, lying on the bed. She could tell from one glance that he was in agony, his face tense and contorted, his body rigid as if trying to hold the pain away from him by sheer force of will. She had sat on the bed beside him, stroking his hair, trying to help him relax. She had asked if there was anything he wanted. And he had told her.

'He was in so much pain. He was in *agony*. He – he asked me to help him.'

She heard her mother's gasp, Danny's whispered, 'Jesus!', but she kept her eyes lowered. It was the only way she could get through this.

'He asked you to help him how?' Kit asked.

'He was dying,' she said, her voice shaky, 'and he asked me to help him.' She looked into his eyes, willing him to understand, to not make her say the words.

Then his eyes widened. 'He wanted you to … help him die?'

'He told me where the pills were, downstairs in the dresser. He asked me to make him a mug of coffee and crush them all into it.'

'Oh my God, Romy!' Marian's hand flew to her throat. 'What did you do?'

Romy took a deep breath, steadying herself as a fat tear rolled down her cheek. 'Nothing,' she said finally. 'I did nothing.'

For minutes, she had simply sat, numb with horror, pins and needles of fear prickling her skin as her father had begged and pleaded with her. He had clutched her arm tightly, his hand claw-like, biting into her skin. He had told her it would be okay – no one would ever know. 'Yesterday, I could have gone and got the pills myself, but today I don't have the strength.' He had cursed himself for not doing it when he had the chance. But no one would know he hadn't stored the pills up himself when he was able. She could help him and it would be all right. While he had begged and wheedled, Romy had just kept shaking her head silently, tears spilling down her cheeks.

'I couldn't do it,' she said, her eyes welling up with tears. 'He was screaming with the pain, and he looked at me like—' she gulped '—like he *hated* me. But I couldn't do what he wanted.'

While she spoke, her eyes drifted around the table and the look on Ethan's face caused her to falter. He looked stunned – almost like he was in shock. He certainly wasn't taking her revelation calmly. She turned away from him in confusion. She knew she wouldn't be able to continue if she looked at him.

When she refused, her father had become angry. He had cursed her, told her to fuck off if she wasn't going to help him, the little energy he had left lighting the spark of fury in his eyes and fuelling the venomous words he had spat at her. 'We've talked about this,' he'd said. 'I thought I could rely on you. Why are you being so stupid and irrational now when you've always agreed with me about this?' Romy thought back to the discussions they used to have over Sunday lunch. They *had* talked about this. Had she agreed with him? She couldn't remember. But it didn't matter because then it was just an *idea*. The reality was altogether different and every sinew and synapse of her being rejected it.

Eventually, she couldn't bear it any longer and she had prised his hand off her, running to the door. In the doorway, she had turned and looked back at him, and the bitterness and contempt in his face had chilled her to the core. She had left the room, closed the door behind her and run down the stairs as if something was chasing her. She didn't know how long she had sat in the kitchen, hugging herself as she had cried, her whole body shaking.

Finally, the tears had subsided and she got up and put on the kettle. She had pulled out one of the drawers and the bottle of pills was there where he had said it would be. She had picked it up, reading the label, the warnings against exceeding the stated dose. Then she had tossed it back in the drawer, wiped her eyes and made two mugs of coffee while she gathered her courage to face him again. She couldn't do what he wanted, but she could at least be with him. She shouldn't leave him alone at a time like this, no matter what he had said to her. She had made her way back upstairs, dreading the hope she might see in his eyes when he saw the mug, perhaps thinking she had changed her mind and was going to help him after all.

'When I went back up, he—' she gulped '—he was dead.'

She chanced another glance at Ethan, but she couldn't see his eyes. He was frowning down at the floor. She wished she knew what he was thinking. She felt panic build up inside her, sure that somehow she was losing him, but not knowing why. She blinked tears from her eyes, and discovered she was shaking. Maybe Ethan felt it too, because he reached out and rubbed her back lightly. She wished he would take her in his arms, but he seemed almost absent.

'Oh, Romy!' Her mother's eyes sparkled with tears. 'I'm so sorry. He should never have asked you to do that. But you didn't do anything wrong. You have nothing to blame yourself for.'

'He died all alone,' she said in a small voice. 'I just shut the door and left him there because I was too much of a coward, and he died alone when he shouldn't have.'

'You don't regret it, do you – not doing what he wanted?'

'No,' she whispered. She knew she couldn't have lived with that.

'Well, he wouldn't have wanted you to do anything you'd regret. And he knew he could count on you to be strong. I think that's why he asked you – because he trusted you completely.'

'But he was wrong, wasn't he? I let him down.'

'No, he wasn't wrong. I don't mean that he could trust you to do what he wanted. I mean he could trust you not to.'

'You didn't see his face – the way he looked at me.'

'He was in so much pain, Romy – he wasn't in his right mind. We'll never know for sure what he was thinking, but I do know that he loved you. And he knew you could stand up to him. He never asked me, and I was the obvious person. Danny?' She looked at her son questioningly.

'No,' Danny shook his head.

'Do you think if he'd lived longer, he'd have forgiven me?' Romy asked, wiping away the tears that were now streaming from her eyes.

'I don't think he'd feel there was anything to forgive. He would only want you to be true to yourself, and you were. The real question is do you forgive him?'

Romy was caught off guard by her mother's question. She hadn't consciously realised it herself until now, but she knew immediately that her mother was right. It wasn't so much that she was afraid her father died hating her for refusing to help him. *She* had hated *him* for asking her. She resented him for burdening her with all that guilt, for pushing her into running away. But he had been deranged with pain – he hadn't been himself. If he had had time, he would have forgiven her. Well, she had time …

She nodded, wiping her tears away with the back of her hand. 'I do. I forgive him.'

✳

Ethan seemed agitated and preoccupied for the rest of the evening, and Romy could tell he was anxious for their guests to go. As soon as everyone had left he shot up and disappeared into the bedroom without a word. When she had cleared the table, Romy followed him. She felt completely drained by the evening's events, but she had to talk to him. She needed to know why he reacted so strangely to her story.

The door of the bedroom was open, and Ethan was kneeling on the floor, rooting through one of the packing boxes.

'Sorry,' she said, leaning against the door jamb. 'That was a bit heavy for Sunday dinner.'

He glanced up and smiled at her absently, almost not seeing her.

'I'll learn some jokes for next time.'

He stood and came over to her. 'Sorry I sort of zoned out back there,' he said, pulling her into his arms. There was something strange, almost quizzical, in his eyes as he looked at her – as if he was seeing her for the first time, trying to figure her out. 'Come here,' he said, pulling away and taking her hand. 'I want to show you something.'

She let him lead her to the bed. 'Wait here,' he said, pushing her down onto it. 'I have to find it first.' He planted a soft kiss on her forehead before returning to the boxes.

The room was even more of a mess than before. A couple of boxes were already open, their contents spilling onto the floor, and now he was on his knees again, rummaging through a third, flinging random bits of jumble in every direction – PlayStation games, scarves and belts, shoes that flew through the air and landed with a thud on the carpet.

'Damn,' he mumbled to himself, 'it must be in here somewhere. Unless Mom ...'

Romy sat on the edge of the bed, hugging her knees, and wondered what the hell was going on. 'Can I help?' she asked. 'If I knew what we were looking for ...' She trailed off as a long black leather glove landed at her feet.

Then Ethan's frantic movements stopped suddenly. He unfolded himself from the floor and turned to her with something in his hand. Romy stood as he came towards her, not meeting her eyes, looking down instead at what he was holding. She noticed his hand was trembling slightly as he held it out to her.

'Is this yours?' he asked softly.

Romy saw her own hand shaking as she reached out to touch it. She didn't need to inspect it, she already knew what it was – the mask she had worn to David's Hallowe'en party. She gasped, and cupped a hand to her mouth, her eyes welling up with tears as she sank back down on the bed. She looked at Ethan and nodded. 'It was you,' she whispered.

'When you were talking about what happened the night your father died ... I'd heard that story before.'

'You were at David's party? You're—'

'Darth Vader.'

'I didn't think you knew David.' Then she gasped. 'You and Katie—'

'Oh, yeah.' He rubbed the back of his neck, squirming uncomfortably. 'I met her at an MSF fundraiser. She did a lot of charity work.'

They were talking in breathless murmurs, skirting

around the main issue because it was too overwhelming to take it all in at once.

'I thought I'd never find you.'

'You wanted to find me?'

Romy nodded. 'So much.'

Because now that she had, she knew it was true. Even when she didn't know who he was, she had always wanted to find *him*. 'I'm so glad it's you,' she said, looking up at him, her eyes shining with tears.

'I'm glad it's me too,' Ethan said hoarsely, his own eyes filling with moisture.

He pulled her up into his arms and drew a ragged breath. 'You called your baby Luke,' he began, a catch in his voice.

'It seemed appropriate.'

'Romy, does this mean what I think it means? Luke—'

She nodded. 'He's yours,' she sniffed.

'We used protection.'

She shrugged. 'It doesn't always work.'

'I'm so sorry. If I'd known ... He's really mine?'

Romy nodded. 'You're a dad.'

Ethan swiped away his tears with the heels of his hands. But if she'd been in any doubt about how he felt, the big goofy grin that split his face in two put her mind at rest.

She grinned back at him through her tears. 'This is good news, then?'

'The best. You know how much I love you both. I wanted to be a father to Luke anyway. But this—' He broke off, shaking his head wonderingly. 'I just wish ...'

'What?'

'I wish I could have been there from the start. I wish I could have been with you when you were pregnant,' he said, reaching out and lightly touching her belly. 'I wish I could have seen him the day he was born.'

'I know. But you can be there all the days from now on.'

'What if we'd never—' Ethan gulped. He didn't finish the thought, but she knew what he was thinking.

'But we did,' she said soothingly. 'Come on,' she touched his hand. 'Let's go and tell him.'

They tiptoed down the corridor to the room where Luke was sleeping and stood on either side of the cot, gazing adoringly at him – *their son* – as he snuffled in his sleep, oblivious to the momentous goings-on around him.

'Say it,' Romy whispered, smiling across at Ethan as he leaned on the cot, resting his chin on his hands.

He smiled back at her. 'Should I do the voice?'

'No!' she hissed. 'Don't do the voice.'

'Why not?'

'It'll freak him out.'

'But he's asleep.'

Oh, all right then. Do the voice if you want.'

Ethan took an unsteady breath, but when his voice came out it was shaky and nothing like an intergalactic warlord's.

'Luke,' he said, 'I am your father.'